Emma Rous spent her childhood in England, Indonesia, Kuwait, Portugal and Fiji, and she grew up wanting to write stories and look after animals. She studied veterinary medicine and zoology at the University of Cambridge, and worked as a small-animal vet for eighteen years before switching to full-time writing in 2016. Emma lives in Cambridgeshire with her husband and three sons.

You can discover more about the author at www.emmarous.com

THE AU PAIR

Seraphine Mayes and her brother Danny are known as the summer-born Summerbournes: the first set of summer twins to be born at Summerbourne House. But on that day, their mother threw herself to her death, their au pair fled, and the village thrilled with whispers of dark-cloaked figures and a stolen baby. Now twenty-five, and mourning the recent death of her father, Seraphine uncovers a family photograph taken on the day she and Danny were born featuring both parents posing with just one baby. Seraphine begins to suspect that they might not be twins after all, and that there was more to her mother's death than she has ever been told. Why did their beloved au pair flee that day? Where is she now? And does she hold the key to what really happened?

3800 19 0015432 3

HIGH LIFE HIGHLAND

EMMA ROUS

THE AU PAIR

Complete and Unabridged

CHARNWOOD
Leicester

First published in Great Britain in 2018 by
Piatkus
an imprint of Little, Brown Book Group
London

First Charnwood Edition
published 2019
by arrangement with
Little, Brown Book Group
London

A catalogue record for this book is available
from the British Library.

ISBN 978–1–4448–4287–6

Published by
F. A. Thorpe (Publishing)
Anstey, Leicestershire

Set by Words & Graphics Ltd.
Anstey, Leicestershire
Printed and bound in Great Britain by
T. J. International Ltd., Padstow, Cornwall

1

Seraphine

AUGUST 2017

We have no photographs of our early days, Danny and I. A six-month gap yawns in the Mayes family album after we were born. No first-day-at-school pictures for Edwin, no means of telling which of us two looked more like him at the beginning. An empty double page marks the overwhelming grief that followed our arrival.

It's a muggy evening at Summerbourne, and the unopened window in the study muffles the distant rasp of the sea and leaves my skin clammy. I've spent the day creating paperwork towers that cluster around the shredder now, their elongated shadows reminding me of the graveyard. If Edwin has finished his packing, he'll be waiting for me downstairs; he disapproves of me doing this so soon, or perhaps disapproves of me doing it at all.

The swivel chair tilts with me as I grab another photo wallet from the bottom desk drawer — more landscape shots of my father's, I expect — and I focus on the wall calendar as I straighten, counting red-rimmed squares. Twenty days since my father's accident. Eight days since his funeral. The packet flaps open and spills glossy black negatives across the carpet, and my jaw tightens. I've lost count of how many days since I last slept.

The first photo is of Edwin on the beach as a child, and I check the date on the back: June 1992, just weeks before Danny and I were born. I examine this four-year-old version of my big brother for any sign of awareness of the family catastrophe that was looming, but of course there is none: he's laughing, squinting against the bright sunlight, pointing a plastic spade towards a dark-haired young woman at the edge of the image.

Photos of seagulls and sunsets follow, and I shuffle through them until I reach the final picture: a domestic scene both recognisable and unfamiliar. The hairs at the base of my skull prickle, and I hold my breath, and the air in the room presses closer, as if it too is straining to absorb the details.

We grew up with no photos of our early days, Danny and I. Yet here is our mother, sitting on the patio at Summerbourne, her face tilted down towards a swaddled baby cradled in her arms. Here is our father, standing on one side of her, young Edwin on the other side, both beaming proudly at the camera.

I bend closer over the image: my mother, before she left us. The details of her expression are hazy, the picture poorly focused, yet she radiates a calm composure from the neatness of her hair, the angle of her cheek, the curve of her body around the single infant. She shows none of the wild-eyed distress that has always haunted my imagination in the absence of anyone willing to describe her final hours to me.

I flip the photo over, and my father's distinctive scrawl confirms it was taken on the day we were born, just over twenty-five years ago. I already know it could be no later, because on the same day Danny and I were born, our mother jumped from the cliffs behind our house and killed herself.

My bare feet make no noise on the stairs.

A holdall squats by the hall table, snagging at my dressing gown as I sweep past. I find Edwin leaning against the wooden worktop in the unlit kitchen, gazing through the wide glass doors towards the shadows in the garden.

'Look at this.' I flick on the lights. 'I've never seen this before.'

He takes the picture, blinking.

'Me neither,' he says. He studies it. 'The day you were born. I didn't know we had this, but . . . yeah, I think I remember it being taken.' It's the first time I've seen him smile in days. 'Dad looks so young. Look at that. Mum looks so . . . '

'Happy,' I say.

'Yeah.' His tone is soft; his attention absorbed in the picture.

'Not like someone who's about to commit suicide.'

His smile fades.

I twitch the picture from his fingers and scrutinise it. 'Why's she only holding one of us? Is it me or Danny?'

'I've no idea. What's this one?' Edwin reaches for the other photo I brought down — him laughing on the beach with the dark-haired teenager. 'Oh, this was Laura. I remember her. She was nice.'

'Your au pair?' I ask. Now that he says her name, I'm pretty sure I've seen her in the family photo album. The young woman who looked after Edwin in those carefree days before we were born, when he still had a mother and no need of the full-time rota of nannies that Danny and I grew up with.

'She's the one who took this,' Edwin says, reaching again for the photo of our mother holding the single baby, but I keep my grip on it and take it with me to the kitchen table. I drop onto a chair and straighten the picture in front of me, smoothing a curled corner with my thumb.

'It's odd,' I say. 'It's staged, like you were marking the occasion. You'd think they'd have made sure both of us were in it.'

Edwin shakes his head. 'I don't know. I suppose — there was other stuff going on we don't know about.'

'But Mum looks so calm here.' I frown at the picture. 'I know . . . I do *know* why we never had any baby photos. Everyone in shock after Mum died. But I can't believe I've finally found one — and I don't even know if it's me or Danny in it.'

'Here,' Edwin says. 'I'll take it — I'll ask Gran about it.' He reaches for it again, but I press my thumb more firmly onto the corner.

'Gran never wants to talk about these things,' I say. 'No one ever does.'

Edwin sighs. 'You need to get some sleep, Seph. Do you want to try one of Gran's pills?

Maybe get dressed tomorrow; go out for a walk or something.' He rubs his eyes briefly. 'Things will get easier, you know.'

'Do you think we could find Laura?' I ask him. 'If she's the one who took the picture, maybe she could tell us . . . ' I bend closer over the image, gazing at my mother's hair, the way she cradles the baby. 'This was literally a few hours before Mum died, wasn't it? This was the day everything here changed.'

'Seraphine,' Edwin says.

I look up at him. 'And we don't know why. And now Dad's gone, we might never . . . ' The injustice of our situation — of growing up without a mother and now losing our father in such a senseless accident — comes crashing down on me again.

Edwin's gaze travels from my unwashed hair to the coffee stain on my dressing gown, and then he squeezes his eyes shut. 'Okay, I'm going to stay another night. I can't leave you like this. I'll ring work first thing and explain.'

'No.' I slide the photo away across the table and roll my shoulders, stretching my neck. 'Don't be silly. I'm fine, honestly. I guess I was just wondering, really, where Laura went. Afterwards.'

Edwin watches me. I concentrate on relaxing my facial muscles, dredging up an expression of unconcerned interest. He sighs again.

'She left after Mum died. I've no idea where she went. And she'd be — what? In her forties by now. Even if you knew where she was, you couldn't just turn up on her doorstep complaining that one of you got missed out of a photo

5

twenty-five years ago. She'd think you were nuts.'

I nod, and Edwin pushes himself away from the worktop, heading to the hall. The corner of the photo lifts again, and I draw it slowly back towards me.

'But if she could tell us what happened . . . '

He pauses in the doorway. 'We know what happened, Seph. Mum was ill. She took her own life. We can't change that.'

I press my lips together.

'Do you want me to stay?' he asks. 'I can stay another night. Or, look — pack a bag and come back with me? Go out with Danny tomorrow, have lunch with Gran. Take your mind off things.'

I grit my teeth. For almost three weeks I've had my brothers and my grandmother staying at Summerbourne with me, handling funeral arrangements and solicitors and condolence visits. I can't begin to express to Edwin how desperately thirsty I am now for solitude.

'No, honestly, I'm fine,' I say. 'You need to go. It's late.' I fold my hands in my lap and try to smile at him. 'I'll go to bed now. I might come up at the weekend.'

'Joel's staying at Michael's — I could ask him to look in on you, check you're okay?'

I can't suppress a groan. 'Oh, please don't.' I'd found it awkward enough shaking Joel's hand at Dad's funeral; I hadn't realised he was staying with his grandfather, our old gardener, Michael, just down the lane.

'Well, could you ask someone over tomorrow?' Edwin asks. 'A friend . . . someone from work . . . ?'

His gaze slides away as I shrug. I've never felt much need for friendships, never nurtured them, and this baffles my big brother. I think of the phrase Danny uses about Edwin occasionally — 'he's not disappointed in you, Seraphine, he's disappointed *for* you' — Danny's wry tone softening the thorny truth of it. Not for the first time, I swallow down my frustrated response. *I'm fine as I am, Edwin. Leave me alone.*

I allow him to hug me at the front door, leaning against him for a moment, inhaling the honeysuckle scent of the fabric conditioner that our grandmother uses on our clothes when she stays here. When I pull back, I keep my gaze lowered to avoid having to look at the tension creases around his eyes.

'Get some sleep, Seph,' he says.

'I will.'

Back in the stale air of the study, I switch on the overhead light and eye up the paper towers. An image of a blue company logo niggles in my memory. I start on the documents that I cleared from the bottom drawer of the filing cabinet this morning, and within five minutes, I'm holding the au pair agency form — faded ink on foolscap paper.

Laura Silveira was eighteen years old in 1991, and her home address was in London.

I type her name into my phone, then try the address, but come up with nothing that convincingly fits a woman who worked here as an au pair over twenty-five years ago. I carry the form down to the sitting room and pull out the family photo album that covers 1991 and 1992, gingerly turning the pages that show life at Summerbourne during her eleven months of employment here, up until the blank double page when we were born.

She appears in only half a dozen pictures. The clearest is labelled 'Edwin with Laura' in my mother's spiky handwriting, and as I tilt the page to peer at it more closely, the ancient adhesive gives up, and the photo slides free of its transparent cover and into my hand.

I gaze at Laura's image. In the other pictures, she's on the margins, glancing away, the focus on Edwin and frequently his best friend, Joel. In this one she smiles at the camera as she holds Edwin's hand in front of the rock pools. She's tall, athletic, with a mass of dark hair tied back. The agency document says she was taking a year out to resit her A levels following 'difficult circumstances at home'. I study her face. Were there complex emotions within her smile? To me, she simply looks happy.

The sun has set, but the heat of the August day lingers. I prop the family photo on my bedside table, and the eyes of my so-much-younger father and brother follow me as I roam restlessly around my room.

It was never a taboo subject exactly, my mother's suicide, but we were only given a limited amount of information as we were growing up. Seeing her in this picture, gazing calmly down at her indistinct bundle, contradicts everything I've ever imagined about that day, and reminds me forcibly that there's no chance now of ever hearing the full details from my dad.

But if Laura was there — if Laura saw what happened between this photo being taken and our mother jumping — perhaps I don't have to spend the rest of my life not knowing after all.

I shove the previous night's nest of sheets off the bed and stretch out flat on my back, my fingers splayed, as I wait for a hint of breeze from the open window.

Inside the red-black of my eyelids flicker the faces of children who were a few years above me at the village school — sly-tongued kids who used to call Danny and me the sprite twins, and ask me repeatedly why I didn't look like my brothers. Vera, my grandmother, used to tell me they only taunted me because I reacted with fury, unlike Danny, who could shrug off any teasing with a laugh.

Bird chatter rouses me, creeping through my window with the first rays of sunlight, and I'm not sure whether I was asleep a moment ago or just lost in my thoughts. A plan is already unfurling behind my gritty eyelids. By seven o'clock I am showered and dressed, with more energy and purpose in my limbs than I've felt in the three weeks since Dad died. I tap Laura's old postcode into my GPS and join the flow of traffic from the coast to the capital, a three-hour journey that often swells to four.

Laura's old address turns out to be a neat terraced house with a semicircle of brightly stained glass in its front door. There's a small park across the road, surrounded by green railings that gleam in the late-morning sunshine as if they've just been painted. I hesitate on the pavement, imagining suspicious eyes watching me from behind the pristine net curtains. For several heartbeats I consider walking away, but I grit my teeth and knock.

The man who answers is grinning before I even finish my question.

'I'm looking for a Laura Silveira who lived here twenty-five years ago. Do you happen to know where I might find her?'

He has a large hooked nose and a bald head, and he fills the narrow doorway.

'You from that posh family she used to live with?' he asks.

I blink at him. His gaze travels over my linen shift dress down to my cream ballet pumps, and he curls his lip, still grinning.

'Wait there. I'll get her mum. She knows where she works.' He shuts the door in my face.

Water drips from a hanging basket of petunias next to the door, and an earthy puddle shimmers on the block paving underneath. Traffic at the top of the road drowns any sound from within the house. I'd prefer a quick answer, but part of me hopes Laura's mum will query my intentions first; I like to think my own mother wouldn't have handed out my details to a stranger. A memory niggles at me: my grandmother Vera scolding me when I was a teenager for passing on an acquaintance's phone number without their explicit permission.

The door swings open, and it's the man again, a slip of paper poking out from between his thick fingers. I glimpse cream-carpeted stairs rising behind him, a large circular mirror on the wall, but no woman — no inquisitive maternal figure come to question me. The man narrows his eyes at me and pulls the door closer to his body.

'That's where she works.' He keeps his grip on the paper for a moment as I try to take it. 'Is she in trouble again?'

I shake my head. 'No, not at all.'

He grunts. 'Tell her to ring her mum, yeah?'

'I will. Thanks.'

As soon as he lets go, I fold the paper into my damp palm and hurry away.

The address takes me to a grey three-storey office building on a street in north-east London, and a parking space comes free just as I approach, as if reassuring me that my visit is within the bounds of reasonable behaviour. Once parked, I clamber into the back seat, and my tinted rear windows let me peer into the reception area without being seen.

I study the receptionist. She springs off her stool behind her high desk to fetch some papers, and I'm convinced she's not Laura — she's not tall enough, not old enough. A dusty pavement lies between us, as well as three shallow steps and a pair of tall glass doors that slide open and shut periodically as people enter and leave. I stroke the curved corner of my phone with my thumb, silently rehearsing what I plan to say to Laura: *My name is Seraphine Mayes. You used to be my brother Edwin's au pair. Our father just died . . .* I squeeze my eyes shut against the threat of tears. I'm feeling less capable of this by the second.

The first few tinny notes of an ice-cream van

float down from the park at the far end of the street, and an image of my brothers rises in my mind: both tall men, with the sort of open, friendly faces that people warm to instantly. For a moment I wallow in a sensation of separateness, of being different to them, of being disconnected from everyone. I grind my teeth. This is my chance to find out what happened back at the start, on that day we were born. No one else has ever been willing to tell me the details. But Laura might.

I realise I want to see Laura first. I want to see what she looks like before I approach her, before I ask her the question that might change everything.

I ease out of my car and head away down the street before looping around to approach the office building from the direction of the park. A cloud of cool air embraces me as I enter.

'How can I help?' the receptionist asks, her eyebrows rising into pointy arches.

'I have a delivery for Laura Silveira,' I say.

A young man leaning on the desk looks sideways at me, and the receptionist's gaze drops to my hands.

'Where is it?' she asks.

I curl my fingers. 'In the van. She needs to come and check it first. We'll bring it in if she wants it.'

The receptionist exchanges a glance with the young man, who coughs into his hand.

'What is it, then, top secret?' she asks.

I step right up to the desk, summoning my grandmother's iciest expression.

'Are you going to call her down, or do you want me to go back to the depot and have my boss ring your boss?' I tap my nails on the smooth counter. The receptionist settles back in her chair slightly.

'Sure. I'll call her. And you're from . . . ?'

'I'll wait outside,' I say.

I march through the glass doors and down the steps, turning left, restraining my gait to a fast walk until I'm confident I'm out of their sight. Then I cross the road and loop back, pulling my hair loose from its bun and shielding my face as I duck through the slow traffic to dive into the back of my car. I scoot across to peer through the window.

The lift doors open, but it's a grey-haired man in a shirt and tie coming out, calling something to the receptionist. My dress sticks to my skin. I wait.

The lift doors open again, and this time it's a woman. Tall. Broad shouldered. Easily mid-forties. Her dark hair is tied back at the nape of her neck, and she wears black trousers and a shapeless cream blouse, flat black shoes. Her gait as she walks towards the desk seems heavy, although she's barely overweight. I can't be certain she's the same person as the fresh-faced au pair in our family photo album, but it's possible.

The receptionist says something to her, and she turns and looks sharply through the glass towards the casual shoppers strolling along the pavement, and the row of parked cars within which I'm hidden. I shrink down in my seat behind my tinted glass, half closing my eyes. She steps closer, and the doors slide back, and now she's standing two metres away, scanning left and right, frowning. There are no vans in sight. Behind her, the receptionist says something to her lanky companion, and he smirks. My nostrils flare.

I study the woman through the brush of my eyelashes. No visible make-up. Strands of grey along her parting. Two vertical frown lines between her eyes. A silver locket hangs around her neck, but there are no rings on her fingers.

She ventures down the steps to look as far as she can along the street in each direction, and her scowl gives way to something more wary. Before I have had enough of scrutinising her, she whips round and stalks back into the building, back to the lift without even glancing towards the pair at the desk. I uncurl and rub the fingernail crescents from my palms.

I have found Laura.

Now that I know what she looks like, when she comes out again, I'll be able to catch her and introduce myself. I tie my hair back up, keeping my gaze fixed on the building. As one o'clock approaches, employees emerge from the lift and spill out onto the street, peeling off cardigans and jackets as they squint up at the sky, pulling phones from bags and pockets. Laura doesn't reappear. Eventually I clamber into the driver's seat and turn on the air-conditioning. I can wait.

If I was in Edwin's car now, I would find a spare bottle of water and emergency cereal bars in the glove compartment. If Danny was here, there's no way he'd be able to sit and wait without nipping off to buy some chips. I watch a woman saunter along the pavement, sipping from a takeaway coffee cup, and my stomach shrivels. I ease off my shoes and angle my feet into the sluggish draughts from the air vents.

She'll have to come out eventually.

I think of my own colleagues in Norwich — eating their sandwiches in the cathedral grounds under this same cloudless sky, sharing the usual jokes after a steady morning managing the recruitment company accounts. I miss the soothing routine of my accounting job: the reliability of the numbers, the clear-cut answers. I don't suppose my boss imagines this is how I'm spending my compassionate leave.

I tug the family photo from my bag and peer at the baby again. I know I was the bigger twin when we were born — amusing, since Danny now towers over me — but I can't judge the size of this cocooned infant. Edwin's grin makes my throat tighten: four years old and oblivious to the fact that this was the last day he would ever spend with his mother. Our mother. When I think about her, I picture my heart sending out tentacles, like wriggling strawberry laces, straining to latch onto an emotion. They don't succeed. Her absence left a hollow space inside me.

Laura's reappearance jolts me from my thoughts.

She strides from the lift, and within seconds is out on the pavement, sweeping past me, marching towards the park. I slip my shoes back on and scramble out of the car to follow her. She glances back over her shoulder once, just before she turns into the park, but by the time I reach the gate half a minute later, she's vanished.

A path bisects the expanse of grass, and people lounge around, finishing picnics on either side, but Laura is nowhere in sight. There's a second gate further along the boundary with the street. I set off towards it, keeping to the narrow band of shade by the hedge as my eyes seek out potential hiding places: behind the bandstand? Among those trees?

Back out in the fume-filled street I still can't see her. I rub the back of my neck. Across the road is a small newsagent's, and while I queue to pay for a bottle of water, I continue to scan the pavement outside. A hand on my bare arm makes me flinch.

'You dropped this,' a woman in a head scarf says to me, holding out a coin and ducking away from my expression.

The photo, the one with my mother in it, still lies on the passenger seat of my car when I return, and I drop into the driver's seat and turn the picture facedown. I thought I was being so clever, but I've messed it all up. I start the engine and sit for a moment, gripping the steering wheel, an uneasy thought prickling underneath my frustration. If I contact Laura properly now — ring her, ask to meet her — will she guess it was me who called her down for a non-existent delivery today? Did she spot me trying to follow her? Will she ever agree to talk to me now?

Twenty-one days since my father's accident;

16

nine days since his funeral. I can't make any decisions sitting in my roasting car on this tired, dusty street. I wipe my palms on my dress and tap **Summerbourne** into the GPS. I'll be able to think about it all more clearly when I get home.

2

Laura

AUGUST 1991

Greengages. I always associated my first visit to Summerbourne with those shy green plums, whose ordinary-looking skins hide such astonishing sweetness. In my eighteen years as a city girl, I had never even seen a greengage, but they grew abundantly in the woodland at the back of the Summerbourne garden, and I devoured several that day. They tasted of honey and sunshine and new beginnings.

The full English breakfast at King's Cross station earlier that morning had settled my nerves for a while, but as midday drew near and the train rumbled deeper into the Norfolk countryside, the fluttering under my ribcage increased. I pressed my forehead against the window. Broad, flat fields stretched to the horizon, punctuated by eerily motionless villages and odd isolated houses topped with thatch. Somewhere in the depths of my handbag lurked a cheese sandwich intended for this section of the journey, but the upcoming interview had chased away my appetite.

At King's Lynn, I clutched the letter from Mrs Mayes in front of me as I approached the taxi rank, even though the address for

Summerbourne House was already fixed in my memory in its spiky letters. The taxi driver's vowels rolled and stretched in his mouth, leaving a heartbeat's delay before they settled into words I could understand. I fumbled the letter across to him.

'Oh, Summerbourne, is it?' he said. I climbed into the back.

Despite the roads having only one lane in either direction, we hurtled along between high hedges as if he had a sixth sense for hazards around bends.

'That's just down the drift here,' he said eventually, his tone encouraging, as we left yet another village behind us and swung into a narrow lane. I wound my window down, unsure whether my churning stomach was a reaction to the twisting roads, the looming interview or the sudden fear that I didn't have enough money in my purse to pay him. A heavy, sweet smell filled the car as we passed a field of cows, and the lane curved to reveal a row of small cottages with low front doors, their walls studded with irregular grey stones. Just as I became convinced the lane was narrowing into a dead end, we reached a sign for 'Summerbourne' inviting us to turn right. The driveway widened into an oval of golden gravel in front of the most entrancing house I had ever seen.

From the buttery glow of its weathered bricks to the rounded edges of its broad stone doorstep, every detail of Summerbourne radiated a warm welcome. Lush greenery stretched along the front of the house on either side of the central front door, glossy leaves stroking the ground-floor windowsills. The front door knocker was a large brass ring, solid and plain. There was none of the adornment I had seen on grand London houses, but this only enhanced the impression that Summerbourne sat contentedly in its own bricks and mortar.

A long single-storey wing stretched from one side of the house, angled backwards, its sharper corners hinting at more recent origins. From the far end of this wing a high wall curved to join a stable block that stood at right angles to the main house, fronting onto the oval of gravel. Three of the four stable doorways were fitted with wooden garage doors.

I forgot my anxiety as I stood by the taxi and absorbed the view, and my smile must have revealed my genuine delight to the small, dark-haired woman who emerged from the front door.

'Mrs Mayes?' I asked.

'Call me Ruth,' she said, and paid the taxi driver without fuss. She had an unhurried manner about her — friendly, but as if part of her attention was elsewhere. A little boy had followed her out and peered at me from behind her legs as the taxi purred away down the lane. This child was the reason I had travelled all this way, and I crouched on the gravel in front of him.

'Hello. I'm Laura. Are you Edwin?'

He nodded. 'Did you come on the train?'

'I did.' I tugged my handbag open and rummaged through the contents. 'Look — here's my ticket. Would you like it?'

I wasn't particularly used to young children, and I'd never seen anyone's mood change so quickly. He snatched the ticket and whirled around, whooping, waving it in the air, before catching Ruth's eye and pausing to say, 'Thank you.' Then he launched into a garbled story about a train journey he had taken with his granny — what the guard had said, how fast they'd travelled, what all the different carriages had been for.

Ruth smiled at me over his head. 'Let's show you around.' She indicated the single-storey extension as we approached the front door of the house. 'That's the day nursery, there, and the annexe at the end of it. We'll start in there.'

She led me from the hall, through the kitchen and utility room, into the vast, light-filled day nursery that made up the majority of the extension. A row of floor-to-ceiling windows looked out over a wide lawn that ended in trees in the distance. I tore my gaze from the scene and hurried to catch up with Ruth and Edwin as they paused at the door at the far end of the room.

'The annexe,' Ruth said, pushing the door open and gesturing me in first. 'Did the agency explain the hours? We just want some part-time childcare. We're quite flexible. The other girl I interviewed thought we were too far out in the middle of nowhere.' She sighed. 'We've never had an au pair before.'

I looked around at the high ceilings, the white walls, the generous windows.

'I've never been an au pair before,' I said, and then gritted my teeth as I realised this reply was hardly reassuring. Ruth didn't appear to notice.

Edwin slipped his hand into mine. 'I'll show you everything, Missus Laura Silvey. There's a bed in the bedroom, and there was a *ginormous* spider in the bathroom, but it's gone to live in the woods now.'

The furniture was heavy looking and old, but the rooms were bright and spotlessly clean, and I was glad of Edwin's nonstop chatter as he showed me around. I was primed and ready to answer questions about my limited childcare experience, but I struggled for the right reaction to this casual tour.

'It's all so . . . beautiful,' I said.

Ruth indicated the hob and fridge in the corner of the sitting room. 'The kitchen in the main house will always be available. We're happy for the au pair to eat with us, or not — whichever they fancy.'

We retraced our steps and this time paused in the day nursery long enough for me to take in its contents. Bookcases bulged with games and toys, and there was a large table covered in art equipment, along with two battered sofas and a television and video recorder.

'He does like to play outside as much as possible,' Ruth said. 'But this room's handy for when you want a quiet hour or two.'

The whole ground floor of Mum's house would have fitted inside it.

We rejoined the main part of the house through a utility room that opened into the kitchen. Edwin's artwork covered a corkboard on one wall, and paintbrushes mingled with cutlery on the drainer. Double glass doors opened onto a patio, and I followed Ruth outside, squinting through a dazzle of whirling lawn sprinklers to spot some wooden play equipment in the far corner where the perfectly trimmed grass met the trees.

'We've had a difficult couple of years,' Ruth said as Edwin ran ahead to reach his climbing frame. 'I'm looking for someone to keep him company and play with him when I can't. Most mornings and some afternoons, but I'm quite flexible. No evenings or weekends unless mutually agreed and for extra pay.'

'It sounds great,' I said. 'It doesn't sound like work, to be honest.'

'Wait till he's telling you the train story for the thirtieth time.' She gave me a quick smile. 'But no. He's just full of energy. He needs to be outside climbing and running, but I need to know he's safe.'

We stopped by the play equipment, and watched Edwin launch himself along the monkey bars.

'It's just for a year,' she said. 'He starts school next September.'

'Well, I'll retake my A levels next May, and then I'll be free until I start university.' I tapped a strut of the climbing frame. 'Touch wood.'

'And you have some experience of working with children?'

I hesitated. 'A little. I've done a fair bit of babysitting for my neighbours. I like children.' I waited for her to frown, to exclaim that this wasn't enough, but she was gazing at Edwin as if her mind had already moved on.

'Watch me, Laura Silvey!' Edwin shouted, lining up to shoot down the slide headfirst on his back. He had a false start, so I went over to help him.

We continued our stroll through the garden, slowing at the edge of the woodland to pick our way over the scattered fallen fruit that Ruth told me were greengages. Hundreds more of them hung from the branches overhead, and Ruth and I picked several, passing some to Edwin. They were perfectly ripe, and all three of us exclaimed over their heavenly flavour, spitting the stones away into the undergrowth and wiping our mouths with our hands. The tension in my stomach began to ease.

My early impression of Ruth was of someone self-contained and calm, with a controlled way of moving and speaking. I worried at first that her reserved manner meant she didn't like me, but as we followed the winding path through the trees, I began to suspect this was her natural personality, and I found myself warming to her. She seemed to forget she was meant to be interviewing me; she complained good-naturedly when she caught cobwebs in her hair, and was gentle in her handling of an earthworm that Edwin presented her with. I examined her in brief sideways glances. Below average height and delicate boned, she was the physical opposite of me. I wondered whether she was always this pale. Perhaps it was due to the difficult time she had mentioned.

They showed me the tall iron gate in the back of the boundary wall, but we didn't have time to go out to the cliffs and see the sea.

'Next time,' Ruth said. I was returning her smile before the full implication of her words sank in, and then the remaining tension in my stomach melted away.

We toured the vegetable garden and the apple orchard on our circular route back towards the house, and Ruth introduced me to the gardener, Mr Harris. With his thick white hair and leathery skin, he had the appearance of a person who'd lived outdoors his whole life.

'Mister Michael Harris is Joel's grandad,' Edwin told me.

'You'll have passed his cottage in the lane,' Ruth said.

The older man nodded at me, and I smiled back. I used to love helping my aunt in the garden of her little bungalow, before Mum fell out with her and I was banned from visiting. When Michael slid open the greenhouse door for Edwin to pick a handful of sun-warmed tomatoes, I leaned in to inhale the earthy aroma of humid green growth.

The biggest surprise came at the end of our walk. Sheltered by the back wall of the stable block, encircled by faded timber decking and a hedge of lavender, was a glorious turquoise-tiled swimming pool. The water sparkled invitingly in the August sunshine.

'You're a swimmer, aren't you?' Ruth asked. 'Although the solar heating's pretty puny, I'm afraid. You have to be fairly tough to bear it.'

I smiled. 'I taught myself to swim at a lido when I was ten. It was freezing, but you get used to it.'

'And you swim competitively now?'

'I did, yes. Until . . . my exams, the last few months.' I squint at a single green leaf floating on the surface of the pool. 'I love it.'

'I'm glad,' Ruth said. 'I'd much prefer to have someone who's a strong swimmer. To keep Edwin safe, you know.'

I look at the little boy. 'What do you reckon, Edwin? Do you think we're brave enough to swim in a bit of cold water?'

Edwin did a wild dance to show his enthusiasm for the idea, and Ruth laughed.

'Do you have any questions?' Ruth asked me, and then, 'Have you had lunch? We had ours before you arrived. Come and sit on the patio, and I'll bring some tea out.'

The patio furniture was more substantial than Mum's three-piece suite at home, with sturdy wooden frames and deep cushions. Stone urns brimmed with orange marigolds and blue lobelia. Along with the tea, Ruth carried out a plate laden with squares of chocolate tiffin, cinnamon pastries and slices of carrot cake with thick lemon icing. Edwin scampered off to his sandpit with a piece of tiffin, and Ruth poured the tea.

'I was very impressed by the references from your school,' she said. 'I'd like to offer you the job, Laura. I do hope you'll say yes. I think you and Edwin would get on extremely well together.'

26

I fumbled with my saucer. 'Yes, please,' I said. 'Thank you. That's brilliant.'

'Lovely,' she said. 'Can you start a week from Monday?'

I was finishing my second slice of cake when the peace of the garden was interrupted by sounds drifting over from the front of the house. Tyres crunched over gravel, and a door slammed. Ruth made a noise in her throat.

'My mother's taxi,' she said. She didn't get up. 'Technically, this is her house, and she likes to keep an eye on what goes on. She was angling to meet you. Sorry.' She must have caught my expression, because she added, 'Oh, don't worry, she doesn't visit that often. She comes down from London once or twice a month on the train. Anyway, she'll adore you. I'm sure of it.'

'Granny!' Edwin hurtled towards the woman who stepped out onto the patio, his arms outstretched. Her sleek bob of dark hair was immaculate, her white blouse pristine, but she dropped her handbag and swung the little boy up and hugged him to her chest, laughing.

'Hello, my darling boy.'

I brushed cake crumbs from my lap as I stood.

'Mother, this is Laura Silveira,' Ruth said, remaining seated. 'Laura, this is Vera Blackwood, my mother.'

Vera's handshake was firm, and I braced myself against her appraising expression, struck by an unsettling conviction that she understood more about my personality and my background from that brief greeting than Ruth did after an hour of talking to me. I wondered whether Vera had met the other girl Ruth said she'd interviewed. I found myself assessing Vera in return, wondering how she felt about owning a house like this and yet living elsewhere.

Vera's direct gaze softened when she smiled, and she nodded as she released my hand. She turned to Ruth.

'Sorry to interrupt your interview, darling. How are you getting along?'

'I've offered Laura the job. She's perfect.'

Vera's smile widened. 'How wonderful. I'm so glad to meet you, Laura. Edwin is our pride and joy, and we do so want him to be happy.'

Ruth gave an exaggerated blink and turned to watch Edwin practising handstands on the lawn.

'Ruth?' Vera tilted her head as she scrutinised her daughter. 'You look tired, darling. How are you feeling?'

Ruth sighed. 'I do have a bit of a headache, actually. This sun doesn't help. I might go and lie down now, if you don't mind, Laura?'

'Not at all,' I said. 'Of course.'

'I'm so glad you're going to come and live with us.' Ruth kept her hand on her forehead as she stood. 'Just let me know which date suits you to move in — maybe next weekend? Mother can call a taxi to take you back to the station when you're ready.'

'Oh, but — ' I stopped, ducking my head as they both looked at me. 'I mean, it's a shame, that's all, that the other taxi just left. I should have gone in that one.'

Heat rose to my cheeks. Ruth looked at me

blankly, but Vera waved away my concern with a gentle smile.

'Not to worry,' Vera said. 'Ruth, you go and lie down, and I'll ring for the taxi and keep Laura company until it gets here.'

Edwin trotted into the house after them, and I stayed on the patio, fanning myself with a picture book from the table. When Vera returned, she brought a jug of cold squash with her, and she sent Edwin off to eat an ice lolly on the lawn so as not to drip it on the cream cushions. She poured me a glass, and asked me a few questions about my school and my swimming squad.

'I'm so glad Ruth likes you,' she said. 'She can be rather overprotective of Edwin sometimes. Unsurprisingly, after what happened to his brother — did she tell you?'

I shook my head, the glass at my lips.

She twisted the rings on her fingers. 'Edwin had a twin brother. He died the December before last. In an accident.'

The liquid caught in the back of my throat, making me cough. I covered my mouth with my hand, staring at her. 'No.'

She closed her eyes for a moment. 'It was just after their second birthday. I thought you ought to know. We all miss him terribly, of course. But Ruth has found it particularly difficult, because she blames herself.'

Her tone was matter-of-fact. I couldn't find any words.

'Ruth can be a little . . . unpredictable at times,' she continued. 'I'm hoping she'll get better once you're here. She doesn't like me coming over too often, and Dominic's in the City for work during the week, of course. It's rather lonely for her. Although she says that's the way she likes it.'

I watched her twist her rings, struggling to follow her words, the horror of Edwin losing his brother pulsating in my mind.

She paused to study my face for a moment. 'I think you'll be perfect for her.'

Edwin brought his ice-lolly stick to the table and then scampered back to practise forward rolls on the lawn.

'My number's in the book on the hall table, if you ever need to ring me,' Vera said. 'Ah, that's the taxi.' She rose in one smooth movement. 'Edwin, darling. Come and say goodbye to Laura. She has to go now.'

Edwin slid his sticky hand into mine as we walked through the kitchen and hall, and out to the drive. Vera held her purse in front of her.

'When are you coming back, Missus Laura Silvey?' Edwin asked. I cleared my throat, squashing Vera's words to the back of my mind and concentrating on the serious blue eyes gazing up at me.

'You can call me Laura,' I told him, smiling. I looked at Vera. 'If I'm starting a week on Monday . . . '

'Shall we say Saturday the seventh?' she said. 'Give you time to get settled.'

'Yes, great.' I gave Edwin a quick hug, and climbed into the taxi while Vera paid the driver.

'Safe journey,' she called as we pulled away. I waved to the two of them, craning my neck to keep the golden bricks of the house in sight for as long as possible. The greengage in my pocket I would savour on the train home. I had just over a week to pack and say goodbye to my friends, most of whom were starting new jobs, or themselves packing for university. Then I could put my old London life behind me, and dive into the year at Summerbourne that glittered ahead. Ruth and Vera had both said I was perfect for the job. As far as I could see, the job was perfect for me.

3

Seraphine

Despite my failure to speak to Laura, despite the sharp ache of missing my father, my spirits rise as I drive that last mile to Summerbourne — through the village and out the other side, down the winding lane, cruising between the hedges where we picked blackberries as children, past the flint cottages with their windows propped open, swinging right onto the driveway. Apart from the three years I spent living in shared student houses in Liverpool, Summerbourne is the only home I've ever known.

My stomach growls, but I stay in the car for a minute more, contemplating the familiar yellow bricks in front of me, my gaze skimming over the peeling paint on the windowsills and the nettles in the front beds. Danny and I were the first children to be born in the summer months here for several generations, and despite the Summerbourne surname having been lost via female inheritance many years ago, we grew up proud of being called 'the Summerbourne summerborns'. It made up for the less friendly nicknames anyway.

As well as Summerbourne, my grandmother Vera inherited a smart London house called Winterbourne — apparently renamed as such to amuse a Summerbourne ancestor. When Vera decided a few years ago that she'd prefer the amenities of a luxury city apartment, she gave Winterbourne to Edwin, making the announcement on his twenty-fifth birthday. It's perfect for him — close to his work in Canary Wharf — and he's always made it clear that Danny and I can stay there whenever we want, even gave us our own keys.

But the question of Summerbourne's fate festers inside me like an abscess: I try to wall it off and ignore it, but at moments of weakness it swells and erupts and gnaws away at me. Last month, as Danny and I approached our twenty-fifth birthday, I wondered whether Vera was considering giving the house to one of us, or both of us. How could it be done fairly? And then Dad died the day before we turned twenty-five, and I haven't given it another thought until now, mulling it over here on the drive.

I'm the one who still lives here, and I'm the one who dreams of always living here. I can picture myself growing old at Summerbourne, and although I used to dream of falling in love and sharing it with someone else, I'm perfectly resigned now to living here by myself. Edwin has Winterbourne, Vera has her shiny new city apartment, Dad had his own flat in London when he was alive. Danny works abroad a lot and shows no sign of wanting to settle anywhere. I'm the one who still lives here; I'm the one who loves this house the most.

I fix my eyes firmly on the round door knocker as I leave my car, determined not to glance towards the patch of gravel in front of the garages where last month they had to hose Dad's blood away.

The air inside the house is even warmer than outside, and I fling open windows and back doors. Edwin left food in the fridge for me, and I reheat a bowl of pasta and carry it out to the patio. The lawn is an uneven patchwork of yellow and brown, parched and dejected. The gardening company that Vera hired after Michael retired a few years ago has never come close to re-creating the lush green velvet that Michael achieved seemingly effortlessly.

My phone vibrates with a text from Edwin:

How's your day been?

I consider ringing him, but I can't face confessing that I tracked down his old au pair today, that I tricked her and followed her, and then lost her. I picture Laura's expression as she looked up and down the street, her irritation sliding into unease.

Fine.

I text back.

Tired. Going to bed.

The sky is still light, and I prowl into the kitchen for a beer, deciding instead on a hot chocolate in the hope the warm milk might make me sleepy. I fetch a mug from the shelf, grab the powder from the cupboard, pluck a spoon from the drawer — all without having to really look. Nothing has changed in this kitchen since I used to do this as a child, even as far back as the days when I needed to stand on a chair to reach the mugs and was obliged to ask Edwin or Joel or one of the nannies to heat my milk in the microwave.

I start to carry my hot chocolate towards the day nursery, old childhood habits resurfacing, but then I shake my head and turn instead to the sitting room. A faint breeze from the open window stirs the curtains as I walk in.

On a whim, I send a text to Vera:

Hi Gran, Do you fancy coming down to Summerbourne tomorrow? I could pick you up from the station. I have one of Edwin's quiches in the fridge. Love, Seph x

Surely, Vera must have raced over here that day when she heard Danny and I had been born, excited to see her new grandchildren? Perhaps, now that Dad's gone, she will agree to share some more details of that day with me. Perhaps she can explain why one of us was missing from the photo, and what happened to drive our mother to take her own life.

I wonder about Laura — where she lives, what she's doing right now. I'm torn between frustration at her for evading me today, and a reluctant sympathy after seeing how carelessly the hook-nosed man and her own mother gave up her details. What sort of a life has she had, with people like that as family? I rub my temples. Maybe right now Laura is immersed in the distractions of her own busy home: overseeing homework, cooking with teenagers, opening a bottle of wine with her husband. I chew my lip. Or perhaps she's worrying about hoax deliveries and stalkers. I turn on the television in an attempt to focus on something else, but the phrase 'poor little orphan' bursts out, and I hit the off button savagely, hurling the remote control across the sofa.

And then my phone vibrates with a reply from Vera:

Love to, darling. Pick me up at 12.

I carry my hot chocolate up to my bedside table, where it grows a slimy skin during the night.

* * *

The following day I keep the conversation light all through lunch, until Vera and I have carried our tea out to the patio, hoping for a breeze to relieve the relentless heat. We settle in the shade, and I run my fingertips over the chipped stone rim of the plant pot next to me. A couple of the other pots hold wilting hydrangeas, but this one has only a low fuzz of weeds.

Vera's gaze sweeps across the neglected lawn. 'We need to sort this garden out.'

'Yeah. Um — Gran?'

She starts to pour the tea. 'Hm?'

'Can I ask you about Laura?'

She freezes. Literally holds the teapot an inch above the table and stares at it without moving. I reach out and gently push the pot down until the china clunks on the wood, and then she shakes her head slightly and sits back in her chair, her expression distant.

'Laura who?' she says eventually.

'Laura Silveira, Edwin's old au pair.'

'Darling, I'd really rather not.'

We sit facing the garden for a while, listening to the bees droning in the faded lavender. Vera keeps her chin high, one thumb stroking the rings on her other hand. I run my fingertips over the rough fabric of the sofa cushions, back and forth.

'I'm sorry, Gran, but I can't spend my whole life not knowing about this stuff.'

She acknowledges this with a dip of her head. 'Well, what is it you'd like to know?'

'What was she like?'

Vera sighs. 'She was a young girl who worked here a very long time ago, Seraphine. I hardly remember what she was like. Why do you want to know?'

'She was here on the day Danny and I were born?'

'She helped your mother deliver you, yes. Ruth was ridiculously resistant to the idea of calling a midwife or doctor. It was part of her illness.'

'I'm sorry, Gran, to bring up bad memories. But — what happened afterwards? After Mum died? Did Laura leave straightaway? Edwin doesn't think he ever saw her again.'

She frowns at me. 'Why have you been discussing her with Edwin?'

'Oh, just — I found a photo. In Dad's desk. It made me wonder.'

'What photo?'

I jump up and fetch it from the kitchen. She puts her reading glasses on and stares at it for a long time.

'I've never seen this before,' she says eventually.

'Edwin thinks he remembers it being taken by Laura. But I don't understand why Mum looks so calm, when it must have been just hours before she . . . ' I shake my head. 'And why only one of us is in the picture. Why not both of us? I don't understand.'

The photo trembles in Vera's hand, and she drops it on the table. I snatch it up again, fearful of it being damaged by a stray drop of tea, reminding myself that I must scan it tonight, save it safely in digital format.

'Are you all right?' I ask.

'Yes, darling. It's just a shock, to see that after all this time. It must have been taken not long before I arrived, and everything happened. It's — it's actually quite nice to see a shot of them looking so happy together.'

'So what was Mum like when you got here? What happened?'

She shakes her head slowly. 'She was — confused. Unwell.' She gives me an anguished look. 'I'm sorry, Seraphine. I didn't know she was going to jump until it was too late. I should have saved her.'

I nod, pressing my lips together. The corner of the photo is damp under my thumb, and I switch to holding it by the edges. My mother's face seems more blurry than ever.

'Well, why do you think they took this without both of us being in it?'

She shakes her head slowly, her forehead creased. 'I can't think. Perhaps one of you was asleep and they didn't want to disturb you?'

'Can you tell which of us it is?' I hold the picture closer to her, but she keeps her hands folded on her lap.

'No. I'm not sure. You were bigger than Danny, of course. But I can't tell from that — it could be either one of you.'

'Maybe it's Danny, then. It looks small to me.'

'Maybe.'

'I tried to get in touch with Laura,' I say, and then leap to my feet again as Vera starts to cough. She pushes her chair back and half stands, bent over the table, catching her breath.

'Are you all right, Gran?'

She waves a hand at me. 'Fine.'

'I'll get you some water.'

As I wait for the kitchen tap to run cold, I slide the photo between two pages of a heavy old recipe book to keep it flat. A dragonfly batters against the window, but when I push the pane open it just skitters higher to buzz metallically at the ceiling. I fill a glass.

Vera stands at the edge of the patio, looking out over the neglected lawn, her back to me.

'How did you find her?' she asks.

'I went to her old address, and they told me where she works.'

'Did you speak to her?'

I hesitate. 'No.'

She turns to me, and I think she's going to accuse me of lying, but she steps closer with an expression I've never seen before, as if she's fighting a swell of panic. She twists her rings around and around in front of her chest.

'Seraphine, listen to me. That girl almost destroyed our family. I wish to God Ruth had never employed her. Don't talk to her, Seraphine, please. I can't bear it. I'll answer any questions you have about your birth, about your mother, about anything. Just please stay away from her.'

'Oh, Gran, I didn't mean to upset you.' My hand hovers over her arm for a moment. I weigh up her words, and then I step back.

'Actually, there is something else I'd like to ask you,' I say. 'It's nothing to do with Laura.'

She returns to her seat, easing herself down with a huff. 'Go ahead then.'

'What are your plans for Summerbourne?' I ask. 'In the long run?'

Her eyes widen. 'What do you mean?'

'Can't we just talk about these things? I don't mind either way. But who will get it? Danny or me? I just want to know.'

'Seraphine.' She pulls a handkerchief from the bag at her side and dabs it around her mouth. 'My goodness. What's got into you today?'

I press my lips together and look at her, and she's the first to break eye contact.

'There will always be more than enough money for you to buy your own house,' she says. I sway slightly and grasp the back of a chair.

'Are you saying that Summerbourne will go to Danny?' I ask.

She watches me. She gives the smallest of nods.

'Why?' I whisper.

She opens her mouth, but the sudden flash of pity in her eyes makes me recoil.

I can't bear to be near her any longer. I have a sudden desperate need to see the sea. She calls my name, but I stride across the lawn without looking back, breaking into a run when I reach the cover of the trees, curling my fists as I pound towards the back gate. Summerbourne is my home. *I'm* the one who loves it the most.

When we were young, Danny used to run away from home periodically, triggered more than once by one of his favourite nannies leaving. He would pack a bag with provisions, and sometimes make it as far as the village before he was missed. Dad used to say Danny was ready to go off exploring the world before he even started school.

I, on the other hand, resisted bonding with our nannies, because I understood from a young age that sooner or later they would all leave us. Just like our mother had left us.

People were unreliable, but the house I was born in was a safe, solid constant. I used to pester Dad and Vera for tales of Summerbourne's history, frustrated that Dad knew so little and that Vera seemed so irritated by my questions. I drew pictures of 'my' house obsessively, and dreamed of being its queen and making all the rules. One of Dad's favourite tales was of finding me, aged five, crying with a cut finger — 'Not because it hurt,' he used to tell people, laughing, 'but because I'd told her Summerbourne was in her blood, and she'd been peering into her wound and couldn't see any yellow brick dust.'

I think of Danny now, my laid-back brother, and a loud, harsh laugh escapes me, because I know already what he will say when he hears Vera's decision about Summerbourne: *We can share it, Seph. You can have it, Seph.* The same as he's always said about everything our whole lives.

As ever, the view from the top of the cliffs soothes me. Gulls soar and swoop further along the coastline near the boatyard, but their cries are drowned by the hiss of the waves here on the beach below. The breeze dries my tears, and I turn my attention to the stone tower by the top of the cliff steps: the Summerbourne folly, built by one of my ancestors, used nowadays to store our deckchairs and windbreaks for the beach. I potter around, tugging up a few weeds from the low wall that encircles the tower, bundling the prettier ones together into a bouquet. I run my fingers over the chiselled Latin words by the tower door, and then I sit in my usual spot on the scratchy grass inside the enclosure and rest my back against the warm stone wall.

I think of my grandmother's face as she looked at that photo, and as she told me that

Summerbourne will go to Danny. Despite her faults, I struggle to believe that Vera would favour a male heir for the sake of it. Has she made this decision because Danny has always been her favourite? Cheerful, biddable Danny, who never argued with her or resented her claustrophobic care the way I did. Or could it be something else — could it be related to there just being one baby in that photo? Could it mean she has doubts about who I really am?

I know that Dad was in London on the morning we were born, that he didn't get here until after Laura had helped my mother deliver her babies. We weren't expected until the following month, and there was nobody else in the house apart from four-year-old Edwin.

I push myself up, and take my bunch of wildflowers back to the house, dropping them into an old glass vase on the kitchen table. Vera has gone, presumably in a taxi back to the station. There's a note on the hall table saying,

Please don't be cross, Seraphine. I'll see you next weekend. V x.

I scrunch it up and toss it into the bin before dialling the number for Winterbourne.

I need to talk to my brothers. I grit my teeth against the tiny voice that scratches inside my skull: *But are they your brothers?*

43

4

Laura

SEPTEMBER 1991

Ruth and Dominic Mayes met me at King's Lynn station on my return to Norfolk just over a week later. Dominic was a tall man, all smiles and enthusiasm. He laughed when he lifted my suitcase.

'What have you got in here — rocks?'

'Books,' I said.

'Darling, she's here for a year,' Ruth said. 'This is hardly anything.'

I tried to smile. 'I don't need much.'

Dominic opened the back door of his car with a flourish, ushering me inside. 'Anything you need while you're staying with us, just ask, Laura. Edwin can't wait to see you again. He's made you about five welcome cards this morning already.' I glanced at the empty car seat next to me, wishing Edwin had come with them.

The villages were busier on a Saturday morning than they had been in the week, with people mowing their front lawns and walking their dogs in family groups. Driving through the last village, the one that Summerbourne sits on the outskirts of, Dominic pointed out several landmarks.

'You can walk into the village in fifteen

minutes or so,' he said. 'Or we can find you a bike, I'm sure. Food in the pub's okay. Basics in the shop. Bakery and butcher's down there behind the post office. There's a little pharmacy at the back of the doctor's surgery.'

'That's the school,' Ruth said, turning her head to keep it in her sight.

'The preschool's in the hut at the end,' Dominic said. 'Edwin will do a couple of mornings a week after Christmas.'

'He might,' Ruth said.

'To make some friends before he starts school,' Dominic said. 'Oh look, there's Helen. Hang on a sec.'

He swung into a parking bay alongside the village green, and a woman in a flowing maternity dress huffed her way over as Ruth wound down her window.

'Hot enough for you, Helen?' Dominic called out, leaning into Ruth's shoulder.

The woman laughed. 'I'll say. How are you all getting on?'

'Very well, thanks,' Ruth said. 'You?'

'Heartburn's killing me — must be another curly-haired one, I reckon. I was bad enough with Ralph. But it's all worth it, isn't it?'

I couldn't see Ruth's face, but she made a 'mm' sound.

'Your mother gave me a beautiful little outfit for the baby,' Helen continued. 'Really kind of her. Do thank her again for me, won't you?'

Ruth nodded. 'Of course. Well. We'll see you Wednesday.'

'Have a good weekend,' Dominic said.

The woman's gaze flickered over me curiously, but Ruth waved her fingers and we pulled back out onto the road.

'Helen Luckhurst,' Ruth told me, turning in her seat for a moment. 'Her son, Ralph, does gymnastics with Edwin.'

Dominic slowed the car again, this time to allow a group of people to cross the road in front of us. They waved, calling out greetings.

'Everyone knows everyone around here, I'm afraid,' Dominic said, catching my eye in the rear-view mirror. 'You'll get used to it.'

Ruth wound her window back up.

Edwin hurtled out of the front door when we pulled up at Summerbourne, grabbing me by the hand as I climbed out of the car.

'Come and see my den, Laura. Come and see my kittens. They've got names.'

'Not *your* kittens, darling,' Ruth murmured.

Vera appeared in the doorway holding a glass vase brimming with yellow carnations. 'Edwin, let Laura come in first. Why don't you give her your cards, and Daddy will carry her case to the annexe?'

The family swept me through the kitchen into the day nursery. The door to the annexe was open at the far end, but Vera held Edwin back as I followed Dominic and Ruth through. Ruth placed Vera's flowers on the coffee table.

We stood and looked around together, the moment stretching out in silence as I tried to take it all in. Someone had added bright orange cushions to the little sofa, and a thick sheepskin rug to the floor in front of the gas fire. In place of the armchair that had been in the corner previously, there now stood a desk and a small bookcase.

'It's wonderful,' I said at last. Ruth smiled.

'I meant to get you a desk lamp,' Dominic said. 'I'll bring one down next weekend.'

I felt rather as though I was in a spotlight myself, struggling to assume the correct facial expression under the intensity of the family's gaze. I turned my back on them for a moment to line up Edwin's handmade cards along the mantelpiece.

'No, Edwin.' Vera held on to the squirming boy in the doorway. 'This is Laura's private space, not for you.'

Dominic handed me two keys on a key ring. 'Front door and this door. We'll leave you to unpack and settle in.'

The beseeching look in Edwin's eyes broke through my daze, and I smiled. 'Perhaps I could go and see this den now?' I said. 'And the kittens. I can unpack later.'

Edwin chattered nonstop as he led me back through to the kitchen and out into the garden, leaving the adults behind. I chased him across the lawn, and even once we were hidden in the wooded area I continued to run, weaving through the trees and making him giggle, pumping the blood back into muscles that I'd held rigid all morning. I examined each of the precious objects in his den in turn, and suggested we build our own museum to house them in.

'We can charge money!' Edwin said with glee.

47

He took me to a shed behind the stable block, next to the swimming pool. A cat from the neighbouring farm was keeping a pair of kittens in the gap underneath the shed, and Edwin reached in and stroked the two sleepy creatures with a gentle finger.

'Mummy won't let me bring them inside,' he said. 'This one's called Stripes and this one's called Gordon. They're twins, you know, because they were born on the same day.'

My throat tightened, and I nodded. I'd done the sums: he'd been without his twin brother for almost half his lifetime now, this little boy. Did he still remember him? I watched a series of expressions flit across his face.

The mother cat basked in a patch of sunlight nearby, and Edwin's gaze drifted towards her, and then he flashed me a sudden grin.

'When I'm a grown-up, me and Stripes and Gordon are gonna live in London. Do you want to come?'

We crouched there together, watching the kitten twins and chatting about train journeys and London Zoo, until a bell rang out from the house and Edwin said, 'Lunchtime.'

Saturday lunch at Summerbourne was eaten informally at the kitchen table. Over time I learned that the cooking was left to Dominic when he was there, and the rest of the time Ruth heated things up without enthusiasm, often relying on ready-made meals from the butcher in the village. The dining room was generally used only on Sundays, when Dominic liked to prepare a traditional roast dinner.

I lay awake for hours that night, the conversations of the day swirling insistently through my mind. I swapped pillows around, trying to find one that didn't feel so desperately unfamiliar. Even the sheets felt strange — both lighter and yet somehow scratchier against my skin than my duvet cover at home. A faint scent of honeysuckle was a constant reminder that I was in a strange place, in a strange bed. *I'll get used to it*, I told myself, over and over. *It's better than being at home.*

By the time I emerged into the main house the next morning, Dominic was pressing sprigs of rosemary into a joint of lamb, and a mound of unwashed potatoes sat by the sink. He waved away any offer of help.

'You're not working today,' he said. 'Make yourself at home. Don't let Edwin hassle you.'

Vera was reading the Sunday newspapers on the patio, and Ruth was still upstairs. In the end, I played with Edwin in the garden until the bell rang.

Despite the appetising aromas, my mouth dried as we entered the dining room. Heavy silver cutlery and crystal wineglasses were laid on a red tablecloth, and the family members glided to their places with the ease of long-held custom — Vera at one end, and Dominic at the other. I took the remaining seat, between Edwin and Vera, opposite Ruth. For a moment I thought someone might say grace, but the family launched into serving themselves from the dishes in the middle, swapping them around and murmuring appreciatively as they took their first mouthfuls. The plates were warm. I poured gravy onto Edwin's vegetables for him.

'Alex finally exchanged contracts on the cottage last week,' Dominic said between mouthfuls. 'He's coming down to collect the keys on Saturday.'

Ruth put her fork down. 'Really? When did you speak to him?'

'He was in town in the week. We had drinks with the Mellards on Wednesday night. I told him he should come for lunch next Saturday.'

The potatoes were crispy and golden on the outside, light and fluffy on the inside; I suspected they had been roasted in goose fat. The carrots were glazed with honey. The lamb was so tender it slipped off my fork. I declined the wine that Dominic offered me, and spooned some homegrown mint sauce onto my plate.

'Is that all right?' Dominic was saying.

'Absolutely.' Ruth cut her meat into fine slivers. 'I can't wait to see him.'

'The Collisons' old cottage?' Vera asked. 'I didn't realise he was seriously looking.'

'That's the one,' Dominic said. 'It'll be a nice little escape when he needs it.'

Ruth reached out and put her hand over Dominic's. 'We could have a picnic on the beach on Saturday. Would you pick up groceries from the deli if I phone them an order?'

Vera turned to face me then. 'How are you liking it here so far, my dear? You know you mustn't let Edwin dominate your weekends. I hope you're not feeling homesick?'

I finished my mouthful and shook my head.

'Not homesick, no. I'm very happy, thank you.'

'More potatoes?' she asked.

'Thank you.' I took two.

I retreated to the annexe after lunch to finish unpacking. My paperbacks fitted neatly along the top shelf of the bookcase, textbooks and multicoloured ring binders underneath. I pulled a clip frame from my suitcase and contemplated the familiar photo montage: me and my three best friends — laughing in our form room, posing at the lower sixth ball, doing rabbit ears behind one another's heads. A twinge of nostalgia threatened to open the lid on other, darker memories, and I gritted my teeth and slid the frame back into the suitcase. That was all behind me now.

I angled my chair towards the window so I could watch Dominic and Edwin romp on the lawn.

Dominic reminded me of an easygoing forest animal, like a lean, friendly grizzly bear, with his height and his loose-limbed way of moving; his light brown hair unfashionably long. Perhaps it was also because of the way he would scoop Edwin up into his arms, roaring and pretending to take bites out of the little boy who would giggle and wriggle until eventually Ruth would snap at them to stop.

Usually, Dominic drove back to London very early on a Monday morning, but when Vera spent the weekend in the country with them, he gave her a lift home on the Sunday evening instead. On my first weekend at Summerbourne, they left just before Edwin's bedtime.

'Winterbourne always seems so quiet after a weekend here,' Vera told me in the hall as she waited for Dominic to retrieve her small suitcase from upstairs. She caught my confused expression and smiled. 'Winterbourne. It's the name of my house in London.' I nodded warily, unsure whether she was making a joke.

Monday morning was the start of my official employment, and the bright September sunshine lured us out to the patio straight from breakfast. The plants in the garden shone as if they had been washed and polished overnight. Ruth looked cool in a pale cotton summer dress, and I resolved to use my first pay packet to buy myself some decent clothes, and some pastel nail varnishes to replace my usual dark colours.

'It's going to be a glorious day,' Ruth said. 'We really should make the most of it. Let's take a picnic down to the beach.'

So she and I packed a bag with sandwiches and drinks and a picnic blanket. After much rummaging through a huge built-in cupboard in the day nursery, Edwin emerged laden with buckets, spades and two nets on sticks. Considering the beach is within a few hundred metres of the house, there was more of an expedition feel to the process than I had expected, although at that stage I didn't appreciate how gruelling it would be to have to haul yourself back up the cliff steps in the blazing sun if you forgot something.

We stopped frequently on the way for our intrepid three-and-three-quarter-years-old explorer to examine feathers and snails and butterflies. We paused for a chat with Michael by the back gate.

'Where's Joel, Mister Michael Harris?' Edwin asked.

'Ah, he's at preschool, my man. He'll be round later, I 'spect.'

'Joel's Edwin's best friend,' Ruth told me.

'After Theo,' Edwin said, sticking his bottom lip out. Ruth and Michael exchanged a glance.

'Yes, darling. After Theo. Say goodbye to Mr Harris, and we'll show Laura the way to the beach.'

Once through the gate, an astonishing view of the sea greeted us; my mouth fell open as I stood and gazed at it. The coastline spread out before us, undulating back towards the house and the village to our right, and curving on alongside fields and distant haze to our left. The dark blue water sparkled in front of us to the horizon. It was only a minute's walk along the path to the cliff steps. A squat tower stood near the top of the steps, its walls made with stones the same colour as the bricks of the house out of sight behind us.

'The Summerbourne folly,' Ruth told me, waving a hand at it dismissively. 'We own this strip of land up here, but the coastal footpath is public — you can get to the boatyard this way, or back into the village if you go that way. The beach is public too, but hardly anyone else ever comes here.'

'Can we go up and see the cannon, Mummy?' Edwin asked, hopping from one foot to the other.

'Not now, darling. Let's get down to the rock pools before the crabs have to go to crab preschool.'

Edwin stood still. 'No such thing as crab preschool.'

I peered up at the black barrel jutting over the platform at the top of the tower.

'Not a real cannon?' I asked.

'Kind of,' Ruth said as we redistributed Edwin's beach gear between us so that he could have his hands free to hold the railing down the cliff steps. 'It's called a noon cannon. It's on a sundial. If you set it up right, you can get the sun to shine through a lens at midday and light an explosive, and fire the cannon. Follow me now, Edwin, and hold on very carefully.'

'An actual cannonball?' I asked.

Ruth laughed. 'Goodness, no! It doesn't fire an object. Just makes a loud bang.' She paused on the steps to check that Edwin was holding the railing properly. 'Family legend says Philip Summerbourne, the one who built the house, had it put there so they'd know when it was time to pack up at the beach and head back to the house for lunch. It's such a faff, though, setting it up, I'm sure they hardly ever bothered.'

We continued our cautious descent. Edwin frowned as we reached the sand.

'*Is* there such thing as crab preschool, Missus Laura Silvey?'

'Let's go find some crabs and ask them, Master Edwin Mayes.'

He grinned.

It was a small beach, but postcard perfect in

the summer sunshine. The sand was pale yellow, and a band of rocks along the base of the cliffs bulged out to the sea at the far end of the cove to create a few rock pools. Edwin and I spent a contented hour poking around, scooping tiny fish and bigger crabs into buckets, while Ruth sat on a picnic blanket on the sand with a book, her face hidden by a huge, floppy hat. Edwin sprang between rocks with ease, and I was glad after all for my practical shorts and T-shirt.

The sun was high and fierce by the time Ruth called us over for lunch.

'Look, Mummy,' Edwin said, introducing her to the contents of his bucket, before trotting away to release the creatures back into the pools, and then galloping down to the sea to rinse off his hands.

'Where does he get his energy from?' I asked, flopping down and accepting a sandwich gratefully.

'God knows. I get exhausted just watching him.'

'Do you ever swim in the sea here?' I asked her, conscious there'd been no mention of swimming costumes when we were getting ready at the house.

'Oh, Dominic does. He'll take Edwin for a swim at the weekend. Maybe when we come down with Alex on Saturday.' She smiled, and looked out to sea. 'I used to swim here sometimes when I was a child, but' — she shrugged — 'I wouldn't be that confident to take Edwin in by myself.'

'Can I paddle, Mummy?' Edwin asked, a

sandwich in one hand, too restless to sit down.

'As long as you stay just in front of us, and no higher than your knees, darling. And keep your hat on.'

'Okay, Mummy.' He trotted off. We sat and watched him as we ate. Ruth had put suncream on him before we left the house, and was now applying some to her own limbs. I hesitated when she offered me the bottle, since my olive skin doesn't tend to burn easily, but the harsh glare on the sand was relentless, so I accepted with thanks.

'You're very . . . discreet, aren't you?' Ruth said suddenly, breaking the companionable silence and making me blink.

'What do you mean?'

'Oh, just that you don't ask lots of questions,' she said.

I handed the suncream back to her, ducking my head.

'It's not a bad thing,' she assured me, smiling. 'I meant it as a compliment. You didn't press me on why I don't like to swim in the sea any more, although I could see that you wondered. You haven't asked who Alex is.'

She raised her eyebrows as if to invite a question, and something from our conversation with Michael earlier niggled at me. Something I'd registered, but not yet thought through properly.

'Who's Theo?' I asked.

As soon as I'd said it, I was seized by an awful conviction. Who else might Edwin describe as his best friend, aside from little Joel?

Ruth was lying propped on one elbow, but jerked upright at my question. I could feel my cheeks reddening as she stared at me, and I began to apologise, but she shook her head.

'No, it's fine. You just surprised me.' She eased herself back down again. 'Theo was Edwin's twin brother. He died just after their second birthday, in December the year before last. In an accident.'

I held a hand over my mouth, staring at her.

'I'm so sorry,' I said. 'I should have realised. I shouldn't have asked.'

'It's okay. You weren't to know. He fell from the cliff here, actually.'

My eyes darted to the rocks at the base of the steps.

Ruth drew in a deep breath and then let it out again heavily. 'It's . . . I know it seems strange for us still to come here, but . . . ' She cast her eyes around the beach, choosing her words. 'This is our home. Summerbourne. My home, and Edwin's home. It always has been, and it always will be.'

I wiped a tear from the corner of my eye, and she gazed out to sea. Edwin continued to frolic in the shallows.

'I'm sorry,' I said again.

'Honestly, don't worry. It's everyday life for us. I think about him all the time. When I wake up. When I go to bed. When I'm with Edwin. When I'm not with Edwin.' She trickled sand between her fingers. 'So mentioning him doesn't upset me in that way.'

She closed her eyes for a moment, and

breathed in and out deeply before opening them again.

'Of course, Edwin was so young when it happened, he doesn't remember him really. But we talk about him, to make sure Edwin doesn't look back and think we let him forget. It's a shock for other people when we have to tell them for the first time, that's the thing.'

She passed me a paper napkin to use as a tissue, and I blew my nose noisily. I couldn't think of anything to say that wouldn't make it worse, and shook my head instead.

'Honestly, it's okay,' she said. 'To talk about him. I'm sorry too.'

We watched Edwin play for a while.

'So, who *is* Alex?' I asked eventually, to try to make her smile again, and it worked.

'Ah, Alex. You'll meet him on Saturday. He's an old friend.' She carried on watching Edwin and didn't say any more. I rubbed sand from my shins.

'And why don't you swim in the sea any more?' I asked her, my head partially turned away. She laughed.

'No reason. I was being silly. It's cold, I suppose, and I don't like not being able to see where I'm putting my feet. How boring!' She jumped up and called Edwin over. 'Let's show Laura how to make a Summerbourne sandcastle, shall we?'

'A Mayes sandcastle, Mummy.'

'All right. A super Mayes sandcastle. And when you see Uncle Alex on Saturday, you can tell him all about it.'

I considered asking why, if Alex was a friend, she called him an uncle. But her comment about me being discreet echoed in my mind. We set to work, and a lopsided sandcastle grew and spread until Edwin spotted two figures waving at the top of the cliff.

'Joel's here!' he shrieked, and scampered towards the steps, only pausing when Ruth's sharp voice made him wait for us to gather up all our belongings before she would allow him to start the ascent. Michael waited at the top, holding the hand of a small, dark-skinned boy and not letting go until we were all safely away from the cliff edge.

'Joel!' Edwin squealed, and the two boys clutched each other and twirled around, giggling.

'They can come with me to the orchard,' Michael said, and the boys followed him back to the garden gate, chattering excitedly.

'Joel's mum's gone back to Nigeria to look after her mother,' Ruth told me as we made our way back to the house. 'Chris — that's Michael's son, Joel's dad — he thought it would be easier if he and Joel moved back into Michael's cottage until Kemi comes home. I know it sounds selfish, but it's been great for us over the summer, because the boys get on so well — I haven't had to entertain Edwin while Joel's around.'

'But Joel goes to preschool now?' I asked.

'Yes. Not full time, but we'll see less of him.' She pulled a face. 'Dominic thinks Edwin should go too, but I just don't feel ready. I'd much rather have you here to help me with him.'

I followed her in through the unlocked kitchen doors, kicking my shoes off next to hers, dropping my bags, and accepting a glass of cold orange squash.

'Would you mind awfully if I left you here to listen out for Michael bringing Edwin back?' she asked. 'I feel rather headachy.'

'Of course. That's fine.'

She pottered off along the hall and up the stairs, and I sank down at the kitchen table, wrapping my hands around my cool glass and closing my eyes. I wondered how common Ruth's headaches were, and I brushed away the thought that there might be an element of convenience to them. That was none of my business. I could smell her coconut-scented suncream on my skin, and I rubbed sand from the top of one foot with the bottom of the other, listening to it scattering on the tiled floor in the otherwise silent house. As far as first days in a new job go, this had to be up there with the best.

The rest of my first week passed in a haze of sunny days. We swam in the pool several times, Edwin impressing me with his fearsome doggy paddle and his rudimentary backstroke. We helped Michael tidy some flower beds, collecting seeds into little pots and dividing up some of the bushier plants. We ran races and picked raspberries and built a hideout in the woods in the hope of glimpsing a badger or a fox. On the Wednesday, Ruth took Edwin to his gymnastics class, and I drew up a revision timetable. The three of us made an apple and plum crumble together that evening, and devoured it with custard.

I was astonished at how soon Summerbourne felt like home. I began to fall asleep within minutes of my head touching the pillow each night, and didn't stir until my alarm went off the next morning.

I tried not to dwell on little Theo, Edwin's lost twin. There were no photos on display downstairs. I wondered how the accident had happened. Ruth didn't bring the subject up again, and as that week wore on, she became increasingly distracted by plans for Saturday's picnic.

'Would you like to come with us down to the beach tomorrow?' Ruth asked me on the Friday evening after she'd put Edwin to bed. 'You're very welcome to. But don't feel you have to.'

I looked at her shopping lists on the kitchen table, and thought about the painting that Edwin had done earlier for Uncle Alex.

'You can decide in the morning, anyway,' Ruth said, and she went out into the hall, humming to herself. The microwave beeped, and I took my hot chocolate through to the annexe. I told myself I was undecided, but deep down I knew that of course I would go with them. The lure of a grand Mayes family picnic was much too strong to resist.

5

Seraphine

With Vera gone, I spend Friday evening checking through the remaining contents of the bottom desk drawer in the study, a glass of white wine turning warm and unappetising by my side. Underneath a loose photo of Edwin and Theo in stripy T-shirts, I find a newspaper obituary for my mother:

> Taken from us suddenly on 21 July 1992, RUTH ANGELA MAYES of Summerbourne House, Norfolk, aged just 29. Loving wife of Dominic Charles Mayes, beloved daughter of Vera Ann Blackwood and the late John Blackwood, dearly missed mother of Edwin, Daniel and Seraphine. Reunited in heaven with her precious son, Theodore, and with her father, brother and grandparents.

Flowery words, surely chosen by Vera. Strange that I never knew my mother had a brother. There are too many unspoken stories in our family.

I close my eyes and rotate the chair one way and then the other, consumed by the wish that when I open them, my dad will be standing there, grimacing at the mess in his study, ushering me down to the kitchen where he'll chop vegetables for a huge stir-fry while he talks me through the day's county cricket results. If I could have him back, I'd never question anything again. But when I open my eyes, I am still alone, and the questions remain.

On Saturday morning, I'm in my dressing gown, inhaling the steam from my coffee at the kitchen table, when a car pulls up. My brothers burst into the hall, clattering through to the kitchen, filling the house with noise as they fling down keys and bags and phones and takeaway coffee cups. Edwin bends to hug me, while Danny pulls a loaf from a carrier bag and starts slotting bread into the toaster, eyeing up the level in the cafetière.

'So what's up, sis?' Danny asks.

My sigh is tinged with relief, because, despite the way they get under my skin, I love my brothers fiercely, and they're the only people I can be myself with.

'Did Edwin tell you about the photo?'

Danny nods, shrugging. 'Yep. So?'

'Well . . . ' I glance at Edwin. 'I found Laura.'

Edwin makes an incredulous sound. 'You did what?'

'And also,' I say, 'I had an argument with Gran, and she told me she's going to leave Summerbourne to you, Danny.'

They both stare at me. I count the seconds of silence. Four. Five.

'Okay, hang on,' Edwin says. 'What sort of argument? What did she say, exactly?'

Danny sidles away to get milk from the fridge. I glare at his back.

'She didn't give me a reason. I guess Danny

being her favourite blue-eyed boy is all the reason she needs.'

Danny shuffles round to my side of the table with his coffee, and bumps his elbow against mine as he sits down next to me.

'Why would I want this old place? If she gives it to me, I'll give it to you. Don't sweat it.' He peers at the smoke rising from the toaster. 'As long as I can kip in the day nursery when I'm passing, and you make sure you keep some decent coffee in.'

I lean closer to him for a moment, pressing my upper arm against his.

'It's the principle, though, isn't it?' I say, straightening.

'When you say you argued with her — is she okay?' Edwin asks.

I think of Vera's hand trembling as she looked at the long-hidden photo of her dead daughter. I remember the obituary that implied she also lost a son. I tear a leaf from the bunch of wildflowers in front of me, and watch it darken as I roll it between my finger and thumb. The smell reminds me of the folly in the rain.

'She's fine,' I say. 'You know Gran. She'll be fine. But something else — did you know Mum used to have a brother? I thought she was an only child.'

Danny shrugs. Edwin's eyebrows shoot up.

'Did Gran say that?' Edwin asks. 'It's news to me. What happened to him?'

'I don't know,' I say.

Edwin stares at me. 'And what do you mean you found Laura?'

I shift in my chair. 'I found out where she works. At an insurance firm in the City. What do you remember about her?'

Edwin is still frowning, but his gaze drifts to the window.

'She was fun, she was kind. I don't know what else to say. I remember her living here, and I'm not sure I remember a time before she was here. I suppose they took her on to help Mum after Theo died.'

'September 1991, she started working here. You were three, coming up to four.'

'Well, then.' Edwin shrugs.

'What *do* you remember about the day Mum died?' I ask quietly, watching him. I've asked Edwin this before, of course, particularly when I was a teenager, but he always claimed he couldn't remember much.

He frowns down at his hands now, and I can see that he is trying. Danny and I exchange a glance.

'I think I do remember that photo being taken, the one you showed me the other night. But maybe I've just fabricated that memory, you know?'

Danny raises his eyebrows, and I lift one finger. For all our differences, we've always been good at communicating without words. I'll fetch the photo for him in a minute. He nods. Edwin is still concentrating, trying to remember.

'I think Michael was around that day too. Laura took the photo, but Michael was over by the orchard, and he shouted out — congratulations or something. And I was allowed to have chocolate biscuits for breakfast because of you being born.'

He glances up at me a little sheepishly.

Danny snorts. 'Edwin's famous stomach memory.'

'What else?' I ask. 'Which of us was Mum holding?'

'I just don't know, Seph, I told you. I couldn't even guess. I remember Mum getting upset at some point, and — and I followed her up to the folly.'

Edwin's eyes widen as he replays the scene in his mind, and Danny and I sit still, aware of our breathing, waiting for him to go on.

'She was crying. She said someone was coming to steal her baby.'

'What?' Danny and I say in unison.

Edwin takes a moment to return his focus to us, his face stricken. 'I don't know. That's what I remember. But it can't be true, can it?'

'Of course not.' Danny frowns. 'I mean, I'm sure no one was coming to steal us. But maybe that's what she believed for some reason — maybe she was having hallucinations or something.'

'What else?' I ask. 'What else do you remember?'

Edwin screws his face up, shaking his head.

'Nothing else. Mum told me to go away. I hid in the tower. There was a dead bird. Michael brought me home. I don't remember what happened after. I don't remember Laura leaving.'

'What about before that day?' I ask. 'When

Laura was living here, and Mum was pregnant with us — what was it like?'

'Just — normal, you know. I used to play with Joel a lot, play on the beach.' He thinks for a moment. 'I remember getting my bike for Christmas. And having a ride in Uncle Alex's sports car.'

'Who's Uncle Alex?' Danny and I ask.

Edwin shrugs. 'I don't know. He had a yellow sports car. I loved that car.'

Danny drains his mug and stretches for the cafetière. 'Well, none of that accounts for there only being one baby in the photo. Unless someone did steal one of us' — he looks pointedly at me — 'and then brought her straight back when they realised what a nightmare she was.'

'Danny, that doesn't help,' I snap. 'That's why I thought we should ask Laura. She could tell us exactly what happened that day. She was here.'

Edwin gives me a stern look.

'When you said you found Laura, do you mean you found out where she works, or you actually found *her?*'

'Both. I went to her office, and I saw her.'

'Did you talk to her?' Edwin asks, and I can't tell what he's hoping the answer will be.

'I tried to catch her when she came out of work, but — ' I shake my head. 'I lost her.'

Danny snorts into his coffee.

'For God's sake,' Edwin says. 'Why? What on earth did you expect her to say?'

I jump up and go to the recipe book, sliding the photo out, keeping my back to my brothers

67

for a few seconds, blinking hard. Then I stalk back and lay the picture face-up on the table between them.

'Look. That's Mum,' I say to Danny, and he draws the picture closer to himself with one finger, staring.

'She's just had twins,' I say. 'She's dressed, her hair is neat, I'm pretty sure she's even got lipstick on. She doesn't look like someone who's thinking about killing herself.'

'Seraphine . . .' Edwin murmurs, but he too is frowning at the photo.

'Why did they pose for a family photo with only one of their new babies?' I ask. 'Why do they look so — so *normal*, Mum and Dad, and yet a few hours after this was taken, Mum was dead? I don't understand how it happened.'

Danny slides the photo towards Edwin and sits back, studying my face.

'It's a bit . . . surprising,' Danny says. 'But it was such a long time ago, what's the point of worrying about the details? We know Mum became ill, we know what she did. This photo — if anything, it's reassuring, isn't it? Shows they were happy, for a while at least, before it happened.'

Edwin's voice is quiet as he bends over the picture. 'They thought they had all the time in the world to take more photos.'

'But why only one of us?' I ask.

Danny shrugs. 'Maybe one of us was asleep, inside, and they didn't want to wake us.'

'That's what Gran said.' I can't keep the scepticism from my voice.

Edwin looks at me. 'It's not just that, is it? What's really upsetting you? That Dad kept this photo hidden, never showed us?'

I look at him. At his thick mass of light brown hair and his blue eyes and his Mayes jaw. And then I look at Danny, with his darker hair just as thick, his eyes just as blue, his jaw just as strong. These days they look more like twins than Danny and I ever did.

'I don't think I'm Mum and Dad's baby,' I say, and my brothers sit speechless, staring at me. 'Look at me. My skin's different, my hair's different, my eyes are brown. I think I might be someone else's child.' I press my hands to my cheeks for a few moments, drawing a deep breath in and out. 'What if I'm Laura's baby?'

Danny's mouth falls open, and Edwin shakes his head, but neither can summon an immediate reply. I shove my chair back, scraping it noisily along the tiles.

'I knew you wouldn't believe me.' I stumble out to the hall, then on into the sitting room, looking for a box of tissues. Edwin and Danny exchange words behind me, and then follow me in.

'Seraphine, listen to me.' Edwin perches next to me on the sofa. 'You're not sleeping, you're not eating; it's no wonder you're not feeling rational. Dad's accident — we can't make sense of that. But this — you're not thinking straight. Of course you're Mum and Dad's child. You're our sister.'

Danny waves the photograph at me. 'You look like her, Seph. Look how pretty she was.

Everyone always says you get your looks from her, don't they?' I realise how concerned he is about me when he doesn't follow this up with a teasing insult.

Edwin nods vigorously. 'It's true. Look at you. You even move like Mum did — graceful, not like me and Lummox here.'

I press my lips together, but I stare at my mother's short frame in the photo, not so different to mine, and I think about Laura's height.

'I thought . . . ' I swallow. 'But what if Gran wants to leave Summerbourne to Danny because she knows I don't really belong here?'

Danny coughs. I know he's covering a chuckle, and I glare at him.

'Ah, come on,' he says. 'Can you imagine Gran accepting an interloper at Summerbourne? She'd be outraged!' He draws himself up and does a scarily accurate impression of our grandmother: *'If you're not descended from Philip Summerbourne, you can clear orf!'*

I thump him hard on his thigh, but I'm not crying any more.

'Someone's coming,' Edwin says suddenly, tilting his ear to the hall, and seconds later the doorbell rings. The three of us look at one another.

'I'll go,' Edwin says, and we listen as he greets someone at the door and then calls out, 'It's only Joel.'

I groan. If Joel's staying with Michael, he probably spotted Edwin's car passing the cottage earlier. I'm still in my dressing gown and not in the mood for any visitors, least of all Joel Harris.

Danny opens his mouth to say something, but hesitates, looking from the tissue balled up in my hand to my tear-streaked face.

'Don't look at me like that,' I say.

'Like what?'

'Pityingly.'

He grins. 'Well, you are a bit pathetic, sis.' He hauls himself up and heads for the door. 'I'll shove them through to the kitchen so you can escape upstairs. I'd hate Joel to catch sight of you like this — he'd never come back.'

I stick my tongue out at him as he leaves the room, and then wait until I hear their voices recede into the kitchen before I race upstairs.

Joel Harris is Edwin's oldest friend, and was a constant visitor to Summerbourne when I was growing up. He knew me as well as my brothers knew me, and he was patient with me even when my brothers weren't. The four of us spent hours together in the school holidays, and in the absence of friends my own age I grew to idolise Joel.

I was fourteen when Joel and Edwin left for university. Miserable at school, short-tempered with Danny at home, I began to dream of Joel returning and declaring he'd fallen in love with me. I longed to leave the sneers of my classmates behind, and marry Joel, and live happily ever after with him at Summerbourne.

How I miss the days when love seemed so obvious and simple.

My fledgling romantic hopes were crushed a couple of weeks before my fifteenth birthday. I don't relish revisiting that memory now, but it occurs to me for the first time that something Joel said that day might be linked in some way to what happened when Danny and I were born.

Instead of taking a quick shower, I pad across to the main bathroom and rummage through the cupboard for bath oil as the tub fills. Then I ease down into the hot water to try to recall the details of that day.

It was a hot July afternoon, and Edwin had invited half a dozen university friends to Summerbourne to celebrate finishing their first-year exams. At nineteen, these young men and women seemed impossibly grown-up, drinking beer and cider by the pool, telling anecdotes I couldn't follow, and cracking jokes I didn't understand. I studied the girls through my lashes: the sweep of their hair, their glossy nails, the way they adjusted their bikini straps. I tried to mimic them, draping my hair over one shoulder in the hope of catching Joel's attention, but he had barely glanced in my direction since he'd arrived.

Ralph Luckhurst had cycled up from the village to join in the fun, and he and Danny persuaded several of the guests into the pool to play a game of Marco Polo. Edwin remained sprawled on a sunlounger, arguing lazily with a bearded medic friend of Joel's about politics and the new prime minister. A dentistry student named Ruby, wearing a bright red swimsuit, tried to persuade Edwin to make room for her on his sunlounger. When Edwin refused, she wandered over and sat down right next to Joel.

I close my eyes now, sinking lower in the

bathwater, remembering the twist of pain I'd felt under my ribcage as I watched Ruby rest her cheek against Joel's smooth shoulder. But Joel had been distracted that day, irritable, and I was savagely glad that he only frowned at her when she whispered something in his ear.

'So what's it like, then, being a twin?' Ruby had asked me suddenly, and it had taken me several seconds to switch from being an unhappy observer to an active participant in the conversation.

'Nothing special,' I'd said.

Danny hauled himself out of the pool and flopped down beside me. 'Cheers, sis.'

Ruby and the bearded medic had laughed.

There followed the usual questions — which of us was born first, did we have a telepathic connection, why didn't we look alike. The others in the pool drifted over to hear our answers, and I let Danny do the talking, uncomfortable under the scrutiny of so many pairs of eyes.

Edwin mentioned that I was twice Danny's size when we were born, and I remember the way Ruby leaned against Joel as she giggled.

I tip my head right back to soak my hair now, concentrating hard in an attempt to recall Joel's exact words that day. I'd had the impression he wasn't following the conversation, and I'd been half disappointed at his indifference, until he suddenly spoke.

'My grandad calls them the Summerbourne sprites,' Joel had said.

I sit up, wringing my hair out, frowning.

It was a name other children had called us

when Danny and I first started at the village primary school years earlier. I'd always disliked it, without having any idea where it came from. Over the years, as I learned not to react so fiercely, and perhaps as Danny and I learned to keep our closeness at home separate from our lives at school, the phrase had dropped out of use. For Joel to mention it then, in front of people I thought so sophisticated, and to imply that Michael — an adult — *still* used it to describe us . . . It took my breath away at the time. It still makes my throat tighten now.

I remember staring at him, trying to work out why he'd said it. Joel had always been an ally, never been anything but kind to me. Perhaps he was trying to impress Ruby, I thought. If so, he succeeded.

'Ooh, why are they sprites?' Ruby had said.

'Can they do magic, then?' the bearded medic had asked. 'Or do weird things happen around them?'

'Hey, cut it out,' Ralph had said, pushing his dark curls back from his face, flashing me a concerned look. Ralph and I had only overlapped at primary school for a year or so, but he'd defended me from the taunts of older children several times back then, and I loved him for it. On this occasion, the mildly drunk students ignored him.

'You didn't tell us you had spoo-ooky twins in the family, Edwin.'

'Do us some sprite tricks, won't you?'

'Careful, Ruby — you wouldn't want to make them angry!'

Joel had scowled, not meeting my eyes. 'Something strange happened here on the day they were born, that's all,' he'd muttered.

I release my breath, and the surface of the bathwater sways. *Something strange happened here on the day we were born.*

Joel's words had only encouraged the students' speculation that afternoon. Their mock alarm escalated, and the jokes continued.

I had expected Edwin to cut them off, to explain *that was the day our mother died, actually*, to make them feel guilty. But he joined in the laughter and didn't stop them. And the more they teased, the closer to tears I became, until eventually, I fled, knocking a glass from the poolside table as I ran, covering my ears as I sprinted into the house and up the stairs to sob under my bedcovers. The memory of Danny's easy ability to laugh along with their jokes had made me feel even worse.

I avoided Joel for months after that. Even when Edwin explained that Joel had just found out about Michael's dementia diagnosis that morning, that he'd been preoccupied and miserable about his grandad. Even when Vera left me notes on the hall table saying Joel had rung *again*, and would I please ring him back. I thought about him every day, but I barely spoke to him for the best part of two years.

And then I did the only thing left that could possibly make the situation worse. I kissed him.

It happened at Edwin's graduation party, surrounded by all of Edwin's friends. I drank too much white cider, and I launched myself at Joel without warning and kissed him. In the ensuing confusion, Ralph Luckhurst misread the situation and punched him, and after that Joel no longer made an effort to talk to me at all.

Now he's renting somewhere in the village, apparently, doing locum GP work while he looks for a permanent job. I presume this pattern of work means he can also keep an eye on his grandad while his parents are away. He and I exchange civil words when we have to, and as far as anyone else is concerned, there's no bad feeling between us, but we are certainly no longer friends.

I cup water in my hands and rinse my face repeatedly before I pull the plug on the cooling bath water. I refuse to waste another moment dwelling on Joel Harris.

The summer-born sprites. The Summerbourne sprites. I mull over the phrase as I dry my hair and pull on a dress. *Something strange happened here on the day they were born.* Mum thought someone was trying to steal her baby. Just the one baby. She posed for a photograph with just one baby. She gave birth here at Summerbourne with no midwife present, but wouldn't that have been risky with a twin pregnancy?

I stare at myself in the mirror. Could I get hold of my mother's medical notes, her pregnancy record, after all these years? It's ironic that Joel, as a doctor, might be able to tell me the answer, but I'm not about to run downstairs and ask him. Instead, I'll make an appointment at the village surgery for Monday morning. Pamela

Larch has been the nurse there for longer than I can remember, and she knows everything about everyone around here. Maybe she can help me.

6

Laura

SEPTEMBER 1991

From the moment Alex sprang out of his bright yellow sports car onto the Summerbourne driveway, I detected an undercurrent between him and Ruth. It crackled between them, adding an edginess to the social niceties, pulsing in the mistiming of their reactions to each other.

'I've got the keys!' Alex waved them in one hand, raising a bottle of champagne in the other. 'And I realised this morning it's ten years since we met. Can you believe it?'

Dominic took the bottle and shook his hand, and Ruth stepped forward to kiss him on both cheeks while Edwin danced around him on the gravel.

'Ten years since freshers' week? Good God,' Dominic said. 'We're getting old.'

Alex lifted a bouquet of yellow and orange flowers from the passenger seat, and Ruth smiled at them.

'Freesias,' she said. 'How lovely.' She dipped her face to them.

'And roses,' Alex said. Edwin scuffed his sandal into the gravel, and Alex made a show of clapping his hand to his forehead.

'I almost forgot the most important present of

all.' He encouraged Edwin to feel around under the seats and peer into the glove compartment, until Edwin finally persuaded him to check in the Alfa Romeo's little boot. A yellow toy dumper truck was discovered, and Edwin dashed off with it to test it in his sandpit.

I hovered on the front step until Dominic called me over. Alex took my hand in his.

'Lovely to meet you, Laura,' he said, a trace of the smile from Edwin's antics still lingering on his lips. He was shorter than Dominic but broader shouldered, his muscled arms smooth and brown, his handshake surprisingly gentle. For a moment the three of us blinked in a circle around him, transfixed, as he closed his eyes and drew in a deep breath.

'Ah, can't beat that Summerbourne air,' he declared.

'Too right,' said Dominic. 'Does you the world of good, escaping to the coast after a hard week in the office. You know you've started a trend — the Mellards viewed a really dilapidated place last week. Closer to the beach than yours, though. Lots of potential, apparently.'

Alex grinned. 'Money pit, more like.'

Ruth groaned. 'Can you imagine the Mellards descending on the village every weekend? We'd have to escape into town.' Both men laughed.

I hung back as they made their way through to the kitchen, talking over the top of one another, discussing estate agents and solicitors and surveyors. Dominic was keen to open the champagne straightaway.

'Let's wait till we're on the beach, darling,'

Ruth said. 'We'll have it with lunch.'

I escaped through the door at the back of the hall and joined Edwin at his sandpit. We chatted companionably until the kitchen doors were flung open.

'Five minutes!' Ruth called. 'Are you all set, you two?'

I waved and nodded. She disappeared back inside.

'Can you carry my truck, Missus Laura Silvey?' Edwin asked, patting my arm with his sandy hand. He was trying to make me smile. I hugged him, transferring sand onto my T-shirt. 'Of course I can, lovely boy.'

Between us we carried the picnic essentials to the top of the cliff steps. Dominic retrieved a large beach parasol and a faded fabric windbreak from the folly tower, and the two men made an extra trip up and down the cliff steps to bring everything onto the beach. Ruth directed the placing of picnic blankets and coolboxes, and then she settled in the prime spot under the parasol, kicking off her sandals. The coral pink nail varnish on her toes and fingers matched her dress perfectly.

A lightweight sailing dinghy borrowed from one of the neighbours rested at the base of the cliff, and Edwin repeatedly asked his parents to let him play on it.

'Daddy will take you out on it later, darling,' Ruth said. 'Why don't you see what you can find in the rock pools now with Laura?' Dominic was settling himself on the blanket on one side of her and Alex on the other, and for a brief moment all three of them squinted up at me. I reached for Edwin's hand.

'Let's go!' I said, grabbing a bucket and net, and we raced over to the rocks. I kept my back to the picnic spot while Edwin poked through the first pool, and I hunched my shoulders against the laughter that drifted over the sand towards us. I wouldn't have wanted to sit with them, even if they'd asked me to. I had no desire to share their conversation about house prices, or their in-jokes, or their champagne.

'Don't forget your suncream,' Edwin said, peering at my cheeks.

'Let's find the biggest crab ever,' I said, and set to work lifting the loose rocks, shredding my fingernails in the process, so that he could scoop underneath them with his net. Eventually, Dominic ambled over to admire Edwin's catches and to tell us lunch was ready.

Alex declared the picnic a triumph. It's not the word I would have used. Soggy puff pastry cases containing limp prawns, too big for one mouthful but too fragile to sink your teeth into. Wild rice salad laced with gritty husks. Baguettes with sharp crusts and wispy interiors. Edwin and I sat on our own blanket and polished off the cold roast chicken drumsticks between us.

I declined Dominic's offer of champagne, but watched surreptitiously as both Alex and Ruth sipped theirs slowly, while Dominic knocked back his first glass and poured himself a second.

Ruth reached out a hand as he went to pour a third. 'Don't you think you should save that for after the Topper?'

'Fine. Twenty minutes to let your lunch go down, young man, and we'll take the boat out, okay?'

Edwin bounced up and down. 'I'm going to run to the rock pools twenty times. Watch me, Uncle Alex!'

'Where does he get his energy from?' Alex asked, watching him, and Ruth caught my eye and we smiled briefly at each other.

'Goodness knows,' she said.

Eventually, Edwin slowed down and lost count, throwing himself onto the blanket at Ruth's feet. Dominic yawned and stretched.

'We must remember coffee next time — should have brought a flask,' he said.

Ruth didn't look at him. 'Feel free.'

I agreed with him privately, although I'd have preferred tea.

Alex helped Dominic drag the dinghy to the shore, and then the two men shed their clothes down to their trunks and slid the boat into the surf. Edwin nestled in the central section, bundled into an orange life jacket, and the men's voices floated back to us as they pushed the boat towards deeper water.

Ruth stretched out in her patch of shade, propped up on her elbows, and sighed.

'Isn't this just the perfect day?'

I hugged my knees without replying, watching Alex's arms steady the boat while Dominic hauled himself onto it. The breeze carried Edwin's shrill chatter to us. The vessel looked flimsy on the choppy surface, and I marvelled at the little boy's confidence.

'He'd love to have children of his own, of course.'

I knew who she meant. I nodded, and took my sunglasses off to rub a smear of suncream from the lens, half shocked at this glimpse into Alex's desires, half wanting to hear more. Ruth yawned and sipped her champagne.

Dominic fiddled with the sail, and suddenly, the dinghy leapt into life, shooting away from Alex and bouncing across the waves. Down in its hollow centre, Edwin whooped. Alex shouted encouragement as Dominic swung the boat round and raced back again. Ruth clapped, and we watched them zigzag back and forth for a while.

Alex threw up his hands as he strode out of the sea. 'Your son's an adrenaline junkie!' He shook salt water over the picnic remnants as he towelled his hair. Ruth tilted a glass at him, and he dropped onto the blanket next to her.

I fixed my gaze on the little boat zipping back and forth, burrowing my toes under the sand at the edge of the blanket.

'So am I going to have to go shopping with you?' Ruth said. 'Make sure you don't turn this cottage into a sad bachelor pad?'

Alex laughed. 'It's about as far from bachelor pad as it could be at the moment.'

'I'm sure there's lots we can do with it,' Ruth said.

My neck was stiff. Their feet were in my field of vision: hers pale and delicate with pink varnished ovals; his brown and smooth with nails cut straight across. When he said something in a

83

low voice, she rolled towards him and her toes brushed his shin. I clenched my jaw.

The little boat bobbed closer to the shore, and Dominic slid off into the water to tow it in. A faint wail reached our spot on the beach. I leapt up and met them at the water's edge, taking Edwin from Dominic's arms as he swung him off the boat.

'I swallowed it,' Edwin sobbed, and I helped him up the sand and wrapped him in a towel. Alex poked a straw into a carton of juice for him.

'Unlucky, Edwin,' Dominic told him. 'You did great up till then. That was a monster wave that got you.'

Edwin sniffed and nodded. Dominic poured himself some more champagne and lay back, puffing out heavily.

'I'd offer to take you out, Laura, but that's finished me off,' he said, his eyelids lowered.

'Darling, it's the champagne that's finished you off,' Ruth said.

Dominic raised his head for a moment. 'Alex'll take you if you fancy it? Won't you, Alex?' He settled his head back down on the blanket, easing it left and right to shape the underlying sand into a more comfortable pillow. 'She's a proper swimmer, our Laura — a real athlete.'

I rubbed sand from my shins, frowning.

Ruth nudged Alex with her foot. 'Yes, go on, Alex.'

'You can't stay at Summerbourne without learning how to sail a Topper,' Dominic said, his eyes firmly closed.

Alex looked at me. 'Have you done it before?'

I shook my head. He stood up and stretched, and then held his hand out to me.

'Shall we?'

Ruth settled back onto her elbows with a serene smile, her huge pink-framed sunglasses hiding her eyes. I fumbled out of my shorts and T-shirt, tugging at the black fabric of my swimming costume automatically, wishing I owned something prettier. I'd lost weight when I was ill a few months earlier, and hadn't been able to train at the pool, and this had left me feeling self-consciously sharp angled and untoned.

I kept my eyes fixed on the sea, and then on the boat as Alex and I dragged it into the water together. When he cupped his hand under my elbow to help me climb aboard, the breeze snatched my breath away.

'How d'you feel up there?' he asked.

I looked at the glittering surface of the sea and the dark strands of his hair and the tiny hesitation in his smile. 'Precarious.'

He laughed and sprang up to join me. 'Just relax, and lean with me,' he said. 'You'll get a feel for it in no time.'

The moment the sail went up, we were seized by the elements. The restless mass of water sucked at the hull beneath us, threatening to swallow us, but the wind scooped us up and sent us skimming over the surface, our hair whipping behind us. Sunlight refracted off the spray; everything sparkled. His thigh pressed against my thigh, his shoulder pressed against my shoulder, and the heat from his limbs soaked into my muscles and made my heart swell.

We swayed in synchrony, countering the tug of the sail as the boat shot across the waves. Alex threw his head back and laughed at the sky, and I leaned in closer to him, awed by the power of the wind and his seemingly effortless control over where it took us.

'Like it?' he asked.

'I love it!'

I lost all track of time as we flew over the surface of the planet together.

Afterwards, when it was all over and we were tugging the boat through waist-deep water towards the shore, he asked me how I was enjoying living at Summerbourne.

'Have you fallen under their spell, the golden couple? Are they treating you well?' There was a fleeting intensity in his look. I had no idea how to answer beyond a vague nod and a shrug.

Neither Dominic nor Ruth left the picnic spot to help us haul the boat up the sand, but they greeted us with smiles and congratulations.

'Bravo! What do you think, Laura? Are you a convert?' Dominic asked.

Ruth threw me a towel and indicated the sleeping child by her side.

'We've actually managed to wear him out.' She passed me a plastic tumbler of cool lemonade, and brushed at something on Alex's shoulder as he collapsed onto the blanket next to her.

'That was exhilarating,' Alex said. 'Magnificent. I may have to come down every weekend while the weather's like this.'

'And in the winter,' Ruth said.

'Whenever I can.' He smiled.

'Come and visit me in the week sometimes,' she said, her fingertips resting on his smooth forearm. 'It's so tediously boring here in the week.'

Dominic grunted from his prone position. 'I like the way you pretend you're stuck out here against your will.' He yawned. 'You know your mother's lusting after one of those luxury apartments in Kensington, darling. We can move into Winterbourne whenever you like.'

Ruth angled her hat brim between herself and her husband. 'You know how I feel about the city. It's much better for Edwin to be here.'

Dominic hauled himself up onto one elbow and lifted the lid of a coolbox. 'Beer?' he asked Alex, pulling out a bottle. Alex waved a hand to decline.

Ruth frowned. 'Promise me you'll come down in the week sometimes, in the winter.'

'I do have a life in Leeds, you know,' Alex said. 'A little thing called a job. I can't spend my whole life driving up and down the motorway.' He took a breath as though about to say more, but then gave a small laugh instead. 'Much as I'd love to spend all my free time here.'

'Move down here then,' Ruth said.

Alex pulled a face.

A seagull flapped down onto the edge of my blanket, making me jump. It grabbed a discarded lump of pastry and stalked away to shake it apart on the sand. Ruth sprang to her feet.

'Right, time to head back. I can't bear this heat a minute longer.' She scooped paper plates and detritus into coolboxes and slammed on lids.

'Ruth, Edwin's still asleep,' Dominic said.

'You can carry him, can't you?'

'Well, yes, but not him *and* everything else.'

'Well, come back for everything else.'

She picked up a bag and her hat, and marched off towards the steps, calling out, 'I have a headache. I'll see you back at the house.'

Dominic groaned. 'Sorry, guys.'

'Do you want me to carry Edwin back?' Alex asked.

'No, it's fine. I'll carry him. If you can both bring a bag or two, I'll come back for the rest later.'

We barely spoke on the way back. I stumbled once at the top of the cliff steps, and Alex stepped closer to steady me with his forearm, the bottles sliding and clinking in the coolbox he carried.

'Steady,' he said, and he waited for me to regain control of my clumsy limbs, his smile making my heart rattle. I mumbled an apology, but I carried the glow of our skin contact all the way back along the cliff path, through the trees, past the blushing dahlias and starry-headed asters in their neat-edged beds.

The back doors were open, Ruth's hat abandoned on the kitchen table. Alex declined Dominic's offer of a drink.

'Thanks but I'll be off. I'm driving home tonight. No furniture at the cottage yet.'

'You can sleep here.' Dominic waved a hand vaguely, but Alex shook his head.

'It was a great day. Really. Nice to meet you,

Laura. Give me a bell in the week, Dom.' He let himself out.

Edwin was stirring, and I suggested that I toast some crumpets for his tea, and find him a quiet activity in the day nursery for an hour or so before bedtime.

'You sure you don't mind?' Dominic asked.

'Not at all.'

'Thanks, Laura. I've got that lamp for you, by the way. It's in the boot of my car — I'll bring it in later.' He shuffled out to the hall and up the stairs. I thought about the remaining picnic equipment waiting on the beach.

Alex's sunglasses poked out between towels in one of the bags. I transferred them to the kitchen windowsill. He'd be back to pick them up soon enough, with a bit of luck.

7

Seraphine

I wake early on Monday morning, and set off from Summerbourne on foot, a good half an hour before my appointment with Pamela Larch at the surgery. I've known Pamela all my life, so I'm hoping she won't mind me not giving a reason to the receptionist over the phone. I still remember the receptionist, Hayley Pickersgill, as an eight-year-old, asking me why I didn't look like my twin brother. Asking me whether it was true that Summerbourne was cursed, that witches had stolen my mother's real children, and that my mother had bargained with her soul to try to get them back.

'*But the witches took the real twins anyway,*' she'd whispered, wide-eyed. '*And the fairies left you and Danny, sprite babies, as a swap. Is it true?*'

I was suspended from school for three days after I punched her. One of her teeth was knocked out, although Danny assured me afterwards it was only one of her wobbly baby teeth. Dad had to come back from London to talk to the head teacher, and by the time I was allowed back at school, Hayley had told everyone I was *mental*. I was only six, but I didn't get invited to birthday parties in the village for a long time after that.

I put Hayley Pickersgill out of my mind. The earlier mist has cleared to reveal blue skies with high wispy clouds, the air already warm. The hedgerow along the lane buzzes with insects, and I spot Michael sitting out in the front garden of his cottage as I approach. His white hair is as abundant as ever, but he looks frailer than he did a few months ago, and his face is bordering on gaunt. I raise a tentative hand in greeting.

'My heart alive! It's one of them Summerbourne sprites,' he says as I come into his field of vision, and I scuff my shoe with a jolt at the unexpectedness of it. I resented this nickname for years as a child, but hearing it now in Michael's voice makes me wonder again about its origins. I steady myself against his gate, staring at him. His eyes dart on either side of me, and a crease of worry forms across his forehead.

'I'm Seraphine, Mr Harris,' I manage eventually. 'Seraphine Mayes.'

He screws his face up.

'Have you come about the — what was it?'

'No, no. I'm just passing.' The flickering of his eyes makes me glance away. 'I hear Joel's been staying with you, Mr Harris?'

Michael frowns, but at that moment, Joel's head appears at an open upstairs window.

'Oh, it's you,' Joel says. 'Hang on. I'll come down.'

Michael and I wait in awkward silence for him to emerge, and my pulse jumps as he ducks through the low front doorway.

'Seraphine. Hi.'

He's wearing shorts and a creased grey T-shirt, battered old trainers. This is only the second time I've seen him this year, and I try to absorb all the details without making it obvious. He looks as though he's considering holding out his hand to shake mine over the gate, but changes his mind and tucks it into his pocket.

'Not working today?' I ask. As if I'm suspicious that he might in fact have a waiting room full of patients upstairs in his grandfather's cottage. Even Michael looks slightly taken aback.

'Er — nope. Got a few days off. I'm giving Grandad a hand while Mum and Dad are away.' His eyes narrow as he studies me, and I shrink in my skin slightly. It strikes me that Edwin has probably asked him to look out for me, has quite possibly told him that I've been behaving erratically.

'How about you?' he asks.

'I'm just heading into the surgery, actually. I've got an appointment.' I wince. *Shut up, Seraphine. He doesn't need to know this.*

'I could give you a lift?' he says.

'No, no, it's fine. I wanted to walk.'

'Okay. Well. Give us a shout if you need anything.'

I give a half wave in reply and hurry on. I'm annoyed at myself and at the Harris men. Joel and I are never going to regain our old friendship, but if they didn't insist on calling me names, or colluding with my brother to spy on me, we might manage a more comfortable neighbourly relationship.

The surgery's tiny waiting room is empty.

Hayley Pickersgill gives me a smile that doesn't reach her eyes, and I keep my chin high as I sweep past her and stand in front of the array of posters on the noticeboard, each one precisely fixed with brass drawing pins. At the edge of my vision, Hayley waggles her fingers and beams down at a sparkly ring, and I remember Vera mentioning that she was recently engaged to Ralph Luckhurst. The lump in my throat is hard to ignore. There was a time when Ralph used to tell me I was the most beautiful girl in the world. He deserves so much better than Hayley Pickersgill.

Pamela calls me through to her room. She's a smiley woman with a kind manner, and I've always liked her, even when she used to give us our dreaded childhood inoculations. She always gave us chocolate buttons afterwards.

'Seraphine Mayes, it does my eyes good to see you. You looked just like your dear mama standing out there in the waiting room. I'm so sorry about your father, my dear, such a terrible accident. Martin and I came to the service — I don't know if you saw us?'

I nod. 'Thank you for coming. It means a lot.' I'm reminded suddenly of one of Michael's old stories: Martin was one of the village tearaways my grandmother took under her wing many years ago after breaking up a fight he was in — *Blood from Martin Larch's nose dripped all over Mrs Blackwood's white gloves*, Michael used to tell us.

'It was such a moving service,' Pamela continues. 'I had a chat with Edwin in the church afterwards. Such a fine young man he is. And Danny looked well after his travels. How's your grandmother?'

Pamela has always talked a lot, and isn't any more discreet about her patients' affairs than she believes she ought to be. I'm thinking this can only help my cause.

'Gran's very well, thank you,' I say, and she smiles, the skin on either side of her eyes crinkling.

'So what can I do for you today, my dear?' she asks.

'I'm after my mother's medical notes.'

She sits back in surprise. 'Whatever for?'

I lick my lips. 'Her maternity notes, particularly. I'd like to know whether she had any complications with her pregnancies, and births, you know. In case it might be useful to know for my own . . . future.'

Her gaze flicks to my abdomen. She blinks with professional thoughtfulness, but I can feel the force of her village-centric curiosity behind her eyes. I gesture with my hands palm up.

'Most women — they can just ask their mums, can't they? But I'll never be able to,' I say.

She purses her lips. 'Of course, my dear. I understand. But I'm afraid it's most unlikely your mother's notes still exist. It was all paper in those days, and they'd have been shredded after — well, they're destroyed after a patient dies, you see. A year or so afterwards, maybe. There's no room to store such things in the long term.'

I'm unprepared for her reaching across to pat my hand, and I flinch as she touches me. She draws back. I close my eyes, embracing the swell of disappointment that encourages a tear to spill over and roll down my cheek.

'Oh, there, there, my dear.' She scoots her chair closer to mine and passes me a tissue with a practised flourish from a cardboard cube on her desk, not touching me this time. 'Don't get upset. What was it you wanted to know, particularly? Maybe I can help?'

I dab at my nose. 'I suppose any scan records from the hospital would have been destroyed by now too?' I ask. She nods, her widened eyes fastened on mine.

'Did you know my mother well during her pregnancy with us — with me and Danny?' I ask.

She settles back in her seat with a small satisfied sigh. She'll enjoy repeating all this to Martin tonight, I'm sure. He's a police inspector nowadays — the village bad boy turned good. Between them, Pamela and Martin must see most of the local troubles and catastrophes firsthand.

'Ah, I did, my dear. And in her previous pregnancy too, with Edwin and Theodore. Such beautiful boys. Such a tragedy.' She sighs again, loudly. 'She didn't want to see Dr Motte with her second pregnancy, or anyone else. She went off doctors and hospitals for good after little Theo. They told her he might recover, you know, after he fell. Your poor parents sat by his hospital cot for a week before they turned the life support machine off. Terrible, it was.'

'I didn't know that,' I whisper. I suspect Edwin doesn't know that either. I wish she hadn't told me. I dig my nails into my palms.

'So who did she see, with her second pregnancy?' I ask.

'Now, let me think. I believe she had a scan at a private hospital in London. She didn't want community midwife visits, I know that, and she was determined to have the baby at home. Well, babies, as it turned out, of course.' She laughs, seemingly undisturbed by the hiccup of strangeness in her story. The hairs on my arms rise. I draw a deep breath in through my nose as unobtrusively as possible.

'So — she was expecting just one baby?'

'Well, yes. At least that's what she told people. They'd have forced her to have hospital monitoring if they'd known you were twins, I suppose, and she just wanted to be left alone to have the home birth she wanted. I expect she knew the private hospital wouldn't interfere, or wouldn't even know what went on at this end.'

I release my breath, my shoulders relaxing.

'I promised her I'd go over and help with the delivery if she needed me, because she didn't want strangers there.' She darts me a sharp look. 'I would have gone, but I'd have called for back-up, no hesitation. I wouldn't have done anything unprofessional.'

I give her my best reassuring smile.

'Of course, you two came early in the end,' she continues. 'What date was it?'

'Twenty-first of July,' I say.

'Ah yes. We weren't expecting you until the end of August. But as it turned out, you did well for twins, getting that close to your due date, and your dear mama got the home birth she wanted.'

'And did you see us, on that day? After . . . '

She goes to pat my hand again, but draws back at the last moment.

'Oh, my love. Yes, I did. I dashed up to Summerbourne as soon as I heard the news. Your poor, poor mother. Dreadful, it was. And you so tiny — well, you were quite a decent size, my dear, but goodness me, your brother was a shrimp of a thing. They sent three ambulances out, and fire engines — you know, because of the — the rocks and everything. And in the end they took little Danny off to the hospital. I offered to help, but your father went with Danny, and your grandmother stayed at the house with you and Edwin. A terrible day.'

I'm listening to her with one part of my brain, but another part is scrabbling around for something — the right question, the key fact.

'And Laura?' I ask. 'What happened to her?'

'Laura?' she says blankly. Then, 'Oh, Laura, the nanny? Nice girl. A terrible shock, it was, to her too, of course. She left, went off to university, I believe. Edwin loved that girl — might have helped him if she'd been able to stay on for the summer, but I suppose she couldn't.'

I nod, exhaling. Another thought occurs to me.

'Do you remember a man called Alex, used to visit my parents?'

Pamela's face lights up.

'Oh, I remember him all right. Used to see him around the village a fair bit in those days — he bought the Collisons' old cottage, although he sold it again after your mother died. I remember him coming in here with the nanny once, and your brother.' She nudges my arm, and I manage not to react. 'Ever so handsome, he was. Whatever happened to him?'

I stare at her. 'I don't know,' I say eventually, and she shrugs.

'Shame.'

'Do you mean he came into the surgery here with Laura?'

'Oh yes. Edwin cut himself, and they brought him in, and I put a couple of butterfly strips on it, if I recall. Nothing major. Such a charming man. Pity he left.'

'Can you remember his surname, Mrs Larch?' I ask.

She furrows her brow. 'An Indian name it was, began with a 'K'. Oh, I can't remember. I can ask Martin for you, if you like. Memory like an elephant, that man.'

'Yes, please, Mrs Larch,' I say, getting to my feet. 'Yes, please do, and let me know as soon as you can. I'll give you my number.'

I'm jotting it down, and realise she's looking at me with some bemusement.

'I'm sorry I couldn't help with your mother's notes, my dear,' she says, and I wave her apology away.

'You've been very helpful, honestly. Please do let me know what Martin remembers.'

I hand her my phone number, and she looks at it, nodding.

I feel lighter as I step out of the cool surgery into the bright glare of the village high street. My mother had wanted a peaceful home birth, without excessive medical interference, so she told people she was expecting just one baby even though she knew she was having twins. Laura left because she was going to university; Pamela said she was a nice girl. My mother's mental disturbance could hardly have been Laura's fault.

Several people greet me as I stroll out of the village — people who have lived within a couple of miles of me virtually my whole life; who have seen me as a baby, a toddler, a schoolgirl in plaits. People who came to my father's funeral the week before last, and probably to my mother's funeral twenty-five years before that. I wave to Helen and Daisy Luckhurst as they pass me in their car, and then I tilt my face to the sky as I leave the houses behind me, concentrating on the birdsong in the trees and hedges.

I will go back to see Laura, I decide. I pull my phone from my pocket as I turn into the lane, and the receptionist who answers my call confirms that Laura will be at her office all day. I'll drive back to London and speak to her face-to-face this afternoon, and then spend the night at Winterbourne. If I can persuade Laura to tell me the story of my birth, I might finally relax into a proper night's sleep tonight.

Back at the house, I'm gathering things for my overnight stay when I notice something odd about my handbag. I didn't take it into the village this morning, so it's next to the microwave where I left it when I arrived home on Thursday night. I know I've taken something out of it since then — the photograph — but the buckle on the flap is done up. I know I wouldn't have done the buckle back up when it was just sitting on the kitchen worktop.

My pulse quickens. My phone is in my pocket. But my purse was in my bag, and I curse our laid-back family habit of leaving doors unlocked and windows open. I fumble to undo the buckle, knowing that anyone could have gained access to our house via the back doors over the weekend.

I line up the contents on the worktop. There isn't much, which is normal. My purse is here. My driving licence. The order of service from Dad's funeral, the letter confirming my compassionate leave from work. Lipstick, hairbrush, spare sunglasses — they're all still here. I stroke my fingertips over each item in turn.

But something is missing. Goose bumps rise on my arms. The receipt that hook-nosed man at the neat little house gave me, with Laura's work address scribbled on the back. It was in my bag. *Wasn't it?* I'm almost sure of it. And now it's gone.

8

Laura

SEPTEMBER 1991

A subdued atmosphere settled over Summer-bourne after Saturday's picnic. Ruth's headache persisted through Sunday, and Dominic went out with the boat-owning neighbour after breakfast and didn't return for several hours. The joint of beef the village butcher had delivered on Friday sat untouched in the fridge, and when Edwin and I grew hungry around midday, we ate cheese sandwiches at the kitchen table. Afterwards, we made banana milkshakes laced with honey, and drank them out in his den.

Clouds loomed ever darker as the afternoon wore on, eventually driving us back indoors. Raindrops spattered against the day-nursery windows, and Edwin and I rummaged to find jumpers to pull on.

'Summer's over,' Ruth muttered as she padded into the kitchen to put the kettle on.

Each time I caught sight of Alex's sunglasses on the kitchen windowsill, I remembered the warmth of his skin against mine, and the intensity of his gaze, and the way his smile lingered when he stopped speaking. How close he must have been to me, to have caught me when I stumbled on the cliff steps. I wondered whether he had thought about me at all since the picnic, and then I grew certain that he must see me as a naive, awkward schoolgirl. I had felt so grown-up last year, dating a man six years older than me, but I didn't want to think about that now, and I knew I should stop thinking about Alex too.

I longed to talk to my friends — to giggle with them about ridiculous crushes, and be reminded of our promise that we'd always be there for one another. They'd been there for me when my boyfriend kicked me out of his flat at midnight, and my mum's partner, Beaky, refused to pick me up. They'd been there for me when I was in hospital, when I missed my A levels, when I felt like I'd ruined my entire life. But I was living in a different world now, and my friends had moved on too. Even if I'd known their new phone numbers at their new addresses, the prospect of a telephone conversation in the Summerbourne hall within earshot of Ruth and Dominic was unappealing.

By the time I got up on Monday morning, Dominic had left for London and Ruth's headache had disappeared.

'Let's walk into the village,' she said. 'I need stamps. We could get ice creams from the shop — if it doesn't rain.'

Edwin hopped up and down. 'Even if it does rain, Mummy.'

'I suppose we could sit under the bus shelter to eat them,' she said, smiling.

Our luck held, and we savoured our ice-cream cones on a bench on the village green in the watery sunshine, sprinkling chocolate crumbs down ourselves and competing to poke the ice cream all the way down to the end of our cornets with our tongues. Two elderly ladies stopped to greet Ruth, and made reference to Theo. Edwin remained unruffled while Ruth thanked them for their concern. I wanted to ask her whether Theo was buried in the churchyard beyond the green, but bit my tongue. Ruth's praise of my discretion lingered in my memory.

The threat of autumn receded as the week wore on. I swam in the pool with Edwin and Joel, and Michael taught us the Norfolk words for creepy crawlies.

'Charleypig, erriwiggle, bishy barney bee,' the boys chanted. Edwin had a particular throaty chuckle that I only ever heard when he was around Joel.

When they grew tired of playing outside, we made dragons out of Play-Doh, or drew pirate maps which Edwin stashed in his treasure box. Ruth took Edwin to gymnastics on the Wednesday, and I made a respectable start on my chemistry revision.

The calendar in the kitchen showed **R — reflexology 10 a.m.** for Friday — particularly intriguing since most of the boxes for the month were blank. When I flipped back through the year, there was a similar note once or twice each month. Ruth didn't refer to it at breakfast, but when Edwin and I were gathering containers to go foraging for blackberries, she told us she was popping out.

'I'll be back for lunch. Do you want me to pick

you anything up in town?' she asked.

'No, thanks, I'm fine,' I said.

The phone in the hall rang just after she'd left. I peered through the window: she was in her car, pulling the sun visor down and rummaging through her bag on the passenger seat. I picked up the receiver.

'Hello, Summerbourne?'

'Hi, Laura, it's Alex. How are you?'

The receiver slipped in my hand, and I fumbled to bring it back to my ear.

'Hi. I'm fine. Thanks.'

'Glad to hear it. Is Ruth there?'

I checked: the car was gliding out of the drive.

'She's just gone out,' I said.

'Ah. Do you know when she'll be back? I wanted to drop something round — I'm at the cottage, but I've got to stay in this afternoon for the electrician.'

'She won't be long. But I'm here if you want to come now. If you want to leave it here for her, I mean.'

'Um, okay, I might do that, actually. Thanks, Laura. I'll see you in a bit.'

He hung up. Edwin stood in front of me, one sandal on, a bucket in his hand.

'Who's coming?'

'That was Uncle Alex. He wants to bring something round for your mummy.'

Edwin beamed. 'I'll show him my crocodile pictures.' He lolloped away to the day nursery to find them.

I stood in the hall a moment longer, studying my flushed cheeks in the mirror. I resisted attempting to tidy my hair, and went through to the kitchen to boil the kettle, drumming my fingers on the worktop while I waited.

It was another forty minutes before Alex arrived, by which time Edwin had grown bored and gone to play in his sandpit. He must have heard the crunch of wheels on gravel, though, as he came haring through the house when Alex's car pulled up.

'Whoa there! You get stronger every day, young man,' Alex said. Edwin bounced up and down as Alex opened the sports car's little boot. 'Sorry, nothing for you today, my friend. This is for your beautiful mama.' He lifted out a bouquet of luscious pink roses, tweaking a few to disguise the flattening from their journey.

'They're lovely,' I said, my hands feeling suddenly awkward at my sides.

'Just to thank her for the picnic. It's really nice of you to let me drop them off. Can I put them in the kitchen?' He hesitated, and I remembered that I was the responsible adult of the house and gestured for him to follow me in.

'We're going to pick blackberries, but we waited for you, Uncle Alex,' Edwin said, and I frowned.

'Oh, that was very kind of you,' Alex said. 'And where has your mother gone?'

Edwin shrugged elaborately. 'To see the quacks, most probably.'

Alex raised his eyebrows at me.

I mimicked Edwin's shrug. 'Reflexology?' I felt a flicker of disloyalty to Ruth after her comment about me being discreet, but surely she wouldn't mind me telling Alex. Alex laughed.

'Is that what your daddy calls them?' he said to Edwin.

'Are you coming with us, then?' Edwin asked him. 'To pick blackberries?' He swung one leg as he looked from Alex's face to mine.

Alex checked his watch. 'Where are you going — to the folly?'

I nodded. I was acutely aware of his sunglasses on the windowsill, that I ought to give them back to him. But I held my breath, waiting, willing him to come with us.

'How about I come for a bit?' he said, directing the question at Edwin but glancing at me to check. I released my breath and smiled.

'Sure,' I said, and Edwin cheered and ran to fetch his bucket.

I grabbed keys, but hesitated. 'Shall I lock up or — will you need to get through to your car if you come back first?'

He chuckled. 'Ah, I see we feel the same way — these country folk leaving their houses unlocked all the time — it's unsettling. No, don't worry — you lock up, and if I come back before you, I can always jump the wall by the stables.'

I turned the keys with a smile. We felt the same way.

'So how long are you here for?' he asked as we set off down the garden. 'Au pairing, I mean. Is it a long-term thing?'

'For a year,' I said. I watched Edwin skip towards the trees ahead of us. 'I missed my A levels. I was in hospital. We . . . I decided it'd be

106

good to take a year out before retaking them.'

'Not retaking exactly, is it? If you didn't get to sit them in the first place?'

'No, well . . . ' I pushed away the memory of turning up at the first exam, against doctor's orders, stumbling out again before the invigilator could tell me to turn over my paper.

Alex filled his lungs and gestured at the vibrant garden around us, the cloudless sky. 'Well, you certainly picked a great place for a year out. I wish I'd stepped off the conveyor belt for a year at your age. It's all exams, interviews, work, work.'

I glanced at his expression, hesitating to ask him what it was he did for work, but a whoop from Edwin as he disappeared into the little woods made Alex grin suddenly.

'I might take a year off myself, actually. I think I'd make a pretty good au pair. What do you do all day — pick blackberries, play on the beach? Easy stuff.'

'Hey!' I shook my head, but I couldn't help laughing. He asked me about my university plans then, and he gave me his full attention while I told him about my passion for science and my desire to one day run my own research lab. His gaze remained on my face rather than on the path ahead. I felt as though I walked taller and my limbs moved more gracefully, as if he had high expectations of me and I was rising to meet them.

A piercing scream burst the illusion. My chest constricted. We sprinted through the last section of woodland and found Edwin lying on the ground by the gate, one side of his face streaked with blood.

'Let me look, let me look,' I said, trying to keep his head still as he thrashed around in Alex's arms.

'I fell off,' Edwin wailed.

His blood made my hands slippery. 'We'll have to get him back to the house — I can't see.'

Alex carried Edwin back at a gentle jog, and by the time we had him sitting up on the kitchen table he was hiccupping between sobs and managed to keep still enough to be cleaned up. There was a half-inch gash near the top of his right ear. So much blood from such a tiny wound.

Alex and I looked at each other over the top of his head.

'I think I'd better take him to the surgery,' I said. 'He might need stitches.'

'I'll drive you down there,' he said.

'But there's no room in your car.'

'It'll take two minutes. He can sit on your knee.'

The receptionist when we walked in was displeased, but the nurse who called us through couldn't have been kinder. She cleaned the wound and closed it with tiny strips of sticking plaster, and gave Edwin a lollipop and a sticker for his bravery.

'Can I have one too?' Alex asked, and she actually nudged his chest as she chuckled at him. I gritted my teeth.

We sat for a few minutes on the bench on the village green, giving Edwin time to finish his lollipop. Alex stretched his arm along the back of the bench, behind Edwin's head, and if I'd leaned in a tiny bit, his fingertips would have touched my bare shoulder. Helen, Ruth's pregnant friend, waddled past and smiled at us. Alex ruffled Edwin's hair and then grimaced at me over his head.

'You okay?' I asked.

'I'm just so relieved it wasn't any worse,' he said. I nodded.

A screech of brakes on the high street made us both turn to look, and my heart jolted at the sight of Ruth sprinting across the grass towards us, her car door gaping open behind. A van tooted. Alex stood up.

'My God! What happened?' She dropped to her knees in front of Edwin, who pulled his shrunken lollipop out of his mouth with a pop and giggled at the sound. She looked from Alex to me, and back to Alex.

'What happened?' she asked again, and her voice had dropped an octave; the consonants exaggerated in a way that made my skin tingle.

'He tried to climb the gate and he slipped,' Alex said. 'We were going to pick some blackberries.' He pulled Ruth upright to face him, placed a hand on her shoulder, and then put his other hand gently on her cheek. 'He's fine, Ruth. It was a little cut, but the nurse cleaned it up and he's completely fine.'

She twisted away from him and dropped back down in front of Edwin.

'Tell me what happened, darling?'

'Missus Pamela Larch gave me a lolly,' Edwin

answered, waving it at her and then poking it back in.

'Before that, Edwin. How did you hurt yourself?'

Alex and I exchanged a glance. His forehead was crumpled, and I wanted to squeeze his hand and say, *It wasn't our fault.*

Edwin swung his legs back and forth, avoiding his mother's eyes.

'I fell off the gate, Mummy. I was just trying to climb it. It had the bolt on.'

'It's supposed to have the bolt on, darling. To keep you safe.' She stood up again, without looking at either of us. 'We're going home, Edwin. Put your stick in the bin, please.'

'Ruth — ' Alex said, but she shook off his hand.

'He's all I have left, Alex,' she hissed, as Edwin skipped over to the bin and then sauntered back to take her hand. They set off towards her car.

I looked from Alex to the retreating figure of my employer.

'Go,' he said. I jogged after them. While Ruth fastened Edwin into his car seat on one side, I went round and eased myself into the back seat from the other side. She didn't comment, and didn't speak to either of us on the short drive home.

Something held me back from apologising as we entered the hall, but I touched her gently on her arm.

'Why don't you go and sit down, and I'll bring you a cup of tea?' I said.

After a moment's pause her shoulders sagged,

and she met my eyes briefly.

'Okay,' she said. 'Come on, darling — let's see what's on the telly and have a cuddle.' She led Edwin off to the sitting room.

I hurried into the kitchen and scooped the wads of bloodstained kitchen paper from the table, bundling them into a carrier bag which I stuffed underneath the top layer of rubbish in the bin. Then I dashed through to the annexe and changed into a clean T-shirt, leaving my bloodstained top soaking in cold water in my bathroom sink. I returned to the kitchen just as the kettle finished boiling, and I picked the dried blood from under my fingernails while the tea brewed in the pot.

9

Seraphine

I'm parked outside Laura's office again, preparing to ring her, to ask her to come down and meet me. Across the pavement and through the glass doors, I can see the receptionist stapling sheets of paper together. A young woman who looks like she might still be a teenager collects a pile of letters from the desk and disappears into the lift.

My phone vibrates, and an unknown number flashes up. The words

Dear Seraphine, Martin says that man

make me smile, as I picture Pamela nipping home on her lunch break and collaring her elephant-memoried husband. She's a kind woman.

Dear Seraphine, Martin says that man's name was Alex Jay Kaimal. Lived in Leeds. He sold the Collisons' cottage about a year after your mother RIP passed away. Young Billy Bradshaw handled the sale. Martin spoke to Alex on phone after your mother RIP accident, but he had nothing to add to investigation. Warmest regards. Pamela Larch

I send a quick response:

Mrs Larch, Thank you so much, I really appreciate your help. Seraphine

Then I type 'Alex Jay Kaimal Leeds' into my web browser.

There's a senior executive for an engineering company in Leeds with that name. He's also associated with a private company registered in India, a running club in Roundhay, and as a donor at a charity ball for diabetes research. I can't find a Facebook account for him, but I tap on a thumbnail picture on the engineering company website, and an image of a middle-aged man in a jacket and tie springs up.

He is broad shouldered with a blend of Asian and Caucasian features; his skin a mid brown, his hair dark. His posture exudes confidence, and his serious expression is warmed by the hint of a smile around his eyes. If he was the same age as my parents, he'd be in his mid-fifties now, but he looks younger here — no trace of grey in his short hair. Perhaps it's an old photo, or perhaps he's lucky, or perhaps he's vain. I think of Pamela saying 'ever so handsome', and even on my little screen, I see that he might possess a certain charisma.

I scrutinise his face. *Who are you, Alex Kaimal? What was your relationship with Laura? Why did you disappear after my mother died?*

I sigh and tap away, calling the insurance company in front of me before I can change my mind. The phone rings twice.

'Good afternoon, Crowford Insurance. How may I help?'

'I'd like to speak to Laura Silveira, please,' I say.

'One moment. I'm putting you through.'

The ringtone sounds six times, seven, eight. No answer. The receptionist comes back on the line after the ninth ring.

'I'm so sorry, Ms Silveira doesn't appear to be at her desk at the moment. Would you like me to try someone else?'

I curl forward, bumping my forehead against the steering wheel.

'But I rang this morning.' I struggle to keep my tone calm. 'You told me — was it you I spoke to? You told me she'd be here all day.' I keep my gaze fixed on my knees, not wanting to look across and catch her smiling, although when she speaks again I can hear it in her voice.

'She may have gone out to an external meeting. Perhaps you could try again later?'

I hang up.

If she's gone out to a meeting, she might not come back to the office. But what if she's still in the building? What if she's avoiding answering her phone after she was lured down for a non-existent delivery last week? My forehead leaves a damp patch on the steering wheel when I sit up.

I call Edwin's number, but he doesn't answer. Busy at work. I call the Winterbourne landline in case Danny is hanging out there today — he's been cagey about his plans since he got back from working in Kenya last month, shrugging off questions even before Dad's accident. My twin brother is still looking for his place in life. In a different way to me. I hang up when the Winterbourne answer machine kicks in, and I try Danny's mobile, but again, no answer.

My thumb hovers over Vera's number, but I flick past and in the end choose to send Edwin a text.

Can I stay with you tonight?

Unlike Summerbourne, Winterbourne House is protected with sophisticated locks and a burglar alarm, but I have my own key and I know the code. I'm asking out of politeness.

A reflected glint from the sliding glass doors catches my eye, and it takes me a full second to register that the tall figure striding down the steps in front of me is Laura. It's mid-afternoon, and she has no bag with her, just a white envelope clutched in one hand. She turns sharply to the left, knocking shoulders with a burly man in a suit as she passes, causing him to mutter something crossly to her back. I shove my phone into my trouser pocket and leap out of the car, dodging around other pedestrians to keep her hunched figure within sight as far as the park gate, where she turns in.

I sprint ahead, sweat soaking into my top. I can't lose her again. When I swing through the gate, I spot her instantly, veering away from the main path, hurrying over towards the empty bandstand. I jog along the inner line of the boundary hedge, not following her directly but closing the gap between us. As she reaches the bandstand, she skirts its perimeter and approaches a bench and a bin. I keep my face turned away, towards the hedge, as I jog past, but there are some trees up ahead, and when I reach them, I circle around to get as close to her as I can without being seen.

She doesn't sit on the bench. She tears the envelope open, and her hands are shaking. She tugs out a folded sheet of paper, opens it, and looks at it for a few seconds, and then she turns to bend over, one outstretched arm supported by the top of the bin, and she vomits onto the ground.

I draw a deep breath in, my stomach clenching. What on earth is this? Has she brought this letter out of the office to open away from prying eyes? What does it say?

I creep forward in the undergrowth to get a better view.

She's wiping her mouth on the back of her hand now, and she takes the sheet of paper in its refolded state and rips it in half, and half again, and again. She scrunches the pieces up and shoves them into the bin. Then she does the same with the envelope. She straightens and looks around, not directly towards me, and then she pats the pocket of her trousers and sets off towards the main path that bisects the park. I wait until she's on the path, heading for the far end of the green, before I emerge from my hiding place and start to follow her.

There are family groups playing football and Frisbee, and others sitting around on the grass. I concentrate on keeping Laura in sight, getting steadily closer as she leaves through a gate on the far side. I follow her along residential streets, crossing over once, turning right at the next junction. These are narrow roads with cars parked all the way along each side, and I'm expecting her to notice me at any moment, but she tugs keys out of her pocket as she swings jerkily into the front garden of a narrow end-of-terrace house, ignoring the broad steps up to the front door and instead disappearing down the side alley towards the door of the basement flat.

'Excuse me!' I shout, and I dive through the gate and around the corner of the building. Laura is frozen in position, her hand on the key in the lock, her head turned towards me. I stop with a jolt, and we look at each other for a long moment. She's breathing though her mouth, and there's a sheen of sweat on her face.

'I'm Seraphine Mayes,' I say.

'I know who you are.' Her tone is flat, but her hand trembles as she turns the key and starts to push her front door open, keeping her eyes on me.

'I was hoping I could ask you some questions,' I say, stepping forward as she eases herself through the door, rotating her body so that she's still facing me but is now inside her flat.

'I can't help you, Seraphine. Please go away.'

She starts to close the door, to shut me out, but I put my hand against it, pushing lightly, and she hesitates.

'Please,' I say. 'I just want to ask you about Summerbourne.'

She presses her lips together and shakes her

head slightly. I search her face. It must have been traumatic for her, my mother dying the way she did. But still, twenty-five years on, shouldn't she be happy to meet me — one of the babies she helped deliver?

'You were there when we were born?' I ask. 'Danny and I?'

She turns her face further into the shadows of the dark hallway, and I have to increase my push against the door to counteract hers. If she puts her whole weight behind it, I won't be able to stop her closing it against me, and I desperately try to find words to stall her.

'The photo,' I say. 'Did you take it? On the patio. With only one of us in it?'

Her eyes widen, and I can see that they're brown, like mine; not blue like my brothers'. She twitches the door away from me, and I lurch sideways, unbalanced, knowing any second now she's going to slam it and any chance I have of hearing the truth will be over. I blurt out the question before I can change my mind.

'Are you my mother?'

And suddenly, her face softens, and I read sympathy in her eyes as her grip on the door relaxes and she exhales heavily. I press my lips together, trying to calm my breathing so that I can concentrate on every detail of her reply.

'No, I'm not your mother, Seraphine. How funny you'd think that.' She pauses, and I watch the flicker of expressions on her face. 'I was with your mother when you were born.' She still blocks the doorway, but she reaches out with her free hand and touches me gently on my forearm.

I hold my breath. 'Your mother said you were the most beautiful baby she had ever seen. Like an angel.'

I am aware of tears on my cheeks, but I focus harder than ever on her face, on her fleeting sad smile as she mentions my mother, on the steadiness of her gaze as she says these precious words. Words I've been waiting my whole life to hear. Words I should have been able to turn over and examine every day of my life until they were as smooth as glass pebbles from the sea. Instead, I am lacerated by the glittering surprise of them as I clutch them to me now.

She opens the door a tiny bit, and I remove my hand from it and take a small step back.

'I can't talk to you any more, Seraphine,' she says. 'I'm sorry about your father. I only just heard. Please don't come here again.' The door bangs shut in my face, and I hear the grate of locking mechanisms on the inside.

I wander back out to the pavement, dazed. At some point on her road, I stop to lean against somebody's gatepost, taking deep breaths and trying to clear my head. Eventually, I have the presence of mind to go back and make a note of her house number, and then the street name. I feel empty as I retrace my steps to the park: I came for an explanation, a resolution, but I'm leaving with a sense that Laura was protecting secrets in that dark hall, pushing them into the shadows behind her to keep them from my view. Just inside the park gate, a child drops an ice-lolly stick on the path in front of me, and suddenly, my swelling resentment is punctured

119

by the thrill of an idea.

I jog over to the bin by the bandstand, keeping my feet clear of the mess on the ground as I reach my hand tentatively through the slot on one side, feeling for scrunched-up paper. I'm lucky. I pull out several wadded sections, slightly damp, keeping my face turned away from the smell. On my last attempt to feel for more, the drone of a wasp rises from the mass of rubbish, and I withdraw my arm sharply. I hold the pieces of paper away from my body, and a solitary child watches me with his mouth open as I hurry towards the gate.

Back in my car, I quickly abandon an attempt to piece together the shreds of the letter, and check my phone to find a reply from Edwin:

Course you can. I'll be home around 8.

Winterbourne is the opposite to Summerbourne in many ways. It's formal on the outside, and sparsely furnished on the inside, with none of the clutter that our childhood country home has accumulated over generations. Nevertheless, it has a welcoming calmness that always soothes me as soon as I step inside. When Edwin moved in four years ago, he replaced the old gas burners in the kitchen with a sleek induction hob, but changed little else. Danny is staying here at the moment, but I've no idea where he goes during the day. His motorbike is parked under cover to the side of the house, but when I call his name from the entrance hall, there's no reply.

I place my handbag on the polished wood of

the dining table and begin to peel the layers of damp paper apart and lay them out; the words are machine printed, and form a narrow band across the middle of the page. There's a section missing, but it belongs to the upper right corner of the paper, and I imagine would have been just blank space anyway.

I hold my breath as I look at the two sentences I have recreated, and then a surge of nausea makes me dash to the cloakroom. The stench from the park bin still clings to my hands, and I scrub repeatedly with antibacterial hand wash. I need a hot shower and clean clothes.

I creep back into the dining room, and read the note again.

Dominic Mayes is dead. If you discuss Summerbourne with anyone, your daughter will be next.

I leave the room and close the door softly behind me. My mother said I looked like an angel when I was born, I remind myself. The most beautiful baby she had ever seen. I won't think about the letter until Edwin gets home.

An hour later, I am heading downstairs in fresh clothes, running my hands along the smooth oak banister, stroking the heavy brocade curtains as I pass them on the landing. As I make the last turn on the staircase, a complete stranger — a slim young woman with long white-blond hair — steps out of the cloakroom, sees me, and screams.

Danny appears in the kitchen doorway, a tea

towel over one shoulder.

'Brooke?' He turns to gaze up at me, and then pads across to her with an apologetic grimace. 'I'm so sorry. Meet my sister, Seraphine. She is pretty scary, I know. I had no idea she was here, actually.' He shoots me a dark look. 'Seraphine, this is Brooke from next door.'

I come down two steps. 'Hi.'

'Hi.' Her eyes are pale blue, like a washed-out sky, and she doesn't smile.

'Did the grumpy couple move out then?' I ask Danny. He closes his eyes.

'No,' Brooke says. 'I'm their daughter.'

'Oh. God, I'm so sorry — '

'What are you doing here, Seph?' Danny asks me, his tone cool. 'Does Edwin know you've come?'

'Of course he does.' I take another step down, glancing at Brooke and back to Danny. 'I need to talk to you, actually.' Brooke directs her gaze towards the grandfather clock rather than at either of us.

'Well, Brooke's here for dinner,' Danny says. 'I invited her.'

I carve my thumbnail into the wax on the banister. I wonder whether this is the first time Danny has invited this woman for dinner; he never mentioned her name in all the days he stayed at Summerbourne before and after Dad's funeral. I wonder how well they know each other, and how she'll react to sharing the dining table with a threatening letter that smells like the contents of a warm park bin.

'I went to see Laura today,' I say. Danny stares

122

at me. 'She's being threatened.'

Brooke looks at me directly then. I'm expecting a hint of annoyance, but her expression is strangely serene. She glides over to Danny and kisses him lightly on the cheek, and then picks up a bunch of keys from the hall table.

'We can do dinner some other time,' she tells him, and then switches her calm gaze to me. 'It's nice to meet you, Seraphine. I'm sorry about your father. I'll let myself out.' She leaves without glancing back.

Danny glares at me, and then stalks off into the kitchen where he crashes pans around on the hob. I follow and sink down on a kitchen chair, rubbing my eyes.

'This had better be good,' he says eventually.

'I'll tell you when Edwin gets here.'

He keeps his back to me for a while, but eventually says, 'I miss him too, you know.'

'Oh, Danny.' He turns, and I stretch my arms out towards him. 'I know.'

When Edwin arrives he finds us holding hands at the kitchen table, a mound of tissues between us, our faces streaked with tears. Edwin bends to hug me, pats Danny on the back, and then leaps to rescue the stew which is starting to burn at the base of the pan.

I confess everything to my brothers over dinner: following Laura to the park, watching her read the letter and throw up, confronting her on her doorstep, what she said about our mother. We sit around one end of the dining table, picking at our food, while the pieced-together letter lurks at the other end like an uninvited guest.

I'm feeling increasingly uncomfortable with the route the conversation is taking.

'We should go to the police,' Edwin says. 'Whatever this is about — we should report it.'

'Oh, and what will I say?' I ask him. 'I stalked this woman. I pulled a ripped-up note out of a park bin and stuck it together?' I try to imagine pressing the soggy scraps of letter into Martin Larch's large hands.

'I'm worried, Seraphine,' Edwin says. 'It mentions Dad, and Summerbourne. Going to Laura's house today — you might have put yourself in danger.'

I shove my plate away. 'I'm not her daughter!'

'I know, I know.' He takes my hand, squeezes it. 'I didn't mean it like that. Just that you were there, asking questions about Summerbourne.'

'Plus the small fact,' Danny says quietly, 'that whoever wrote this seems to be implying they caused Dad's death.'

Edwin and I stare at him, and then our eyes are drawn back to the note.

'That's one interpretation,' Edwin says eventually.

'A hollow threat,' I say.

'Yeah, using Dad's accident to try to frighten her,' Edwin says.

'Because we know it was an accident,' I say. 'Don't we?'

Danny turns his stew over and over with his fork. The air in the dining room seems to squeeze inward and then recede, as if Winterbourne itself is listening, considering.

'Of course,' Danny says. 'We know that.'

Edwin sits back.

'Well then,' I say. 'All this tells us is . . . Laura knows something about Summerbourne, and someone wants to stop her talking about it.'

Edwin groans. 'But not necessarily anything to do with us. Who knows what happened that year? It might be something to do with a friend, a boyfriend — nothing to do with our family, just something that happened while she was living in our house.'

'So why mention Dad then?' Danny asks.

'Exactly,' I say. 'She knows something about us.'

Edwin gives me a sharp look. 'No. If you won't go to the police, then you have to drop this, Seraphine. I mean it. You mustn't approach Laura again.'

I grind my teeth, and glance at Danny for back-up, but he looks just as concerned as Edwin.

'I agree,' Danny says. 'She told you herself to stay away from her. You've got to drop it, sis. Promise.'

I close my eyes and think about my father. *Dominic Mayes is dead.* And my mother. *Your mother said you were the most beautiful baby she had ever seen.*

When I blink them open, both my brothers are watching me with a familiar wariness. I sigh.

'I won't approach Laura again — I promise.' I stand and grab my plate. 'I'm shattered. Thanks for dinner. And Danny,' — I scrunch up my face

— 'I'm sorry about spoiling your plans with Brooke. I'm going to bed.'

I scrape my uneaten stew into the waste disposal sink and slide my plate into the dishwasher before making my way up to the bedroom I always use at Winterbourne. Something continues to niggle at me. The stolen scrap of paper with Laura's work address; the threatening letter sent to Laura's work address — is the same person responsible for both?

The weight of the bedspread on my body comforts me despite the heat of the evening, and my breathing deepens and slows as I gaze at the faint cracks in the ceiling, familiar from my childhood stays here. I promised my brothers I wouldn't approach Laura again. A moth batters at the bedside lamp, and I reach out for the switch. But my fingers rest on my phone, and before I turn out the light, I do a quick internet search to find out how long it will take me to drive up to Leeds tomorrow. I promised my brothers I wouldn't approach Laura again, but I didn't say anything about Alex Kaimal.

10

Laura

SEPTEMBER/OCTOBER 1991

It wasn't my fault. I tidied toys and washed dishes while Ruth got Edwin ready for bed that evening. Each time I heard a noise that might have been Dominic's car approaching along the lane, my stomach lurched. *It wasn't our fault.* But if I hadn't let Edwin run ahead out of sight, if I hadn't been so wrapped up in Alex's company . . .

It was an accident. Dominic would understand that. I checked my watch again, and a familiar gravel crunch reached my ears.

'Daddy!' Edwin bounded down the stairs in his pyjamas, launching himself into Dominic's arms. From the kitchen doorway, I could barely make out the crust of blood that edged the plaster strips.

'What's all this?'

'I cut it on the gate, Daddy. I got a lollipop.'

Ruth leant against the wall a few steps up from the bottom, her arms crossed.

'Laura will tell you,' she said.

Dominic looked from her to me.

'He tried to climb the gate. We were right behind him. He must have slipped. It's actually only a little cut.'

'There was blood everywhere,' Edwin said.

Dominic kissed the top of his head and set him down. He forced a smile as he stroked Edwin's cheek. 'What sort of lollipop did you get?'

'A round one, you know. A red one.'

'Strawberry?'

Edwin shrugged.

'Well, don't climb the gate again, Edwin. It's not a good idea. Come on, let's get you back into bed. I'll read you a story tonight.'

Dominic squeezed Ruth's arm briefly as he passed her on the stairs, and she closed her eyes. I retreated to the annexe and went straight to bed, listening to the rain on the window for hours, failing to sink into sleep.

Edwin and I ate breakfast together the next morning, before slipping outside to potter around by the climbing frame. I rubbed my arms while he inched his way up the slide on his knees. The grass underfoot was slippery, and a faint hint of bonfire smoke mingled with the earthy scent from the damp borders.

Dominic joined us, his slippers stained dark with dew, his hands wrapped around a mug of coffee. He stood next to me, and we watched Edwin in silence for a while.

'I'm sorry if Ruth upset you yesterday,' he said eventually.

I shook my head. 'No, not at all. I understand.'

'She's feeling particularly fragile at the moment.'

'She didn't upset me. I feel terrible about frightening her like that. It must be very hard

128

after . . . after what happened with your other son.'

A spasm distorted his face for a moment, and I looked away. He blew out a loud puff of air.

'It's not just that. She's been hoping — we've been hoping — for some happier news recently. A new brother or sister for Edwin. But sadly — ' He cleared his throat.

'Daddy, help me on the monkey bars!' Edwin called.

Dominic handed me his coffee mug, and leapt to Edwin's aid. Any anticipation of comfort evaporated as I discovered the liquid inside was stone-cold.

Vera joined us at Summerbourne the following day; Dominic was preparing a joint of pork and making apple sauce, and Ruth felt too unwell to collect her from the station, so she arrived in a taxi.

'Perhaps we should arrange some driving lessons for you, Laura, while you're here,' Vera said, checking her hair in the hall mirror. In the sitting-room doorway, Ruth rolled her eyes. I smoothed down a spike of hair on Edwin's head, wary of replying.

'Perhaps we should arrange some driving lessons for you, Mother,' Ruth said.

Vera waved a hand dismissively. 'Oh, I'm too old for such things.'

'You're not even fifty! But don't worry about it. Everyone loves driving you places, don't they? It's a real treat for us.'

Vera ignored her. 'Now, Edwin, what have you

been painting this week? You must show me everything.'

If anything, Edwin's injury looked more dramatic than it had on the first day, with a thick scab bulging from the contour of his ear. Vera didn't mention it in front of him, though, and I guessed that either Ruth or Dominic had told her about it over the phone. Once Edwin had shown off his latest pictures and models, he settled at the day nursery table to paint a new scene. Vera beckoned me to the other end of the room.

'How are you getting on?' she asked. 'With the job — with everything?'

'Oh, fine,' I said. 'Great. Thank you.'

She gave me an appraising look. 'Are they working you too hard? You shouldn't be working today at all. Twenty-two hours a week, isn't it?'

I spread my hands, indicating the day nursery and the little boy who sat dipping his brush into paint with his tongue poking out.

'Honestly, it doesn't feel like work. I'm happy being with Edwin when I'm off duty, and it hardly feels like work when I'm on duty.'

She studied my face.

'You're not homesick, stuck out here in the middle of nowhere?' she asked.

I shook my head.

'You're not bored? Missing your friends?' she asked.

'I'm okay. Really.'

'Well. Nevertheless, I shall remind my daughter not to take advantage of your good nature.' She sighed. 'And how would you say

Ruth has been? Edwin's little accident gave her a shock, of course.'

I was saved from replying by Dominic calling us through to the dining room for lunch.

I didn't talk to Ruth properly until the Monday, when Dominic and Vera had returned to London and she and I were sitting in the kitchen, trying to ignore the grey drizzle outside and planning our activities for the week.

'My mother says I'm not to overwork you,' she said, looking at me sideways. I smiled.

'Well, you haven't so far, and I promise to tell you if you do,' I said, and she seemed satisfied with this. She pushed a leaflet across the table to me.

'There's some kind of indoor play centre opened up, look,' she said. 'I thought I'd take Edwin along this afternoon and see what it's like. Let him burn off some energy. They do coffee and cakes.' She paused for a moment. 'You might prefer to stay here and have some downtime, or revise or whatever, but,' she looked at me, 'if you fancy coming along to try the coffee with me, I'd be glad of the company.'

A warm glow spread through my chest.

'I'd love to come.'

As it turned out, the place was dimly lit and overheated, and we had to talk over the noise of wailing babies and shrieking children. But Edwin thoroughly enjoyed the padded climbing struc-ture with its slides and ball pool, and Ruth and I chatted for an hour and a half as if we were friends.

The miserable weather persisted for the rest of

the week, but Edwin and I were happy enough dividing our time between the day nursery and the kitchen.

'My mum used to do lots of baking with me when I was your age,' I told him.

'Did she let you do the whisking all by your own?'

I smiled. 'No. She always had to hold it too. But you can press the button if you like.' His little hands gripped the electric whisk under mine, his elbows jutting out on either side, a fierce determination on his face. The clatter of the metal beaters against the sides of the bowl triggered an unexpected swell of emotion in me: nostalgia, mixed with a powerless anger. Mum and I used to do this all the time before Beaky moved in. Beaky didn't like mess in the kitchen; Beaky didn't like children 'traipsing around to the neighbours with cakes they'll only throw in the bin'. I left enough mixture in the bowl for Edwin to scrape out and enjoy while the cakes rose in their tins in the oven.

We pulled on coats and wellies on the Friday and splashed along the lane to see whether Joel was in the cottage with Michael, but no one answered the door, and we had to splash home again. On the Saturday, I agreed to babysit so that Dominic and Ruth could go out for dinner.

They left their bedroom door ajar, and I couldn't help but glance in after I'd settled Edwin to sleep. There was a single framed photo on the chest of drawers by the window. I tiptoed in. Two blond toddlers in stripy T-shirts, each with an arm over the other's shoulder; the one that looked more like Edwin grinning at the camera, the other sticking his bottom lip out. It must have been taken not long before Theo's accident, I thought. Ruth and Dominic must look at it every morning when they wake up, every evening as they go to bed.

It was the following Monday morning, after Dominic had left, that Alex rang.

'Oh, hello, Alex,' I heard Ruth say as she answered the phone.

I hovered in the kitchen, where Edwin was finishing his Weetabix.

'This Friday?' I heard her say. 'I might be.'

I glanced at the calendar. The square for Friday was blank.

'Yes, all right.' A pause, and then she gave a light laugh. 'Absolutely. So easy. Come over when you're ready.'

I put the kettle back on to boil as she wandered in.

'Tea?' I asked.

'Oh, yes, please. That was Alex. He wants to take me out for lunch on Friday.' She bent to drop a kiss onto Edwin's head.

I attempted a smile, but she shook her head suddenly.

'I don't know why he thinks I'm at his beck and call. Just because we're out in the country doesn't mean we don't have plenty of other things going on in our lives.' She stroked Edwin's hair, frowning. 'I might have to keep you this size for ever and ever, Edwin,' she murmured.

I gritted my teeth. At the picnic on the beach a couple of weeks ago she was begging Alex to visit her during the week, to rescue her from boredom; now she was complaining about him. Edwin batted her hand away and jumped up to take his bowl to the sink.

Alex wasn't mentioned again until the Friday morning, and it was me who brought him up when I saw Ruth checking her lipstick in the hall mirror, and unhooking her raincoat from the cupboard.

'I'm just popping out,' she told me. 'Helen Luckhurst had her baby on Monday. A little girl. They think she has some problems. I'm going to take her some flowers — see if we can do anything to help.'

I stared at her.

'Isn't Alex taking you out for lunch?'

She laughed and waved the question away.

'Oh, Alex — I'd almost forgotten. Well, he can jolly well wait for me to get back. I'll only be an hour or so,' she said, and she picked up her bag and marched out of the house.

I watched her car glide out of the drive, pausing alongside two figures for a minute as she wound down her window and said something, before disappearing towards the village. Michael and Joel ambled up the gravel, and I had the door open before they reached it.

'Please may I play with Edwin?' Joel asked, craning his neck to peer behind me into the house.

'Preschool's closed,' Michael said to me, with a wiggle of his eyebrows. 'He was coming with me to the Matthews' place, but Ruth said you might not mind having him here for a bit instead. Don't want to impose.'

I swung the door open wide and beckoned Joel in.

'It'll make Edwin's day,' I said to Michael, and we exchanged smiles at the shouts of glee that erupted from the kitchen.

It was a blustery morning, and bright bursts of sunshine were interspersed with shade from the scudding clouds. I decided to let the boys play for half an hour in the day nursery, and if Alex hadn't arrived by then, I would take them down to the beach for a run around on the sand. They always seemed particularly full of energy on windy days.

I tried not to clock-watch, but I heard the crunch of Alex's car while the boys were absorbed in their game, and I met him at the door. His expression was expectant.

'Laura, hi. Is Ruth . . . ?'

I chewed my lip. 'She went out. I'm sorry. She left about twenty minutes ago, said she'd be an hour or two.'

He looked so crestfallen, I stepped back without thinking. 'Do you want to come in?' We walked through to the kitchen.

'Do you know where she went?' he asked, his eyes roaming over the unwashed breakfast dishes, the paintings on the fridge, the wall calendar.

I picked up his sunglasses from the windowsill. 'You left these. At the picnic.' I handed them to him. 'She's gone to visit a baby in the village.'

'Oh.' He opened the arms of the sunglasses, closed them again. 'Right.' He thought for a moment, then glanced at me. 'What are you and Edwin up to for the next hour?'

'We were going to go down to the beach. Get the wind in our hair, you know. Would you like to come?'

'Oh, I meant would I be in your way if I stayed here to wait?'

'Oh right. No, of course not.'

'But the beach does sound good,' he said, and then he was smiling, and there must have been a break in the clouds, because the kitchen was suddenly flooded with sunshine.

Edwin and Joel hurtled in.

'Uncle Alex! Look, Joel's here!'

'Excellent,' Alex said. 'I was hoping for two smart boys to show me where the blackberries grow on the way to the beach.' Within minutes I had locked up and we were heading towards the back gate.

'No climbing this time, Edwin,' Alex called out, and Edwin shook his head vigorously as he ran ahead with Joel.

'No way!'

We paused at the folly, craning our necks to peer at the cannon jutting out from the top of the tower.

'Can we go up?' Joel asked, batting his long lashes at me. I looked at Alex, and he looked at Edwin.

'Do you want to, Edwin?' Alex asked, and Edwin nodded, skipping ahead into the stone circle and wrestling to turn the heavy iron handle on the door of the tower. Alex suggested that I climb the spiral staircase first, with Edwin and

Joel following, and he would come last, to catch them if they fell. The steps were perforated iron, and our footsteps clanked and echoed as we climbed. It can't have been more than six metres high, but my heart pounded as we wound our way up.

The wind whipped my breath away as I emerged onto the platform, and I was immensely thankful for the stone parapet that encircled the small space. There was a central stone dais, decorated with carved sea serpents, and on top of it a large sundial, and a contraption with a glass lens, and the black cannon I had glimpsed from down below. The barrel of the cannon pointed out towards the sea, and the four of us shuffled around in an arc between the dais and the parapet so that Alex could show us where the gunpowder went and how the sun shone through the lens onto the powder at the critical moment. Joel was entranced, but Edwin spent more time peering down at the clifftop below.

'Look for Theo,' he said suddenly, and Alex's smile plummeted.

'Hey, let's go down again, carefully, and see if there are any blackberries left,' Alex said.

Back on the ground, the boys went to search in the bushes, squealing when they found each blackberry, stuffing them into their mouths as if they hadn't been fed for days. I gave Alex an enquiring look.

'This is where they were when Theo fell,' he said quietly. 'Ruth helped Theo up first to see the cannon. Then she brought him down and strapped him into the double buggy before getting Edwin out and taking him up. It's something they did every week, but Ruth couldn't manage the staircase with both of them — it's too dangerous.'

I stared at him, wide-eyed. I wanted to tell him to stop, to change the subject. But I also wanted to hear; I needed to know.

'Theo must have unstrapped himself. Ruth was at the top with Edwin when she spotted him toddling towards the edge of the cliff.'

I pressed my fingers over my mouth. Alex's gaze was distant.

'They think he was aiming for the steps, but missed his footing. He fell and hit his head. No other major injuries, remarkably. But he never woke up.' Tears brimmed in his eyes.

'It's awful,' I said. A surge of nausea made me turn away and shuffle to the stone wall, where I sat with my head hanging.

Alex went to help the boys reach a cluster of berries above their heads, and he carried some back for me. They burst in my mouth with a tangy sweetness.

'Sorry,' Alex said. I shook my head. At least now I knew what had happened. And I was practised at keeping bad memories locked away.

There was a Latin inscription next to the tower door, surrounded by a design of waves and sea serpents. I peered at it.

'*A fronte praecipitium a tergo lupi*,' I read haltingly. 'What does it mean?'

He perched next to me.

'A precipice in front, wolves behind,' he said. 'It's like — being caught between a rock and a hard place. Or between the devil and the deep blue sea. No way out.'

A strong gust of wind produced a tattered plastic bag out of nowhere, and sent it flapping across the stone circle. Under my coat sleeves, tiny hairs rose along my arms.

'Why? Was someone trapped here?'

Alex tipped his head back and rolled it left and right, stretching. 'Dominic reckons the Summerbourne who built the house was involved in some dodgy moneymaking schemes. He made his fortune, and then lost it all again, promised some of the families in the village he'd help them get rich, but then made enemies of them when he couldn't pay his bills. The villagers used to say Summerbourne House was — I don't know — not haunted, but unlucky in some way. Have you been into the village much?'

I shook my head.

'You should ask them,' he said. 'Ask anyone in the village about Summerbourne. Their eyes light up — honestly. They were brought up on stories about this place. Not just the murky history of it, but fairy stories too. What do they call them here — sprites, is it?'

'Yeah.' I'd heard Michael blame sprites when his seeds got mixed up in the greenhouse. Edwin was fascinated with the idea of seeing one, catching one. I pictured them rather like the gremlins from the movie I'd loved when I was eleven or twelve. 'But fairy stories? A bit weird for adults to talk about, isn't it?'

'God knows what really happened here.' Alex grinned at me. 'They never actually tell you that,

139

of course — they probably don't remember themselves any more. The first time I met my neighbour at the cottage, he told me to watch myself coming up here. I said, 'I'm only going for a picnic.' He virtually crossed himself.'

I hugged my arms around my chest. 'They're probably just jealous. In the village. The people who lived here would always have seemed . . . '

'More privileged?' Alex said. 'You're probably right.'

I frowned at the inscription. 'Still, a strange saying for that Summerbourne ancestor to pick. It sounds like he regretted his behaviour, if it made him feel that trapped.'

'I quite like it,' Alex said, leaning towards me a little as he dropped his voice. 'It always strikes me as quite apt for the family. Don't you think they're a bit like wolves, our friends in the house there?'

I glanced towards Edwin, but the boys were oblivious to our conversation, feasting on blackberries and giggling, their chins dripping purple.

'What do you mean?' I liked the way his mouth curved upwards on one side in a half smile.

He leaned closer. 'You know. Dominic thinks he's the alpha male, out hunting in the City all week, returning triumphant on a Friday night to feed his pack. But everyone knows Vera's the real alpha, with all the real money and power. She's the one who oversees the pack, brings new blood in to make it stronger. I bet she turned up at your interview, didn't she? To inspect you before

Ruth gave you the job?'

I licked my lips. 'After Ruth offered me the job, actually. But, yes.'

'There you go. She's got half the village eating out of her hand, that woman — she's always rescuing people, helping people out, and then she calls in the favour when she needs it, or when the family needs it.'

'What are you, then?' I asked. 'New blood?'

When he laughed, his elbow bumped against mine. 'Hardly. I'm not obedient enough for that, anyway. No, I'm just a lone wolf, roaming through their territory. We circle around each other every so often, and then I go off and look for a more suitable pack.'

'But you haven't found one?'

'Not yet.' His mouth half curved again.

I turned to watch the boys for a minute, aware that our sleeves were still touching.

'So what am I?' I asked.

'Ah, you. You're an omega. A lowly caregiver.' He squinted sideways at me. 'You're not a threat to them, so they treat you well.'

I frowned. 'What do you mean?'

'The pack always comes first,' he said. 'It's more important even than the individuals in it. If you threaten the pack, you know what they'll do to you.'

I watched his mouth as he spoke, the flash of his teeth. He leaned towards me again, his gaze on my lips, his voice a whisper. 'You wouldn't stand a chance.'

Edwin skidded to a halt directly in front of us. 'Can we go to the beach now?'

Alex eased away from me. My heart was jumping.

'Are you sure you've had enough?' Alex asked Edwin. Dark purple juice stained all around both boys' mouths and ran in streaks down the fronts of their coats.

'My tummy's full,' Edwin said, and behind him Joel clutched his abdomen dramatically and nodded.

'Well then.' Alex launched into a passable Robin Williams imitation. '*Carpe diem*. Seize the day, boys! Let's get down to the beach.'

Edwin and Joel whooped, and we abandoned the folly and scrambled down the steps to the sand. The boys raced around in the wind, shrieking, stretching their arms out like aeroplane wings.

I had brought nothing with me, and I suffered a twinge of self-recrimination, knowing that Ruth would have thought to bring a picnic blanket, a flask of tea. But seeing the boys run made me want to join in, so I knocked Alex's arm with the back of my hand and shouted, 'Race you to the rocks!' and set off at a sprint.

'Hey!' I heard him shout behind me, and his shoes pounded the wet sand as he tried to close the gap, but I beat him.

'God, I've got to get fit before I turn thirty,' he panted, hunching over with his hands on his knees for a minute. Then, 'It!' and he whacked me on the arm and hared back towards the steps. Edwin and Joel joined in, and we played tag on the beach until we were all exhausted and the boys began to clamour for their lunch.

'You can't be hungry again already?' Alex

asked them, laughing.

I gave the boys the usual instructions to climb the steps carefully, one behind the other, holding on to the railing. As I was about to start after them, Alex caught hold of my wrist. He reached down and picked a spray of tiny purple flowers from the clump of sea lavender at the base of the steps, and he tucked it behind my ear.

'Perfect,' he said.

I swayed towards him, convinced he was about to kiss me, my heart juddering at the nearness of him, my scalp tingling from his fingers settling the flower stalk in my hair. His lips parted.

'Laura!' Edwin called from above. We swayed apart. I dragged my gaze to where the boys waited ten steps up the cliff. 'You're s'posed to be right behind.' Edwin's purple-stained lower lip jutted out, a mix of crossness and anxiety in his expression.

Alex gestured to me to start climbing. 'We're right here,' he told Edwin. 'Good job, boys. Keep going now, nice and steady.' He continued to chat to the boys on the way back to the house, and I kept my gaze on the ground, wishing I understood whether it meant something or nothing — the flower, the leaning towards, the pulling away.

My mood sank further as we reached the lawn and saw the kitchen doors were open. Ruth appeared in the doorway and watched us approach.

'Mummy!' Edwin yelled, running towards her. Alex kept his chin high, his focus directly on Ruth, no sideways glance at me. I tugged the flowers from my hair and slowed my stride.

Ruth kissed the top of Edwin's head. 'Go and wash your hands and face, darling, and take Joel with you. You can play inside then until your lunch is ready.' When she straightened, her gaze was fixed on Alex.

'Ruth. You look wonderful.' Alex opened his arms as he walked up to her. She allowed him to kiss her on each cheek, her expression taut. I hesitated on the patio, turning to look out at the garden.

'Are we still on for our lunch date?' he asked her, and I could tell he wasn't confident of her answer.

'Why not?' she replied after a heartbeat's pause, and then, 'Laura, please make sure Edwin eats a sandwich before any more fruit, won't you?' By the time I had turned to acknowledge this, they were walking away side by side, and I heard Alex's car engine start up a minute later.

There was a bird-pecked apple on the patio table, and I picked it up and examined it. I thought of Ruth saying 'at his beck and call', and I pressed my thumbnail through the wrinkled green skin into the spongy flesh. Alex didn't deserve someone who made him wait, who made him feel guilty when he hadn't done anything wrong. He deserved someone who would race with him on the beach in the wild wind and laugh at the sky. He deserved someone who loved him — someone who was free to love him.

In the kitchen I prepared ham sandwiches for myself and the boys. I sliced two unblemished apples into perfect crescents, and arranged them on a plate alongside a mountain of chocolate fingers. Afterwards, while Edwin and Joel were pushing trains around a wooden track in the day nursery, I escaped to the annexe and slid the wilting purple flowers that Alex had given me between pages of my heaviest textbook and pressed them flat.

11

Seraphine

I love waking up at Winterbourne. I love lying with my eyes closed and listening to the soft rumble of traffic outside, the snatches of phrases from cyclists whizzing by, the leisurely comments drifting up from neighbours as they emerge from their houses. This morning there is high-pitched yapping from a little dog, and then the clatter of the bin lorry as it begins its stop-start progress down the street. I trace the familiar embroidery pattern on the bedspread with my fingertips like I used to on childhood visits to Gran. Even the scent of the wood polish on the mahogany bedside table takes me back to being seven years old again, and for a moment I pretend that all is well and my dad is still here, pottering around in the kitchen downstairs, brewing his coffee and reading his newspaper.

By the time I descend to the kitchen, Edwin has left for work. Danny is frying bacon, yawning.

'How many are coming?' I ask, eyeing the panful.

'Funny. I need energy. Brooke's taking me on a walking tour of the city with some friends of her parents.'

I raise my eyebrows. 'Friends of her parents? How serious is this?'

He ducks his head. I'm not used to seeing Danny embarrassed, and it gives me a little jolt of amusement, alongside some other more protective emotion. He shrugs.

'I like her, that's all,' he says. 'Listen, sis. I was thinking, about last night. That letter. And Dad's accident.' He looks at me, hesitating.

'Hm?'

'Dad said something a few days before he died. When I first got back. He said he had something he wanted to tell us, when we were all together.'

'What do you mean?' I ask, pouring milk onto my muesli.

'I don't know. He said he was glad we were all going to be together that weekend, our birthday weekend. There was something he wanted to tell us.'

I pause with my spoon halfway to my mouth.

'Well, what was it?' I ask, then see his expression and add, 'Okay. You don't know.' I put my spoon down slowly.

Dad's accident happened on a Thursday, the day before Danny and I turned twenty-five. He'd driven over to Summerbourne to start preparations for the family party we had planned for the Saturday. We think he might have been trying to rescue one of the farm kittens from the garage roof. He fell off the ladder onto the driveway and hit his head and died.

Edwin and I were at work that day — Edwin in London and me in Norwich — but Danny was freshly returned from working abroad and was catching up with friends in the village, so he was the first of us to arrive at Summerbourne and find him. It was Danny who had to watch the paramedics shake their heads. It was Danny who had to talk to the police, phone the rest of us, ward off the curious neighbours, pick me up off the gravel when I got home.

'Did Dad say anything to Edwin about this?' I ask eventually, but Danny shrugs.

'I'd forgotten about it until this morning. Do you think it means anything? No one was there when he fell.' He looks down then, blinking at the bacon he's laid out on his bread. 'That's what I keep thinking. No one was there. How can we be sure it *was* an accident?'

'Danny!' I push my chair back and get up, walk to the sink, turn around and walk back. 'The police *said* it was an accident.'

'I know.'

I can tell that, like me, he is remembering our conversation last night: the implication in the letter that Dad's death was far from an accident, and my insistence that this was a hollow threat. I attempt to summon back that certainty now, but there's a tremor in my voice.

'You can't think . . . someone killed him? Murdered him? Because of this thing he was going to tell us?' I concentrate on breathing, trying to push the distressing image from my mind. 'Please, Danny. It's not true. It can't be true.'

We hold each other's gaze, and I feel as though I'm waiting for him to leap up and grab me by the shoulders and tell me it *is* true, it's horribly true. But as he's just pointed out, no one was

148

there; how can we be sure either way?

Danny breaks eye contact first. 'I'm sure you're right, sis.' He sighs. 'This is probably a normal reaction. Looking for someone to blame, or whatever. I shouldn't have said anything.'

He takes a bite of his bacon sandwich. I tip my muesli into the sink, flushing it down the waste disposal. Through the window I glimpse a slim figure with white-blond hair gliding past the railings and pushing open the Winterbourne gate. I turn back to Danny.

'But you think he might have been going to tell us something about all of this?' I say, waving my hand towards the dining room. 'This weirdness. Laura.'

The doorbell rings. My twin brother sits and looks at me for another moment, and then gets to his feet, still holding his sandwich.

'I don't know what to think any more,' he says, and pads out to the hall with me close behind. He turns to me as I start to climb the stairs.

'What are your plans for the day?' he asks. 'Are you going back to Summerbourne?'

'Yep.'

He gives me a long look.

'Don't do anything stupid, will you?' he says. The doorbell rings again.

'What, like going on a walking tour of the city on the hottest day of the year?'

He pulls a face at me, and I dash up out of sight before he swings the front door open. From the privacy of my bedroom, I ring Alex Kaimal's work number, and a friendly-sounding man assures me that he's in the office all day. The address is on an industrial estate in a suburb south of Leeds. I hope Alex is going to prove easier to talk to than Laura.

I shower and dress and wait upstairs until I hear Danny and Brooke leave, and then I set off. Roadworks stretch the journey to over four hours, and when I eventually switch my engine off in front of Alex's steel-framed block of a workplace, I realise my stomach is growling. I can't afford to mess this up. I need to get on with it. I brush my hair, apply lipstick, and attempt to smooth the creases from my dress before I leave the car.

At one end of the low-ceilinged reception area is a horseshoe arrangement of chunky padded chairs in sherbet colours, and a water dispenser. At the other end, a woman and a man murmur into phones behind the reception desk. I catch the man's eye as he hangs up.

'I'd like to see Alex Kaimal, please,' I say. 'Quite urgently. Could you ask him to come down and meet me?'

The man smiles. 'Sure. Is he expecting you?'

'No, I — I did mean to e-mail him, but . . . ' What can I say? I was afraid if Alex saw my name on the e-mail he'd refuse to see me? After the reception Laura gave me, I'm not confident that Alex is going to welcome me wholeheartedly.

The receptionist is unruffled. 'Who shall I tell him . . . ?'

I swallow. 'Seraphine.' He holds his smile as I press my lips down on my surname at the last moment. 'Harris,' I say. I grip the counter.

After a murmured conversation into his

phone, he cups his hand over the mouthpiece and tilts his head at me. 'I'm sorry. Mr Kaimal's in a board meeting. His secretary says you can make an appointment for next week if you like?'

I fight the urge to snatch the phone from his hand and force myself to smile, as if it doesn't matter in the least. 'It's fine,' I manage, and I turn away as he replaces the handset. I feel light-headed and walk over to the water dispenser, glancing at the lift as I pass. Could I march confidently into it without being challenged? The receptionist is busy again, paying me no further attention; I think I could. Could I open every door on each floor and peer inside without someone stopping me? I grit my teeth. Probably not.

I press a jet of chilled water into a plastic cup, and choose a seat with a view of the lift doors. I'll wait. I know what Alex Kaimal looks like, and I'll catch him as he leaves the building. I browse through several magazines over the next hour, and nobody says a word to me. Around half past four, a young woman with a pink streak in her dyed black hair walks in and smiles at me, but she takes a seat at the far end of the horseshoe and concentrates on her phone.

I count thirty-four people out of the lift before it opens to reveal the man I'm waiting for. He's slightly heavier in the face, clearly older than in the company photo, but this is definitely Alex Kaimal. I get to my feet, but the woman with the pink and black hair is closer to him, and she rises between us and says, 'Hi, Dad.'

151

'Kiara,' he says, smiling.

They embrace briefly. They're oblivious to me. I follow them outside.

'Mr Kaimal,' I say, but it comes out as a croak, and he doesn't hear me.

'Mr Kaimal!' I call, louder. The daughter turns first.

When Alex Kaimal finally swings round to look at me, we stand facing each other wordlessly. Cold needles prickle down my neck and arms. His frown deepens as he stares at me. The girl looks curiously from one of us to the other.

'Can we help you?' she asks me. I can't tear my gaze from his face.

'I'm Seraphine Mayes,' I manage to say. 'I'm Dominic and Ruth Mayes's daughter. I think you were a friend of my parents.'

His demeanour changes then. His eyes widen, he draws in two deep quick breaths, and he takes a step backward, holding his hands up as if to defend himself.

'Dad?' his daughter asks, but he doesn't take his eyes off me.

'You can't be,' he says eventually. 'You can't be. Ruth died.'

I step forward, warily.

'I know. She died on the day I was born,' I say.

He starts to shake his head, slowly at first and then more violently.

'No. No, it's impossible,' he says.

'Dad?' his daughter says again, and he reaches for her hand without breaking eye contact with me.

'We need to go,' he says, taking another step backward.

'My brother Edwin remembers you,' I say.

An expression of pain distorts his face.

'Why do you say it's impossible?' I ask.

He shakes his head, his mouth slightly open, no sound emerging.

'Have you been in contact with Laura?' I ask. 'Did you send her a letter?'

'Laura?' he blurts. 'No. What?'

Then he regains some composure and takes a step towards me, and then another, his eyes stretched wide, his face thrust forward.

'Who *are* you?' he demands, and I'm convinced that at any moment he's going to snarl at me. I stumble backward. The young woman tugs at his hand, pulling him away.

'Dad, stop it. We need to go. Please, let's just go,' she says.

He relaxes slightly and examines me all the way down to my feet and back up again in a swift moment.

'I don't know who you are,' he says, his voice gravelly, 'and I don't want to talk to you. Stay away from me. Stay away from both of us.'

They cling on to each other as they hurry away from me, crossing the car park and climbing into a car. Several men and women have stopped outside the building and are eyeing me curiously. I'm shaking. *Impossible*, he said. It's *impossible* that I'm my parents' child. The conviction that this man is right claws at me, firing off the same three words over and over again in a staccato rhythm at the back of my brain. *Who am I?*

12

Laura

OCTOBER/NOVEMBER 1991

When Alex dropped Ruth home after their lunch date, she went directly to her bedroom claiming a headache. I'd been making flapjacks with Edwin and Joel, and I chewed on a crispy corner piece as I watched the yellow car glide away down the lane. I guessed from Ruth's headache that her outing with Alex hadn't been a success.

That night, Dominic arrived at Summerbourne in a jolly mood, but the following morning he came off the phone and into the kitchen with his mouth in a flat line.

'That was Alex. He can't come for lunch after all. He's got to go back up to Leeds right away — some crisis at work.'

Ruth shrugged. 'Oh well. All he could talk about yesterday was the work he's having done on the cottage. It got boring. I wish he'd just ring you when he's in that sort of mood — he's your friend.'

Dominic frowned. 'Come on, you've known him as long as I have. Have you upset him again? I got the feeling this work crisis thing was an excuse.'

'Well, if informing him that I'm not his employee, I'm not at his beck and call to sort out

154

his interior decorating problems counts as upsetting him, then yes. Maybe. It's his own fault.'

My jaw tightened. I was in the kitchen to fetch a beaker of water for Edwin, and I kept my eyes down and padded back out towards the day nursery. But I hovered out of sight in the utility area between the two rooms.

'For God's sake, Ruth. He doesn't *need* your help. He's excited. He wants to include us in his project.' There was a sharp edge of exasperation in Dominic's voice. 'Why do you always do this?'

'You have no idea what it's like for me stuck out here in the week. Do you think it's all fun and games? I gave up my career for this.'

I held my breath. Ruth had told me about the banking career she left when she had the twins; about how much she loved it, how much she missed it. I gripped the door handle of the day nursery, upset at how dismissive she was about the days she shared with Edwin and me.

'So let's move into Winterbourne, then,' Dominic said. 'Get Edwin into the school the Mellard kids go to. You could pick up some part-time hours, see how it suits — '

There was a scrape of chair leg on tiles.

'I'm not taking Edwin away from Summer-bourne,' Ruth said. 'Never.'

I slipped into the day nursery and kept Edwin out of their way for the rest of the morning.

Ruth remained preoccupied even after Dominic returned to London that Monday. Edwin and I fell into a routine of playing outside every morn-ing — in the garden or at the beach, or at the

155

playground in the village if we fancied a walk and a trip to the shop. We'd return to the house for lunch, and then choose a project for the afternoon: creating models from cardboard boxes, baking biscuits, designing treasure hunts. There was no part of me that minded working longer hours than I was supposed to; the busier I was, the less chance I had to feel lonely or to dwell on what had and hadn't happened with Alex at the base of the cliff steps.

Ruth often drifted into the kitchen as Edwin and I were eating lunch, and she seemed to enjoy Edwin's happy chatter as he told her what we'd been up to, but for three weekends in a row she complained of a headache when Dominic was home. I didn't hear either of them mention Alex's name.

Vera phoned on a Tuesday towards the end of the month. 'Would you mind awfully taking Edwin to his gym class tomorrow afternoon, Laura? I'd like to come down and take Ruth out for lunch. Have a proper chat with her.'

'Of course,' I replied. 'No problem.'

'Thank you, my dear. I don't know what we'd do without you.'

Edwin wasn't fazed by having to walk to his gym class. Helen Luckhurst was there with her solemn son, Ralph; her new baby daughter, Daisy, muffled in a sling against her chest. She bought me a polystyrene cup of grey coffee, and quizzed me about daily life at Summerbourne while we watched the children wobble along beams.

'Does she act like a proper mum, though

— Ruth — when she's at home?' She widened her eyes at me, waiting for my reply, her lips parted.

'What do you mean?' I asked.

'I mean, she always seems so — cold. Especially since she lost her other little boy. Does she blame Edwin for that? For distracting her? Does she still love him, do you think? I mean, really, deep down, like a proper mum?'

I inhaled sharply through my nose, and turned away. When she realised I wasn't intending to answer, she shrugged and wandered off to chat to someone else.

Ruth and Vera were still out at lunch when Edwin and I got home. I settled him in front of his favourite cartoon video in the day nursery, and was in the kitchen when the phone rang.

'Hello, Summerbourne?'

'Hi, Laura, it's Alex.'

'Oh. Hi.' I stretched the spiral cord between my fingers. It was three weeks and five days since he'd tucked the flowers into my hair, leaning in so close to me, smiling his half smile at me. Had he been counting the days too?

'I just wondered — is Ruth there?' he said. The telephone cord sprang back at me, bouncing briefly up and down with a rhythm like a laugh.

'No, sorry,' I said. 'She's out.'

'Ah. Would you mind giving her a message?'

I picked up the pencil kept on the hall table for that purpose. 'Of course.'

'Could you tell her I'm at the cottage now until Sunday. If she wants to pop round before the weekend, she'd be very welcome. My neighbours tell me there's a Halloween party on in the village tomorrow night — do you know if she's thinking of going? Or perhaps I should wait until the weekend.' He paused. 'Perhaps I should give Dominic a ring.'

'Okay,' I said. 'I'll tell her.'

'Great. Thanks, Laura. And thanks for the trip to the beach the other day — it was fun.'

I scored a deep grey groove into the pad of Post-it notes.

'Yep. Okay. Bye.' I hung up.

Alex at cottage, I wrote on the pad. **Party tomorrow night?**

Ruth stalked into the day nursery to find us when she and Vera got back.

'How was gym, darling?' she asked Edwin, bending to kiss him.

'Good, Mummy.'

She had bright red patches high up on her cheeks, and she narrowed her eyes at me over Edwin's head.

'Get rid of her, please,' she hissed.

'Who?' I asked.

'My mother. Persuade her to go home. She's going on and on about us making a fresh start, moving into Winterbourne. I can't bear to sit next to her at dinner. Please, Laura.' She gave Edwin another kiss and marched out of the room. I trailed after her.

Ruth headed directly upstairs. Vera was leaning by the back doors in the kitchen, gazing out at the garden.

'Is everything all right, Mrs Blackwood?' I asked. She straightened and smiled at me.

'Absolutely. Quite all right, thank you. I don't think I will stay for dinner after all, though, my dear. Would you mind phoning for a taxi for me?'

I went out to the hall. The block of Post-it notes displayed a fresh blank sheet.

The following morning, Edwin and I had clomped into the hall from the garden, shedding wellies and coats and bundles of autumn leaves, before we realised we were interrupting Ruth on the phone. She held her hand over the mouthpiece and waited for us to take our finds through to the day nursery before she resumed talking. A while later she wandered through to admire Edwin's collage.

'Laura, I know I said I'd take him to the Halloween thing in the hall this afternoon, but I don't suppose you'd take him for me, would you?'

Edwin looked from her to me, his glue stick poised in mid-air.

'Yeah, of course,' I said.

'Oh, thank you. You're a lifesaver. I want to nip into town and buy a costume for the village do tonight. Lots of the neighbours are going, apparently.'

Edwin said, 'Can I come?'

'Tonight?' Ruth ruffled his hair. 'No, darling. Sorry. It's for grown-ups only. Laura will look after you here — maybe you could do apple bobbing or something?' Her vague tone sharpened as she met my eyes. 'That is, if you don't mind babysitting?'

I shook my head. 'That's fine.'

Edwin put his pirate costume on after lunch,

159

and I drew him a curly mustache and dots of stubble with a black eyeliner pencil. I dropped a torch into my bag before we set off. It was the half-term holiday, and the village hall was overrun with children in fancy dress, from pillowcase ghosts to red-horned devils, and everything in between. Helen Luckhurst introduced me to Kemi Harris, Joel's mum, recently returned from Nigeria. Kemi thanked me for the biscuits I'd helped Joel bake to welcome her home, but Edwin was tugging at my arm, so I left her chatting to Helen and accompanied him on a tour of the hall.

He gripped my hand hard as he queued for games, his eyes wide as he watched the shrieking gangs of children rocketing around the echoing space. He had a turn at biting doughnuts hanging from strings, and then a go at sliding his hand into the lucky dip barrel where slimy toy bugs hid among the sawdust. Two little wizards who pounced on him turned out to be Joel Harris and Ralph Luckhurst, but Edwin hid his face in my cardigan and didn't want to join in their play.

I wrapped his scarf around his neck and pulled his hat tightly over his ears before we set off for home, but the sharp air crept underneath our layers and pinched at our skin. I stopped to wipe his nose as we passed the last house before our lane, and a car slowed to a halt. It was Ruth.

'Good timing!' she said as we clambered in. I fumbled to do Edwin's buckle up with my numb fingers. 'How was the party, darling?'

Edwin jutted his lower lip out.

'I found the most marvellous witch costume,' she said. 'And Alex has some floor-length black cloaks for us. It will go perfectly.'

Later, when I had made cheese on toast for Edwin and bathed him and was reading him stories in bed, Ruth danced into his bedroom. She wore a pointed black hat and a maroon and black velvet dress, and when she spun around, the skirt whirled up into ripples. Her nails and lipstick were blood red, her eye-shadow was dark, and her eyes shone.

'Don't like it.' Edwin buried his face into my shoulder. Ruth stopped dancing.

'It's only Mummy, Edwin,' I said. 'It's just a costume. Isn't it a pretty skirt?'

Edwin shook his head without looking.

Ruth put her hands on her hips. 'Well, Alex is picking me up in a minute. Don't wait up for me, Laura — just keep the annexe door propped open. I'll see you in the morning.'

'Have a nice time,' I said.

She swished out of the room, and Edwin rubbed his fists into his eyes.

'I don't like Mummy like that,' he said.

'Me neither,' I whispered. 'But she'll be back to normal tomorrow, don't worry.'

I read him more stories, and sat with him afterwards, stroking his hair until he fell asleep. Then I cleared up the kitchen, covering the top of the half-empty red wine bottle with a square of foil.

I dragged my pillow and blankets onto a sofa in the day nursery to be closer to Edwin if he needed me, but my sleep was undisturbed. A grey mist swirled outside the curtainless windows when I woke, the sun barely breaking the horizon. In the hall, Ruth's black boots lay on their side, shining wet. Beads of water glistened on the tiles in a pattern that suggested a larger pair of boots had recently stood next to them. I planned to make a cup of tea and retreat to the annexe, but something caught my eye through the hall window on my way back to the kitchen. I took a couple of steps closer and peered out through the gloom.

Something swayed under the trees at the entrance to the drive. Was that people out there? I stepped closer to the glass, blinking. Two figures hovered at the corner of the lawn. All traces of sleep left me. I backed towards the phone, my heart thumping. Should I call the police? Should I wake Ruth? My feet grew chilled on the tiles while I hesitated. Perhaps I should go back to bed, wait for the sun to come up properly. Probably they were innocent neighbours and had already wandered away down the lane.

A faint squeal cut through my indecision then — a high-pitched squeak that repeated itself twice more. It sounded familiar. I crept back to the window. Michael stood facing the figures, and he slowly lowered his wheelbarrow. There was something wrong with the swaying shapes, I realised — they weren't people standing on the ground.

I grabbed wellies from the cupboard, hauled my coat onto my arms. My hands shook as some instinct made me press the door handle down before looking for the keys. The door swung open. My stomach lurched. I stepped outside.

Michael watched me approach, his expression grim. The rising sun was beating back the mist, and it was clear now that the two figures were shapes hanging from the branch of one of the ash trees. I stepped closer.

'They're not real,' I whispered. Michael made no response but stood with his gaze fixed on me, as if waiting for me to do something. I stretched out trembling fingers and felt velvet — wet, black velvet. The cloaks that Alex and Ruth had worn to the party, hung up by their hoods.

I made a noise like a laugh, from relief rather than humour, but when I turned to Michael, his face was more severe than ever.

'That ent right,' he said. He shook his head, no longer looking at me. I stumbled away then, back to the house, locking the front door behind me. I dragged my bedding back through to the annexe and lay under my blankets until I heard Edwin's cartoons blare out in the day nursery an hour later. When I looked out to the driveway in the grey daylight, the cloaks were gone.

Edwin and I stayed indoors all morning. The yellow sports car announced itself with a scatter of gravel while we were making sandwiches for lunch. I pushed the sitting-room door open and peered into the shadows.

'Alex is here,' I said.

Ruth sprang up, her hands on her cheeks. The doorbell rang. She whisked the curtains open and ran her fingers through her hair.

'I told him not to come back,' she said. She

straightened her shoulders. 'It's fine. Let him in.'

He stood empty-handed on the doorstep, his gaze flicking past mine to search the hall behind me, his dark hair slick in the drizzle. I stepped back to allow him in, and nodded at the sitting-room door. Edwin and I ate our sandwiches in the day nursery and watched cartoons all afternoon, not venturing into the main house again until the car had gone.

Dominic arrived late that evening with bags of groceries in his boot. He was dicing onion and crushing garlic the next morning when he asked, 'So, what time's Alex coming?'

Ruth leaned against the sink with her back to us. I peeled Edwin's banana for him and gestured for him to follow me out.

'I'm not sure he is coming,' she said.

Dominic paused with his knife poised. 'Why not?'

Ruth shrugged.

A minute later Dominic strode into the day nursery, where Edwin was laying out fresh sheets of paper for painting.

'Hey, Edwin. Fancy a trip into the village to see Uncle Alex?'

Edwin scrambled off his chair. 'Yes, yes!'

Dominic gave me a flat smile. 'It's the weekend. You shouldn't be working. I'm afraid we take advantage of you far too much.'

'I don't mind,' I said.

'Do you want to go out somewhere? I could drop you in town?'

An image of my friends flashed into my mind. The four of us who used to spend our Saturdays hanging out at the shopping centre, scraping money together for chips, gossiping about the other kids at school.

'No, I'm good, thanks. I'll . . . ' I indicated the annexe door with my head.

'Okay.'

I stood by the table after they'd gone, wondering what my friends were doing at that very moment. My throat ached with self-pity. Hazel would be taking notes in a Saturday-morning lecture, I suspected; the first year of medicine was pretty lecture-heavy. Jo had joined the police, and I pictured her on a weekend shift, gulping down scalding coffee before dashing out to an urgent call. Pati would almost certainly still be asleep in her student bedsit, unlikely to surface until mid-afternoon. They'd all have new friends by now, new in-jokes, new futures mapped out. I doubted they had time to spare a thought for me.

A movement in the garden tugged me back to the present, and I stepped closer to the tall day-nursery windows. Ruth was wandering out across the lawn in her baggy grey cardigan and slippers, seemingly oblivious to the November chill. She disappeared among the trees. I was alone in the house.

In the kitchen, raw onion and garlic lay abandoned on a chopping board, filling the room with their odour. I plucked two paperbacks from the bookshelf in the sitting room and took them with a cup of tea to my annexe.

The sound of cartoons alerted me to Edwin's return a couple of hours later. He didn't acknowledge me passing behind his sofa, his eyes fixed on the screen. I filled the kettle, but tiptoed to the doorway with it in my hand, holding my breath. Dominic's voice floated from the sitting room.

' . . . thinking of selling it,' he was saying. 'After such a short time. It's ridiculous. He knows it's a good investment even if he doesn't want to use it himself.'

I couldn't make out Ruth's reply.

'Well, something has upset him, that's for sure,' Dominic said.

Ruth said something like,' . . . his own life.'

'You've picked a fight with him again, haven't you? Made him think we want him here, then told him you don't. Well, I hope you're satisfied.' I heard the creak of the sitting-room door, and I dashed across the kitchen, clattering the kettle onto its base.

'*He* should move into Winterbourne,' came Ruth's voice. 'With you and my mother. You'd like that, wouldn't you? You and Alex. You could suit yourselves then.'

I abandoned the kettle and crept back to my rooms.

Dominic headed back to London on the Sunday morning. Ruth kept to herself that week, and I took Edwin out of the house as much as possible. Michael introduced me to quinces, another fruit I had never encountered. Edwin and I picked some and I hacked them into pieces to stew with apple, but it was their fragrance that attracted me the most: an aroma that reminded me tantalisingly of Turkish delight jellies and the

Earl Grey tea that Vera drank. I kept a couple on my windowsill in the annexe, stroking their fuzzy yellow skins when I passed them, inhaling their beguiling scent as if it was an antidote for the tense atmosphere in the main part of the house.

Dominic and Ruth argued again the following weekend, and Dominic sought me out on the Sunday afternoon.

'I'm really sorry about all this, Laura,' he told me, his lips tugged downwards. 'I think Ruth could do with getting away from here for a little while. Is there any chance you'd consider looking after Edwin full time for a few days? I might book a mini break for her to go on with Vera.'

I nodded. 'Of course. Whatever helps.'

He pressed his lips into his flat smile.

'God, I don't know what we did to deserve you. Thank you. I'll pay you at double rate for all the extra hours, overnight, all of it,' he said.

I opened my mouth to protest. That would be a ridiculous amount of money for the minimal extra work it would entail. He held up a hand.

'Really — it's the only way I can justify it,' he said. Edwin whizzed down the slide and ran head-on into his father's legs. 'It's danger money,' Dominic added, his smile reaching his eyes this time.

The weekday atmosphere in the house lightened after that. Ruth told me she and Vera were going to stay at a luxury country house hotel for a few days, and she began to eat meals with us again. She asked Edwin questions about his morning activities, and sometimes she took him out with her in the afternoons so that I could study. Often, she walked down to the beach with Edwin in the early evenings, saying it helped clear her head. She asked me to babysit on Saturday nights, and she and Dominic went out together, coming home late. I dozed in the day nursery until they came in, and then took myself off to the annexe.

But as the date of her mini holiday approached, she withdrew again, her behaviour distracted and restless. I did my best to reassure her that Edwin would be fine with me, but she barely listened: that didn't seem to be the source of her anxiety. I knew Dominic thought she was miserable about not being pregnant again, and Vera thought she was ill with depression and ought to see a doctor, but I wasn't convinced about either of these theories. If Dominic was right about Alex putting his cottage back on the market, I guessed that Ruth was feeling guilty about pushing him away. I wondered if she missed him, and if she might attempt to entice him back to Summerbourne. I was torn between wanting to see him again and hoping I never would.

I checked the clock constantly on that last morning. Dominic had taken the day off work to collect both women and chauffeur them to the hotel. I wondered if Ruth was building up to a refusal to go.

However, she seemed resigned to the trip by the time Dominic arrived, and she gave Edwin a fierce hug before joining Vera on the back seat of the car. It was a grey Thursday afternoon, spitting lightly with a cold rain, and Edwin and I huddled in the doorway to wave them off. Edwin's bottom lip wobbled as the car purred away.

'Is Daddy coming back after?' he asked. We gazed down the lane together.

'I don't know,' I said.

13

Seraphine

One hundred and forty miles of road lie between Alex Kaimal's office and Summerbourne. Questions run through my head in a relentless loop as I allow the GPS to guide me home. Why did Alex look so shocked when I told him my name? Was he telling the truth when he denied contacting Laura? Why did he say I was *impossible*?

Who *am* I?

The pounding at the base of my skull worsens with every mile.

A dead bird lies on my front doorstep when I finally reach home. I nudge it with the tip of my shoe. Spindly pink toes and black beak point to the sky; its eyes are half closed and sunken. I crane my neck to look for a mark on the window above — perhaps it stunned itself against the glass and failed to recover from the impact. When I step over it into the hall, a single black feather wafts across the tiles ahead of me, and my breath catches in my throat. I slam the door shut behind me. I could have sworn that feather was already inside the house when I opened the door. *I'm losing my mind.* I turn my key in the lock, and stand on tiptoes to wrestle the rarely used bolt across.

My neck muscles tighten more with every

minute that passes, drawing my shoulders up under my ears. When I fumble for a packet of painkillers in the kitchen cupboard, Vera's pot of sleeping pills tumbles out onto the counter. I swallow a couple of ibuprofen tablets, and then stand in front of the open fridge for several minutes, concentrating on taking slow, deep breaths as the chilled air washes over my skin. The tubs of cold pasta that Edwin left for me stare sullenly out. As the interior of the fridge reaches room temperature, I kick the door shut and rummage through the pantry for a packet of crackers.

A flurry of movement in the garden makes me jump. I press my forehead against the glass doors, peering at the overgrown bushes along the edge of the lawn. A band of pink still decorates the sky, but dusk is merging into night, and it's difficult to distinguish shapes from shadows. A fox, perhaps? When I turn back to the brightly lit clutter on the kitchen surfaces, my gaze falls on Vera's pill pot. The lozenges inside are tiny — could they really be powerful enough to override the whirling thoughts in my brain? The prospect of surrendering to a night of dreamless sleep is too much to resist, and I gulp one of the pills down with a glass of water, barely feeling it as it slips down my throat.

I munch through another cracker as I pace around the house, checking that all the windows and doors are locked. The drug begins to work sooner than I expected. Or perhaps it's my own exhaustion that makes my eyelids droop as I haul myself up the stairs. A numbness sloshes through my thoughts, dragging them under the surface of my consciousness. I throw myself onto my bed without undressing, and slip into a deep sleep.

Images of the sea fill my mind as I gradually wake in the morning. Bright sunlight bounces around my room, and an intermittent buzzing grows more familiar until I realise it's coming from my phone. It takes me a further minute to focus on the screen.

A text from Pamela Larch:

I thought of something else. It's not very nice, I'm afraid. If you can pop down to the surgery this morning, we can have a chat. Pamela

What on earth does 'not very nice' mean, coming from Pamela? Did she type something else, something more specific, and then change it to this blandest of warnings? A nurse who deals with cancers and amputations, death and mental breakdowns. What would count as 'not very nice'?

My legs are heavy as I plod down the stairs, and I'm desperately thirsty, but I'm seized by an overwhelming need to see whether the dead bird is still on the doorstep. The stiff bolt hurts my fingers, and when I finally swing the door open, I am momentarily blinded by the sun's glare. The bird has gone. I scan the drive. Perhaps a cat took it in the night, or a fox. Something catches my eye on the narrow curve of lawn that borders the circular driveway. I take a few steps towards it, but the sharp stones under my bare feet make me wince. It looks as though marks have been burnt into the scruffy grass.

My heart pounds as I haul myself back upstairs to my bedroom window. The letters scorched into the lawn are angled as if designed to be read from this exact viewpoint. Chills creep along my arms as I stare at the word they form: STOP.

I stumble back down to the kitchen and try to think of innocent explanations while I pop more ibuprofen tablets through their foil seal, waiting for the kitchen tap to run cold. Village kids messing around? One of my brothers playing a joke? A rogue act by the unreliable gardening company? There must be a rational explanation. The pills make me gag. I have a sudden urge to escape from the house, to put some distance between myself and those blackened letters while I work out what to do. The surgery will already be open, so I'll head straight there and find out what it is that Pamela has remembered. I hold my breath as I dash out to my car, my line of sight squeezed between the damaged grass on one side and the spot where Dad's head hit the gravel on the other. The steering wheel is clammy under my fingers, and I accelerate past the flint cottages although no neighbours are in sight.

As ever, the surgery is quiet. Hayley Pickersgill stares at me from behind her desk, and I blank her, painfully aware that I'm still wearing yesterday's rumpled clothes and haven't brushed my teeth this morning, let alone my hair. My head pounds. Pamela's door is open, and when I peer in, I catch her scrolling through her phone.

173

The staff here have too much time on their hands, I think.

'Seraphine, come in. Please, sit down.' Pamela's bright eyes scrutinise me, and her mouth tightens.

'Pamela.' I attempt a smile. 'You said you remembered something?'

She repositions herself in her chair. 'Well, I wasn't sure whether to mention it. Martin thinks I shouldn't.' She frowns. 'But it might be relevant. To what you want to know — about the pregnancies and births in your family, I mean.'

I nod, gripping the plastic arms of my chair, watching her.

'It's something people used to talk about when I was little,' she says. 'In the village. In the playground at school. Your mum was a few years older than us. In the top class, I think, when Martin and I were in the infants. But we knew all about her. You know what the village is like.'

I nod again.

'Well,' she says. 'She had a twin. Your mother, I mean. She had a twin brother.'

'Oh right,' I say. 'Yes.' The brother mentioned in my mother's obituary. 'Do you know what happened to him?'

'Well, he died, you see.' She's twisting a pen over and over in her hands, and she looks down at this now rather than at me. 'Before he was born. Your grandmother was pregnant with twins, but only Ruth survived.'

'Oh.' I stare at her. 'That's so sad. Gran never said.'

'I don't remember his name,' she says. 'I'm sorry.'

I shake my head. 'Well, it was before you were born. It must have been terrible for Gran.' I think about Vera, and the way she always makes a point of referring to Danny and me as the Summerbourne twins. I feel guilty to remember how it sometimes irritated me, now that I know she lost her own twin baby, as well as her grandson Theo.

'But,' I say, 'why did Martin think you shouldn't tell me?'

Pamela fiddles with her pen again. 'Well, not that bit. It was what the other kids used to say, you see. They used to . . . to say mean things to her about it. Nasty things.' She swallows. 'They said that Ruth strangled him.'

My mouth falls open. 'What?'

'He was born dead, you see, with the cord around his neck. They said she wrapped it round his neck while they were still inside the womb together — twice around his neck, they said — and then she choked him to death. On purpose.'

I stare at her. 'But that's . . . ridiculous. Horrific. How could they say that?'

'I know,' she says. 'And of course it's not true.'

'Well, of course not.'

'But I think that's what reminded people of . . . the other stories. The old stories.'

Her fingers are still now. She waits, and I sense she is giving me a chance to walk away, to say I don't want to hear.

'What old stories?' I ask.

'That twins never survive at Summerbourne,' Pamela says.

She meets my eyes then, and her expression is apologetic, almost fearful.

I try to keep my voice calm, but my pulse is jumping. 'That's . . . What do you mean?'

'The original Summerbourne, the man who built the house,' she says. 'He got into financial difficulties, apparently, nearly went bankrupt. He had baby twins, and they say he cheated people in the village. Claimed he'd paid them for goods and services when he hadn't, that sort of thing.'

I watch her. 'This was a very long time ago.'

'I know,' she says. 'So the story goes that it was a local stonemason that built the folly for him, did all those carvings and everything. And the village blacksmith made the cannon for the sundial. And when it was all finished, Mr Summerbourne, he said a certain price had been agreed, and the stonemason and blacksmith said it was double that, and they argued — you can imagine. And the villagers threatened to knock the whole thing down. But when they went up there, all angry, Mr Summerbourne had parked his baby twins inside the circular wall, right up against the tower, in their baby carriage. Fast asleep.'

I'm transfixed despite myself. 'Go on.'

Pamela blows out a puff of air. 'Well, the villagers turned back. They were decent people; they didn't want a scene with the babies crying and everyone shouting and all that. So they cut their losses and went home. But that night . . . ' She frowns at me. 'That night, one of them babies disappeared from its cot in the nursery at Summerbourne. Vanished, just like that.'

I swallow. 'What happened?'

'They never found a trace. No sign of a break-in; everyone had an alibi. People said the fairies had taken him as a punishment.'

A laugh escapes me. 'Right. Okay. Fairies obviously much more likely than a human being with a grudge.'

Pamela's look is almost disapproving. 'I'm just telling you what they say. That from that day on, the Summerbourne family hasn't been allowed to keep its twins. Your mother's twin brother — died in the womb. Your older brother Theo — fell over the cliff. And you and Danny . . . '

I stare at her. 'Me and Danny what?'

'Well, some people say your poor mother bargained with her life to try to keep both of you safe . . . '

I shove my chair backward, scrambling to move away from her. 'How can you say that?'

'And some people say . . . ' She stretches a hand towards me. 'I'm sorry, Seraphine, but you wanted to know . . . '

My heart is pounding. I stumble backward until the door handle jabs into the small of my back. 'What?'

'Some people say it didn't work. That someone took your mother's real babies anyway. That you and Danny aren't real Summerbourne twins at all.' She tilts her head, her expression sympathetic. 'I'm sorry, Seraphine, and I'm sure it can't be true, but I feel you ought to know that that's what people say.'

I fumble for the door handle and finally wrench it open. Hayley straightens in her seat as I lurch into the waiting room, her mouth falling open. Out in the high street the sun is high and fierce, and everything around me shimmers with heat. Houses and cars and lampposts look strangely distorted. I'm not certain whether I've actually woken up this morning, or whether I'm trapped in a nightmare.

14

Laura

NOVEMBER 1991

Dominic did return to Summerbourne after dropping Ruth and Vera at their hotel. It was already dark, and he brought the crisp chill of the November night into the hall with him.

'Guess where we're going tomorrow,' he said to Edwin. 'I'll give you a clue: lots of water and lots of fishes.'

'The sea!' Edwin shouted.

'The aquarium,' Dominic said. He gave me a quick grin. 'Didn't fancy going back to work just for one day.'

When I came down from putting Edwin to bed, Dominic called me into the sitting room. The curtains were open, and he was gazing out at the sky, his back to me.

'It's a blue moon tonight,' he said. 'Come and look.'

I stood alongside him. Warm air rose from the radiator and mingled with the cold breath of the glass.

'It doesn't look blue.'

He chuckled. 'It's an old farmer's term. When a season has four full moons instead of three — it doesn't happen very often — the third one is called a blue moon.'

'Oh. I didn't know it was an actual thing.' I thought about it. 'Why isn't it the last one that's called the blue moon? The fourth one is the extra one, surely?'

He gave me a sideways glance. 'I've no idea. I never thought about it like that.'

I leaned closer to the window to peer at it, my breath misting the glass.

'I'm shocked,' I said. 'That it's not actually blue.'

'Wait till you see a black moon.' He turned to me, his hip against the windowsill. 'Next summer. I'll find the date for you. You'll be quite overwhelmed.'

'Oh.'

He smiled. 'Some people say a blue moon is just a second full moon in a calendar month. Much more common.'

I sucked in my breath. 'How dare they!'

A bark of laughter escaped him, and he swivelled further round to lean back against the radiator. The surprise in his eyes blinked into a more focused gleam.

'There's more to you than you let on, isn't there?' he said.

'I don't know what you mean.'

'You never talk about yourself. Your home.'

I shrugged. 'I don't think about it much.'

'To a lot of people it's the most important thing about them. Where they come from. Who their family is.'

'Not to me,' I said.

'You lived with your mum, before this?'

I nodded. 'And Beaky. Her partner. He doesn't like me.'

Dominic's eyebrows shot up. 'Beaky?'

'Yep.'

He studied my face. 'Was it that bad?'

I walked away, pausing at the coffee table with my back to him. An opened bottle of red wine waited on it, two glasses by its side. Dominic's sleeve brushed against mine on his way to the sofa.

'Join me?' He picked up the bottle and tilted a glass towards me questioningly.

I hesitated. The sitting-room door was ajar, the curtains open. I rubbed my arms.

'I'll light the fire,' he said. 'We should celebrate the blue moon. Here, sit.'

I pulled the curtains closed before sinking onto the sofa. The wine was warm, and I swirled it around my mouth, trying to get used to the bitter furriness of it as I watched Dominic crouch over the hearth with a box of matches. He coaxed a pile of kindling into flames, then arranged logs over the top. A billow of smoke puffed into the room, carrying an aroma of something musty and old.

'So what do you want to do with your life, then?' he asked as he sank down next to me with his own full glass. 'After you finish here, after your biochemistry degree or whatever?' I curled up in my half of the sofa and sighed.

'I don't know. Travel, maybe.'

'With your friends?'

I shrugged. 'I don't know. We used to talk about it. They've probably made new plans by now.'

'You're very good with Edwin. I can see you

181

settling down and having a family of your own one day.'

The heavy flavour of the wine had grown on me, and I drained my glass. 'Yeah.'

'But meanwhile, the world is your oyster.'

'I'd walk away from everything if I could,' I said. 'Start again. Be someone new.'

'Reinvent yourself?'

I looked directly at him then. His expression was open, no glint of judgement in his eyes. I held his gaze for a moment, and then nodded.

'Yeah. That'd be nice.'

He considered this, and didn't press me further. The combination of wine and warmth and companionable silence helped my muscles relax, and I shifted into a more comfortable position. He refilled my glass, and we sat and watched the flames dance over the puckering logs.

'Funny thing, life,' he said eventually. His voice was low and scratchy. 'One minute you've got everything you ever wanted, and the next minute . . . ' His pupils were dilated in the low light, reflecting the flickering yellow of the fire.

'Theo,' I said.

He tipped his head back, staring at the ceiling. 'Did Ruth tell you how it happened?'

'Alex told me.'

'I think about it all the time. I think about him all the time.'

I leaned towards him, and placed my hand over his. His hands were broader than Alex's, and not as smooth; his knuckles bore smudges of soot from the fire, and it made him seem vulnerable somehow.

'I'm sorry,' I said.

He rolled his head forward, tucking his chin down and studying my hand. He turned it over, running his thumb over my palm. A tingle spread through my body, and I savoured the sensation.

'You know, it's funny,' he said. 'I thought — that day we all went to the beach. When you went on the Topper with Alex. I thought maybe you two might . . . ?'

I shook my head, tried to smile. 'Nope.'

'Ah.' He stroked my palm again, and then looked at me. 'You wanted to?'

When I didn't answer straightaway, he turned his attention back to my hand. I closed my eyes to concentrate on the feeling of his thumb running along the underside of my fingers, crossing my palm, stroking circles on the inside of my wrist. I felt as though I was floating, as if my muscles had melted.

'Someone like him would never be interested in someone like me,' I said, without opening my eyes. I was picturing the way Alex watched Ruth's movements, from under half-lowered lids, his concentration intense. I was picturing the way he'd stood on the doorstep in the rain, the day after the Halloween party, his clothes dripping, craning his neck for a glimpse of her.

The stroking stopped, and I opened my eyes to find Dominic brushing a strand of hair from my cheek.

'Then someone like him is a fool,' he said.

I watched his lips as he leaned towards me. His fingers traced through my hair to the back of my head. We paused with our faces an inch apart.

'We shouldn't,' he said. 'But you're just so . . . ' His lips brushed against mine, and he drew back, and the sudden movement drew a cold draught between us where the warmth of his chest had just been. I put one hand behind his head and pulled him back down towards me.

It had been a long time since I'd done this. I thought of Alex as we kissed, at first. *We could have . . .* But this wasn't Alex. This was someone who wanted me, who really wanted me right now. The deeper I kissed him, the deeper he kissed me; and the faster I tugged at his clothes, the faster he tugged at mine.

And I didn't mind that he wasn't Alex any more. I was only aware of the flames and the shadows, and his unfamiliar body against mine. I focused on the moment, with no thoughts of the barriers that ought to separate us, and no consideration of the consequences. We wanted each other. We needed each other.

'Don't go,' I said, as he rolled off me afterwards.

He kept his back to me, putting a distance between us even while our bodies were still cooling. The fire had dwindled to flakes of ash. He dragged the curtains apart with a harsh clatter of metal hoops, and rubbed at the condensation on the glass. His hair took on a silvery tint in the moonlight.

'When is the next blue moon?' I asked from the sofa.

He shook his head. His shoulders were

hunched. I wrapped my arms tighter around my knees.

A scuffling sound in the hall made us both jump, and I snatched my cardigan from the floor and drew it up to my chin. Dominic stalked to the door, but his posture relaxed as he peered into the hall.

'Nothing there.' He turned to face me for a moment, his eyes dark in the shadows. 'We can't let this happen again, Laura.'

I swallowed. 'I know.'

'Are you . . . ?' He indicated my abdomen, frowning.

My heart bumped painfully against my chest wall. 'God, yes. I'm on the pill.'

'Good.'

He left then, the stairs creaking rhythmically as he climbed. A door clunked shut above. I curled up on the sofa, stroking the palm of one hand with the thumb of the other, my eyes wide open and dry. The chill of the sea trickled through invisible gaps around the window frame, and the blue moon gazed down unblinkingly at the dead fire and my shivering skin.

15

Seraphine

I stumble as I cross the road to my car. A sharp pain stabs at my temple, and the metal of the door handle is too bright for my eyes, too hot for my hands. I touch my fingertips to my throat, surprised to find nothing physical restricting my breathing. Helen Luckhurst bustles over the road towards me.

'Seraphine? Are you all right?'

I pretend I haven't heard her and brave the scorching metal, diving into my car and slamming the door between us.

I crawl along the lane to Summerbourne in second gear. Michael stands at his front gate and lifts a hand in vague greeting. I swerve up onto the grass verge just after the cottages and stare at him in my rear-view mirror. Edwin thinks Michael was there that morning, when my mother was posing with that single baby for the photograph. I climb out and walk back to his cottage.

'Morning,' Michael says, his eyes narrowing as I place my hand on the gate.

'Good morning, Mr Harris. Do you remember me? I'm Seraphine Mayes?'

He squints at me.

'You used to call me and my brother the Summerbourne sprites,' I say.

His eyes widen slightly, and he looks back over his shoulder and calls out, 'Joel! Joel!'

For a long moment nothing happens, and I wonder what on earth I am doing here, upsetting this old man. He was such a figure of authority in my childhood, such a fascinating source of facts and stories that I could cry now at how rapidly his dementia has progressed recently, at the confusion on his face as he looks at me. But then Joel ducks out of the cottage doorway. He has smudges of dirt on his T-shirt, and a shine of sweat on his forehead, and he's not smiling.

'Seraphine.' There's an edge to his voice, and out of nowhere I am engulfed in a wave of regret so overwhelming I can't draw breath. I have pushed Joel away for so long that we act like distant acquaintances, and yet if I could choose one person in the world at this very moment to be by my side — to be *on* my side — I would choose him. But it's too late. I tear my gaze from his face, and focus on the grass by my feet, willing air into my lungs.

'I just . . . ' I say. *It's too late, Seraphine. You're too late.* 'I wanted to talk to Michael . . . But not if . . . '

Michael's demeanour has relaxed since Joel's appearance. His anxiety gone, he beams suddenly, wagging a finger at me.

'Oh, I remember you,' he says. 'Seraphine Mayes. The little sprite.'

Joel opens his mouth, a horrified expression forming as he looks from Michael to me, but I interrupt him.

'It's okay. Honestly.'

I meet Joel's gaze for a second, and he seems moderately reassured, his shoulders relaxing slightly. He indicates a pair of wooden chairs.

'Well, have a seat in the shade, if you're sure. I'll get you a drink.'

He disappears inside again, and my breathing steadies. Michael is already settling himself into his chair, huffing and puffing, and I perch on the other one.

'These are lovely,' I say, nodding at the profusion of pink Busy Lizzies that spill from a terracotta pot on the table between us, but Michael doesn't appear to hear.

'Oh, Seraphine Mayes,' he says. 'She can bear a grudge, that one, that's for sure. Everything's always someone else's fault.'

I clear my throat, checking over my shoulder, hoping Joel didn't hear that.

'I'd really like to hear about the day we were born, Mr Harris. The Summerbourne sprites? Do you remember my mother, Ruth?'

Michael leans forward with a grunt, to pinch a dead flower head off a plant, but he smiles as he leans back, rolling it between finger and thumb.

'Oh yes, she were a good woman, Ruth. Kind. Helped me out no end when I had this young'un to look after.' He points his chin at Joel, who has reappeared with two tall glasses of lemonade. 'Such a tragedy, her going over the cliff like that.'

'Grandad, please,' Joel says, placing the glasses on the table.

'It's okay,' I say.

Joel steps back into the cottage and returns

with a third chair and a glass for himself, and sits a little apart from us. I twist in my seat to face Michael.

'Go on, Mr Harris,' I say. 'Can you tell me about that day? About what happened to Ruth, and what happened to her babies?'

Michael shoots me a sly look then. 'Ah, about the sprites, is it? Ruth's baby got stolen, and the fairies took pity on her and gave her little sprite twins. What d'you think of that, then?' He sits back, looking pleased with himself.

One baby stolen? This doesn't even match the story Pamela told me.

'But, Mr Harris, it's a . . . an interesting story. But what really happened? There's no such thing as fairies.'

I give him a tentative smile, but his face darkens.

'Don't you be so sure, missy. I seen witches at Summerbourne. Witches that hang in trees and steal babies. I burnt their cloaks, you know. Those twins weren't right.'

Joel makes a noise in his throat, but I speak first, leaning closer to Michael.

'Which twins weren't right, Mr Harris — me and Danny? What do you mean?'

'Summerbourne ent never allowed to keep its twins,' Michael says, and his gaze drifts to the end of the lane and the Summerbourne chimneys that can just be glimpsed over the hedgerow. 'One of them, or the other of them, maybe. But not both. Ruth and Robin — the fairies couldn't let them both live, could they? And — what was his name — the little blond boy who toddled right over the edge of the cliff?'

'Theo,' I whisper.

'That's it,' Michael says.

'And what about us, Mr Harris? What about Danny and Seraphine?'

'That weren't right,' he says slowly. 'Oh, that family, they wanted their twins again. But what they did weren't right. I saw the midnight woman come.'

'Midnight woman?' I prompt. He doesn't react. The phrase is vaguely familiar, something in the local dialect. 'A midwife, do you mean? But my mum didn't have a midwife.'

Michael leans forward to peer at me suddenly.

'Where did you really come from, my dear?' he asks me. 'You're not a Summerbourne twin at all, are you?'

There's a loud crack, and suddenly my hand holds only the lower half of my lemonade glass. Curved shards of the upper half skitter away across the tabletop and tumble to the grass beneath.

Joel jumps to his feet. 'Are you okay? Are you hurt?'

I can't catch my breath. And I'm staring at Joel, because, despite the look of repulsion in his eyes, there's no surprise. He's heard all this before.

'Are you okay?' he asks me again, easing the jagged-edged base of the glass from my fingers.

'I'm so sorry,' I say. 'I must have — misjudged . . . '

Michael tries to stand, distressed. 'Joel? Who is this?'

Joel bends over Michael's chair, blocking me from his sight.

'It's all right, Grandad,' he says gently. 'Sit back down. Everything's fine.' He sweeps the shards of glass away from Michael's end of the table, into the jagged base section, and Michael relaxes back in his chair and sighs.

'You're a good boy,' Michael murmurs, and then turns to pluck another dead flower head.

My heart continues to judder as Joel walks with me back to my car.

'I'm sorry,' he says. 'He's getting worse. He doesn't mean anything by it.'

His gaze rests on my car, and suddenly I'm acutely conscious of how dirty it is. 'I shouldn't have asked him those questions,' I say. 'It was my fault.'

While Joel's focus remains on the car, I seize the opportunity to examine him in sideways glances. He's tense, but underneath that he looks tired, the stubble on his face adding to the impression that he hasn't been getting enough sleep. I have no idea what else is going on in his life these days. It hurts to see him looking so unhappy.

'Are *you* all right?' I ask eventually.

He looks at me then, and his dark eyes shine with emotion. I lean closer to him despite myself. He shakes his head.

'He loved telling all the old stories when I was a child, you know? Down at the pub, everyone gathered round him — he was the expert on all the local folklore. Some of it he got from his grandmother, I think, and some of it I expect he made up. He loved being the centre of attention. Thrived on it.'

I nod. I have no memory of ever being taken to the village pub when I was a child, but I remember Michael spinning tales to Danny and me when he paused for a mug of tea in the Summerbourne garden. He could conjure images in our minds quite effortlessly — sneaky pirates, angry fairies, kings and queens and wicked witches.

'And he told newer stories too,' Joel says. 'Gossip, you'd call it, really, mixed in with fanciful embellishments. Some of it maybe too real, too close . . . '

I watch his forehead crease as he remembers.

'Ruth and Robin,' he says. 'And Theo. Especially Theo, like it was all some horrible nursery tale. It gave me nightmares. I used to wonder sometimes — ' He squeezes his eyes shut. I wait. 'I used to worry that maybe it was *me* who undid Theo's straps. I used to think I could remember seeing him fall.'

I stare at him. 'Joel, no. That's impossible. You were two years old then. You wouldn't have been out there on the cliffs on your own.'

He looks at me for a long moment, and then draws himself up, seems to give himself a shake.

'I know. Of course, it's ridiculous. It just — it brought it back, hearing him just now, those horrible stories, and I'm — ' He cuts off whatever else he was about to say.

I want to tell him I'm here for him. To tell him everything will be okay. I reach my fingers towards his, and he catches hold of them, and for a moment we stand there, linked, and my pulse rate soars.

'I wish . . . ' he says, and his eyes search mine, and I hold my breath as I wait for him to continue. But his gaze slides over my shoulder to the cottage garden where Michael still sits, and my fingers slip from his, and then we both take a deep breath and turn to look at my car.

'I'm so sorry about your dad,' Joel says eventually, and all I can do is nod, and then I climb into my car and leave him standing there, his figure a blur in my rear-view mirror as I drive the final hundred metres back to Summerbourne.

In the shed behind the stable block, I knock over rakes and hoes in my hurry to pull out a gardening fork, leaving a jumble of wooden handles criss-crossed behind me. I march back to where the letters scar the front lawn and stab the tips of the fork into the sunbaked ground, stamping on the horizontal bar in an attempt to drive the prongs further in. I manage to lever up clumps of earth and twist the top layer of grass and soil until the word is obscured. *Kids*, I tell myself. *Just kids from the village, messing around.*

I sit at the kitchen table with a mug of strong coffee, waiting for my tears to stop. I think about Joel growing up listening to Michael's stories — all the drama and sorrows of their neighbours turned into gruesome tales to entertain and scare little children. I never saw any malice in his tales when I was a child, but of course he'd have saved the Summerbourne stories for a different audience. How many of the villagers grew up hearing about Summerbourne sprites and curses and ill-fated twins?

And suddenly, I wonder whether Michael is capable of scaring people in other ways, despite his memory lapses and his failing strength. Does he have more lucid days? Could he have sneaked onto our front lawn under cover of darkness and scorched a warning into the grass with weed killer? But Michael seemed happy enough to talk about our family history today, even if his accounts were jumbled. The 'STOP' message can't have been from him. I shake my head.

'Just stupid kids,' I say aloud. But the possibility of a more sinister explanation continues to gnaw at me. I still don't know what happened here on the day I was born; I still don't know why Mum and Dad appeared to be celebrating one baby rather than two. What if someone is warning me to stop asking questions? What are they trying to hide?

The sun is high, and Vera's pills glint at me from their square-shouldered pot, and I decide that a soak in the bath might make me feel better. I carry my mug upstairs, but at the entrance to the bathroom it slips from my grasp. Scalding coffee splashes up my legs, and shards of crockery fly in all directions, but my gaze is fixed on the mirror over the basin. A message is scrawled in dark red lipstick across it:

STOP ASKING QUESTIONS OR LOSE YOUR FAMILY.

Someone has been here, inside my house.

All doubt vanishes with those seven red words. Someone has been here, inside my house, and they want to stop me finding out the truth.

I step back onto a sliver of broken mug, slicing my heel. The adrenaline that's making my heart hammer overrides any pain. I need to tell someone. I need help. I need to call the police.

My phone's downstairs somewhere. On the kitchen table? I stagger lopsidedly down the stairs, gripping the banister, leaving a trail of blood spots behind me. There's no handset on the landline base in the hall. Did I leave it somewhere? My mobile lights up seconds before I reach it, cheery green and blue notifications oblivious to my fear.

I tap nine twice, but hesitate before the third one, straining my ears for any sound in the house, feeling the drumming of my pulse start to ease. Is a message on a mirror an emergency? I need to think.

This was the first time I'd been in that bathroom since I came back from London and Leeds: I collapsed in bed fully dressed last night, and shot out to see Pamela this morning after finding the scorch marks in the lawn. The lipstick message might easily have been written forty-eight hours ago; the perpetrator surely long gone.

I picture a police car skidding onto the drive; me leading frowning officers upstairs, pointing at some lipstick writing. The police officers annoyed or — worse — amused. I clench my jaw.

The non-emergency number, then. The local

police station. Martin Larch.

I'd have to tell Martin about the letters burnt into the grass as well, of course, and the address that was taken from my handbag. Which means I'd have to tell him about tracking down Laura, and the threatening letter she received, and its mention of Summerbourne and Dad. I'd have to explain about the photo and the missing baby, and my fear that I'm not really Seraphine Mayes at all.

Can I face that?

As I have done many times before in moments of doubt, I turn to the fail-safe mantra of my childhood: Edwin will know what to do.

I dial Edwin's mobile, but it rings on and on unanswered. I try Winterbourne, then Danny, then Vera. No one picks up. For a brief moment my thumb hovers over Dad's number, which I still can't bring myself to delete, and then I let the phone clatter onto the table. I could run back to Michael's, ask Joel to come and take a look at the mirror — but what would I say to him? What could he do?

I should ring the police. I press my phone back into life. The earlier text was from Pamela:

I'm sorry if I upset you this morning. I hope you're all right. Pamela

The blue notification is a Facebook friend request. I've been avoiding social media even more than usual, conscious there may be birthday messages from acquaintances who hadn't heard about my father, followed by a trickle of awkward condolences.

I tap on the notification, and a picture of a young woman pops up. A young woman with a pink streak in her short black hair. I sink onto the chair, the phone trembling in my hand.

You have a friend request from Kiara Kaimal.

I tap on the picture. Her profile has high security settings: just her name and photo, and a background picture of a turquoise sea beneath a cloudless blue sky. I hesitate over the accept button. A tiny red flag indicates a string of unread messages, and I open the list. A message from Kiara Kaimal sits at the top.

Hi, I hope you don't mind me contacting you. My father won't talk to me about you, but I have a feeling that you might have some connection to my mother. My mother died when I was very young. I don't remember her. My father used to tell me he was too sad to talk about her. But I think there must be something he's not telling me. Can we meet? I'll understand if you'd rather not. Best wishes either way. Kiara Kaimal

197

16

Laura

NOVEMBER/DECEMBER 1991

Life at Summerbourne acquired a prickly edge after the night of the blue moon. Dominic was full of mumbled apology and regret the next morning, sending Edwin out to play in the garden so that he could explain to me with an earnest expression that it must never happen again.

'Ruth can never find out,' he said, his voice husky, his eyes managing to meet mine for a split second before sliding away again.

'Of course not,' I said. 'It was a stupid mistake.'

I held out my hand after he left, watching it for several seconds. The tremor was mild. My breath seemed too shallow that morning, as if I was tiptoeing a narrow path between looming guilt on one side and a sense of hurt indignation on the other, trying to avoid provoking either of them. Neither would do me any good. Either could see me dismissed from Summerbourne.

I continued to watch my hand until the tremor was almost imperceptible. If anything, Dominic's words had brought me relief: my greatest fear had been that he would fire me. I'd lived at Summerbourne for not quite eleven weeks, but already I felt like a different person. Here, I was respected, listened to, treated kindly. The thought of being banished, having to spend the rest of the year at Mum and Beaky's house until I could escape to university, was a huge incentive to put this awkward episode with Dominic behind me.

In optimistic moments over those next few days, I hoped Ruth would return from her holiday refreshed and positive. As it turned out, she came back pale and withdrawn, and spent the subsequent few days in bed feeling unwell. I had tried to forget Dominic's baffled declaration the previous month that Alex was considering selling his cottage, but Michael informed me that Billy Bradshaw had told *him* that Alex had been into the estate agent's recently and had a private chat with the boss.

'But he can't really be thinking of selling it!' I was aware of the distress in my tone but too shocked to hide it. 'He only bought it in September. Maybe he went in to talk about something else.'

Michael's eyes were bright. 'Had a barney with Mrs Mayes, that's what they're saying. Won't want to visit down here no more if he's not welcome at Summerbourne.'

'But . . . ' I pressed my nails into my palms. 'They've fallen out before, haven't they? Ruth and Alex. They'll make up again?'

'We'll see.' Michael grinned. 'It's them sprites, you know, stirring up trouble at Summerbourne as usual. Don't you go upsetting them, young Laura, or they'll make you pay too.'

I didn't like it when Michael talked like this. It was the sort of nonsense that had started to creep into Edwin's dreams. I'd had to ask Michael not to mention the cloaks again, after he'd told Edwin and Joel about finding them in the trees, and about how difficult it had been to dry them out before they'd burn on the bonfire. Green sparks came out when he burnt them, he'd told the boys. Edwin had had a nightmare that night, about witches circling him in the folly tower, flying faster and faster on their broomsticks until their cloaks burst into green flames.

In the house, Alex's name wasn't mentioned at all. Dominic returned each weekend, and we were perfectly civil to each other, but all the previous warmth between us had disappeared.

I threw myself into decorating the day nursery for Edwin's birthday party, preparing for half a dozen children from the village to come and play pin the tail on the donkey and pass the parcel.

'I don't suppose you'd make him a cake, would you?' Ruth asked me. 'I usually do it, but . . .'

'No problem. I'd love to.'

Edwin helped me cut and arrange slabs of chocolate sponge cake into the shape of a '4' and then cover it in chocolate buttercream. I supervised him hacking the crusts off sandwiches and arranging pink wafers on plates, while I speared chunks of cheese and pineapple onto half a grapefruit to make a hedgehog centrepiece. Edwin selected the glacé cherry for its nose.

Vera travelled down from London to help at

the party, and she squeezed my hand and told me I was a *'true gem'*. The young guests were well-behaved, although some of their parents took full advantage of the white wine that Ruth offered them, causing her to complain about them afterwards.

'Did you see how much Helen knocked back?' she said. 'I caught her in the hall, reading through the names in the address book — can you believe it?'

'She's worried about her daughter,' Vera said. 'Daisy's going to have long-term problems. I'm sure it was good for Helen to take her mind off things for a couple of hours.'

'Well, it's a good job Kemi was happy to drive her home again. She was in no fit state.'

Vera sighed. 'Be nice, Ruth.'

Dominic arrived home after the party had finished, scooping an armful of wrapped presents from his boot, and booming, 'Where's my Summerbourne winter-born?' as he stepped into the house.

We had crisp, cold days in December when the clifftop sparkled with frost, and seagulls harassed us on the beach, demanding food. Edwin and I still spent several hours outside each day, wrapped up in coats and hats; I wore gloves lent to me by Ruth, and Edwin had mittens attached to a length of string that ran through his coat sleeves. I knew every inch of the Summerbourne grounds by then, and much of the surrounding countryside too. Michael was around less, but now and then we would catch sight of him, and if I knew he was out there, I would take him a mug of steaming tea.

I avoided the first couple of family Sunday lunches in December, pretending to want a break but secretly trying to minimise the amount of time I had to spend in Dominic's presence. However, Ruth asked me if I would join them on the Sunday before I was due to go home to Mum's for Christmas, and I reluctantly agreed. Vera was there for the weekend, and Ruth made a particular fuss setting the table, snapping at Edwin when he moved the napkins. We were still eating, murmuring over last mouthfuls, when Dominic clinked his fork against his glass.

'We have a little announcement to make,' he said, smiling around at us, his eyes sliding from Vera's anticipatory smile, over my blank expression, to Edwin's look of surprise. Ruth nodded at Vera, and I put down my cutlery.

'We're going to have a baby,' Dominic said, beaming. 'You're going to have a little brother or sister, Edwin.'

I stared at Ruth, trying to keep my breathing calm. Hidden by the tablecloth, my nails pressed into my palms.

'Oh, that's wonderful news,' Vera said, clapping her hands, and Edwin performed a comedy fall of amazement from his chair, making Ruth laugh.

I thought of the photo of the little twin boys in Ruth's bedroom. This was good news. Of course this was good news.

'Congratulations,' I said.

A hubbub of excited baby talk broke out.

'How far along are you?' Vera asked.

'Oh, it's early still,' Ruth said. 'A few weeks.'

'A summer-born Summerbourne!' Vera exclaimed, and Dominic chuckled.

'Exactly,' he said. 'About time we had a summer-born around here.'

'A boy baby or a girl baby, Mummy?' Edwin asked.

'We don't know, darling. We'll have to wait and see.'

'It might even be twins again,' Vera said, and a short silence fell.

'How are you feeling?' I asked Ruth, and she smiled gratefully at me.

'Lousy!' she said. She did look rather pale, and somewhat separate from Dominic and Vera's mood of gaiety.

Edwin began to suggest names for his new sibling.

'Are those all names from *Thomas the Tank Engine*?' Dominic asked him with mock suspicion.

'Of course, Daddy!'

Ruth declined any pudding, but Vera ate two portions, a highly unusual occurrence. I had never seen her look so delighted.

I slipped away from the family as soon as I could, but passed Dominic in the kitchen as I headed for the annexe.

'It really is lovely news,' I said, and he smiled at me, a trace of our old friendship around his eyes, but his lips pressed slightly too tight in acknowledgement of the other thing.

'Thanks, Laura,' he said.

I felt increasingly out of sorts during the

afternoon, and I abandoned my textbooks and retired to bed early.

A few days later, I was sitting in the kitchen with Edwin on my lap, my suitcase by the door, waiting for Ruth to drive me to the station, when the phone rang.

'Mother,' I heard Ruth say.

'Then you'll have to cancel it,' she said.

'I'm having the scan where I choose,' she said. 'No, I'm not telling you.'

There was a longer pause.

'I'm not listening any more. I know what I'm doing. If you try to override me in this, I'll — '

After a few seconds more, she hung up.

She was white-faced when she stepped into the kitchen. I slid Edwin down from my lap.

'Go and draw me a picture, would you, lovely boy? For me to take home for Christmas?' I asked him. His gaze swung to his mother and back to me.

'I want to see the trains,' he said.

'You will. In a little while. I'm just going to make Mummy a cup of tea first.'

He sighed and trotted off. Ruth sat at the table with her head in her hands, and I made her a milky tea. She looked up and smiled wanly when I placed it in front of her, and then grimaced and slid it away.

'Thanks. Sorry. I've gone off it,' she said. 'That was my mother, trying to get me to see some doctor she knows. She's dead set against me having a home birth, but there's no way I'm setting foot in a hospital again.'

The colour was returning to her cheeks until I

asked, 'When do you think your due date is?' She reached out suddenly and grabbed my hand.

'Oh, Laura. I can't talk to anyone.' She began to cry — loud sobs, hunched over the table, her tears leaving dark stains on the wood.

'What's the matter?' I asked.

She made a groaning sound, as if her abdomen hurt.

'Ruth! What's wrong?'

'It's Alex's baby,' she whispered, holding on to my hand still, squeezing it. Her eyes were closed. 'It's Alex's baby, Laura. What am I going to do?'

My lungs were compressed. I couldn't breathe. She opened her eyes then and gazed at me mutely, her face tear streaked, her hair in disarray. I heard a raspy sound and realised it was me, trying to draw air in.

'That's impossible,' I managed eventually.

She released my hand. 'Oh God. It's all such a mess.'

'But — ' I almost asked, *How?* but changed it in time. 'How can you be sure?'

'I'm sure. I wish I wasn't, but I am. It was the week my mother tried to talk me into moving us all to Winterbourne. I was so angry, so miserable. I went to the Halloween party with Alex. And he was . . . he was nice to me, Laura. He's the only person who's ever really liked me for who I am. My mother wanted me to marry him, you know. She told me Dominic would never love me the way Alex did.'

I shook my head. She was wrong. I knew how much Dominic loved her, how desperately he wanted her to be happy. But then the memory of

205

him leaning towards me, kissing me, made me curl my fists. I felt sick.

Ruth groaned. 'I hate that she was right.'

'No,' I said. And then, 'What are you going to do?'

'What can I do? Fudge the dates a bit. Not that Dominic will do the maths. Hope the baby doesn't look too much like Alex. Oh, God.' She rested her forehead in her hands for a minute then sat back up and held her arm out, rolling it over to reveal the blue veins in the whiteness of her inner wrist. 'Do you think our skin colours might balance out to match Dominic's?'

An incredulous noise escaped my lips.

'Ruth, this is madness.'

She showed no sign of having heard me. 'Alex's sisters all have lighter skin than him. Half Indian, half good old Yorkshire. If I'm lucky . . . ' She frowned, her gaze unfocused. 'He's always been jealous of them, you know — his sisters. They're all settled with children — so many nieces and nephews. He pretends his job is everything, but I know he longs for a family of his own . . . '

Suddenly, she lunged forward, gripping my arm tightly this time, her nails digging into my skin.

'Ow!'

'You mustn't tell anyone,' she hissed, her eyes narrow, a fleck of her saliva hitting my cheek. 'Never. Not Alex. Not my husband. No one.'

I shook my head. 'Of course not.'

She squeezed even harder. 'Promise?'

'I won't tell anyone,' I cried, pulling away,

standing up, and turning my back on her. Red marks swelled on my arm.

Behind me, she wiped her face, combed fingers through her hair, composed herself. I watched her reflection in the window as she straightened up and called out to Edwin.

'Edwin, darling. Come and put your shoes on. It's time to take Laura to the station.'

Edwin ran in with a picture for me: it showed me and Ruth and Dominic on one side of a Christmas tree with Edwin on the other. A large wiggly shape overlapped our heads.

'It's a sea serpent,' he said. 'It's going to gobble us up for its Christmas dinner.'

17

Seraphine

I can't think straight, here in the stale heat of the kitchen. Kiara's message is too much to take in. The word burnt into the grass; the lipstick writing on the mirror; Laura's intimidating letter that I fished from the bin: I wish I'd never started any of this. I want to go back to the way things were before I found the photo. I want to be left to mourn my father without questioning whether he *was* my father.

I need to clear my head. I need to go to the cliffs.

The door keys are slippery in my fingers as I double-check that everything is locked. Despite my certainty that no one could be living in the annexe without my knowledge, I lock that door too and hide the key in the kitchen. The garden has a frazzled feel in the mid-afternoon sun; insects dart above the weeds in the borders, and a clump of red-hot pokers sags wearily over the lawn. The rounded sweet scent of old-fashioned roses drifts along with me as I make my way to the back gate.

The sea breeze calms me, as always, and I sink into the long grass at the base of the folly tower, wriggling to create a more comfortable seat, soaking up the warmth from the stone at my back. This is my spot, even in the winter. This is where I come most days after work, when Edwin thinks I should be out socialising, meeting people — *the occasional party won't kill you, Seraphine*. I frown. Edwin has never really understood me. Not the way Danny does. Not the way Dad did.

Dad had flexible part-time working hours in London, so he used to come down to Summerbourne for a few days each month and stay with me. We'd eat together when I got home from work, go on day trips together at weekends when we felt like it, but he didn't mind me heading out to the cliffs when I wanted time alone. If I'm not my parents' daughter, do I really want to know? My dad is my dad. He always was and he always will be. I don't want different parents. I want to be the same person I always thought I was.

I close my eyes and wait for my thoughts to settle. But there it is again, that question, despite my efforts to quash it: who am I?

I spent so much of my childhood feeling like an outsider. Edwin and Danny made friends effortlessly, playing out on the village green in big gangs after school. I felt awkward when I tried to join in, uncomfortable with how casually the other children seemed to treat one another's feelings. I wanted all the games to be fair, but they weren't, and although I knew my complaints were an overreaction, it took me a long time to learn how to control my temper. I overheard two women discussing me in the village shop once, suggesting I might have been a gentler child if only my mother had been around to care for me. I knocked tins flying as I charged into their aisle to inform them they were wrong and stupid.

The girls in my class mostly ignored me, the older children in the playground taunted me, and the only place I ever felt happy was at home: at Summerbourne. I used to leave the phone off the hook in the holidays to stop village kids from inviting my brothers out, and I savoured the days when it was just me, Danny, Edwin and Joel, with the garden and the lane and the beach as our playground. Those were the days I felt accepted and safe.

I try now to remember precisely what it was the village children used to tease me about. The implication was that either Danny or I, or perhaps both of us, had come from somewhere else. That we weren't Ruth's children. Which Dad always assured us was ridiculous, of course. But there was also teasing about a child-stealing witch in a long black cloak, and fairy babies, and somehow the numbers never added up.

One or two babies born, one or two babies stolen, two children left to show for it — how does that make any sense? How did the truth blur into such bizarre fiction? What facts were the wild stories based on?

My cheeks and shoulders glow with the threat of sunburn, and I haul myself up. On the pale crescent of beach below, a man throws a ball for a black-and-white dog. A seagull swoops over the dog's head, and although it's too far away to catch the sound, I can see that the dog is barking. The carefree scene makes my lips tighten with a tug of envy, and I move around the tower to sit in its shade.

If I let all of this go, if I stop asking questions, what will life be like? I will have the predictable, soothing routine of my job. I'll have family dinners with Edwin, Danny and Vera. I might never have to move out of Summerbourne, whether or not Vera gives it to Danny. I will have a photograph of the day I was born without knowing whether I'm the baby in it. Life will be calm and safe. Unresolved but safe.

But what if Kiara can tell me something — some seemingly trivial fact, perhaps, about her father or my family — that provides the key to everything else making sense?

I retrieve my phone from where it bakes in the dry grass and scroll through Kiara's message again. It seems reckless to agree to meet her without telling the police about the threats I've received. But as soon as I go to the police, a chain of events will be triggered, and they'll have to question Alex. And that might frighten Kiara off, and ruin my chance of finding out the truth.

When I eventually stand up again, the man and the dog have gone. I can turn a full circle without glimpsing another living soul in any direction. I brush the dust from my dress and make my way back to the house, bolting the heavy garden gate behind me, scanning the windows as I approach. Nothing moves.

Indoors, I prowl through the rooms, one by one. The landline handset sits on the coffee table in the sitting room, flashing with a message from Joel. He recites his mobile number in the precise

211

manner of a doctor speaking to a recalcitrant patient. '*Call me if you need anything.*' I listen to it several times.

I come close to calling Edwin's number again, but I'm afraid suddenly that he'll insist I delete Kiara's message and heed the warnings. I'm not sure I'm ready to make that decision after all.

I stand in front of the lipstick message for a long time, the floor tiles sucking the heat of the day out of me through the soles of my feet. I don't want to lose my family. But I do need to know what happened on the day I was born. I do need to know who I am.

The china fragments clink together in the dustpan. I mop the tiles, and scrub smudges of coffee and blood from the carpet. Then I spray lemon-scented cleaner all over the mirror, and sigh as the angry red words dissolve with a gentle wipe. A soft sea breeze whispers through my bedroom window as evening falls, and I make my bed with fresh linen sheets before dropping into a dreamless sleep.

No further threats appear overnight, and in the morning I carry my coffee out to the patio and reply to Kiara:

Yes, please, let's meet up. Could you come to Norfolk on Saturday? Midday for lunch?

Ten minutes later she replies:

Yes, okay. Let me know your address.

I ask her:

Do you mind if my brothers join us?

I don't receive a reply until late afternoon:

That's fine. I'm going to leave a note for my dad so he knows where I've gone. He'll see it on Saturday evening.

It occurs to me that she's not sure she can trust us: she wants back-up in case we're luring her into something sinister. As I'm thinking this, I hear the rumble of tyres on gravel, and I dash back into the house to peer through the hall window. An unfamiliar car completes a three-point turn at the entrance to our drive, and glides off down the lane. I glance at the phone on the hall table, thinking of the message Joel left yesterday.

'Joel? It's Seraphine.'

'Oh, hi. Hang on a sec — ' There's a muffled noise in the background and I wonder whether he's still at Michael's cottage.

'Sorry,' he says. 'Are you okay? You got my message?'

'Yeah. Thanks. Did Edwin ask you to check up on me?'

'Well, yes.' I think I can hear a smile in his voice. 'But also, I wanted to apologise for yesterday. Grandad. Those stories.'

'It's fine, really. It was my fault.'

There's a pause. 'Did you — is there anything you need?' he says.

I've wandered with the handset into the kitchen, and my gaze rests on my handbag, its buckle undone as usual.

'You haven't seen anyone suspicious in the lane recently, have you?' I ask.

'No, why? What's happened?'

I hesitate. 'Oh, nothing. I don't know. I'm just feeling a bit jumpy, being here on my own, I guess.'

I perch on the arm of a chair, tracing scratches in the wooden tabletop with my thumb.

'Do you want me to come over?' he asks. I try to analyse his tone of voice. Not keen. Maybe reluctant, or maybe just wary. I swallow.

'No, it's fine. I'm going to ask Edwin and Danny to come down for the weekend. I'll let you go. I'm fine. Everything's fine, really.'

He starts to say something, but I hang up, my heart thudding. *I'm fine. I'm fine.* We're so *polite* to each other these days, so distant. I wish I'd never called him.

I know I need to talk to Edwin, although I'm determined not to tell him yet about the lipstick warning or the burnt grass. I want him to come and meet Kiara with me — both him and Danny. I want to present a united front to Alex's daughter, in case she springs something on us we're not prepared for.

I stand under the hot water in my little en suite shower room until the temperature starts to fall, and then I pull on clean clothes. I can't put it off any longer. I call Edwin's mobile.

'Hey, how're you doing?' he says.

'I'm okay. Can you talk?'

'I'm just on my way to meet Danny and Brooke,' he says, and I can hear the rhythm of his breathing as he walks. 'Thought we'd have a drink out, it's such a nice evening.'

I'm not sure why I feel so unsettled by Danny's new girlfriend. He's never been one for serious relationships, but this one seems different somehow. Brooke gives the impression she's someone who gets what she wants.

'Edwin, listen. I need to tell you something.'

'Oh God, Seraphine. You haven't been to see Laura again?'

'No, of course not,' I say, and there's a pause. I hear a heavier exhale as if he's just sat down.

'Okay. Talk,' he says. 'I'm listening.'

I push the image of the lipstick writing from my mind, and try to decide where to start.

'You still there?' he asks.

'I went to see Alex. Alex Kaimal.'

'You what?' he says, his voice a sudden boom so that I have to tilt the phone away from my ear.

I lean back on my bed as I wait for him to digest this.

'Bloody hell, Seph. What did he say?' he asks.

'He said I was impossible.'

'What?'

I sigh. 'He knew Mum and Dad, but he didn't know who I was. He said I couldn't possibly be their daughter.'

'Seraphine . . . '

'Edwin. He had a girl with him. His daughter. She's called Kiara.'

'Seraphine, you can't just approach strange men. It's harassment.'

'It was fine. The thing is — Kiara, his daughter, she wants to meet up with us. I've

215

asked her down here for lunch on Saturday.'

Edwin groans, the tail end of it sounding more like a growl. 'Alex's daughter? Seriously? Why?'

'She just . . . she'd like to meet us. And . . . ' I think about Kiara's message; she lost her mother when she was a baby too. 'You know, she might be able to tell us something. Will you and Danny come down and be with me when she arrives? I don't want to do it by myself.'

I wait, listening to my own breathing, gnawing at my lip.

'I promised Gran we'd have a family weekend at Winterbourne,' Edwin says eventually. 'She wants you to come too, Seph. I'll do us a roast on Sunday. It'll do you good.'

'But Saturday? Please. I really need you here.'

There's another drawn-out silence, and eventually he sighs and says, 'I suppose we could come. I'll talk to Danny.' And then more softly, 'We'll come.'

I close my eyes. 'Thank you.'

'Look, I'll try to leave work early tomorrow, head straight to you. Just don't do anything else crazy until we get there, okay?'

I'm on my feet, looking out of my bedroom window down the lane towards Michael's cottage.

'Of course not,' I say. 'Have a nice time with Danny and the Ice Maiden.'

Edwin hangs up.

I'm preparing cheese on toast a while later, shaving the hardened crusts off the block of cheddar, when the doorbell rings. Joel stands there: shoulders hunched, eyebrows raised as if

216

he's not sure of his welcome. My eyes flick towards the damage on the front lawn, but I've parked my car to shield it from this angle. He holds out a carrier bag of shopping — some bottles, bars of chocolate, fruit, biscuits.

'I said I was fine,' I say, but I stand back and let him in. He walks through and puts the bag on the kitchen table.

'Just checking,' he says. He glances at the cheese I've been hacking. 'I'll leave you to it.'

'No, stay,' I say, pulling items out of the bag, keeping my back to him while I wait for my pulse rate to settle. 'Thanks. It's nice of you.' I offer him a bottle of beer, and he accepts. 'Look, I'm going to toast this cheese, and then you can report back to Edwin that I'm cooking for myself.'

He takes the chair at the end of the table, granting me the smallest of smiles. His stubble is gone, but he still has deep shadows under his eyes.

'How's Michael today?' I ask, keeping my tone light.

Joel sighs. 'Not too bad. Two more weeks till Mum and Dad get back. It's easier when they're here to share it.'

'Does it mean you can't work, while they're away?'

'No, I can do some. I've been taking a few locum shifts.' He rubs his eyes briefly. 'I just check him before and after.'

'You can't get someone in? I wouldn't mind sitting with him if you need help.'

He smiles at me properly then, and my knife

curves out of the block of the cheese too soon, making me jump.

'Ah, thanks, but he's all right by himself really. He doesn't even try to cook any more.' His eyes flick to my cheese shavings. 'He just potters in the garden mostly, or takes a walk over the fields. It's nice of you, though. I'd have thought you'd had enough of listening to him.'

I shrug. 'I'm tougher than I used to be.'

Our eyes meet, and I have a disconcerting sensation that I'm fourteen again. He looks at me as though he can read my thoughts, and I force myself to turn away and sort out my food.

The grill is heating up, but the handle of the grill tray is broken. Joel twitches the pair of oven gloves from its hook near his chair and passes it over to me, and I slide the tray under the heat.

'I remember Edwin breaking that handle,' he says.

I poke the tray in a little further. 'Really? When was that?'

'Making toasties after school one day, when we were about ten, I guess.' He relaxes in his chair a little. 'Freezing cold day. We put them under the grill and forgot to watch them, messing around. It was when you had that German nanny. The one who used to sing all the time. Do you remember?'

I shake my head.

'You must have been five or six. She was really nice. You don't remember her?'

'We had so many. I wasn't like Danny. I tried not to get attached.'

He blinks at me. 'Well. Anyway, the toast

caught fire — proper flames, it was pretty scary — and Edwin yanked the tray out and dropped it. Broke the handle. We got a huge telling-off.'

'I'm not surprised.'

Joel's gaze roams around the kitchen. I wash up a couple of plastic tubs with my back to him, keeping half an eye on his reflection in the window. He looks more at home here than I do. The tick of the kitchen clock seems louder with each minute of silence.

'Do you remember Laura?' I ask him suddenly, turning to face him. 'The au pair Edwin had before Danny and I were born?'

He shrugs. 'Yeah, vaguely, I think. She used to bake cakes with us.'

'How about Alex? Alex Kaimal?' I ask.

'No, who's he?'

'Do you remember Danny and me being born?'

He gives me a long look.

'Seraphine — ' he starts, but I cut him off.

'Oh, okay. Edwin's said something, hasn't he? What did he say? Keep an eye on poor Seraphine, she's lost her marbles, thinks she's a changeling?'

'Seraphine,' he says calmly, 'your toast is burning.'

I jam my hands into the oven gloves and yank the tray out from under the grill, clattering it onto the chopping board. I throw the back doors open, and then I lean against the doorframe, facing the garden, swallowing down the lump in my throat as the smoke drifts past me to curl away with the breeze.

'I don't really remember you being born,' Joel says from his seat behind me. 'Sorry. I remember it being me and Edwin, before we started school, playing here. Just happy memories really. And then after we started school, it was always . . . sad here, in your house: two screaming babies, your dad all spaced-out, Vera fussing all the time, new nannies starting and leaving. I mean, it got better, of course. Not that you screamed *all* the time, I don't mean that.'

I turn around, try to smile.

'Oh, Gran always says I was a horrible baby, it's okay,' I say.

'You were pretty fierce back then. Do you remember Edwin and me teaching you and Danny to ride your bikes? Before you started school. Felt like it took us the whole summer holiday, and you had a huge tantrum every time you fell off. You'd stamp your feet and shout at us, blaming us.'

I shake my head slowly. 'I don't remember that.'

Joel pulls a face. 'Probably just as well.'

'I bet Danny was a dream to teach.'

He doesn't reply, but the corners of his mouth pinch up in confirmation.

I reach for the chocolate biscuits he brought, and hold them out enquiringly, but he stands up.

'Thanks, but I'll get going. I just wanted to check you're okay. I hope I haven't made you feel any worse.'

I walk as far as the front door with him, and as he steps outside, he turns to face me, not saying anything for a moment. There's a faint sinuous

220

scar just under his jaw — a pale indentation in his dark skin — and without thinking, I reach up and touch it with my fingertip.

'How did you get this?' I ask.

His pupils widen, and he takes hold of my hand, pulling it down gently.

'From the glass, that day,' he says, his eyes searching mine.

I look at him blankly. 'What day?'

'Seraphine.' He draws in a deep breath, still holding my hand. 'That day I upset you by the pool, when the others started teasing you and you ran away. The glass you smashed — it cut me.'

I'm shaking my head now, feeling cold.

'No one . . . I didn't . . . '

'It's okay,' he says. 'Long forgotten. Except it made me realise just how harmful Grandad's stories could be. I'm sorry. I tried to fix things afterwards, but . . . '

I stare at him. Is it true? How could I have hurt him and not known about it? The hairs on my arms rise, and the air around me seems to shift and relayer itself, as if Summerbourne itself is sifting through its memories.

'You're cold,' Joel says. 'I'm sorry. You should go in.'

He drops my hand and steps back, but I catch hold of his sleeve before he can escape.

'Don't go,' I say, and then he's wrapping his arms around me and holding on to me as if he thinks I'm about to fall.

'Hey,' he says. 'What is it?' There's a trace of wariness in his voice, and my heart thuds with the realisation that he thinks I've lost the plot — him, Edwin; everyone thinks I'm going crazy.

Maybe they're right.

But he doesn't let go of me. We go into the sitting room and sit side by side on the sofa, and he keeps his hand over mine the whole time. 'Tell me.'

I'm not sure where to start, or how much he already knows from Edwin. I want to trust my instincts: that he won't go behind my back to Edwin, that he'll understand I need to talk to Kiara before getting the police involved, that he'll be on my side. I barely know him any more, but my desire to confide in him is overwhelming.

He nods at me, his dark eyes serious.

'Someone broke into the house,' I say, and it all spills out: Laura and Alex and Kiara; the message on the mirror, the word burnt into the grass, the address stolen from my handbag, the dead bird on the doorstep. My fear that he'll think I'm making it up. My fear that I really am making it up. He listens intently without interrupting, and when I finally finish speaking, my throat aches.

'I believe you,' he says, and it's like a warm blanket draping over my skin. I keep hold of his hand and lean back on the sofa, watching his face as he thinks, and I find myself marvelling at how different he seems and yet how familiar.

'Who has a key?' he asks, and I'm reminded of how practical he's always been, how single-minded when confronted with a problem. 'If you think you locked the doors on Monday and there's no sign of forced entry, you have to make a list of all the people who hold a key to Summerbourne. The cleaners obviously do?'

'Vera sorts that out. It's not a regular contract. Sometimes it's someone from the village, sometimes an agency.'

'What about the plumber, electrician? Or the people who did the food after your dad's funeral?' He squeezes my hand as he mentions my dad.

'I don't know. Vera sorts out the maintenance stuff — I mean, it's her house. I've never really had to — ' I take a deep breath, cringing at how spoiled I sound. I want to add, *It's not my house — it'll never be my house*, but I realise that's hardly the point. I raise my chin. 'Does Michael have a key?'

Joel frowns, and shakes his head slowly. 'I don't know.' He shifts his position to face me more directly. 'Look, I understand why you don't want to tell the police before you've spoken to Alex's daughter. I get it. But I'm worried. You shouldn't be here by yourself until we know who did these things. The thought of someone . . . '

'Edwin and Danny are coming tomorrow,' I say.

'Good.' He looks down at my hand in his, and I can tell he's choosing his next words carefully. 'But tonight. Is there someone you can go and stay with? Or . . . ' He glances up at me. 'You could come back to Grandad's with me now. Take my bed. I'll sleep downstairs.'

I'm trying to concentrate on his words, to form an opinion so I can give him an answer, but I'm distracted by the nearness of him, the rise and fall of his chest under his T-shirt, the mesmerising motion of his eyelashes as he tilts his head.

'I wish . . . ' I say.

His small movements cease. His gaze locks onto mine. It's a long moment before his chest begins to rise and fall again. 'You wish what?'

'I wish we'd sorted it out,' I say. 'I wish I'd listened to you when you tried to say sorry.'

'I wish to God I'd never said that stupid nickname,' he says. 'I had no idea . . . '

'How badly I'd react?'

He blinks at me, and I try to smile back.

'I'm sorry,' I say. 'For pushing you away.' I want to say more, but my voice dries up. The moment stretches out in silence, and I close my eyes, concentrating on the heat from his body, the feel of his hand on mine.

'I missed you, Seraphine,' he says, and when I open my eyes, he brushes a tear from my cheek. But a second later he is on his feet, and there's something about the tension in his brow and the set of his jaw that spins my memory back to a hazy autumn evening in the Summerbourne garden: the four of us squinting against a low sun, Edwin trying to persuade us to sneak out to the folly, Joel objecting: *'We're not allowed. We'll get into trouble.'*

His eyes are serious. 'Let's concentrate on keeping you safe tonight, okay? We can't fix everything in one evening. If you don't want to come back with me, is there someone in the village you could . . . ?'

I blink at him.

He clears his throat. 'Okay. So . . . Grandad's?'

I tilt an ear towards the hall, straining for any unfamiliar sound in the house. The hairs on my arms remain settled.

'Will you stay here?' I ask him. 'With me?'

When he doesn't reply immediately, I'm afraid he's going to say no. My gaze slides to the door.

'I'll have to pop back to the cottage and let Grandad know,' he says. 'But sure. Okay. I can do that.'

It's only after he's gone to check on Michael that I allow myself to replay his words: *I missed you, Seraphine.* But he doesn't want to talk about that tonight. By the time he returns, I am clearing up the kitchen, wiping the surfaces and tipping my rubbery cheese on toast into the bin.

He has brought back some thick slices of ham wrapped in the white greaseproof paper of the village butcher's shop. He makes me a sandwich, and while I munch my way through it, we share a beer at the kitchen table. Our conversation is stilted at first, trying to find safe ground in the small news of the village and the mild drama of the current heatwave, but soon we are reminiscing over shared childhood experiences, and we begin to relax.

'Do you remember our signal system for raiding the greenhouse?' Joel asks.

'The birdcalls? A wood pigeon if it was your grandad coming, a seagull shriek for my gran.'

'Wasn't it a seagull whisper you ended up doing that time your gran did show up?'

'Well.' I demonstrate my refusal to accept responsibility with a wave of my bread crust.

'You were bound to get caught sooner or later.'

He laughs. 'We were always so hungry in those days. I mean, big meals, and then an hour later we'd be starving again.'

'Remember corn on the cob and potatoes on the bonfire?'

'They were the best.' He sips his beer. 'With melted butter, and we had to use the camping forks 'cause your gran didn't want the good cutlery lost outside. I still can't believe you made us take the whole bonfire apart that time.'

'I definitely saw a hedgehog under there.'

'And yet . . . ' He spreads his fingers.

I'm laughing now. 'I really did see it, you know.'

'Sure,' he says. 'And Edwin really didn't mind his potato being raw.'

'I gave him some of mine, I'm sure.'

'It was usually me you shared things like that with,' he says, and suddenly, our eye contact feels heavy. I look down at my empty plate.

'Because I liked you.' I shrug. 'You weren't as annoying as my brothers, anyway.'

'You know, I had to go that night.' His voice is lower now. 'After Edwin's graduation party. I was always going to go straight back to uni that night — I was in the middle of exams still.'

I nod slowly. 'Okay.'

'But I should have come back. Talked to you about it.'

We look at each other.

'It was my fault,' I say. 'I mean, I didn't know Ralph was going to hit you, but . . . '

'We could start over. Try again.'

I stare at him, my pulse skipping. Does he mean friendship? Does he mean more than that? I open my mouth, but I can't think how to respond.

'I know,' he says. 'You need to get through the next couple of days first.'

I realise I'm nodding.

'Well.' He puffs out a breath. 'Let's hope this Kiara woman can sort everything out.' He gives me a small smile. 'I'll still be here afterwards. I'm not going anywhere.'

A short while later, I show him up to the guest bedroom, feeling suddenly shy in the shadows on the landing.

'Night, Seraphine,' he says. His pupils are enormous in the dim light. I'm forcibly reminded that he is the one — the one I have always, deep down, wanted to share my life at Summerbourne with. I'm so tempted to reach out and run my fingertips over the smooth skin of his arm, to step closer, to hold on to him. When I force myself to look away, I notice the moonlight glinting on a small shard of broken china nestled up against the skirting board.

'Good night,' I whisper, and I retreat to my bedroom. I'm tired of puzzling over the threats; I'm tired of keeping secrets from Edwin and Danny; I'm worried about Kiara coming for lunch the day after tomorrow. But Joel's presence across the landing makes me think that perhaps it's going to be okay. And we'll sort everything out between us. Once this is all over and done with. Once I know for sure who I really am.

18

Laura

DECEMBER 1991

Christmas at Mum's was miserable. Beaky interrogated me on a range of subjects: Dominic's job; whether Vera would hand Summerbourne over to Ruth one day; whether the family had given me a Christmas bonus. I had only applied for the au pair job at his insistence — I still remembered his exact words on the day I left hospital and moved back home: *Get down the agency first thing tomorrow. Let's see how you like looking after someone else's brat.* Now that he realised I was genuinely fond of my small charge, he grew increasingly critical of the slightest change in me and mimicked anything I said in a mock upper-class accent.

'Oh, we don't do it like this at Summerbourne,' he would say. And then, 'I saw your ex down the Feathers again last night. Had a nice chat with him. He couldn't remember your name.'

'Don't listen to him, love,' Mum told me afterwards. 'He's just not used to you growing up yet. Just don't go on too much about this Summerbourne, yeah? It gets his back up.'

I spent most of the fortnight in my old bedroom. My Bon Jovi posters had been peeled off the walls, and Beaky's boxes of duty-free wine took up most of the floor space, but my bed was still there, with my swimming trophies lined up along the shelf above it. I sat cross-legged on the bed with my textbooks open, wondering if my ex-boyfriend remembered shoving me out of the door, calling me an attention-seeking bitch. He was the total opposite of Alex.

My thoughts drifted frequently to the way Alex looked at me when he asked me about myself, and the way he listened to me with a half smile forming. I wondered whether he would come back to Summerbourne, and whether he knew yet about Ruth's pregnancy. I thought about Ruth on the beach saying, 'He'd love to have children of his own, of course.' My notes grew dimpled with tears.

On Christmas morning I hid in that room to unwrap my presents from the Mayes family: a beautifully soft lamb's wool scarf with matching gloves from Ruth and Dominic, an address book from Vera, and a box of chocolates from Edwin. Mum cooked a turkey with roast potatoes and chipolatas, but my stomach was unsettled all day, and I could only pick at the meal and duck away from Beaky's permanent glare.

My birthday two days after Christmas was uneventful. Mum gave me a book, and some pyjamas that were too small for me. My friends were all busy, and I hadn't mentioned the date to the Mayes family. I read my new book in my room and munched my way through the chocolates. When Pati, Jo and Hazel called by a couple of days later, I told them I was too unwell to come out. I didn't feel like explaining Summerbourne to anyone else, and I didn't relish hearing about their new lives either.

Returning to Summerbourne was like waking from a bad dream. I travelled back on New Year's Eve — or Old Year's Night, as they called it in the village — so that I could look after Edwin while Ruth and Dominic attended a party at Kemi and Chris Harris' house. I felt as though I ought to be paying them for having me back rather than the other way around.

Edwin danced around me in the hall as Dominic paid the taxi driver behind me.

'Laura! I got a red bike from Father Christmas. Can we go out and play?'

The last day of the year was cold and grey, and the interior of the house offered a warm welcome, but I was desperate to wash my lungs out with fresh Summerbourne coastal air.

'Get your coat on then, quick,' I said, and we took his new bike out for a tour around the garden, giggling at his wobbly progress and delighting in being reunited.

After Ruth and Dominic had left for the party and Edwin had fallen asleep, I wandered around the sitting room and browsed through the family's Christmas cards. There must have been over a hundred — arranged along the mantelpiece, the bookshelves, the sideboard. Eventually, I found one from Alex: **Have a great Christmas,** it said. **Hope to see you in the New Year.** He won the prize for the blandest message.

I turned up the volume on the television in the

sitting room and listened to Big Ben strike midnight with my face pressed against the window in the hall, watching fireworks explode over the village. The Luckhursts were close neighbours of the Harrises, and I suspected that both Joel and Ralph would still be up, enjoying the celebrations with their parents. I was glad Edwin was safely tucked up asleep in his bed.

'Happy Old Year's Night,' I whispered to the darkness. A lone ball of light flared and swooped in a downward arc, leaving a trail like a silver scar in the sky. I was tempted to make a wish, as if it was a falling star. But it was just a firework, and anyway — I didn't know whether to wish that Alex *would* come back or that he wouldn't.

19

Seraphine

Joel knocks on my bedroom door early on Friday morning and carries a mug of coffee in to my bedside table. I've been awake for a while, mulling over last night's conversation, and I wish now I'd got up sooner and brushed my hair, put on something more attractive than this old grey T-shirt of Edwin's that I adopted because it's so comfortable. I pull my sheet closer to my chin, and he smiles down at me.

'I have to go — check on Grandad before I go to work. You going to be okay till Edwin and Danny get here?'

I nod.

'Be careful,' he says. 'Ring me if you need me.' He pauses at the door on his way out. 'Oh, and you look gorgeous, by the way.'

The coffee is the perfect temperature, and I smile into it. But as the caffeine sharpens my thoughts, I am struck by the certain knowledge that Michael *does* have a key to Summerbourne. When Edwin still lived here, before he moved into Winterbourne, he lost his key at the beach one weekend. He'd joked afterwards that he'd been preparing to survive on the fruits of the greenhouse until I got home, cursing his bad luck that none of the usual doors or windows had been left unlocked. But in the end, he said, he'd jumped the wall by the stable block and walked down to Michael's cottage, and Michael had produced a huge set of assorted keys, one of which had opened Summerbourne's front door.

Because they trusted him, I told myself. Dad, or Vera, or Mum — one of them must have given Michael a key at some point, *because they trusted him*. It might even have come from Vera's parents — Vera celebrates her seventy-fifth birthday next year, and I would guess Michael to be ten years older. He might have been living in that cottage, working for Vera's parents, long before Vera inherited the house. The old village postmaster once told me my great-grandparents threw scandalous parties here during the 'fabulous fifties': naked dancing on the beach, he told me; babies conceived under cloaks around the campfire; eerie singing from the top of the folly. No wonder Summerbourne has never shrugged off its reputation for being a world apart from the rest of the village.

I try to picture Michael Harris watching me drive away from Summerbourne on Monday, shuffling down the lane, letting himself in, climbing the stairs, writing with lipstick on the mirror. I throw off my sheet and head for the shower. It's beyond ridiculous.

Joel has left me a note on the kitchen table: **Eat breakfast**. I blast some instant porridge in the microwave and force it down. Then I push my lurking anxieties to the back of my mind and concentrate on scrubbing the kitchen and running the vacuum cleaner around the ground floor. I don't need to rely on Vera remembering to send in cleaners. I throw open every window and all of the back doors, and the fresh sea breeze clears the stale air from the house.

Until last month, my solitude at Summerbourne was interrupted regularly by visits from Dad. If Edwin came with him, he and Dad would happily spend a Sunday morning preparing a roast dinner, and if Vera joined us, we would shake out the old red tablecloth and make an event of it. Danny spends the odd week here too, in between overseas volunteering projects; he makes popcorn when I get in from work, and we binge-watch old movies together.

But I rarely have other visitors. Perhaps I don't feel the same need for friends that other people do. Outside of my family, the only person I ever longed to be close to was Joel, and I made a total mess of that. When acquaintances in the village ask me to the pub, or a party, or a barbecue, I make my excuses. I prefer my own company. Today, I try to convince myself, as I count napkins and swipe cobwebs out of corners, that this is the reason for my growing nervousness about Kiara's impending visit. Not that I'm frightened of what she might say. Not that I'm frightened I might regret ever meeting her.

While I'm peering into the fridge, wondering if the pasta salads are still safe to eat, my phone beeps with a text from Danny:

Ok if I bring Brooke along tonight?

As if I don't have enough to worry about already with Kiara coming tomorrow. Does this mean Danny's serious about this woman? Has he told her yet that the house will be his one day?

I slam the fridge door shut, empty-handed.

Would love to see Brooke sometime but this weekend not really best time. Hope you agree? S

Much later he replies:

Ok no worries.

Mid-afternoon, the house is more or less visitor ready when the doorbell rings. A van stands on the drive with the driver's door hanging open, Luckhurst Landscape Gardening printed on the side. My surge of adrenaline doesn't recede. Ralph Luckhurst? What's he doing here?

'Hi,' he says. He stands a couple of metres back from the step with his hands in his pockets. He's grown a beard since I last saw him, and its effect in combination with his dark curls is dramatic. He looks so much older, more serious than ever. 'Sorry. I promised your gran I'd take a quick look at the back lawn, but I can do it some other time. It's just, you know, my mum asked me to check you're okay as well.'

'I'm fine,' I say automatically, staring at him.

He's like a stranger, these days. Always kind to me when we were children, his interest in me grew more intense as the years passed. Five years older than me, he used to wait for me outside my sixth form college when I was seventeen, offering to take me to the cinema or out for a drink. I said yes a few times, trying to convince myself I fancied him, trying to take my mind off Joel.

Ralph had been there at the pool party and knew I'd spent the subsequent two years trying to avoid Joel, so when he saw us kissing at Edwin's graduation party, he assumed that Joel was harassing me and reacted accordingly. Joel left the party with a black eye, too shocked to listen to my drunken apologies. Ralph and I maintained a lopsided friendship for another year, but we drifted apart when I left for university. My romantic life has always been a disaster.

Ralph squints towards the patch of damaged grass when I tell him I'm fine.

'Good,' he says. 'My mum said you looked upset the other day, that's all, but I'm glad you're fine.' He takes a step back.

Warmth spreads across my cheeks as I picture myself staggering out of the surgery the day before yesterday. What must Helen have thought? And of course, Hayley Pickersgill would have told him about it too. His fiancée. I grip the door handle more firmly, ready to send him on his way.

'I'm really sorry about your dad,' he says then, his voice low, and for a fleeting moment I glimpse Ralph as a teenager again: always ready to help anyone in need despite the constant responsibility of caring for his mother and sister. I was so angry with him after he punched Joel at Edwin's party that night, but I never doubted it was because he cared about me. He kept checking up on me in the days and weeks

236

afterwards, long after Joel had disappeared. I swing the door open wider.

'You might as well look at the lawn now, since you're here.'

He glances back at his van. 'I should have rung first. I can come back at a better time.'

'Please. I haven't seen you in so long. And I'm going a bit crazy here on my own, to be honest.'

He puffs out a big breath, and his gaze runs over the upstairs windows. 'Sure, okay.'

I fill two glasses with cold water from the kitchen tap, and he follows me out to the patio. I settle in a chair and watch him pace out over the lawn, stooping to poke at it a couple of times. When he joins me back on the patio, he's restless, jiggling his leg as he squints out at the garden.

'It's bad, isn't it?' I say, following his gaze. 'Not like when Michael Harris used to do it. I wish Vera would get rid of the current gardeners. Would you take it on, if she asked you?'

He clears his throat. 'Actually, she thinks I should concentrate on the design side of the business in the long term. But she did cancel their contract a few days ago. That's why . . . I'll get the lawn treated at least, while she finds someone else to take over.'

'Oh.' I nod slowly, determined not to show him how taken aback I am that he knows more about my grandmother's plans than I do. There's a note of respect in his voice when he mentions her that makes me feel guilty for not having apologised to her after our argument last week. She's helped his family a lot over the years, and he's obviously grateful. 'Gran said — didn't she help find Daisy a job recently, in the village?'

'That's right. At the baker's. She loves it.'

'Great,' I say. We sip our drinks and stare out at the garden. I don't want to ask him about the rest of his life, about Hayley and his wedding plans. I wish I hadn't invited him to sit down; he could have been on his way by now, reporting back to his mother and my grandmother. Yellow dandelion heads shiver as a breeze strokes the lawn, and an idea occurs to me.

'If someone sprayed normal weed killer on all this,' — I gesture to the scene in front of us — 'would it kill the grass too?'

'Well, you've got to use the right stuff.'

'What I mean is, what *would* kill grass? Like, burn grass?'

His fidgeting stops, and he frowns at the lawn. 'What do you mean, burn?'

'I mean, if you used the wrong weed killer, say, could that leave burn marks in the grass?'

He nods. 'Yeah, of course. Or a propane torch.'

'What's that?'

'A weed burner.' He looks directly at me for the first time, his forehead creased, as if he's looking for some sign in me. 'Why do you ask?'

I feel as though I've missed something; our wires are crossed.

'No reason,' I say. 'Why do you say it like that?'

He settles back in his chair, his gaze still on me. 'I had one stolen from my van the other day. A propane torch.'

'What?'

'Yeah. One of the tools I bought from Michael Harris, actually, when he stopped working. Joel helped him sell some of his stuff.' He says Joel's name with a slight awkwardness.

I stare at him. 'Did you report it to the police?'

He studies me for a moment. 'Is there something you want to confess, Seraphine?'

'No!' I say, but I can feel the heat in my cheeks. 'Don't be ridiculous. What would I want with a weeding tool?'

He runs his hand over his beard as he glances at the lawn, and the sudden flash of amusement in his eyes triggers a stab of regret in me for our lost friendship.

'Fair point,' he says. 'No, I haven't reported it yet. I'll mention it to Martin when I see him. I was stupid — the van wasn't locked — and it's the only thing they took. I thought it was probably kids mucking around. Or someone just' — his smile has gone — 'borrowed it.'

He eases to his feet, the empty glass in his hand.

'Who would have borrowed it?' I ask.

He looks at his watch and grimaces. 'I really need to run, sorry. Thanks for the drink.' I have to make an effort to keep up with his long strides back through the house.

'You're not going to answer me?' I say as he opens the front door, and he turns to me with a startled expression.

'What?'

'Who do you think might have borrowed a weed burner from you?'

239

His eyes search mine, and he leans towards me, and when he speaks I hear the genuine concern in his voice.

'I'm really very sorry about your dad, Seraphine. He was a good man. We all miss him. Just . . . let me know if there's ever anything you need, anything I can do.'

He swings round and jogs to his van.

I lean against the kitchen sink for a long time, waiting to make sense of it. I've had so many off-kilter conversations this past week — not just with Ralph, but with Laura, Pamela, Alex, Michael — do they all know something I don't know? Do they have an agenda, an ulterior motive? Is it personal? Is it me?

I don't find any answers. The clock in the hall chimes, and I lift my chin, shaking off the circular thoughts. I make a cup of tea and prowl around the house, poking through the sideboard in the sitting room and browsing through the family photo albums again. I wander back towards the day nursery, an old memory niggling at me.

A walk-in cupboard opens into one corner of the room, and I have to replace the light bulb inside it to get a good look at the contents. It's like a time warp in here, with the games and toys of several generations muddled together. I know what I'm looking for, and after a couple of minutes, I ease out a cardboard box, a bit bigger than a shoebox, decorated with glued-on postcards and tickets and drawings. This was Edwin's treasure box.

I carry it over to the battered old nursery

table. In my memory, the pictures stuck on the outside were colourful and exotic, but in the bright sunshine of this room now they look faded and tatty. I lift the lid gingerly.

There are shrivelled pinecones inside, and conkers. A pebble that has an 'S' shape gouged into it. Tickets to the pantomime, the aquarium, Madame Tussauds waxworks. Train tickets — many, many train tickets. Programmes for primary school productions — *Edwin Mayes as The Innkeeper*. Certificates for swimming, for a spelling competition, for karate. And a bundle of cards and drawings at the bottom. I would guess Edwin stopped squirreling things away in here when he was around seven or eight. Danny and I caught chicken pox when we were six, and I remember Edwin digging the box out and letting us browse through its contents when we were housebound feeling itchy and grumpy.

I ease out the bundle from the bottom and flick through the drawings. Almost all of them show people, ranging from stick men to more sophisticated figures with detailed expressions. I wonder what it says about me, that I used to draw Summerbourne so obsessively when I was a child, but rarely people. Danny used to design complicated mazes. Not for the first time, I wonder how different our personalities might have been if we'd grown up with a mother.

I pause at a simple drawing of two figures, one labelled with an 'E' and the other with a 'T'. Edwin and Theo. They each have a yellow spiral of hair. A later picture shows 'Daddy, Gran, Edwin, Sefn, Dany'. There are several featuring

241

Edwin and Joel surrounded by animals.

There are postcards from Vera in London, and from our paternal grandparents in Scotland who died a few years ago. I open a Christmas card and read: **Dear Edwin, I am at my own home now, but I miss you loads. Happy Christmas and I'll see you soon. Love from Laura xxxx**

I check all the others. There's no further mention of Laura, and none of Alex.

Just before nine in the evening, I hear a car on the drive. My brothers have arrived. I'm tempted to run out and tell them all about the burnt grass and the lipstick message, but I steel myself against it. Edwin and Danny make a noisy entrance, dropping bags onto the floor I cleaned earlier, scattering possessions over the kitchen worktops I'd so diligently cleared. I grit my teeth.

'You told me you were coming straight back here,' is the first thing Danny says to me. 'Alex bloody Kaimal? What the hell's got into you?'

'At least I'm doing *something*,' I snap back. 'I need to know what happened that day.'

Edwin holds up his hands between us. 'Hey, you got beer in for us, thanks,' he says, grabbing a bottle and pulling the bottle opener from the drawer.

'Joel brought them, actually,' I say.

'Is he coming tonight?' Edwin asks.

I shake my head.

Danny opens two more bottles and passes one to me. 'Come on then, spill.'

'Come and see what I found, first.'

They follow me through to the day nursery.

The sun is setting, and the pink and gold light bathes the contents of Edwin's treasure box laid out on the table. It's a strangely beautiful scene, and yet for some reason makes me wish I had never unearthed these memories, or perhaps just makes me wish that Dad was still alive and we were gathered here for happy reasons. Edwin moves forward with a murmur of recognition.

'I haven't seen this for years. Where did you find it? Look at these.' He shuffles through the cards and the tickets, holding a couple of them up to show Danny.

'I remember this,' Danny says. 'I started my own treasure box, but I could never be bothered to collect things for it.' I lean my shoulder lightly against his as we watch Edwin leafing through his old drawings.

'That's you two,' Edwin says, holding up a brightly coloured picture, 'flying on gigantic birds.'

'Of course,' Danny murmurs.

Edwin pauses at another one, and then places it separately on the table and stares at it. I recognise it from earlier — a bird with a beak and legs and spindly toes, and a person lying next to it with a sad face. Unusually, it's all in black crayon, except for a red patch on the bird's body.

'Theo and the robin,' Edwin says quietly.

My eyes widen.

'What robin?' Danny asks.

'I don't know,' Edwin says slowly, shaking his head. 'Gran said something about it that day, on the cliffs.'

'Robin was Mum's twin brother,' I say. 'He died before he was born. The cord was wrapped around his neck.'

They stare at me.

'How did you . . . ?' Edwin says.

'Pamela told me. She also told me . . . ' I feel light-headed suddenly. I can't say it aloud to my brothers — that twins never survive at Summerbourne, that that's why Theo died, that no one in the village believes we're the real Summerbourne twins. I take a deep breath. 'Look, it doesn't matter. I'm glad you're here. I just hope Kiara can tell us something useful tomorrow, that's all.'

Edwin and Danny watch me. I concentrate on keeping my breathing calm, conscious of the other secrets I'm keeping from them: the letters burnt into the lawn, the writing on the mirror.

Edwin sighs. 'What time is she coming?'

'About twelve.'

'And then you'll come back with us for a Winterbourne lunch on Sunday, yes?'

I nod, pressing my nails into my palms.

Edwin is fiddling with the layers of tickets and postcards glued to the box lid, and he suddenly sits up straighter, ripping a train ticket off completely.

'Look at this.' He gives a short laugh. Freshly revealed is a flimsy grey square of shiny paper with a grainy white pattern on it. He peels it off the box and bends over it for a moment, then pushes it across the table towards us. It's an ultrasound image. With *Ruth Mayes* and

10/02/92 printed across the top. And it shows a baby. One baby.

Goose bumps spring up along my arms.

Danny and I look at each other and then back at the scan picture.

Which of us is it?

'Shit,' says Danny.

'I don't believe it,' I whisper.

We stare at it in silence.

'Can you get individual pictures of twin babies?' Danny asks eventually.

I rub my hands over my face. 'I don't know. We could ask Joel.'

'Why did you have this?' Danny asks Edwin. 'Did Mum give it to you?'

Edwin shrugs. 'I guess so.'

'Would you remember if there were two pictures of two babies?' I ask.

'Oh, Seraphine, I don't *know*,' Edwin says.

Without further discussion, we abandon the table strewn with Edwin's memories and carry our beers through to the sitting room where we slump on the sofas.

'Is there shopping coming in the morning then?' Edwin asks eventually.

'Yeah, between nine and ten. I ordered stuff for risotto, if you don't mind cooking?' I pause, trying to picture the four of us sitting around the dining table, eating lunch, piecing together clues. 'I should have told Joel to come before twelve if he wants to see you. Can you text him and say?'

Edwin nods.

'I can't believe she's driving all this way because her dad used to know our parents,'

Danny mutters. Then he sighs and pats me on the arm. 'Anyway, I'm sorry, sis,' he says. 'I can see you've got it bad.'

'What?'

'Mentionitis,' Danny says, shaking his head.

Edwin says, 'Danny . . . ' in a warning tone.

I narrow my eyes at my twin brother.

'I have no clue what you're on about, Danny.'

'Mentionitis. With Joel. You've mentioned him at least fifteen times since we arrived.'

'Oh, shut up. Idiot.' I whack him with a cushion. He's laughing, and I can feel my cheeks reddening, but I'm suddenly reminded of something else. 'Hang on, truce. I need to ask you both something.'

Danny groans. I look at Edwin.

'You remember that day by the pool, when you had that party, with your university friends, and Joel called us sprites?' I ask.

Edwin raises his eyebrows; Danny just blinks at me.

'Yeah,' Edwin says eventually. 'It was ten years ago, but yeah, of course I remember.'

'What happened after I left?' I look from one to the other. 'Did Joel get hurt?'

Edwin tilts his head back against the sofa and looks at the ceiling. Danny's gaze slides sideways, and he waits.

'You knocked a glass off the table as you ran away,' Edwin says quietly. 'Deliberately, it looked like. Maybe not, I don't know. A piece of glass flew up and cut Joel under his chin.'

I stare at him. The air feels too thick. 'I never knew that. It was an accident.'

They're both quiet.

'So what happened then? Did he need stitches?'

'We got Michael.' Edwin rolls his head forward again. 'The nanny would have made a fuss. Michael took Joel to the doctor. He got stitched up. It was fine.'

'Lots of blood, though,' Danny says.

I look at the bottle of beer in my hand, and slowly place it on the coffee table. 'Why didn't you tell me? Nobody ever told me.'

Edwin sighs, and Danny makes a small noise in his throat.

'You always turned everything into a drama, Seph,' Danny says, his gentle tone at odds with the weight of the words. 'Who knows how you'd have reacted. You spent the rest of that summer hiding from Joel anyway, and biting our heads off if we tried to talk to you about it. It was generally easier not to tell you stuff like that.'

The fact that neither of my brothers adds, *It still is*, merely deepens the silence that follows.

20

Laura

JANUARY TO MARCH 1992

Vera began to visit more frequently in the New Year — at least once and sometimes twice a week. Each time she arrived, she found an excuse to take me out of Ruth's earshot and ask, 'How is she?' I felt sick at being put on the spot like that, unwilling as I was to describe Ruth's odd behaviour, yet reluctant to lie that everything was fine. I began to dread her visits.

Ruth took Edwin to his first settling-in session at the pre-school. The following day I heard her on the phone cancelling his place for the rest of the term.

'Thank you so much. We'll try again after Easter.'

She didn't mention a reason to me, and I didn't ask.

She hired a man to come and paint the day nursery, and then after he had moved all the furniture and covered it in dust sheets, she sent him away, claiming she couldn't bear the smell of the paint. Privately, she told me, 'I didn't like his eyes. I didn't trust him.'

She spent ten minutes chatting at the front door with a red-haired traveller woman one afternoon, allowing the warm air of the house to be sucked out into the January gloom, and she bought a pair of beautiful glass candlesticks from her. Afterwards, she smashed the candlesticks in the kitchen sink, grinding the glass with a rolling pin and flushing it down the drain.

Yet frequently, she was seized by buoyant moods. She sang as she pottered around the kitchen, making up nonsense words to entertain Edwin. She stopped taking him to gymnastics, but she often joined us on the beach despite the cold weather, and we'd all have hot chocolate together on our return to the house.

I might have told all of this to Dominic, but he never asked. He had a wary manner about him those days — sometimes watching me without seeming to actually see me.

'I know you've been discussing me with Mother behind my back again,' I heard Ruth say to him. 'You both use identical phrases — it's pathetic. I'm fine. We are fine. I'm having my scan on the eleventh of February, and I'm happy with my doctor. You've got to let me do this my way, Dominic. Trust me to know what's best for my baby.'

'Our baby,' Dominic said, and then I heard her weeping and him murmuring soothing words.

I agreed to look after Edwin from a Sunday evening until a Tuesday evening so that Dominic could take Ruth down to London for a couple of days and accompany her to her scan. On the Monday afternoon, I had Edwin and Joel kneeling on chairs at the kitchen table, stirring cake mixture, when a taxi pulled up on the drive.

For a minute, I thought it was going to be Alex. I hovered in the kitchen doorway, watching through the hall window, waiting for him to step out and look up and perhaps catch my eye. But it was Ruth who emerged, handing money to the driver, marching up to the front door with a broad smile on her face.

'Guess what?' she said, bustling in and shedding her coat, checking her hair in the mirror. 'It's just one baby, and all is well.'

Edwin galloped from the kitchen to wrap his arms around her middle, and Joel hung back in the doorway, a streak of flour on his cheek.

'Well, that's wonderful,' I said. 'I thought your scan was tomorrow?'

'Oh, it was, but I popped in this morning, and they said they could do it today. I couldn't say no. It was so magical to see it. Him or her. I must ring Dominic straightaway and tell him.'

I brushed the flour from Joel's cheek, and ushered both boys back into the kitchen.

'Could Dominic not go with you, then?'

'No, like I said, it was a spur-of-the-moment thing.' She licked her lips. 'Would you like to see the scan picture?'

I looked properly into her eyes for the first time. A suspicion that she might not have actually had a scan had been unfurling inside me, and I hadn't anticipated this offer of proof. But she was already reaching into her handbag, pulling out a little square image, handing it to me.

I held it gingerly. It showed a fuzz of white on black, and had Ruth's name and the date at the top. She leaned over it, her hair beneath my chin.

'That's the head,' she said, 'and that's the backbone. The legs are up there, and that's part of an arm, you see?'

'It's amazing.'

'You could see the little heart beating,' she said. 'It was perfect. And, you know, I thought I might be disappointed it's not twins, but I think it will be easier this way.'

'Yes,' I said, blinking unexpected tears away. My only personal experience of a twin relationship was a decidedly negative one — my mum's virtually estranged sister whose occasional postcards from exotic locations made my mum scowl. So it was ridiculous to feel sad for Edwin, sad for this new sibling of his. 'And you don't know if it's a boy or a girl?'

'No. I don't want to know. I want to meet this baby when he or she is ready to be met. Enjoy the moment.'

I nodded. 'And did they tell you a due date?'

She froze.

I bit my lip. When she eventually moved, it was to twitch the picture from my grasp.

'End of August,' she said, and then looked at me.

'Okay.'

'I need to ring Dominic. Would you mind getting back to the boys?'

'Of course.'

I closed the kitchen door, not wanting to hear any of that conversation.

Later, when Edwin and I had returned from delivering both Joel and a box of fairy cakes

251

safely to Michael's cottage, Ruth showed Edwin the scan picture.

'That's your baby brother or sister,' she said, smiling.

He wrinkled his nose at it. 'It's not very good.'

'The baby will look much nicer when he or she is born, I promise,' she said.

'I'm going to do a drawing of my baby,' Edwin said, heading off to the day nursery with the picture. 'I'll stick this on my treasure box.'

'Good idea, darling,' Ruth said. I must have looked surprised, because after he'd gone, she added in a slightly defensive tone, 'Dominic can still see it when he gets home. It's my baby at the moment. Once it's born, he'll fall in love with it, and everything will be fine.' She went upstairs to have a rest.

Later that afternoon it began to snow heavily, and for a number of days, the three of us didn't leave the grounds of Summerbourne. On the eve of Valentine's Day, Ruth made much fuss at the discovery of a parcel of sweets on the doorstep.

'Oh, Edwin, look. Jack Valentine has left us a present.'

She and Edwin were in high spirits that evening, eating the sweets and peering out of the windows to look for footprints in the snow from the mysterious gift giver. I had to confess that Jack Valentine had never ventured as far as my home in London, but evidently, here he was just as important as Father Christmas and the Tooth Fairy.

Ruth begged Dominic not to risk driving on the icy roads to get home for the weekend, and in the end he agreed to stay in the city. Snowed in for several days at Summerbourne, we made popcorn and watched movies and built snowmen, raiding the freezer for fish fingers and pizzas, going to bed early and getting up late. On the day the snow finally melted, I had to suppress a twinge of disappointment that our mini holiday was at an end. But the Summerbourne woods had never looked more beautiful than on that day: snowdrops huddled in clumps on either side of the path, and the dark skeletons of the plum trees showed off delicate white blossom against the palest of grey skies, promising that spring was on its way.

When Dominic returned the following Friday evening, he was full of plans for booking a real holiday for the three of them before the baby came.

'I don't want to go abroad,' Ruth said. 'And I don't want to leave it too close to my due date. And I'd rather take Laura too, to help with Edwin.'

I was in the kitchen with them, but I abandoned my washing-up and moved to the door, avoiding eye contact with Dominic.

'Wait,' he said. 'Laura, it's not that I don't want you to come.' He turned towards Ruth again. 'I just think it would be nice to be just the three of us. Special.'

Ruth sighed, and Dominic shot me a pleading look. I rested a hand on the doorframe.

'I could do with a week at home, to revise,' I said.

'Well then,' Dominic said, turning back to

Ruth. 'There you go. Let's take a look at the Center Parcs brochure.'

As it turned out, I went home to Mum's for longer than originally planned. Edwin came down with a cold and a cough, and then Ruth and I both caught it. It left me feeling drained and lethargic, and I spent three weeks recuperating at Mum's, during which time Ruth, Dominic and Edwin had their holiday. Thankfully, Beaky went down to Kent for a couple of weeks on a job, so Mum and I got along better than we had for ages, but I still kept to my room for much of the time.

A certain reluctance to return to Summerbourne began to grow in me. I wasn't sure I could summon enough energy to face more of Ruth's mood swings, Dominic's awkwardness or the ridiculous jolt of desperate hope I felt every time the doorbell rang, wondering if it might be Alex. I browsed local job adverts, and considered applying for part-time waitressing or bar work.

'But I thought you loved it there?' Mum asked when she caught me underlining phone numbers in the local paper.

'I do. I did. But this would bring in money too, and I could pay you rent. I could revise at home then, for these last few weeks.'

'You don't need to pay rent, love.'

'Beaky thinks I do.'

Mum sighed. 'He just wants you to learn to take responsibility for yourself.'

I slammed the paper onto the coffee table and stood up. 'I made one mistake. How long do I need to keep paying for it?'

'He just thinks — '

'I don't care what he thinks.' I glared at her. 'You sound just like him, you know that?'

I barricaded myself into my bedroom for the rest of the afternoon, shoving Beaky's wine boxes up against the door. I half hoped Mum might attempt to coax me out, but she didn't. I pulled out the resignation letter I'd written to Ruth and Dominic that morning, and it trembled in my hand as I read it through. I hadn't signed or dated it yet.

When Beaky got back a few days later, I turned up the television volume to drown out the noise of him ranting to Mum in the kitchen. He stalked in and turned the set off with a snarl.

'We're not a hotel. You're well enough to work. You need to go back and get on with it.' His lip curled as he looked me up and down. 'Your mum says you've barely moved since you got here. I thought you were gonna get fit at this posh mansion, playing tennis all day with your snobby friends. Got fed up of you, did they?'

I rang Summerbourne that evening, and headed back the next day. The unsigned resignation letter remained tucked at the back of my biology ring binder. I dozed on the train, but my spirits lifted as the taxi approached the house. Edwin burst from the front door and flung himself into my arms with a whoop of joy.

'He's been rather difficult,' Ruth told me a few minutes later, out of the little boy's earshot.

'More than ready to go to school,' Dominic said.

Ruth gave my arm a quick squeeze. 'It's good

255

to have you back.' She smiled, and I was sure then that I had made the right decision in returning. My life was tied up with Summerbourne now. It was in my blood. It wasn't the sort of connection I could just walk away from.

When I found Ruth sobbing over a box of baby clothes a few days later, distressed by the mould that had bloomed on them in the attic, I took charge. I rang Vera and arranged for her to come and look after Edwin the following day, and Ruth and I went shopping in Norwich together. After months of baking and curling up indoors, with no daily training sessions at the pool any more, I had lost the sharp angles I'd arrived at Summerbourne with. When I looked in the mirror, I was pleased that I no longer had dark smudges under my eyes, and I relished the idea of buying some new clothes and make-up, and perhaps even a floppy sun hat to match Ruth's.

Ruth and I spent a happy couple of hours trying on clothes and then cooing over Babygros and choosing a whole new set of essential nursery items. Ruth bought us tea and cake in the department store restaurant afterwards.

'Thank you for doing this,' she said.

'It's been fun. I can't wait to find out if it's a boy or a girl now.'

She gave me a sudden intense look. 'You will stay with us the whole summer, won't you? After the baby comes? It'll be perfect — lazy days in the garden, down to the beach every day. We must make the most of it, before Edwin starts school and you have to leave us.'

My last forkful of cake hovered over the plate as I glanced around at the bags and boxes of baby equipment surrounding us, and then I smiled at her.

'Sounds like we have the perfect summer ahead,' I said, and she returned my smile, her hand drifting down to her gently rounded abdomen. But that last mouthful of cake turned to glue on my tongue. I forced it down with the dregs of my tea, determined to be optimistic about the next few months: Ruth's baby would have a great father in Dominic; Dominic might become less awkward with me; Alex might come back to Summerbourne . . .

I placed the cup carefully down on the saucer and leaned forward to admire a tiny cardigan that Ruth had pulled from one of the carrier bags. Alex might come back to Summerbourne.

'Are you okay?' Ruth asked.

'Yeah, fine,' I said. 'Worn out from all that shopping!'

She laughed, and turned to catch the attention of a staff member, asking him to carry our purchases out to the car for us. And all the while my insides squirmed, as if a sea serpent was rearranging its coils inside me.

21

Seraphine

Edwin and I unpack the grocery bags together on Saturday morning. As ever, the effect the fresh ingredients have on him is powerful: he smiles as he rubs his thumbs over the onions, flexes the celery, sniffs at the Parmesan, and inspects the prawns. He's in his element, relaxed and happy; at moments like this, he reminds me so much of Dad.

Danny is still in bed. I set out cutlery and glasses on the old red tablecloth in the dining room, fussing with napkins, irritated by my inability to be calm like my brothers. I'm wearing a new cotton dress, but I can't find my sandals that go with it, and when the doorbell rings, I answer it barefoot, distracted.

Joel stands there with a bunch of hydrangeas.

'From Grandad's garden,' he says. 'For the table.'

'Oh.'

'Everything okay?'

I realise I haven't moved. When I reach for the flowers, our fingers brush against each other, and I come close to blurting out a jumble of questions: *Did you really not know Michael has a key for Summerbourne? Why didn't you hit Ralph back at Edwin's party after I kissed you? Did you know Michael's old weed torch was stolen from Ralph's van last week? What did you mean when you said we could start over? As friends? As more than friends?*

'Edwin's in there,' I say, indicating the kitchen door, and I escape to the dining room with the hydrangeas. The pink flower heads are full and heavy, droplets of water still clinging to their petals. A wave of nostalgia washes over me: for Summerbourne's formerly beautiful garden, for the days when Michael ruled over it with cheerful authority, and for a time when Joel and I were friends and life was uncomplicated.

A whole hour before she's expected, Kiara arrives. I happen to be passing through the hall, still barefoot, and I freeze, watching her through the window as she unfolds herself from the driver's seat. She wears some kind of silky black sleeveless jumpsuit, and delicate heeled sandals which must surely make driving difficult. She's tall and slender, and I realise the word I'm really searching for is *elegant*. I swallow.

Danny has come down the stairs behind me in old shorts and T-shirt, bleary-eyed, and he whistles now as he peers through the window past the visitor.

'Nice wheels.'

Edwin is at the kitchen door, with Joel standing behind him, both watching curiously. When the doorbell rings, Danny gives me a shove in the small of my back.

'Your idea, sis,' he says.

I take a deep breath as I swing the door open.

'Kiara. Hi.' I do my best to smile at her. Her hair is how I remember, with the pink streak to one side, but up close, I am transfixed by the tiny diamond stud in the side of her nose, and the rows of similar sparkles in her ears. She thrusts a box of Belgian chocolates at me.

'Hi. I'm sorry I'm so early. I allowed extra time, and then the roads were so clear.' She sounds nervous, and I'm not proud of the fact that this helps me relax a little. I turn around as she steps into the hall, ready to make introductions. I glimpse Edwin passing the vegetable knife he was holding to Joel, who places it carefully on the worktop behind him. They move properly into the hall then too.

'This is Danny,' I say, 'my twin brother.'

'All right?' Danny says, and Kiara smiles and nods at him.

'And this is Edwin, our older brother,' I say.

Edwin reaches out a hand and shakes hers.

'Pleased to meet you. I remember your father. I liked him a lot,' he says.

Her smile widens. 'Hi.'

'And this is Joel, a neighbour,' I say. 'He's not staying.'

Edwin coughs, as Joel shakes Kiara's hand too.

'Nice to meet you,' Joel tells her. Is her gaze lingering on his face? Does he think she's attractive? I'm regretting this visit already.

'Well, I don't know about anyone else, but I need coffee,' Danny announces. 'Would you like one, Kiara?'

She smiles at him. 'I'd love one.' She follows him through to the kitchen.

As Edwin joins them, I stand alone for a minute in the hall with Joel, listening to the polite chatter between my easygoing brothers and this stranger. I don't look at Joel directly, but he watches me, a serious expression on his face. In the end, he steps closer and touches the back of my hand with his fingertips, and finally, I do look at him.

'Good luck,' he says, with the briefest of smiles, and then he leaves.

Edwin has resumed his chopping of ingredients when I enter the kitchen. Danny is pouring milk into coffee mugs, and Kiara is studying the old photos on the noticeboard.

'It must have been lovely, growing up with so much family history around you,' she says. She sounds wistful, but as I gaze around at the worn surfaces in our kitchen — the battered wooden doors of the cupboards, the chipped tiles on the floor — I have a sudden mental image of her standing in a pristine hightech kitchen in her own home this morning, white marble and stainless steel glinting all around her.

'Family history's not all it's cracked up to be,' I mutter into a pocket of silence, and they all stare at me. No one replies.

The kitchen doors are open, since it's another hot, cloudless day, and the three of us take our coffees out onto the patio while Edwin begins to cook the risotto.

'Such a fabulous garden,' Kiara says, seeming genuinely enraptured, and for a moment I am able to ignore the scruffy grass and neglected borders and appreciate the beauty of it alongside her. We stroll along the paths and show her the orchard, the vegetable garden, our old play areas, and the gate to the cliffs. We offer to take her down to the beach later.

We carefully avoid the subject of our parents until we're back indoors with Edwin, seated around the dining table, tucking into our lunch. The hydrangea heads droop towards the tablecloth in the heat.

'This is divine,' Kiara says, of the risotto. 'And I wish I didn't have such a strange reason for being here. But can you tell me why you came to see my father?'

She looks directly at me, and I put my fork down carefully, wipe my mouth.

'The day that Danny and I were born,' I say, 'our mother had a mental breakdown. We don't know quite what happened, but she ended up committing suicide, jumping from the cliffs behind the house. We were only a few hours old.'

Kiara brings one hand to her mouth. 'Oh, I'm so sorry.'

'Yeah. Well, our dad only ever worked part time after that, and we had our grandmother and various nannies here to look after us, so — it was okay.' I try to smile. 'I mean, we had one another, you know? But then Dad had an accident last month. He fell off a ladder and — and he died. A freak accident.' Danny is sitting next to me, and he slides a hand over mine under the table.

I realise all three of them are watching me, and that my brothers are waiting for my explanation with as much wariness as Kiara. Why *did* I go to see her father?

I draw in a deep breath. 'I think our mother

might only have had one baby that summer. I found a photo of her holding just one baby. And people always said ... there were always rumours when we were growing up that something odd happened. And there was a girl working here at the time — Laura Silveira — who I thought might be able to tell us ... Do you know the name?'

Kiara shakes her head slowly. 'She's the woman you accused Dad of sending a letter to?'

'I didn't accuse him. I asked him.'

'But he didn't,' Kiara says.

'Someone sent Laura a letter after our dad died, saying that if she spoke about Summerbourne to anyone, her daughter would be in danger,' I say.

'Who is her daughter?' Kiara asks.

We all look at her. At her willowy frame, her cheekbones, the texture of her hair. I've seen Laura's olive skin, and Alex's brown, and this young woman is paler than either of them, but what does that prove?

I shake my head. 'We don't know.'

'You think it might be me?' Kiara asks, frowning. 'Or you?' she adds, staring at me. 'I don't understand.'

'I'll get the photo,' I say. 'Hang on.'

I rise and head to the kitchen, and for a moment I contemplate the doors that stand open to the garden. I could walk out right now, escape to the cliffs, abandon any further conversation with Kiara, set my sights on rescuing my old life. What's left of my old life. A faint waft of humid air reminds me that it's even hotter out there than it is here in the house.

I turn to the sink and run my wrists under cold water until my head feels clearer, and then I return to the dining room with the photo, and pass it to Kiara.

'That's our mother, with one of us, presumably — me or Danny. With her new baby, anyway. Apparently, she was convinced before she died that someone was trying to steal her baby.' I give a short laugh. 'And yet they ended up with two of us.'

Kiara scrutinises the picture. 'You look like her,' she tells me. 'You look like your mother.' I feel tears well up suddenly.

'Thank you,' I whisper.

Danny shifts on his chair. 'So what did your dad tell you about your mum?' he asks Kiara. 'When were you born?'

She passes the photo back to me carefully. 'Twenty-first of July 1992,' she says.

The three of us stare at her.

She stiffens. 'What?'

'That's . . . ' Danny shakes his head.

Edwin pushes his chair back a little, putting his hands on the table as if about to get up, but then he stays in that position, his face turned away.

I manage to start breathing again. 'That's our birthday,' I say eventually. 'Danny and I were born that day too.'

Kiara looks around the room, up at the ceiling, back down again. 'Oh.' There's a long silence.

'Okay,' Danny says eventually. 'So we were all

born on the same day. What do you know about your mum?'

Kiara closes her eyes for a moment. 'She died soon after I was born,' she says, her tone flat, as if she's reciting. 'In India. My dad brought me to England when I was very young, used my Indian birth certificate to get me a British birth certificate, since he's British. I've looked at both the certificates, many times, but my mother's name on the Indian document is smudged, illegible, and the British document says 'unverified'. He says he loved her, but it hurts too much to talk about her.'

Edwin turns to stare at her, his eyes wide.

'Was she Indian?' Danny asks. 'Your mother?'

'No, British too.'

'So why were you born there?' Danny asks.

Kiara shrugs. 'I wonder sometimes whether I really was. It seems a convenient story.'

Edwin says, 'I used to call your father Uncle Alex. I'm sure he used to visit us here the year you were born. I remember him being here with Laura. He never brought a girlfriend or a wife here that I remember.'

'He was friends with Laura,' I say. 'They took you to the doctor once, Edwin, when you cut yourself, do you remember? Pamela Larch told me.'

Edwin looks at me blankly, but Kiara sits forward.

'Is that why you wanted to talk to him? Because he was a friend of Laura's?' she asks.

I nod. 'I thought Laura might have told him something about us after she left here, or they might still be in touch and maybe he could persuade her to talk to me. I thought he might know something. I didn't know he had his own daughter, and his own secrets.'

'So, let's get this straight,' Kiara says, and we sit up a little in our chairs in response to her tone. 'Your mother had a baby on the twenty-first of July 1992. So did my mother. Your mother believed someone wanted to steal her baby. You were brought up as your mother's twins, but you don't think you can be.'

We're all watching her. I'm holding my breath.

She pauses. 'Okay. All three of us were born on the same day. Your parents had one baby, but acquired a second one. Or, possibly, your mother had one baby that was stolen, then acquired two more. Both of our mothers died around the same time. Unless your mother *was* my mother?'

She looks from me to Danny.

'But I look nothing like the lady in the photo, and that would leave both of you with no known parents, and yet you do both look like your parents . . . '

Her shoulders slump. She shakes her head in defeat.

'Well, I'm glad we sorted *that* out,' Danny says.

I glare at him, and then Kiara pulls a face, and then Edwin snorts, and suddenly, we're all kind of laughing, united in our bafflement.

'We could be triplets?' Kiara says. 'Your mum's baby was stolen, and my mum gave her two of her triplets?' She's holding up her hands now, searching for inspiration. 'Was there a pregnant neighbour? A distant relative? An orphanage nearby?'

'I know we're old-fashioned out here in the countryside, but we weren't born in the nineteenth century,' Danny protests. 'There's no workhouse in the village.'

Kiara smiles, then shrugs. 'I give up then.'

Edwin stands up. 'Can you hear something?'

We listen, and I do hear someone shouting. Behind the house somewhere. We follow Edwin out, through the kitchen, and onto the patio. Two figures stumble from the trees at the back of the lawn.

'It's Joel,' Edwin says, and starts to run. Danny and I follow at a trot, leaving Kiara standing on the patio. I'm halfway across the lawn before I realise that the person Joel is supporting is Laura. What on earth is *she* doing here? As I get closer, I see blood on her head and her blouse, and blood on Joel's shoulder and hands.

'Call an ambulance,' Joel shouts. I stumble as I look down at my dress: no pockets, no phone. Edwin, who is closer to them, turns towards us, and Danny nods at him, spins around, and sprints back towards the house.

'What happened?' I ask as I reach them. Edwin supports Laura on her other side, and the two men lift her between them and carry her towards the house. Laura's eyes are almost closed, but she's moving her lips. She's dazed and distressed, and not fully conscious.

'I found her by the folly,' Joel says, panting with the effort of supporting her. He has a smear of blood on the side of his face. 'Head trauma. Need to get her to hospital.'

'It's Laura,' I say to Edwin, stupidly, keeping pace with them.

He grimaces, looking as if he might say something and then shaking his head.

Danny finishes speaking into his phone as we reach the patio, and he and Kiara lift a table to one side so that Joel and Edwin can manoeuvre Laura around into a sitting position on one of the sofas. Laura's eyes are more open now, and she's making an effort to focus on our faces, her head smearing blood across the cream cushion as she turns it from side to side.

'Can you get me a clean tea towel?' Joel asks, and I run and grab one from the kitchen drawer.

'Shh. Keep still,' Joel says to Laura, folding the fabric and holding it over her wound.

Laura has fixed her gaze on Edwin now. She says his name questioningly, but it's a raspy croak.

He kneels down in front of her. 'Laura.' He tries to smile. 'What happened?'

She shakes her head and winces. 'I don't know. I think . . . something fell on me from the top of the tower.' She looks around, and her fingers twitch towards me. 'Seraphine.' I take her hand and squeeze it gently.

'What are you doing here, Laura?' I ask, but she doesn't respond. She's gazing at Danny and Kiara, who are standing side by side behind the table. A fresh trickle of blood runs down her cheek as she tries to sit forward, and my heart thumps painfully. *Stop asking questions or lose your family*. Someone attacked this woman just behind our house. Is this the danger I have put my own family in? Could Edwin or Danny or Vera be next? Or me?

A single strident note sounds from the lane, and Joel hurries into the house to open the door for the paramedics. Laura moans and leans her head back against the cushion. One hand closes over the silver locket hanging around her neck.

The rest of us exchange wide-eyed looks.

'Who did this?' I ask. Edwin, Danny and Kiara shake their heads with bewildered expressions.

Joel returns with the paramedics, and we stand back as they bustle around, easing Laura onto a stretcher, asking her gentle questions. She murmurs something, but she doesn't open her eyes again. As they start to carry her away, I pick up a folded piece of paper that has fallen from her trouser pocket, holding it out towards their retreating backs, but there's no point trying to give it to Laura in this state. I decide to keep it and return it to her when she's recovered.

I hear Joel offering to accompany her in the ambulance, but they say no, the police are on their way and will want to talk to him. We all stand and watch as the ambulance pulls out of the drive and rumbles off down the lane.

Joel turns to me then, calm despite the blood that covers him.

'Do you mind if I get cleaned up?' he asks, and I gesture to the stairs. Edwin goes up with him to lend him some clean clothes.

As I trail after Danny and Kiara, who are wandering back to the patio, I unfold the note from Laura's pocket. My eyes skip down to the name at the bottom, and my heart jolts painfully. I read it through twice, quickly, trying to make sense of it.

Dear Laura,
I desperately need your help. Please will you meet me at midday on Saturday at the folly at Summerbourne? I will explain everything then, but you know I would not ask unless I really needed you. Come the back way, from the boat hire place. I'll meet you by the tower.
Yours,
Edwin

Edwin, my big brother, who is upstairs finding clean clothes for his best friend, Joel. His best friend, Joel, who would do anything for him, and who left our house before midday today and returned covered in Laura's blood.

22

Laura

MARCH TO JULY 1992

The garden, the lane, the village — wherever I walked that March, I was faced with the nodding yellow heads of daffodils promising more cheerful times to come. Everyone in the village predicted that Ruth would start to bloom soon — surely, they said, she deserved a few months of radiant well-being before this pregnancy was over. They were wrong. She suffered aches and twinges; she slept badly by night and napped resentfully by day; she was prone to outbursts of tears and occasionally hysterical laughter. Meanwhile, Edwin's behaviour deteriorated, with frequent tantrums and wild declarations that nobody loved him. Even on good days he took to whining when he didn't get his own way.

All three of us had coughs and colds again through April, and much as I wanted to get Edwin outside to play every day, it was frequently impossible due to either wet weather or the fact that we felt too unwell. We baked biscuits and cakes when we felt up to it, the warm, steamy atmosphere in the kitchen soothing our symptoms as we waited for the oven timer to ping. Even a stroll into the village to collect a prescription, or to choose treats to cheer ourselves up, felt like an effort.

There was no further mention of Edwin attending preschool after Easter, but as the weather grew warmer in May and Michael increased his hours in the Summerbourne garden, we began to see more of Joel again. Only Joel could bring that deep chuckle out of Edwin and make his blue eyes sparkle with mischief, and I begged Michael to bring him over as often as he could. Kemi, Joel's mother, wanted him with her on the days she didn't work, but this left us with a pattern of three days a week where Joel spent the afternoon with us, and Edwin's mood improved enormously.

I withdrew from most of their family activities at weekends, claiming that I wanted to revise for my exams. I returned to Mum's for the exam fortnight, and for once Beaky left me in peace to concentrate on my final preparations. I'd dreamed of a career in scientific research since I was at primary school, and I needed an A and two B grades to get onto my chosen biochemistry degree course. The maths and biology papers went well, and the chemistry practical wasn't as hard as I'd expected. I headed back to Summerbourne cautiously confident that I'd achieve my grades.

Despite no longer having the revision excuse, I continued to avoid family meals at weekends. On Saturdays, I caught the bus into Norwich, spending some of my accumulated pay on clothes and make-up, and going to the cinema by myself. When I grew bored of this, I sat in the city library and immersed myself in a novel for hours without interruption. It was refreshing to see different faces around me, even if they were all strangers.

It was during one of those library visits that I hunted out a book with a lunar calendar. Sure enough, June had two new moons that year — one on the first of the month, which I had already missed, and then another on the thirtieth of the month — the black moon that Dominic had mentioned. It was only when I examined the diagrams that I understood there would be nothing to see. A new moon has its sunlit face turned completely away from us: it would indeed appear black in the dark night sky — as invisible up there as I frequently felt down here on the ground.

The black moon was on my mind as I made a second round of toast for myself and Edwin on that last day in June. The sky was a glorious blue, the sun cheerful, and I felt better than I had done in months. We devoured several slices of toast and marmalade between us.

'Guess what?' I said. 'It's a special day today. Something's going to happen that doesn't happen very often.'

His gaze travelled around the kitchen as he munched on a huge mouthful of toast. He shrugged, spraying crumbs across the table. 'What?'

Something tightened inside me suddenly, and I drew a deep breath. It was a bad idea to mention the black moon to Edwin. What if he said something to Dominic at the weekend? I didn't want Dominic to think I was dwelling on what we'd done that evening — or worse, to think I was talking to Edwin about it.

'Oh, just look outside. It's a proper summer's day at last. I think we should walk into the village and buy some sweets. What do you think?'

Edwin nodded, dropping his last crust onto his plate. 'Can we go to the playground?'

'Of course.'

'And look through the fence? See if Joel's there?'

A few weeks earlier, we had stood outside the preschool field, watching the children participating in a sports day with their sacks and hula hoops and space hoppers.

'Yep. We can do that too.'

Ruth preferred to rest at home, so Edwin and I set off together. The sickly smell from the rapeseed fields had faded now that most of it had been harvested, and the scent of lavender from the front gardens of the flint cottages stayed with us all the way into the village. As the village green came into sight, Edwin and I spotted the low yellow car at the same time.

'Hey, isn't that . . . ?' Edwin tugged on my hand, pointing. I stared. It was almost eight months since we'd last seen that yellow car at Summerbourne. Eight months is a long time for a child who's not yet five. But Edwin liked cars, and Edwin liked Alex.

'It's Uncle Alex's car!' Edwin shouted.

I felt like a clockwork figure, as though someone had wound me up with a key months ago, kept hold of it tightly until this precise moment, and then let go. Whirring cogs drove my heart in a *thud-thud-thud* rhythm. All I could think was: *Has he missed me? Has he missed me?* Edwin and I looked up and down the street and across the green, but Alex was nowhere in sight.

'The shop, Laura?' Edwin tugged on my hand.

The bell jingled as we pushed the door open, warm bread and coffee smells greeting us. And there he was, down at the far end of the right-hand aisle, the top of his hair just visible over the rows of tins. My clockwork heart kept drumming.

Edwin trotted down the middle aisle, and then there was a squeal of delight and an exclamation of surprise, and Alex was walking towards me, his arms outstretched.

'Laura.' He kissed me on each cheek. His skin smelled of soap and limes; his hair was shorter.

'Laura said something special was going to happen today,' Edwin said. 'She knew.'

'Oh, really?' Alex smiled at me, and I pulled a face as if to say, *Yes, maybe I did know.*

Edwin bounced around him. 'Laura only lets me get two things, Uncle Alex, but I really, really want a chocolate egg as well.'

Alex assumed a sympathetic expression, but said to Edwin, 'I think Laura knows what she's talking about. Come on, choose your two things, and we can go and sit in the sunshine, and you can tell me everything you've been up to since I last saw you.'

He held my elbow lightly as we crossed the street outside the shop, Edwin holding my hand on the other side.

'So how're *you* doing?' he asked, slowing down by the bench and frowning at me slightly.

'I'm fine. Great,' I said.

'Hm. They looking after you properly up there?'

I checked his expression but found no trace of humour. 'I'm the one looking after Edwin, remember?'

'Yeah,' he said. 'I know. So, how's Ruth?'

My clockwork juddered to a halt. How could I have forgotten about Ruth and the baby? Or more precisely, his connection to Ruth and the baby. I bit the inside of my lip. *Of course he didn't miss me.* I was pathetic. Edwin ran off to play, and I sank onto the bench, and after a moment Alex perched next to me, watching me.

'She's all right,' I said. I glanced at him. Did he know?

'Good,' he said, nodding with raised eyebrows as if waiting for more, but I leaned back and focused my attention on Edwin, who was climbing the steps of the slide.

'And Dominic?' he asked.

'Yep, he's fine.' I waited four or five seconds. 'They're excited about the baby, of course.'

'Baby?' Alex swivelled round, his knee bumping mine. 'She's pregnant?'

I nodded.

'Bloody hell.' He leaned back and ran a hand over his face. 'Sorry,' he added. 'I mean, that's great. One baby or . . . ?'

'Yes, just one.'

'Good. Okay.' He sat back again. 'How far along is she?'

'Quite far,' I said. I waved to Edwin at the top of the slide. 'She's due in August. End of August.'

He kept his gaze on the houses at the far side of the green. An elderly man walked past us, a small terrier dragging behind on its lead. A cold sensation was spreading through my chest, and suddenly, I couldn't bear to sit there any longer.

'We should be getting back.' I stood and beckoned to Edwin.

Alex rose too. 'Do you think . . . ?' he said.

I waited.

'Do you think Ruth would mind if I walked back with you?'

I glanced at Edwin. 'I think you probably should ring her first,' I said.

He nodded, rapidly. 'Yeah, okay, good idea. I'll do that.'

'Bye, Uncle Alex,' Edwin said, squinting up at him.

Alex ruffled his hair. 'Bye, Edwin. Say hi to your mama for me.' As we walked away he added, 'Good to see you both.'

We paused briefly outside the preschool for Edwin to say hello to Joel and Ralph through the fence. They were being called inside for story time. Edwin complained at me all the way home: 'You didn't let me play long enough. You didn't let me have a chocolate egg. You didn't let Alex come home with us.' The sun was too hot for my long-sleeved shirt, and my skin itched.

Any thoughts I might have had about avoiding the subject of Alex when we got back to Summerbourne were instantly quashed by

Edwin yelling, 'Guess who we saw?' as he leapt onto Ruth's prone figure on the sofa. She needed a glass of water before she was able to speak properly.

'How did he look?' she asked me, and then before I could answer, 'I don't want to see him.'

When the phone rang that evening, I heard her saying, 'I just don't think it's a good idea,' in a low voice as I ushered Edwin upstairs. Feeling childish, I crossed my fingers under Edwin's towel as I watched the water run into his bath. If Alex went back to Leeds for good, it would leave me with one less thing to worry about.

Alex's name wasn't mentioned for the rest of the week, nor over the weekend. Dominic took Ruth and Edwin out for Sunday lunch at the pub in the village, leaving me to enjoy a luxurious nap on the patio.

On the following Monday afternoon, I was on the phone to Vera when I spotted a figure lurking near the end of the drive in the lane. Vera was reeling off a list of symptoms, wanting me to say whether Ruth was suffering with them or not.

'She hasn't mentioned anything like that,' I said. 'Hold on please, Vera. I think there's someone outside.'

I rested the receiver on the table and went to peer through the window. It was Alex, his hands in his pockets, staring at the house.

'Vera, sorry. No, no one there. Yes, she'll probably be up before teatime. I'll get her to ring you. Bye.'

When I opened the front door, he shuffled up the gravel, glancing at the other windows, looking like he was trying not to make too much noise.

'What are you doing here?' I asked, frowning at him.

'I have to talk to you, Laura. Please.' His hair was unkempt, his eyes restless.

I shook my head. 'You can't come in. And I have Edwin and Joel here. I can't come out.'

'Please, just — ' He caught hold of my fingers, held on to them, his eyes pleading. 'Please tell me, Laura. Is there something I need to know about this pregnancy?'

I should have snatched my hand away immediately. I should have closed the door on him and walked away.

'There is, isn't there?' he asked.

With me up on the doorstep and him hunched on the gravel, I was slightly taller than him. I pulled my hand free, but I hesitated. Laughter from Edwin and Joel drifted out from the day nursery. I thought about Alex's unborn child upstairs, biding its time, growing and stretching and waiting to be born.

'I can't tell you,' I whispered.

He stared at me for a long moment. 'It's my baby, isn't it?' he said.

I pressed my lips together. I wasn't sure whether it was him swaying, or me. He leaned closer, his hand once more reaching for mine.

'Laura. Tell me.'

I held my breath. His fingers wrapped around mine. I nodded.

He stumbled backward then, letting go of me. I expected him to show anger, or distress, or some other kind of negative emotion. But elation seemed to rise inside him, and he drew himself up, his chest inflating, his eyes shining.

I slumped in the doorway. I was no longer taller than him.

'I need to see her,' he said. 'I need to talk to her.'

'No.' I tried to close the door, but he put one foot up onto the threshold and stopped me.

'I need to talk to Ruth.' His voice was louder.

A creak of floorboards above pushed my heart rate higher. Edwin and Joel appeared in the kitchen doorway, and Edwin stepped forward hesitantly when he saw who the visitor was.

'Uncle Alex? Why are you shouting?'

Alex's eyes clouded for a moment, and he stepped back uncertainly.

I slammed the door and yanked the bolt across the top.

'Pass me the keys, Edwin,' I said.

Edwin's eyes were wide, but he did as I asked.

A floorboard creaked again, and I heard Ruth's bedroom door open. The gravel crunched outside, and from the window I watched Alex march away towards the lane, his hands raking through his hair as he went.

I ushered the boys back into the kitchen as Ruth plodded down the stairs. Her hands supported her bump, and she had a line down one cheek from a crease in her pillow.

'Who was that?' she asked.

'Alex.'

'What did he want?'

I steeled myself to maintain eye contact. 'He

wanted to know if — ' The boys were chattering quietly in the kitchen, but I was unable to form the words. I looked at her bump.

She sank down on the steps, her face a ghastly white.

'What did you say?' she asked.

I shook my head, my hands making a hopeless gesture.

'You told him? You told him, didn't you?'

I closed my eyes, holding on to the doorframe.

Ruth wrapped her arms around her abdomen and rocked back and forth.

'What have you done?' she said.

'I'm sorry. He asked me outright. I couldn't lie.'

Her gaze was unfocused as she rocked, and I'm not sure she even heard me. 'What have I done?' she said. 'What am I going to do?'

23

Seraphine

The police arrive while Edwin and Joel are still upstairs. Martin Larch, and a younger officer I don't recognise. Danny introduces Kiara to Martin, and Martin gives her a searching look, and then glances at me.

'I knew your father, a long time ago,' Martin says to Kiara. 'And he knew the lady who has just been assaulted. I'm rather interested to know why you happen to be here today.'

Kiara is jittery. 'I have no idea what's going on,' she says, and Danny puts a hand on her arm the same way he does to me when I'm upset.

Edwin and Joel clatter down the stairs.

'You're the one who found Ms Silveira, Dr Harris?' Martin asks Joel.

Joel says, 'Yes.' He's had a shower and is wearing some of Edwin's clothes. I examine him in brief glances, searching for an indication of guilt or innocence, not wanting to meet his eyes.

'It might have been better if you'd waited before washing,' Martin remarks. 'Could you bring your clothes, please?'

Edwin starts to protest, but Joel waves a hand.

'It's fine. I'm sorry. I didn't think. I'll go and get them.'

The young police constable accompanies Joel back upstairs.

Martin looks at each of us in turn. 'Well, this is a bit of a mystery,' he says. 'I don't suppose any of you know what Ms Silveira was doing here today, or who might have bashed her over the head? Anything you'd like to tell me?'

I wait for one of the others to say, *It's Seraphine's fault: someone warned Laura not to talk about Summerbourne, but Seraphine wouldn't stop asking questions.* I can't tell Martin that Laura had a note from Edwin luring her here, even though I know Laura might be telling that to a police officer at the hospital at this very moment. And I'm afraid that if I tell Martin anything else he will tug on it until he unspools all the events of the past ten days, and then he too will look at Edwin and Joel with suspicion.

There must be another explanation.

Martin watches us, and we stand in silence. As the seconds tick by, a conviction grows in me: the signature at the bottom of that note wasn't Edwin's. Whoever sent it had to have known about Laura's fondness for Edwin all those years ago and used that to lure her to the isolated clifftop. I roll my shoulders back. We stand in silence. We shake our heads.

In the end, Martin questions Joel first, and then the rest of us, and as we account for our movements during the day, I have a strong mental image of Martin placidly absorbing each detail into his elephantine memory.

'Why did you invite Miss Kaimal here?' Martin asks me. 'Without her father. And why today?'

In the air between us hangs the unspoken

283

ending of his sentence: *today, of all days?*

'I spoke to Alex after you gave me his details,' I tell him. 'I thought it would be nice to spend some time with his daughter. Our parents were friends, after all.'

Martin's expression doesn't change. He looks at Kiara, then at Danny, then back at me.

Joel's story is that he'd gone to the cliffs to look for Michael, who had failed to return from a walk, and he spotted Laura collapsed at the base of the tower. In his medical opinion, he thinks she'd only just been hit. A team of police officers are already out on the cliffs, examining the site of Laura's attack, and Martin alerts them to Michael's latest disappearance. Of course, Martin and the Harrises have known each other their whole lives, and I can see the sympathy on Martin's face as he makes the call. His colleagues on the cliffs report no sign of the old man.

'I'll probably need to talk to you all again in the morning,' Martin says before leaving. 'Better you stay here, Miss Kaimal, please. Just until we know how Ms Silveira is doing.'

Kiara is visibly distressed. 'I need to phone Dad,' she says as soon as the police car has gone. Edwin, Danny and I retreat to the day nursery to give her some privacy to make her call.

'Shit,' Danny says, throwing himself on one of the sofas. 'What the hell was all that about? Why did Laura come here — and why today? What kind of maniac did that to her?'

I've brought my bag through, and I pull Laura's note out slowly and hand it to Edwin.

'Laura dropped this.'

Edwin opens it, reads it, his mouth falling open.

'I didn't write this,' he says, staring at the letter and then at me. 'This isn't from me.' He passes it to Danny, his eyes still on me.

I step towards him and take both his hands in mine. His feel cold. 'I know,' I say. 'I believe you. But who did?'

Edwin shakes his head.

'Joel?' I whisper.

'No!' Edwin snatches his hands from mine and strides over to the window, keeping his back to me, his shoulders hunched. The contents of his treasure box are still strewn across the table, and, unable to settle and unwilling to break the silence, I collect them together distractedly and pack them all back inside.

I join Danny on the sofa then, curling up at the far end, wrapping my arms around my knees. My mind keeps returning to Joel, no matter how hard I try to stop it. Joel, who knew I had been asking questions about the day I was born. Joel, who had access to Michael's key to Summerbourne. Joel, who knew that Ralph had a propane torch in his van and could have 'borrowed' it. Joel, who was free to wander up to the folly in the middle of the day at the exact same time that Laura happened to be there.

I squeeze my eyes shut. I'm worried I might be sick.

Edwin's phone beeps from the kitchen, and he goes through to fetch it. 'Joel's found Michael, back at the cottage,' he says as he walks back in.

I don't open my eyes. Who's to say Michael wasn't there all along?

Kiara appears then, eyeing us as if we're dangerous strangers, the camaraderie of our lunch together all but forgotten.

'My dad's on his way,' she says.

We acknowledge this with nods, watching her. She moves slowly towards the table, where Edwin's treasures box sits, its lid now closed.

'I wish I'd never come,' she says quietly.

'You can stay in the annexe,' Edwin says. 'With your dad, tonight. I'll show you.' But when he goes to turn the handle, he finds the door locked.

'I hid the key,' I say. Yet again, they all look at me wordlessly. I stalk out to retrieve it from the kitchen, and hand it to Edwin without further comment. Back on the sofa, I listen as Edwin opens windows in the annexe, making small talk. I can barely hear Kiara's muted replies. I leap up again.

'I'll get fresh bedding,' I tell Danny.

Later, when we've made up the bed and laid sheets and blankets out on the annexe sofa, we have cold drinks on the patio, and it surprises me how relieved I am to see that Kiara has regained some composure. Eventually, Edwin heads into the kitchen to set about making an evening meal. I am unsettled, jumpy. I half expect the phone to ring at any moment, announcing that Laura has remembered who attacked her. *Not Joel. Please, don't let it be Joel.*

As we finish our supper, a car pulls up on the gravel, and Edwin opens the door to Alex. Kiara throws herself into his arms. He looks older than when I saw him a few days ago — his face taut, his eyes taking in each of us in turn as if we are the enemy.

'I'm Edwin, sir,' Edwin says to him. 'Do you remember me? I believe I used to call you Uncle Alex.'

Alex's face crumples slightly, and he holds Kiara at arm's length to check that she really is all right, and then says to Edwin, 'Yes, I remember you very well, Edwin. I was hoping I'd never have to talk to you about what happened back then, but . . . ' He sighs. 'I do see Kiara's point, that she has the right to know where she comes from.' He looks at his daughter, and then back to Edwin. 'Kiara told me about Dominic — your dad. I'm very sorry. But has Laura really been attacked? What was she doing here? What happened?'

'We don't know yet,' I say, watching him, watching the shifting of his facial expressions, searching for any signs of guilt. I am wondering how we can be sure that it wasn't him up on the cliffs today, lying in wait for Laura. He stares back at me.

'Who are you again?' he says. 'I mean, who are you *really*?'

I take a step back, bumping into Danny. This is basically the same question that Michael asked me three days ago — *Where did you really come from, my dear?* In one form or another, it's the same question people have been asking me my whole life. What is it about me that makes me such a puzzle?

Edwin clears his throat. 'This is Seraphine, my sister,' he tells Alex, 'and Danny, my brother. They're twins.'

Alex gives a strange bark of a laugh. The three of us stand very still.

'Whose twins?' he asks eventually.

'Ruth and Dominic's,' Edwin says with authority, and then his eyes dart towards us and his brow creases. 'Or at least . . . '

'What did you mean just now,' Danny says, 'that Kiara has the right to know where she comes from?'

Kiara glances at Danny and back to Alex. 'Dad?'

Alex is shaking his head now, backing away from us towards the front door, pulling Kiara with him. 'I can't do this. I'm sorry. We need to go.'

Kiara pulls her arm from his grip and moves back to stand with us. 'Dad. The police said I have to stay here tonight. Please. Just tell me whatever it is. It's not going to go away now.' Alex's shoulders sag.

In the end we all move into the sitting room, and Alex and Kiara take one sofa while Edwin, Danny and I sit in a line opposite them. Alex refuses any refreshments. He's grim faced, but Kiara holds his hand, and I have a strong feeling he is replaying an event in his mind as he gazes up at the ceiling behind our heads. Eventually, he looks down and focuses on the pile of books on the coffee table between us instead.

'Your mother and I . . . ' He clears his throat and starts again. 'I was in love with Ruth. From when I first met her. Before she married your father, and afterwards. I won't try to justify what we did.' He shakes his head, glances up at us briefly. 'We had an affair. I'm sorry.'

I'm sitting in between my brothers, and each of my hands creeps into one of theirs.

'She became pregnant,' Alex says. 'With my child.'

A chill slides down my spine. I hold my brothers' hands tighter.

Alex looks at Kiara. 'When she had you — during her pregnancy with you, and after your birth — she was very unstable — mentally unstable. Dangerous. I couldn't leave you with her — how could I? I came to see you, to meet you, on the day you were born, and Ruth wasn't even here — she'd left you already. You were perfect, Kiara, so — so beautiful. I took you home with me. To keep you safe. I had no choice.'

I am barely breathing. *Kiara was Ruth's daughter. Kiara was the baby in the photograph. Kiara is the person I thought I was.*

So who am I? And who is Danny?

Kiara stares at Alex, tears sliding down her cheeks.

'She was my mother,' she says. 'You took me from her? She killed herself because of you?'

'No,' Alex tells her. 'I didn't know she was going to do that. I had to put your safety first, Kiara. Dominic was never here. If he'd been here when I came to see you, even — maybe I wouldn't have taken you. We could have sorted out a custody arrangement. If I'd been certain you were going to be safe. But I didn't take you on a whim — it wasn't like that. I'd planned it all. I hired a private midwife, to help look after you in the early days. I bought all the equipment you needed. Formula milk, clothes, nappies. I even changed my car so it would be safer for you. I wanted you so much.'

'So much that you kidnapped her,' Edwin says. I've never heard his voice so cold.

Alex draws in a deep breath. 'It wasn't kidnap. I told you, I found her alone in the house with the au pair. Both Ruth and Dominic had gone out somewhere, left her already. She was hungry. I told Laura to tell Ruth and Dominic to phone me when they got back. We'd discuss it, come to some arrangement. I did want to be the primary parent, yes, of course — but I would never have stopped her mother from seeing her.'

'You told Laura?' Edwin asks.

'Yes, Laura, the au pair. She'd been left here, looking after the baby, all by herself.' Alex turns back to Kiara. 'You were a few hours old, and they'd already left you with the teenage help. I said to Laura, 'Get them to ring me, we'll talk.' But they never rang. I had a little cottage here in the village then . . . I'd been trying to sell it, but when I found out Ruth was pregnant with you, I thought it could be a good base for us in the early days. I set up a nursery there, got everything ready. The midwife and I took you back there. But of course that evening I heard what Ruth had done.'

Edwin lets go of my hand, and I think he's wiping away tears, but then he lurches forward and snarls at Alex across the coffee table: 'What she'd done *because of you.*'

Alex gives him an agonised look. 'No, no. I never wanted that.'

Kiara hunches over, burying her face in her hands. Alex looks from her shaking shoulders to Edwin, and the battle to keep control of his emotions rages on his face.

'I still thought Dominic would ring,' he says eventually. 'Once the shock of Ruth's death had worn off, I took you back to Leeds the next day, Kiara. I didn't speak to anyone in the village, we just left. Dominic knew my number in Leeds. For months, every time the phone rang, I thought it was going to be him. But it never was. I thought . . . he must have found out you weren't his. He must have decided he didn't want you. So I sold the cottage in the village. I never talked to anyone about any of it. I never mentioned the name Summerbourne again.'

My throat hurts. I take a deep breath. 'What else happened? I don't understand. If Kiara was the baby Ruth had that day, then . . . ' I look at Danny. 'Who are we?'

Alex really scrutinises me then. My hair, my face, my body. He barely looks at Danny. It's odd. An expression passes across his face fleetingly, a widening of his pupils and a flaring of his nostrils. He looks away, and then he shakes his head.

'I really am sorry if the things I did affected you,' he says, his eyes still averted. 'I would help you if I could. But I honestly — I'm sorry — I have absolutely no idea who you are.'

24

Laura

JULY 1992

The day after I confirmed Alex's suspicion that the baby was his, he delivered a letter to Summerbourne. I hid behind the kitchen door, holding my breath, as he pushed it through the letter box. Once his car had roared off down the lane, I carried the envelope up to Ruth, and she made no attempt to hide its contents.

> *Dear Ruth,*
>
> *I appreciate this has not worked out the way we might have chosen, but I am delighted about the baby, and I fully intend to play an active role as his or her father. Please can we arrange to meet, to discuss how we are going to sort out visits in the early days, and a longer term shared custody plan, etc.? I am happy to meet with both you and Dominic together if you prefer. I feel confident we can come to an amicable arrangement.*
>
> *With all best wishes,*
> *Alex*

She stared into the distance for a long time, and then tore the paper into tiny pieces and burnt them in the fireplace.

Two more letters came that week, and he rang

the house every day. After a while, neither Ruth nor I would answer the phone, and then on the Friday we had an anxious Vera arrive in a taxi unexpectedly, concerned because she had been unable to make contact. Ruth gave her lunch and sent her away again, adamant that she didn't want visitors in the house.

Vera squeezed my hands just before she climbed into the taxi. 'Ring me. Any time. Day or night. And look after her. Please.' I nodded.

Alex stayed away over the weekend. Dominic came home with a boot load of disposable nappies and a moses basket for the day nursery, as well as a home birth kit in a canvas bag. Ruth kissed him when he carried them in. He took Edwin out all day on the Saturday, and gave no indication that he was aware of Alex's return to the village.

'What's the matter with her now?' he asked me while he peeled potatoes for Sunday lunch.

'Just tired, I think.' I made a sandwich and retreated to my annexe, leaving them to it.

Michael had warned us a heatwave was coming, and sure enough, the air was already heavy and warm when we woke up on the Monday morning. Dominic had left at six o'clock for London, and by nine o'clock Ruth and I were sitting in the shade on the patio, watching Edwin play in his paddling pool on the lawn. Ruth was still in her nightshirt, and she pressed her hand to her bump and groaned.

'I was quite enjoying being able to drink tea again, but I think the caffeine's woken it up,' she said. 'Ouch.'

She didn't show any reaction to the sound of a car pulling up on the drive, and I followed her example and ignored the doorbell. We kept our eyes fixed on Edwin, straining our ears for the sound of an engine starting up again.

But Alex was determined that day. He must have climbed over the wall by the stable block. We whipped our heads round when he appeared from that direction, and he strode up the path towards us. His lips were pressed into a smile, but his fingers were curled.

Ruth rose and pointed at him. 'Get out. Get away from my house.'

Edwin stood in his pool, dripping, staring from one to the other.

'We need to talk,' Alex said. His tone was calm, but the tension in his face suggested this took effort.

Ruth turned towards me. 'Phone the police, Laura. Tell them someone's broken into my property.'

'Your mother's property.' Alex gave a short laugh. 'I wonder if she'll press charges when the police explain to her that I'm the father of her grandchild.'

'Mummy?' Edwin said.

I knocked Alex's elbow as I pushed past him, a towel in my hand.

'Hey,' I said to Edwin, draping the towel around his shoulders, 'shall we get some ice cream and watch a video?'

'But I want to play here.' His bottom lip protruded.

'We can put chocolate sauce on it,' I said. He

slid his hand into mine. Ruth continued to glare at Alex. I took Edwin straight through to the day nursery and settled him in front of the television, his trunks spreading a damp patch onto the sofa.

'I'll be back in a minute,' I told him. 'I'll put lots of chocolate sauce and sprinkles on. Just stay here, okay?'

Straight from the freezer, the ice cream was too solid to scoop out. I placed two bowls on the worktop, then hovered by the kitchen table, watching Ruth and Alex through the open doors. Ruth still stood on the patio, her hands held protectively over her bump, while Alex was several metres back on the lawn, his feet apart and his hands in his pockets.

'You haven't told him, have you?' Alex was saying. 'I can't believe you're this close to your due date and you haven't told him yet.'

'I'm not due for another five weeks,' Ruth said coldly. 'And it's not yours.'

Alex tilted his head back and squinted at the sky. 'For God's sake. If you won't talk to him, I will. I know this is going to be hard for you. But the baby is mine.'

'You're wrong.'

'I'm the father. I'm not going to let you cut me out.'

'I'll tell Dominic you're threatening me. You're making it up. You're deluded.'

Alex shook his head. 'I'm not the deluded one, Ruth.'

She stepped off the patio and advanced on him, one finger jabbing towards his chest. Her voice dropped, and I crept closer to the doorway, holding my breath.

'If you don't leave right now,' she said, 'I will take myself and my baby to a place you will never find us.'

Her finger was an inch from his shirt. He stepped back, raising one hand slightly as if to ward her off.

'What are you talking about?'

'You know exactly what I'm talking about.'

He stared at her. 'No, Ruth. I don't.'

She made a shrill sound, almost a laugh, and stepped to the side, moving around him, swivelling to keep her finger pointed at him. 'It's your choice, Alex. You can accept that this is nothing to do with you. Watch this baby grow up like you've watched Edwin, as a family friend. But if you push me — if you threaten me — I will go. And I'll take my baby with me.'

She swung round then, as fast as her distended abdomen would let her, and set off for the end of the garden with a rolling gait.

'What do you mean?' Alex called after her. 'Ruth? Where are you going?'

Her mouth twisted into a distorted smile as she looked back at him over her shoulder. 'To the cliffs,' she shouted.

Something clattered at my feet, and I looked down, my heart racing. A black-handled knife spun on the tiles, knocked from the draining board.

Alex took two steps towards Ruth's retreating figure then stopped. He raked his fingers through his hair.

I stumbled over to the ice-cream container, and scooped out two portions with trembling hands. When I got back to the day nursery, Edwin was absorbed in his cartoon and didn't look up. I fumbled as I placed the sauce bottle on the nursery table, and the sprinkles pot went flying, sending hundreds and thousands of multicoloured strands skittering across the floor. Had Ruth really just threatened to kill herself and her unborn child? Perhaps I had misunderstood. Perhaps her words had meant something different to Alex. A column of scalding acid rose in my chest, and I bent over the table, gripping the edges.

'Laura?'

I swung round, trying to straighten but failing. Alex stood in the day-nursery doorway, a hand on each side of the doorframe as if it was holding him up. Sweat shone on his forehead, and his face had a greyish tinge.

'Did you hear what she said?' he asked me.

I managed to straighten up properly. I nodded. Our eyes didn't quite meet. Edwin continued to gaze at his screen.

'You've got to help me.' Alex's voice cracked. 'The baby isn't safe with her. She's gone to the cliffs. You've got to get her back.'

I gestured to Edwin. 'I can't. I can't leave him here alone.'

'If I follow her, I'm afraid of what she'll do. I'll stay here and watch him.'

I stared at him.

He exhaled heavily. 'You don't trust me.'

'No,' I said. 'It's not that.'

'What, then?'

'I have to stay with him.' Despite me not using his name, Edwin's concentration broke suddenly, and he knelt up to peer over the back of the sofa, frowning at us.

'Where's Mummy?' he asked.

'She'll be back soon,' I told him. I held my hand against his cheek for a moment, stroking it with my thumb. Once he'd settled back down, I forced my legs to propel me to the doorway until I stood directly in front of Alex. His pupils were wide, his breathing rapid.

'Go home,' I told him. 'She'll come back once you've gone.'

'Laura . . . '

'Just go. You've done enough.'

He left. Within minutes of his car retreating down the lane, Ruth appeared from the direction of the stable block. I guessed she hadn't gone to the cliffs at all, but had circled within the boundary of the garden to listen for his car leaving.

'Are you all right?' I asked her.

She held out her arms as Edwin scrambled off the sofa and scurried into them.

'I'm great,' she said. 'I'm starving, actually. I think six small meals a day are the way forward at the moment. Who's for pancakes?'

We gobbled them with golden syrup and lemon juice, out on the patio, gorging ourselves until our chins were sticky and our stomachs bloated. Then we sprawled on the cushions in the shade, sucking sugar from our fingers and dozing, resembling nothing more than a pack of wild animals sated after a successful kill.

25

Seraphine

Edwin avoids being in the same room as Alex for the rest of the evening, and Danny goes off to phone Brooke, so it falls to me to show Alex and Kiara to the annexe and hand them the key in case they feel the need to lock themselves in. They do: I hear the lock click before I've even crossed the day nursery. Back in the kitchen, I consider these strangers we have allowed into our house: I have warmed to Kiara, but something about Alex troubles me. I bolt the door on the kitchen side, blocking their access to the main part of the house overnight. Suspicion works both ways.

Upstairs, Edwin has just come off the phone to Vera.

'I told her Laura had been found here, injured,' he says. 'But I didn't mention Alex and Kiara and everything else. Not yet. It's too complicated. She's going to come down tomorrow, and she wants you to go back with her, Seph. Please do — let her look after you for a couple of weeks.'

'Okay.'

I step forward and rest my forehead against his chest for a minute. His heart rate is fast, I think, or my perception of time is skewed. I've grown up with the expectation that my big brother can always make things better. But he can't this time. He's not even my big brother this time. He's *her* big brother.

I want to talk to him about that, but I don't know what to say. He seems distracted, distant. But as I pull away, he murmurs, 'I don't care who your parents are, you know. You'll always be my sister.' I hold back my tears until I'm in my bedroom.

It's too hot for bedcovers, but I curl up in the middle of my mattress, my head tucked towards my knees, like a defensive creature trying to deter predators, trying to shut out the world. Will Vera still want me to go back to London with her when she finds out I'm not her real granddaughter? Will she end up giving Summerbourne to Kiara? This is all my fault. If I'd stayed away from Laura, never met Alex and Kiara, I could be mourning my father properly now with the support of my brothers. Instead, I've discovered that Edwin isn't my brother at all, and I've no idea whether Danny is either.

Does this story have to come out? Do we need to tell people? Will Kiara want to meet her grandmother, claim her inheritance, keep her newfound older brother to herself?

The worst thing of all is: I have lost the certainty of my family without gaining the truth I was seeking. No one knows where Danny and I came from. *I still don't know who I am.*

I wake early and tiptoe down to the kitchen to pull the bolt back before making three coffees and carrying them up to Edwin and Danny. Alex and Kiara can fend for themselves.

Danny is still in bed when the police car arrives a couple of hours later, but the rest of us congregate in the sitting room to hear Martin's news, none of us wanting to be the first to sit down.

Martin watches Alex as he enters. 'I suppose you can vouch for your whereabouts around noon yesterday, Mr Kaimal?'

'Headingley Golf Club,' Alex says.

Martin's lips twitch, and his colleague jots something down in her notebook.

I pull the note from my pocket then — the note that Laura dropped — and I hand it to Martin.

'Laura dropped this yesterday. It's not Edwin's signature. He didn't write it.'

Martin studies it and then frowns at me. He waits for his colleague to produce a clear plastic evidence bag and drops the note into it before he says, 'And you didn't give this to me yesterday because . . . ?'

I blink down at the rug and shuffle my feet. 'I'm sorry,' I mumble.

Martin murmurs to his colleague, and she leaves the room, taking the note in its bag with her. Then he tells us that Laura is recovering well, but didn't see who attacked her.

'It appears the attacker used a sizeable stone from the parapet wall at the top of the tower,' he tells us. 'Some of the stones up there are quite loose. We believe the attacker dropped the stone onto Ms Silveira from above. It caught the side of her head. Another inch to the centre and the result could have been much worse.'

'When can she leave the hospital?' Edwin asks.

'This morning,' Martin says. 'They're discharging her as we speak. She was rather hoping to see some of you again before she goes home, so I wondered whether a couple of you might be happy to go and collect her?'

Edwin and I exchange glances.

'So you don't think any of us are a risk to her, then?' Edwin asks.

'Our information points elsewhere,' Martin says evenly.

'Seraphine and I will pick her up then,' Edwin says. He doesn't so much as glance at Alex.

Once Martin and his colleague have left, Kiara and Alex argue over whether to leave immediately or to stay and see Laura.

'She was there when I was born, Dad,' Kiara says. 'If Edwin doesn't mind bringing her here first, I'd really like to meet her.'

Edwin makes no comment to this, but when he and I arrive at the hospital, he puts a hand on my arm before I climb out of the car.

'Wait. I'm not sure about this.'

I frown at him. 'She's expecting us now. We can't just leave her here.'

'No, I mean I'm not sure about asking her . . . questions. We could just . . . I just think we need to be certain we want to hear it before we ask her.'

I think about the lipstick message on my mirror, and the blood trickling down Laura's face and neck. The dead bird on my doorstep. The anonymous letter in the bin.

'Because we might not like the answers?' I

shake off Edwin's hand and rub my temples. 'Or because whoever attacked Laura might do the same to us?'

Edwin's forehead is furrowed. 'I don't know. I'm just . . . I have a bad feeling about all this.'

'You think we're in danger?'

He holds his palms up. 'I don't know. It sounds crazy. But maybe I should just take her straight back to London, and you get a taxi home. And I'll tell her I don't want to hear anything in the car.'

I watch him. 'Or we could both drive her back to London.'

He gives me a small smile. 'Yes. Of course. Or you drive her back, Seraphine, and I'll get a taxi home. I'm not hiding anything here, you know. I just want to . . . ' He pinches the bridge of his nose suddenly, squeezing his eyes shut. 'That note wasn't from me. I swear. I just want to protect you. Protect all of us.'

We sit in silence while a couple unlock their car in the space next to ours and climb in, adjusting their sun visors and fussing over seat belts before they eventually reverse away. I lean over and press my forehead against Edwin's shoulder.

'I know,' I say. Another car begins to manoeuvre into the vacated space, exhaust fumes billowing behind it. My hands feel damp, and I glance at them with a sudden fear that they're covered in blood. *Stop asking questions.* We should stop. I should stop. Edwin's right. We should walk away from all of this, before it's too late. Before more damage is done that we might

303

never recover from. I straighten and look at him.

'But I think we have to ask her, Edwin. Don't you? How else are we ever going to put this behind us?'

Laura waits for us on a bench outside the accident and emergency department, looking vastly better than yesterday, with a neat bandage around her head and a sharp glint in her eyes.

'Are we stopping off at Summerbourne first?' she asks as Edwin holds the rear car door open for her.

He glances at me and back to her, his jaw tense. 'Would you like to? A quick cup of tea, maybe, before we take you home?'

Laura nods decisively. 'I'd like that.'

I join her on the back seat and turn to her as Edwin starts the engine. An image of her head wound hovers in my mind, and it's an effort not to stare at her bandage.

'I feel responsible for dragging you into this,' I say. 'I'm sorry. It was me who rang you at work last week, and — um — pretended to have a delivery for you.'

She looks at me calmly. 'I guessed that, Seraphine, after you pounced on me outside my flat.'

'How did you recognise me that day? You said you knew who I was.'

She sighs. 'I've looked you up, online, you know. Over the years.'

'Because you were there at my birth?'

'Yes.' Her gaze remains steady.

'You know the threatening letter you got that day was nothing to do with me? And Edwin

304

didn't write the note asking you to meet him at the folly,' I say.

Her eyes widen. 'I realise someone tricked me to get me to the folly — I know Edwin would never hurt me. I didn't mention the note to the police. I told Martin I'd heard about . . . ' She hesitates, and gives me an anguished look. 'I told him I'd heard the news about Dominic, and I just fancied a trip to the beach, to reminisce. To say goodbye.' She frowns. 'But how . . . ? Don't tell me you fished that nasty letter out of the bin in the park?'

I nod, looking down. 'I'm sorry.'

'Did you tell the police about that?' Edwin asks her from the front.

'No,' she says, and then she turns her head and watches the scenery out of the window for a while.

'Do you have *any* idea who attacked you?' I ask, but she presses her lips together. She shakes her head, and her fingers creep up to the locket at her collarbone. I want to ask her about her daughter — the one mentioned in the anonymous letter. I want to tell her that I know Alex took Ruth's baby, and ask her whether she knows that he never returned her — the original Seraphine, whom he renamed Kiara. Most of all I want to ask her whether she knows who I really am — who Danny and I really are. Where did we come from? But her closed expression makes me hesitate. Perhaps when we're sitting with a cup of tea on the patio at Summerbourne.

'Alex and Kiara might still be at the house when we get back,' I say softly, and her eyes widen, but she passes the rest of the journey in silence.

As we leave the village behind us and make our way down the lane towards Summerbourne, Laura sits up taller.

'Are you okay?' I ask. She nods.

A police car is pulled over on the verge just before the cottages, and as we approach Michael's home, we see Martin leaning on the gate, speaking into his phone. Inside the little front garden, Joel faces him. Martin raises a hand in casual greeting as we pass, but Edwin doesn't slow the car. My eyes meet Joel's for a split second through my window. He doesn't smile.

Danny opens the front door as we pull up onto the drive. Edwin helps Laura out of the car, and she looks frailer here in the Summerbourne sunshine than she did back at the hospital, her bandage glaringly white against the waxy sheen of her skin.

'Gran's here, and she's furious,' Danny says in a hushed tone as he approaches.

'Why?' Edwin asks.

'Because of her.' Danny indicates Laura, and then flashes her a small apologetic grimace. 'Sorry. But I think it'd be better if you just left now, Edwin. Take her home straightaway.'

Laura hasn't taken her eyes off Danny.

'No,' I say. 'She's coming in. She's welcome here. We need to sit down and talk.'

Danny looks from Edwin to me and back again, hesitating.

Then Vera appears in the doorway. Her lips are

pulled back over her teeth, her shoulders are drawn up under her ears. For a moment I'm concerned that she's ill in some way, and I glance at Edwin, expecting him to rush to her aid, but he's rooted to the spot. She stalks towards us, one stiff step at a time, a quivering finger pointed towards Laura's chest.

'Get away from my house,' she says. Her voice has the chill of the sea in it; the hiss of sand against rocks. 'Get away from my family.'

Laura presses her back against the closed car door.

'Gran — ' Edwin says.

In Vera's other hand is a slim metal pipe. She swings it upwards until it points at Laura's chest. The other end curves like a shepherd's crook with a small cylinder attached, but it's not until a flame bursts from the tip, hissing towards Laura, that it dawns on me that this is a weed burner. Ralph's stolen propane torch.

For a long, breathless moment, the rest of us stand motionless. I can't tear my eyes from the flame. Then Edwin reaches out a hand slowly.

'Put it down, Gran. Give it to me.'

Vera waves the jet of fire closer to Laura, and the blue flame reaches for the buttons on her cardigan. Laura flattens herself against the car, twisting her face away.

'How dare you?' Vera spits the words at Laura. 'How dare you come anywhere near my family after all this time? We don't want anything to do with you.'

Edwin eases in front of Laura, flinching at the heat, forcing Vera to take a step back. A rasping sound comes from my throat, and Danny grabs my arm as I sway towards Edwin.

'I'll take her home now,' Edwin says. 'Gran. We'll go right now. She never needs to come back.'

But Vera shakes her head, glaring at him and Laura in turn. 'She'll try to tell you something in the car. Something not true. I'm not having it.'

Alex and Kiara appear in the doorway behind her, and the movement breaks my focus. But Alex pulls Kiara back indoors immediately, reaching into his pocket as he slams the front door shut.

'Gran, stop it,' I say, as Danny tugs on my elbow. 'Let her go home.'

Vera blinks, and then slowly turns to me. The propane torch sinks, and the flame now points towards my shins.

'This is all your fault, Seraphine,' she says.

My throat constricts. 'Don't say that.'

'Everything was fine until you tracked this woman down.'

I shake my head. 'No, it wasn't. Dad died. It wasn't fine.'

Vera lifts her chin. 'We're a happy family, aren't we? We're successful. Look at the three of you. You make me proud every day. But that isn't enough for you, is it? Everything I've done, I did it for you three. But you, Seraphine — you just can't see that, can you?'

'But if the truth — ' I say.

She gives a tight laugh. 'I was the one who looked after you, remember, all those long nights after Ruth died. The truth never came into it

— you were so young and helpless — why would it make any difference where you came from?'

A shiver runs down my spine. This is the first time my grandmother has acknowledged the possibility of something being amiss, of our identities not being certain. I try to embrace her meaning: that it doesn't matter to her, that she loves us anyway. But it's not enough. Her love for us doesn't give her the right to hide the truth from us.

'You were ours,' she continues. 'Our children. Oh, I know they said things in the village, I know that, but they missed the point. It doesn't matter. We don't need to know. I don't *want* to know.'

The torch and its flame rise as she talks, but my resentment overrides my fear.

'You always thought it was me who didn't belong, didn't you?' I sway towards her, and she dips the torch away, startled. 'All these years, you thought Danny was your real grandchild, and I wasn't.'

She blinks. 'No. It wasn't like that.'

I stare at her. She has no idea about Kiara. But I want to understand where her suspicions about Danny and me came from, in case it gives a clue to our true origins.

'But you're giving Summerbourne to Danny. You're scared of what Laura might tell me.'

The flame dips further. Vera's tone is almost reasonable, almost convincing.

'I'm giving Summerbourne to Danny,' she says, 'because I want him to settle down. You know I don't like him being away, overseas all the time. I told you I'll buy you your own house,

Seraphine. Somewhere nearby. I never knew which of you . . . ' She glances at Danny and back to me, starts again. 'This way you'll both be here. Close. Safe.'

I stare at her. 'But — ' I don't know which aspect frustrates me the most: that she doesn't care that my attachment to Summerbourne is so much stronger than Danny's; that she thinks she has the right to manipulate Danny's life choices; that she didn't foresee that Danny would hand the house over to me anyway. She's devoted so much of her life to keeping us *safe*, and yet so little to actually understanding us.

I grasp at the sentence she failed to finish.

'What do you mean, you never knew which of us . . . ?' I ask her. 'You mean you doubted both of us?'

Vera flinches but holds my gaze.

'It's not important,' she says. 'I've never known anything, not for sure. *She* knew something' — she shoots a look at Laura — 'but it's none of her business, or anyone else's. You're both my grandchildren. And even if you're not — ' She swings the torch back up, back towards Laura's chest, but when she turns her face to me, her expression slides into something close to pleading. 'I just didn't know, Seraphine. Ruth told me — I mean, she was ill, of course, confused, but she told me — that she'd done something terrible.'

'What?' Edwin lurches towards her. 'When? Gran? When did she say that?'

Vera grimaces. 'When I was trying to talk her away from the cliff edge. She was talking nonsense, about someone coming to take her baby. I thought she'd become obsessed with the village tales — you know, those awful things they used to whisper. That twins never survived at Summerbourne — one or the other, yes, but never both.'

'No,' Edwin says, his voice hoarse.

'It wasn't that,' I say, but I think only Danny hears me. He grips my arm tighter.

'She was confused,' Vera says. 'Hysterical. I tried to persuade her, I tried to pull her away from the edge, but every time I reached out, she — ' She shudders. 'And she had a moment. Her foot, at the edge. She shoved me away. She said, *I've done something terrible, Mother.* I couldn't — I didn't ask her. It was too late. She stepped back.'

Edwin groans and turns his face from her. Danny's grip on my arm is tighter than ever.

The torch sways, and for a moment I think she's going to turn it off, that it's all over. But when she speaks again, her voice is harsh.

'It didn't matter after that, whether one of you had come from somewhere else. And it doesn't matter now. We're fine as we are. That's why I have to get rid of this woman.' Vera raises the torch and swings it at Laura, and the flame roars louder. 'She wants to break our family apart, and I won't let her.'

Laura screams as the flame singes the fabric of her cardigan.

'Gran!' Edwin grabs for Vera's arm, but Vera swings the torch towards him and he stumbles back. Laura lifts a flap of smoking fabric away from her body with trembling fingers.

A car door slams in the lane behind us.

Vera jabs the torch at Edwin to keep him back, and then swings it in a wild arc towards Laura's face. As Laura raises her arm, a deep voice calls out from the lane behind us.

'Vera Blackwood.'

The torch sways, inches from Laura's bandage and her hair. Vera's focus jumps to a spot behind us. Danny and I hold on to each other, and I keep my gaze fixed on the flame.

'Martin?' Vera says.

The steady crunch of gravel comes closer, and Martin Larch brushes past me, stopping in front of Vera.

'Ah, Mrs Blackwood,' he says. He looks around at the scene as if he has all the time in the world. 'This is a rum'un, eh?'

Vera lowers the torch slowly, and finally, I feel I can breathe again.

Martin beams at Vera benignly. 'Well now. This reminds me a bit of that day you caught me and Billy Bradshaw fighting, out by the boat sheds, all those years ago, d'you remember?'

Vera's pupils are enormous. She nods slowly.

'Sixteen, we were, me and Billy. Remember what you said to me? 'Violence never solves anything, Martin Larch,' you said.'

Vera stares at him. The flame droops to the gravel where the stones shimmer and crackle.

'And you found me that Saturday job, Mrs Blackwood. And made me go back to school. I'll never forget your kindness.' Martin reaches out slowly with his broad hand. 'Now let me return the favour. Let me take that now, eh? And we can go and sit down and have a little chat.'

For a long moment, I'm not sure whether she's heard him. Then she sighs. She flicks the switch to turn the flame off, and he takes the contraption from her.

Martin turns to look at someone behind us. 'They on their way?'

Edwin, Danny and I twist around, and Joel is there, walking calmly up the drive, his phone in his hand.

'Any minute,' Joel says.

Nothing is quite in focus. Next to me, Danny hunches over suddenly as if he might be sick, and then stays in that position, hands on knees. I try to step sideways, but stumble, and then Joel is right next to me, catching me by the elbow. Edwin has gone across to Laura, who still leans against the car door, her face a sickly greenish colour.

Martin takes Vera by the arm and leads her towards the end of the drive, but she appears to have second thoughts.

'Actually, I'll stay here, thank you, Martin. You can take the weed burner, but I'll stay here.'

'Mrs Blackwood, we need to ask you a few questions,' Martin says.

Vera draws herself up. 'There's no need, Martin. Everything's fine.'

'Can you tell me why you asked Ralph Luckhurst to collect you from King's Lynn station and drop you off at the boatyard yesterday morning, Mrs Blackwood?' There's a sharpness in Martin's tone that wasn't there a

313

moment ago. 'And then asked him to collect you from the boatyard again a couple of hours later?'

I give my head a small shake. What's Martin going on about?

'That's none of your business,' Vera says, her chin high.

'Can you explain why there are traces of gunpowder on the passenger seat of Mr Luckhurst's van, Mrs Blackwood? The same type of gunpowder we found on the block of stone that was loosened from the wall of the folly parapet and dropped onto Ms Silveira's head yesterday. I imagine it'd be pretty hard to climb up so close to that cannon without getting some of the old gunpowder on your hands.'

I can't take this in; I feel like I'm two steps behind. Ralph Luckhurst. My grandmother's greatest fan, her loyal ally. A link between Laura's attacker and Ralph's van. Is this all his doing?

'Don't be ridiculous,' Vera tells Martin, but her face pales.

'Can you explain why a letter requesting Miss Silveira's presence at the folly yesterday matches a letter found in Mr Luckhurst's van concerning his sister Daisy's interview at the bakery? Same paper, same ink, same font. The note in the van was signed by you, Mrs Blackwood. Will we find your fingerprints on both letters, do you think?'

The remaining colour drains from Vera's face. I sway backwards, and Joel catches me under my elbows. Vera sags, slowly crumpling into a shrunken version of herself, her head bowed. I

314

see Edwin flinch, but he stays where he is; he doesn't go to her.

'Gran?' Edwin says. 'You didn't write that note?'

Vera shivers briefly. She doesn't raise her eyes.

'I just wanted to talk to her,' she says eventually. 'To persuade her not to get involved. I might have — leaned against a loose stone while I was waiting for her. It wasn't deliberate.'

Laura raises trembling fingers to the bandage around her head, staring at Vera with an expression of disbelief.

Martin makes a sound in his throat. 'Another question for you, Mrs Blackwood. When I spoke with you after your son-in-law Dominic's accident . . . ' He articulates the word with careful emphasis: *acc-i-dent*. 'When I asked you where you were that morning — why did you fail to mention that Mr Luckhurst had driven you here, to Summerbourne, from the station? Mr Luckhurst tells me that when he came back to collect you, you were exchanging cross words with Dominic here on the driveway. You sent Mr Luckhurst away again, and later called him to pick you up from the boatyard.'

Martin's words rattle inside my head, louder and louder. Ralph drove Vera here. Vera and Dad had an argument. Before Dad's *accident*.

'No,' Edwin says. 'Gran? No.'

Vera's voice is small, distant.

'I knew it would look bad. That's why I didn't tell you . . . ' Her head sinks as she talks, and she doesn't seem to notice Laura straightening up and stepping forward. A bubble of noise, halfway between a laugh and a cry, escapes from Laura's throat.

'And you tried to make out that *I* was the threat!' Laura says.

Vera's head jerks up. The two women stare at each other, and then Vera deliberately turns her head away, her expression tight with contempt.

'I can assure you, Martin,' Vera says, 'Dominic was fine when I left him.'

My mind is still scrambling to catch up. Martin takes a deep breath.

'Vera Blackwood,' Martin says, 'I am arresting you on suspicion of the attempted murder of Laura Silveira.'

I sway backwards. The sunlight is so bright I can barely see him.

'And also on suspicion of the murder of Dominic Mayes,' Martin continues.

I try to draw a breath, but the air's too thick, my throat too narrow.

'And also, based on old evidence reviewed last night,' Martin says, 'on suspicion of the murder of your daughter, Ruth Mayes, in 1992.'

A voice says, 'No.' I think it must be Edwin.

Joel holds on to me. The world sways around us.

'You do not have to say anything,' Martin says, 'but it may harm your defence if you do not mention when questioned something which you later rely on in court. Anything you do say may be given in evidence.'

My knees buckle, and I lean against Joel, peering through the unbearable light towards Vera. She opens her mouth and draws in a deep breath, and then she exhales in a long sigh that rolls towards me like an icy wave crashing over my skin.

Edwin's face is grey. Danny's eyes meet mine for a moment, and then he bends over and retches repeatedly. For a long moment, there is no other sound. No other movement. Laura's eyes are fixed on the gravel at her feet.

'Let's get you down to the station, Mrs Blackwood,' Martin says then, his voice remarkably gentle, and we watch as the blue light flashes along the lane towards us. The gravel sprays in impressive arcs. Martin eases Vera gently into the back seat, protecting her head from the doorframe with his large hand.

The sun scorches my retinas and hollows out my skull.

In the silence that blooms behind the police car's fading growl, a gull takes off from the garage roof with a great flapping of wings, and I watch it fly away until it's a speck in the sky, somewhere out over the sea. Then the front door opens and my attention is tugged back to the land: to the broad-shouldered man and the tall young woman with the pink streak in her hair; the two strangers who stand on the doorstep of Summerbourne as if they belong there.

Laura gazes at Alex and Kiara, and her hand rises to the locket around her neck. She clears her throat before glancing at the rest of us.

'Shall we go inside?' she says. 'I think I'd better tell you everything.'

26

Laura

JULY 1992

Ruth told everyone her baby was due towards the end of August. Privately, I knew the end of July was more likely. Dominic continued to come home on a Friday night and return to London on a Monday morning, and Vera visited for lunch on Tuesdays or Wednesdays. The rest of the week, we suited ourselves.

On the Monday following Alex's unwelcome visit — the twentieth of July — Ruth asked me to take him a note.

'Make sure you put it straight into his hands,' she told me. 'If he's not in, don't post it through the letter box — bring it back.'

I glimpsed an anonymous list of demands: paternity claim to be renounced, visits to be of appropriate duration and frequency for a family friend, no hints ever to be made to 'the father'.

'Do you really think this is a good idea?' I asked.

She scowled. 'He has no choice. It's my decision.'

'I just can't see him accepting his own child calling him Uncle Alex.'

'Just give him the note, Laura. Whose side are you on?'

The water from the taps had developed a rusty brown colouring that day, so Ruth and Edwin waited in for the plumber while I plodded into the village in the early-afternoon heat. I passed Helen Luckhurst outside the shop.

'How's Ruth? Any better?' she asked.

'She's great,' I said. 'Thanks. I'd better get on.'

At Alex's cottage, the yellow sports car was nowhere to be seen. A stranger opened the front door: a woman in her fifties, looking me up and down with hostile eyes.

'Are you Ruth?' she asked.

'No!' I bit back an incredulous laugh. 'Where's Alex?'

He appeared from around the side of the cottage, tugging a pair of gardening gloves off his hands.

'Laura. Hi.'

The woman folded her arms and continued to stare at me. I pressed my bag more tightly to my side.

'Can we talk? In private?' I asked him.

The flash of hope in his eyes made my stomach turn over. I followed him into the low-ceilinged cottage, through a small living room to an even tinier room at the back. It smelled of new paint, and there was a cot in the corner, made up with fresh white bedding and a brightly coloured bumper. A baby bath and changing mat sat on the floor next to it, alongside packets of nappies and a soft toy rabbit. My mouth fell open, but no words came out. He closed the door.

'Do you like it?' he asked.

319

I swallowed. 'It's . . . I wasn't expecting . . . '

He wound a dial on the cot mobile, and a tinkly lullaby tune filled the room as the teddy bears on the hanging frame rotated.

'I've done the same at home in Leeds,' he said over the music. 'A bigger room there, of course. And I've bought a family-friendly car. But we'll play it by ear. If the child is safe at Summerbourne, then he or she can just come here for short visits at first.'

He finally read the shock in my expression.

'What's wrong?' he said. 'The woman out there — she's a private midwife. She's going to help me in the early days. I'm not leaving anything to chance.'

I handed him Ruth's note, and stood by the window as he read it. A scruffy blackbird darted out from the undergrowth and snatched a worm from the freshly turned earth of a flower bed. A noise of contempt accompanied the scrunching of paper behind me.

'She still thinks I might back down?' he said.

I turned slowly. 'She hopes you will.'

'How can I?'

I shook my head, but his hand shot out suddenly and grabbed me by the wrist, pulling me closer until his face was only inches from mine.

'You've got to help me, Laura. She's not rational. I'm afraid she's going to hurt the baby.'

I tried to jerk my arm from his grasp, recognising in his expression the same wild desperation I had seen in Ruth's when she read his letters.

'You've got to tell me,' he said. 'The moment it's born. Do you understand? I need to know as soon as it happens.'

'Let go of me!'

He blinked, and released his grip. 'I'm sorry. I'm sorry. But promise you'll tell me.'

I backed towards the door, rubbing my wrist. He was just as deluded, just as irrational as she was. All this time I had imagined a compromise could be reached — that I could help them reach it, even, and they would both be grateful. How naive I was; how immature and useless.

'I'm going home, Alex.'

His forehead creased. 'Okay.'

'I mean I'm resigning. Going back to London. Dominic's on annual leave next week, and then there'll be his paternity leave. They don't need me any more.'

His eyes widened. 'You can't. You can't leave. I need your help.'

For a split second I was tempted to close the gap between us; to take hold of his hand and promise to help him; to tell him we could do this together. We could look after this baby together. Me and him.

I shook my head. 'I've got to go.'

The midwife frowned over a crossword in the living room, ignoring me as I hurried past her to the front door. Alex put his hand on my arm as I stepped outside, and I swung back to him, assuming he was going to say goodbye.

'Do you think I should ring Dominic?' he asked.

I gave an involuntary laugh and turned my

back on him, stumbling on the uneven path. I crossed to the shady side of the lane and began the long trudge back to Summerbourne. My eyes stung, my throat hurt, and my whole body ached. I would probably never see Alex again, and he didn't even care.

The taps were running clear when I eventually got back, despite the plumber not finding a cause for the earlier discolouration. Edwin and Joel were in the garden, playing an elaborate game involving the sandpit and the paddling pool, and Ruth beckoned me to join her in the shade. The apricot tree in the sunny corner of the patio was heavy with fruit, and a freshly picked bowlful lay on the table between us.

'Well? What did he say?'

I sank my teeth into a sun-warmed apricot and wiped juice from my chin before replying. 'Nothing really.'

'Is he going to do it? Agree to my terms?'

'I don't know.'

She huffed. 'I thought you'd have some kind of answer for me, Laura.'

'I gave him the letter. I tried . . . If you want to know what he thinks, you'll have to talk to him yourself. I'm sorry.'

I threw my fruit stone into a flower bed and stalked off to the annexe. Inside the top drawer of my desk, tucked between sheets of revision notes, was the resignation letter I had so carefully written and not yet dated. I decided I would wait until Dominic arrived home on Friday evening at the start of his annual leave, tell them both then, and leave on Saturday morning. It would be less painful than a protracted goodbye, as far as Edwin was concerned. Deep down, I knew that I had to get home. No matter how displeased Mum and Beaky were going to be, I needed that sanctuary away from the people here.

When Ruth knocked lightly on my door that evening, I hurried to open it, not wanting her to step inside and notice that I'd already packed the books from my shelves.

'Would you be a darling and put Edwin to bed for me?' she asked. 'I'm getting lots of Braxton Hicks. I'd like to lie down and see if they'll ease off.'

'Sure. I'll be up in five minutes.'

Edwin wore his new pale blue pyjamas, given to him by Vera the previous week. He had managed to do all the buttons up without help and was pleased with himself. He knelt on his duvet and wrapped his arms around my neck, burying his face into my hair, and we had a long cuddle without saying anything. I sat by his side after his story, stroking his hand until he fell asleep.

In all the time I'd lived at Summerbourne, I'd never locked my annexe door, and this was the first night anyone ever came in and woke me up.

'Laura.'

I dragged my mind up out of a deep sleep. Ruth was shaking my shoulder, her face looming round and pale above me.

'Laura. I need you. It's started.'

My whole body trembled. I dragged my dressing gown on and stuffed my feet into my slippers, frightened thoughts rattling through my mind. I was astonished when I realised that Ruth's mood was one of suppressed excitement. She turned lamps on in the day nursery and laid towels on one of the sofas, pausing to close her eyes and breathe through a contraction every couple of minutes. My feelings about Ruth had ranged from admiration to frustration over the preceding eleven months, but in the early hours of that morning, I was awestruck by her composure.

Her self-assurance calmed the buzzing of my nerves, and after a while I fell into a rhythm to match hers. Between her contractions we chatted about inconsequential matters, sometimes exchanging stories of funny things Edwin had said, making each other smile. As each new muscle spasm began to build, she turned her focus inward, and I breathed along with her, my own abdomen tightening in sympathy.

The night sky was shading into pink when she announced she needed to push. The atmosphere in the room slid into something urgent I wanted to escape from.

'Let me call someone,' I said. 'I can't do this.'

She buried her nails into my arm. 'You have to,' she hissed. 'It's coming.'

It was the last coherent thing she said for a while. She knelt on the sofa, holding onto the back of it, and I paced up and down behind her, fighting the urge to open the door and run. As her vocalisations grew louder, I picked up a towel. There was nobody else. I had to do this.

The head came first, and after another push the rest of the baby followed: pink and long and lean, all slimy and slippery. I caught it with my towel and fumbled, laying the bundle on the floor while Ruth sagged down onto the sofa. She held her arms out wordlessly, and I scooped the towel and its contents up and placed them in her arms.

'It's a girl,' she breathed. She wiped the little face, and a single tear slid down her cheek. 'She's the most beautiful baby I've ever seen.'

The baby's eyes were open, her chest rising and falling gently. I could see nothing of Alex in her round face, her rosy skin. Her tiny lips parted repeatedly, but no sound emerged.

'Are you hungry, baby?' Ruth said.

She rewrapped the little body in the towel and settled back in the corner of the sofa to latch her onto her breast.

'Pass me the bag,' she said, barely glancing at me. 'The placenta will come in a minute. I'll need to cut the cord.'

I squeezed my hands together. 'Do you want me to ring Dominic?'

The briefest flicker of a frown was replaced with a smile. 'Yes. Go.'

In the dim light of the hall, I pushed the heels of my hands into my eye sockets. *Don't cry*, I told myself. *Get a grip*.

I ran my fingertip down the worn tabs of the address book on the hall table, pausing on the 'K'. I gritted my teeth. The number for Dominic's London flat was scrawled on the inside front cover, and I dialled that.

'I'm on my way,' Dominic said. 'Three hours tops.'

By the time I carried tea and toast back through to Ruth, the baby was asleep, the umbilical cord tied off, and Ruth was stroking the tiny face with one finger.

'I'm going to call her Seraphine,' she said. 'She looks like an angel.'

Edwin came downstairs shortly afterwards and padded through from the kitchen, rubbing his eyes and looking at the scene with surprise.

'Come and meet your summer-born sister, darling,' Ruth said, smiling at him. He stuck his thumb in his mouth and scowled. I led him back to the kitchen and made him some porridge, but he refused to eat it.

Dominic's car roared onto the drive just after nine o'clock. It promised to be another warm day, and Ruth had settled herself on the patio with the baby in her arms. Dominic's smile was broad as he bent to kiss her, and then to kiss the baby's head.

'Was it awful, darling?' he asked.

'Of course,' she said. They smiled at each other. 'I couldn't have done it without Laura,' she added, and Dominic gave me a grateful grimace before intercepting Edwin as he wandered past on the lawn. He swung the little boy up in the air and tried to make him laugh, but Edwin burst into tears.

'What on earth's the matter?' Dominic asked.

'I wanted a brother,' Edwin wailed.

Dominic suppressed a smile. 'She'll be just as good as a brother. Even better. She'll be your best friend.'

Edwin sniffed. 'Joel's my best friend.'

'Well, okay. But your sister, Seraphine, says you can have chocolate biscuits for breakfast, to celebrate her arrival. What do you think of that?'

The corners of Edwin's mouth crept upward. 'Okay.'

Dominic rocked the baby and sang to her while Ruth went upstairs to have a shower. I retreated to the annexe to wash and dress, and to finish my packing. I lifted my resignation letter from its drawer and laid it on the desk; it took mere seconds to date and sign. I was still contemplating the finished result when I heard Dominic call me from the day nursery. I flipped the letter facedown.

'Oh, Laura. You wouldn't mind just taking a picture of us all, would you? While the baby's settled, before she needs feeding again.'

I followed him out to the patio and waited for them to arrange themselves into a little happy family tableau. Dominic put a new film in the camera and wiped chocolate from around Edwin's mouth. A familiar squeak drifted across from the far corner of the lawn as Michael emerged from the trees, pushing his wheelbarrow towards the vegetable garden.

Edwin shouted, 'Mr Harris! I've got a new baby!'

Dominic and Ruth both turned and waved to Michael, and he called out congratulations.

'Take a couple,' Dominic said as he handed me the camera, but I felt neither physically nor mentally able to concentrate on getting a good shot. I pressed the button once and handed it back.

'I don't feel well, I'm sorry,' I said.

'Goodness, you should have said.' Dominic frowned at me. 'Go back to bed. You must be shattered. Ruth, I'll go and ring your mother.'

I was trailing after him into the house when he swung back in the doorway as if he'd just remembered something.

'Oh, I'll let Alex know too. He rang me last night — he's at the cottage, wanted me to let him know as soon as we had news.'

The colour drained from Ruth's face. The baby had just latched on to feed, but jerked her head back and began to cry, as if she'd detected the sudden change in Ruth's mood.

'No,' Ruth said. 'Don't. Not Alex.'

Dominic blinked at her. 'Oh. Okay.' He glanced at me. 'He asked me to remind you to get in touch with him, Laura. Keep your promise, he said.' He smiled, and I realised he was enjoying the hint of romance this suggested. When it became clear I wasn't going to respond, he shrugged. 'I'll go and ring Vera, anyway.'

I was poised to follow him in, but Ruth's glare froze my limbs. I wanted to protest my innocence, to claim that I had no idea what promise Alex was talking about, but it took all my effort just to stay upright. She scrambled to her feet with the crying baby pressed against her shoulder and advanced on me, her body quivering.

'You traitor!' she hissed. She jabbed my collarbone with her free hand as the baby wailed. 'You deceitful little snake. I trusted you. And you've been on his side all along, haven't you? Haven't you?'

I shook my head, and as I stepped back my foot caught on the leg of a chair and I stumbled.

'I can't believe I trusted you,' she said. 'You betrayed me.'

She shoved me hard in my chest, and I fell backwards onto the stone slabs. A sharp pain gripped my abdomen, and I curled over on the ground, trying to catch my breath.

'Go,' she said, tears streaming down her face. 'Pack your things and go. Leave us alone. I never want to see you again.'

27

Seraphine

I can't tear my eyes from Laura's face as she finishes telling us about the birth of Ruth's baby, Seraphine.

I'm Seraphine. Aren't I?

But Alex took Seraphine away.

Laura starts to cough and flaps a hand. Her face below the bandage is blotchy; her voice has weakened. Edwin earlier carried a dining chair into the sitting room so he could perch next to her armchair, and he leaps up now to fetch her a glass of water.

Edwin has insisted we don't speculate further on Vera's arrest until we have more information from Martin, but I'm struggling to process Laura's story while images of Dad's accident and my mother's suicide jostle in my mind.

I look across at Alex on the opposite sofa. If I'm Seraphine, then this man is my father. But he's oblivious to my gaze, his eyes fixed on Kiara next to him.

Kiara opens her mouth as Edwin returns with the water for Laura. I'm expecting her to say, *So who am I?* but instead she says, 'So, I'm Seraphine?'

I make a choking sound, and everyone looks at me.

'Yes,' Alex says, turning back to Kiara.

Laura puts her glass down, shaking her head. 'No,' she says.

Kiara stares at her. Next to me, Danny's expression darkens. I am aware of Joel flexing his fingers on my other side. Alex's eyes slide towards me for a fraction of a second before flicking back to Kiara.

'Are you okay?' Edwin asks Laura.

She nods.

'You'd better carry on, then,' Edwin says.

Laura clears her throat.

28

Laura

JULY 1992

I staggered back to the annexe, groaning at the pain in my abdomen, making for the bathroom to splash water on my face. As the muscle spasm eased, a sudden gush of fluid onto the floor sent a shock wave of cold terror over me. My suitcase was packed, my employer had just sacked me, but I wasn't able to run away from this. At some deep level I'd understood for months that this day was coming, that it was inevitable. There's only so long you can remain in denial about a new life growing inside you.

In later years, I read all I could on denial of pregnancy, from dry scientific papers to sensational tabloid articles, and all the parenting forums in between. It happens in around one in four hundred pregnancies, and sometimes persists right up until delivery. The underlying causes are poorly understood, but the only doctor I ever discussed it with told me that mine was a classic case: isolated from friends and family, surrounded by people wrapped up in their own problems, at a stage of life not compatible with rearing a child. The fact that I was taking the contraceptive pill, and that I'm tall and gained weight all over without a distinct bump, made its persistence all the more possible.

I lost all track of time on those hard bathroom tiles. Sometimes curled on my side, sometimes crouched on all fours, alternating between intense contractions of muscle and pauses for gasping in more oxygen. My mind surrendered to my body, and my body knew exactly what to do. A scream filled the room as I pushed the child out of me, and some period of time later it occurred to me that the noise must have come from my own throat. I opened my eyes. The tiny infant lay motionless in the corner under the sink, a blue tinge to its skin, the cord between us pulsing feebly.

A faint noise in the background had barely registered in my consciousness, but suddenly, a voice outside the door snapped me out of my stupor.

'Laura? Are you all right in there?'

It was Dominic. I tried to sit up, but my hand slipped on the tiles. Pain shot through my elbow. The door handle creaked.

'Bloody hell.' For a moment he filled the doorway. Then he was on his knees, bending over the baby, clearing slime from its nose and mouth. He rubbed it with the hand towel.

'Come on. Come on.'

A wet splutter came from the tiny body, followed by a wheezing sound. The blue sheen faded as it filled its lungs with air.

Dominic cradled it against his chest and stared at me. 'Is it mine?'

I closed my eyes. I nodded.

I was vaguely aware of him scuffling and

murmuring, but was jolted awake again by something bumping my side. Dominic leaned against my arm, pressing the baby onto my T-shirt.

'He's hungry. You need to feed him.'

Despite my reluctance and the baby's feeble appearance, some shared primeval instinct helped him achieve a few minutes of sucking. Dominic retrieved Ruth's birth kit from the day nursery and cut the cord. All I could think about was my suitcase and my escape route, but when I finally looked at Dominic's face, I was surprised to see no anger there. His eyes glistened as he gazed at the infant.

'My son,' he said.

As soon as the baby relaxed into sleep, I pulled my T-shirt down and pushed him into Dominic's arms, sliding away across the floor to put a gap between us.

'I can't,' I said.

Dominic stroked the baby's head, and his voice was soft, entranced. 'It's okay. He can stay here. He's Edwin and Seraphine's brother. He belongs here at Summerbourne.'

I stared at him. 'But Ruth — '

'It's not up to Ruth. He's my son. He'll stay here.'

I looked at the spindly limbs and wrinkled skin; the vulnerability of this tiny child.

I shook my head. 'I can't.'

But Dominic's eyes were glowing now, and he smiled as he rewrapped the baby in a clean towel.

'Ruth'll be upset, I know, but we'll work

something out. We can tell people the truth if she wants to, but she probably won't want to. Better to tell everyone we had twins again. It's what everyone wanted, what we all hoped for.'

My thoughts were jumbled. Upset? Ruth would be incandescent. I tried to picture her absorbing the news, examining the evidence, realising just how extensive my betrayal of her had really been. I curled over on the tiled floor, clutching my abdomen. Deep at the back of my mind, I held on to my flimsy guarantee of protection, the one defence I had against Ruth: *I knew her secret.* She wouldn't lose sight of that fact. If I had no other way out, I could tell Dominic in a matter of seconds that Seraphine wasn't his.

Dominic managed to tear his gaze from the baby to scrutinise me. 'Take a shower, Laura. Get cleaned up. Ruth's upstairs having a nap while Seraphine sleeps. I'm going to nip to the station to catch Vera in a bit — she's coming for lunch; she has no idea yet. I'll take Edwin with me and give her the good news.' He smiled down at the baby again. 'You know, I might just tell her we had two, and then when we get back I'll explain it all to Ruth. She'll understand it's the best way. We'll sort it out.'

I groaned as a spasm seized my abdomen.

'Afterpains,' he said. 'Have you got some paracetamol? When you're ready, I'll get a taxi to take you straight back to your mum's. You can sleep on the way. By tonight, you'll be tucked up in your own bed, and this'll all be behind you.' He gazed down at the baby again. 'Come on, my little summer-born boy.' But in the doorway he hesitated, looked back at me. 'Do you want to give him a name?'

I shivered. There was a name I had always thought I would use if I ever had a son.

'Danny,' I said.

Dominic released a breath. 'Danny. Daniel. I like it.' He seemed to forget where he was for a moment, gazing down at the baby, cupping the tiny head in his hand. 'Hey, little boy. This is your home, Danny. You're going to grow up here with your brother and sister, and you're going to be very happy. Aren't you?' He kissed the baby's forehead, then turned to me, blinking. 'Get dressed. I'll get some clothes on this one, and put him in the moses basket in the day nursery for now. I'll talk to Ruth when we get back.'

29

Seraphine

Danny crashes his knee against the coffee table as he barges out of the room, setting the empty mugs and glasses on the tray rattling. I scramble after him, calling his name. He doesn't slow until he's out of sight of the house, round by the back of the stable block. The shed door hangs open, and when he slams it with the heel of his hand, it bounces back at him. He slams it again, harder.

'Danny.' I touch his shoulder, but he shakes me off.

'Go away.'

He presses his forehead onto the shed door, breathing heavily. Bees drone in the lavender hedge, and one bumbles out and zigzags towards me. I shoo it away.

'Danny.'

'She's a liar. She wants — she's trying to worm her way into our family. I don't want to hear any more.'

I swallow. 'I'm sorry.'

'Why is she doing it? Why is she saying these things?'

He turns to look at me, slumping against the wooden door. I shake my head, watching him.

'Why did you go looking for her?' His voice is quieter now but deeper, scratchy. 'Why did you do this to us?'

My vision blurs suddenly. 'I just want to know who I am! Can't you see? I'm not Seraphine. Alex took Seraphine. I still don't know who I am.'

Danny's chest rises and falls rapidly. Even though we're a couple of metres apart, I reach out a hand to him. 'Come back with me.'

He laughs without humour. 'No way.'

'Please, Danny. I can't do this by myself.'

'Don't then. You started this, remember. You don't need me. I'm not even your — '

'Don't say that.'

'We're not related.' He makes the same laughing sound again, but there are tears on his cheeks now too. His voice comes out as a harsh whisper. 'I'm not your brother.'

We stand facing each other for the longest moment, our breathing in unison, our eyes locked.

'You are,' I say.

He shakes his head, his mouth forming a grimace that looks almost apologetic.

'Go,' he says. 'Go on, go back in. You need to hear the rest. Maybe Alex *is* your father. Maybe he isn't. Go back in and ask her.'

'Not without you.'

He chews the inside of his cheek. 'I can't.'

'Please, Danny.'

He growls. 'Don't.'

'Please. I can't do it without you. I need to hear the rest. I need to know.'

He closes his eyes, and I wait. The scent of lavender is overwhelming. We are metres away from where Joel told those students we were the

338

Summerbourne sprites. If Danny doesn't say something soon, I'm going to lie down on the warm grass right here and never get up.

'Okay,' he says eventually. 'Okay. But after this I never want to see that woman again.'

The clink of ice in glasses and the gentle hum of conversation adds to the surreal atmosphere as Danny and I sidle back into the room in which our relationships are being torn into shreds. Edwin gives us a flat smile, and Joel passes me a glass of iced water as I sink onto the sofa next to him. Joel's solid presence reminds me that my childhood was real; my childhood was *mine*. No matter what Laura tells me, no matter where I came from as a baby, my experiences as a girl called Seraphine living in this yellow-bricked house will still be valid. Won't they?

Alex is murmuring to Laura in a dazed tone, as if he can't quite remember why he's here. 'I knew there was something wrong with you when I came back that summer. You looked — different. I knew something wasn't right.'

'I put on two stone,' Laura says, and there's something about the brief widening of her eyes that makes me think she's suppressing exasperation — with herself or with Alex, I can't tell. 'I had to buy new clothes, baggy clothes, stretchy leggings. I told myself it was the long winter indoors, not swimming any more, all the baking we were doing. It's hard to explain.' She frowns intensely, absorbed in her thoughts. 'It's like — on one level, I knew. I knew a baby was in there, that it was going to have to come out at some point. But I — ' She shakes her head.

'You didn't know what to do about it?' Alex suggests.

'Not even that, really,' Laura says. 'I just — it didn't seem fair. I know that sounds childish. But it didn't seem fair, that it had happened . . . ' She waves a hand, composes herself. 'I'd taken the pill. It just didn't seem fair.'

'Did nobody guess? I can't believe someone didn't work it out.'

'I didn't exactly mix with many people that year. Your midwife saw it, I think — the way she looked at me. She thought I might be Ruth at first, when she opened the door to me. But in the village, I was just the Summerbourne nanny — a minor character, not very interesting because I refused to give them the gossip they wanted about the glamorous Mayes family.'

'Dad.' Kiara places a hand on Alex's arm. 'Seraphine and Danny are back.'

Alex blinks at us.

Edwin is still perched next to Laura's armchair, and he takes her empty glass now and sets it on the coffee table.

'Are you okay to carry on?' he asks her.

Danny makes a low growl in his throat, but I think I'm the only one who hears it, and I squeeze his hand.

Laura settles back in her chair. 'Yes,' she says. 'I'm nearly done.'

30

Laura

JULY 1992

As Dominic's footsteps receded, I hauled myself onto my hands and knees in preparation for a new contraction. I knew I still needed to deliver the placenta. But instead of a final stage of pushing, I felt like I was being dragged backwards in time. The strength of the spasms built up again, and again I lost all sense of time and place, until it was over and I was shaking on the bathroom floor.

A second tiny infant lay blue and motionless at my feet.

I leaned against the bath for a while, trying to steady my breathing. Strength flowed back into my limbs as my body finally expelled the placentas. The baby twitched, and I slithered across the wet tiles and hooked my finger into its mouth the way I had seen Dominic do with the first one. There were no towels left, so I peeled off my T-shirt and dried its body as well as I could. A little girl. I held her to my breast while my mind raced ahead. It barely seemed possible that Ruth would accept one illegitimate child of Dominic's. There was no chance she would agree to a pretence of triplets.

Could I take her with me? I gazed down at her

as she sucked. Back to Mum and Beaky, and a house where appearance was everything and mistakes were not to be tolerated?

It was impossible.

They would never let me live there with a baby. We'd be homeless, without family or support.

It was the shivering that finally made me struggle to my feet, my limbs stiff with cold from the tiled floor. I fumbled with the equipment Dominic had left behind and managed to tie off and cut the baby's cord. She had fallen asleep, and I shuffled to my bedroom and placed her on the middle of my bed, immediately collapsing next to her. I watched her chest rise and fall, her head turn from one side to the other. There was no way out of this. Dominic was going to return and find us, and there could be no happy ending.

Eventually, I decided I couldn't bear to be found like this, naked and bloodstained. I hauled myself to the shower and crouched under the hot water, gripping the edge of the shower screen as I swiped at bloodstains on my legs, worried I was going to faint. It took me an age to get dressed afterwards, my muscles complaining and refusing to cooperate. When my hairbrush clattered to the floor, the baby startled.

I carried her through to the day nursery and found a note from Dominic in the moses basket:

Danny unsettled so am taking him to station with me and Edwin. Everything will be ok.
D

I was still shivering as I fumbled a nappy and clothes onto the baby and settled her in the basket. Standing over her, watching her tiny eyelashes flicker as she dozed, I felt a cold calmness filter down through my thoughts. I would stop the futile task of trying to work out how I could fix this, and instead concentrate on one plan: escape. If I could just stay upright, persuade my unsteady legs to carry me on through the day nursery, past the unwashed dishes on the kitchen table, all the way to where the phone sat on the hall table, I could call for help.

In the hall, no sound came from Ruth and her baby above. Dominic's car had gone from the drive, and the house was still. I rested my fingertips on the phone, determined to stay on my feet, fearful that if I allowed myself to sit down I might never get up again.

Even if I could think of a lie that would persuade Mum and Beaky to come and get me, it would take too long. I needed to talk to the taxi company, ask them if they had a driver free who could take me all the way to London — immediately. I needed to leave before Dominic got back and found the second baby. But the taxi base was in King's Lynn; there was virtually no chance they could get here before Dominic did. I needed someone closer. Someone in the village.

My finger stroked down the alphabet tabs of the address book and paused on the 'K.' Alex would come. My suitcase would fit in his new 'family-friendly car'. Alex owed me that much, after everything I'd done for him: letting him know he was going to be a father, liaising back and forth between him and Ruth, keeping his secret safe from Dominic. Alex would help me.

He picked up after the second ring, his voice a boom in my ear. 'Hello?'

'Alex,' I whispered.

'Laura? Is that you?'

I sank onto the chair next to the hall table, my knees trembling. 'Alex, can you come? I need you.'

There was a pause, and then what sounded like a laugh. 'She's had it, hasn't she? I'm on my way.'

'No,' I said. 'No.' But he'd already hung up. The receiver fell into my lap. I looked up to find Ruth standing halfway down the stairs, holding her baby. She stared at me.

'Ruth,' I said. I managed to stand.

'You told him, didn't you?'

'I didn't — I didn't mean to, Ruth, I swear.'

'He's coming for her, isn't he?' Her face was white.

I curled my arms around my abdomen. 'I just want to go home.'

She came down the last few steps, her knuckles bloodless against the yellow baby blanket, her eyes darting around the hall.

'I need to hide her,' she said. 'Where can I hide her? I can't let him take her.'

The baby gave a high-pitched, reedy wail.

'Shh, shh,' Ruth said, and then pushed the baby at me. 'Take her. Hide her. Keep her quiet. Please, Laura.'

I didn't want to hold the child, but she quieted in my arms. She felt solid, heavy compared to the two I'd just given birth to, her sturdy legs drawing up towards her body and then stretching out strongly. She turned her face into my neck, her mouth open, making pecking movements.

'She's hungry,' I said, and the baby confirmed this with another creaky cry.

Ruth strained on tiptoes to wrestle the bolt across the top of the front door. Her face was white, her forehead glistened with sweat. She pressed her brow against the window, peering down the drive towards the lane.

'What am I going to do?' Her whole body quivered. 'He'll be here any minute. He's going to take her. I can't let him take her.'

A wave of dizziness hit me, and I leaned back in the chair. The baby gave a full-voiced wail. When Ruth spun around, her pupils were enormous.

'Give her to me.' She snatched the child from my arms, and then we both heard it: the growl of an approaching car engine. Ruth stood motionless in front of me, clutching the now-silent baby to her chest, and she kept her gaze locked on mine as we held our breaths and listened. The engine roared, then cut out amidst a rattle of gravel. Two car doors slammed, one sharp crack after the other. I braced myself against the crash of the door knocker.

'Ruth? It's Alex. Can you let me in please?' His voice was loud but controlled.

Ruth kept her back to the door, her eyes on

me. My heart thudded.

'Who's that with you?' she shouted.

'She's a maternity nurse. I just want to see my baby.'

There was a thump on the front door; the letter box rattled.

'She's not yours!' Ruth yelled.

There was an exchange of murmurs outside.

'She's a girl? Ruth? Let me in. I just need to see that she's safe.'

Ruth drew herself up and swung around to face the door, and with our eye contact broken, I was free to curl over in my seat, hunching my body against another spasm of abdominal pain.

'She's not yours!' she shouted again. 'Go away!' She swayed for a moment, and I rocked sideways in my seat, thinking to catch her, but she seemed to brace herself and didn't look at me again. Instead, she set off into the kitchen, the baby moaning against her chest. Moments later I heard the distinctive scrape of patio chair against paving slab, and the baby's cry faded into the garden. The doorbell chimed, not once but repeatedly, and then the knocker crashed down again.

'Let me in now,' Alex called, 'or I'm calling the police.'

I looked at the bolt across the top of the door. I had a wild idea of flinging the door open, clambering into Alex's car, and insisting he take me home. But the pain in my abdomen made me curl over again. Even if I'd found the strength to stand and reach the bolt, I didn't have the strength to distract Alex from his goal.

Gravel crunched outside, and I strained my ears — were they moving away from the door? I remembered how easily Alex had jumped over the wall by the stable block, and I was unsurprised after a further minute to hear his voice in the back garden at the kitchen doors.

'Ruth? Hello? Where are you?'

He was inside then, brushing past me, tugging the bolt back and opening the front door. The midwife barged in with an infant car seat in one hand and a large brown medical bag in the other.

I hauled myself to my feet, and Alex caught me by my upper arms, squeezing them, almost shaking them.

'It's a girl?' His mouth stretched into a pleading grin. 'I've got a daughter?'

I wasn't prepared for the tears on his cheeks. I nodded.

The midwife had moved around us into the kitchen and now loomed in the doorway. 'There's a baby blanket dropped on the lawn,' she said.

Alex gripped me harder. 'Where's Ruth?'

My knees trembled and threatened to give way beneath me.

'Laura?' he said, swaying his face in my field of vision, trying to make me look at him properly. 'Where is she? Tell me.'

'Did she run out?' the midwife asked.

Alex shook me, less gently this time. 'Has she gone to the cliffs?' His voice was hoarse.

My whole body trembled. I wanted him to look into my eyes and see everything that had happened to me and realise that I was the one who needed him. Ruth and her baby would be fine. I was the one who needed him the most.

'Did she take the baby to the cliffs, Laura?' His voice was much louder suddenly, his grip on my arms fierce. 'Tell me! Did she take the baby with her to the cliffs?'

I nodded. 'Yes.'

He released me, and as my hand shot out to steady myself on the hall table, I knocked the telephone onto the tiled floor with a smash. Alex sprang away from me, hurrying into the kitchen, and I stumbled to the doorway to watch him jog out to the garden. The midwife began to follow him, but then she made a startled noise and swung back.

'Stop!' she called out to him. 'Wait — come back!'

Alex hesitated at the edge of the patio. 'What is it?'

A smile crept over the midwife's face, and she beckoned him back inside. 'Listen,' she said. 'I can hear her.'

I held on to the doorframe with both hands, my body rigid, and all three of us listened to the thin wail that floated from the direction of the day nursery. The midwife shot me a dark look, but Alex's eyes were bright with wonder.

'She's in there?' All his former urgency evaporated, and he pushed the door open and padded through the utility area to the day nursery quite tentatively, as if wary of startling the source of the noise. I caught my shoulder on the corner of the wall as I followed, and the jolt of pain stiffened my limbs. As the three of us hesitated at our end of the day nursery, a spindly white-clothed arm rose and waved feebly from the moses basket, and my heart battered in a frantic rhythm.

'No,' I said. But Alex and the midwife were already halfway there, closing the distance between their hungry expressions and my tiny daughter.

My throat constricted as they loomed over her. I had to explain. They had it wrong. It was all such a mess. I watched as Alex placed his fingertip in the baby's palm, and her fingers closed over it immediately. He turned shining eyes to me.

'She's beautiful,' he said, and his mouth curved into a smile that I hadn't seen since our carefree racing on the beach months earlier. 'Perfect,' he said. 'What's her name?'

My throat closed. The future hovered like a boat about to raise its sail, waiting for my next words, suspended between elements, tugged by guilt and love and desperation. Should I tell him the truth: that his daughter was outside with Ruth, probably on the clifftop, waiting for her next feed, oblivious to the adult battles waging around her? Should I tell him that this beautiful, fragile child holding onto his finger was unexpected, unwanted, nameless; not his?

I opened my mouth.

'What?' Alex said. 'Haven't they even named her yet?'

The baby whimpered, and he turned back to her.

'Hey, little one,' he cooed. I held my breath.

He stroked the back of her hand with his thumb. 'What shall we call you? Kiara? Do you like that name? You do, don't you?'

When I closed my eyes, rectangles of light from the tall windows glowed inside my eyelids. It took all my effort to force my eyes open again, to make myself watch.

The midwife parted poppers and peeled back sticky tabs. She tutted, and murmured to Alex, and they bent their heads closer over the basket.

'What time was she born?' the midwife asked, not bothering to look at me. 'When was she last fed?'

'Where's Dominic?' Alex asked me.

'She's cold,' the midwife said.

'Does Dominic even know she's been born?' Alex asked.

'We need to get her warmed up and fed,' the midwife said.

Alex gently extracted his finger from the baby's grasp, and as the midwife began to poke the tiny limbs into different clothes, he turned to me with a frown of concern. I peered around him as he approached. The woman was flipping back the straps of the car seat and sliding her hands into the moses basket.

'You look terrible, Laura. I'm so sorry you got caught up in all of this.'

He stepped in between me and the car seat, blocking my view.

'Laura, listen. I'm going to take her with me. To make sure she's safe. Okay? Tell Ruth, tell Dominic — to ring me. We can discuss where we go from here.'

The high-pitched whine of the telephone handset leaked into the room, drilling through my ears and filling my skull with its screech.

'Are you listening? I can't leave her here. D'you understand?'

The midwife swung the car seat sideways as she moved towards the door, hiding the baby's face from me. Alex gave my hand a brief squeeze, frowning.

'This is not your fault, Laura. Okay? Get them to ring me.'

The noise in my head swelled and pulsed. Loud, desperate, relentless. It took me an age to reach the window by the front door. They were gone. Alex and the midwife and my baby daughter were gone.

31

Seraphine

I am Seraphine.

I *am* Seraphine. I am Ruth's daughter. I am the baby who went with my mother to the cliffs. My real father thought he'd taken me — rescued me — but he hadn't. I stayed here at Summerbourne, with a man who wasn't my real father.

I stayed here at Summerbourne and grew up with people whispering behind my back, neighbours scrutinising my looks, friends asking me why I was so different to my brothers, children teasing me that I came from somewhere else.

I stayed here at Summerbourne where I belonged.

Laura looks at her lap while she talks. Edwin, perched next to her, is poised as if expecting her to topple out of her chair at any moment. The three of us on our sofa — Danny, me and Joel — alternate between gazing at Laura and staring at Alex and Kiara opposite. My relief at being Seraphine — the real, original Seraphine — rushes through my arteries, while a proper understanding of what this means for those I love lags behind, like a poison I am trying not to absorb.

Alex is shaking his head, his breathing rapid,

and by the time Laura finishes speaking, his face is contorted. He bends forward in his seat as if gripped by pain.

'No,' he says hoarsely. 'No.'

Kiara sits straight-backed, her hands curled into fists, her eyes fixed on Laura.

'So you're my mother?' she says eventually.

Laura meets her gaze and nods.

'And Dominic was my father,' Kiara says. It's not a question.

'I'm not — ' Alex staggers to his feet. 'Why are you doing this?' He reaches his hands out towards Laura, pleading with her to retract her words, to offer some alternative explanation.

'Dad,' Kiara says, and then there is an awful moment when Alex's gaze slides towards me, slipping over my hair and my face, and quickly away again. I feel as though I have swallowed a large, cold pebble. Whatever else Kiara was going to say dies in her throat.

I'm too distracted by my own thoughts to realise Danny is about to speak, and his harsh voice sends a jolt though me.

'So you left us.' He's speaking to Laura, but he doesn't look directly at her. 'You let *him* take your daughter, and you left me here, and you went home and put it all behind you.'

Laura draws herself up. 'I know I can't say anything to make it better, Danny. Telling you I'm sorry doesn't help. But I *am* sorry, and I've been sorry every single day since.'

Danny growls deep in his throat. 'My father — ' he says.

Laura sways forward slightly. 'Your father

loved you. From the moment he saw you.'

I can feel the vibration in Danny's arm next to mine, and I turn my head and press my face against his shoulder, squeezing his hand.

Alex tries to pull Kiara to her feet, but she shakes her head.

'No. We need to talk about this. Here, now.'

Joel eases himself up as Alex swings towards Laura, and he and Edwin stand on either side of her as Alex lunges forward. She grips the arms of her chair and doesn't flinch.

'How could you?' Alex spits, looming over her. 'Kiara is my daughter. I'm her father. How could you do this to us?'

Slowly, Laura pushes herself up, stepping between Edwin and Joel so that she's face to face with Alex, her dark eyes flashing beneath her bandage.

She lifts her chin to him. 'We all did bad things, Alex. You, me, Ruth, Dominic. Just because we haven't been arrested like Vera, doesn't mean we got away with it.'

Alex's face slowly crumples. Laura's posture softens, and she touches his arm lightly.

'We need to put the children first now.' She sighs. 'I know that's what we thought we were doing back then, or at least that's how we justified it. But we need to concentrate on that now.'

'And if they want nothing to do with you?' Alex asks, his tone surprisingly gentle.

Laura's gaze drops. 'I wouldn't blame them. I've never looked for anything different.'

A silence falls, and I realise Kiara is watching

Danny. I squeeze his hand. But he's frowning at Laura, looking at her directly for the first time.

'So what happened after that?' Danny says. 'After Alex left with Kiara? What happened when Dad got home?'

Edwin steadies Laura's arm as she sinks back into her chair.

Joel settles next to me. 'You all right?' he asks quietly. I'm not. But I nod anyway.

Alex hesitates, but Kiara holds her hand out to him, and in the end he sits back down.

'Martin thinks Gran killed them,' Danny says. 'Mum.' He acknowledges the wrongness of the word with a tightening of his lips. 'And Dad.'

Edwin holds up a hand. 'Danny. Don't. We don't know anything yet. Martin may well be wrong about all of it . . . '

'Oh, for God's sake, Edwin, face facts.' Danny's tone is harsh. 'She was here, with Dad, the morning he died. She was with Mum on the cliffs. She admitted she pushed the stone — '

'No!' Edwin says. He takes a moment to compose himself. He's always had a much closer bond to Vera than I ever did, and his loyalty to her now is almost more than I can bear.

Danny makes a visible effort to calm himself. He stretches his fingers over his knees and frowns at them, and eventually, he looks up at Laura.

'What happened when Dad got home?' he says. The protest in his voice is gone, replaced with a coldness that makes it clear he resents having to ask her anything. 'What happened when he got back from the station and found . . . ?'

For a long, still moment, the rest of us try to straighten the facts in our minds. Did they find anything amiss, Dominic and Vera, when they returned to Summerbourne from the station?

'Dad didn't know about Kiara,' I say quietly. 'He took Edwin and Danny to the station, and he left me here, and I was still here when he got back. Wasn't I?'

We all look at Laura, and she takes a deep breath.

32

Laura

JULY 1992

I sat at the kitchen table after Alex and the midwife and the baby had gone. I ate a bowl of cornflakes with milk, and then a second one, wiping tears from my cheeks between mouthfuls. No figure appeared from the back of the garden, but I had neither the physical nor the mental strength to go out and look for Ruth and Seraphine.

I guess I'd been sitting at that table for around fifteen minutes when Dominic's car pulled up on the drive. Vera appeared in the kitchen first, carrying Danny in the infant car seat, and Dominic and Edwin clattered in behind her. Dominic didn't make eye contact with me, but muttered something about Ruth and headed off upstairs.

Vera cooed at Danny as she lifted him from the car seat. 'Where's your mummy, little baby boy? Are you hungry? We need to fatten you up, don't we?'

The chair scraped the tiles as I stood. My baby son. When he whimpered, my hand reached towards him involuntarily. Vera frowned at me.

'Laura, you look dreadful. Were you up all night? You should go back to bed.'

'Where's Mummy?' Edwin asked, peering out at the garden.

Dominic strode into the kitchen. 'Where are they, Laura? Where's Ruth?'

My knees gave way, and I dropped back onto my chair. I pointed through the open doors. 'She went out.'

'What?' Dominic said. He and Vera exchanged glances. 'Why?'

The baby boy whimpered again. I shook my head, watching the tiny mouth open and close.

'How long ago?' Vera asked.

Dominic said, 'Did she take Seraphine with her? Laura?' and when I didn't respond, he turned to Vera. 'I'll go and find her.'

'Do you have bottles?' Vera asked him. 'Formula?'

Dominic shook his head.

'I'll come with you,' Vera said. I thought she was about to hand the baby to me, but Dominic intercepted, scooping him out of her arms and carrying him to the day nursery. A creaky cry trailed behind him as he returned, and he shut the door firmly.

'Sit tight. We'll be back in a few minutes.' He rested his hand on my arm for a moment, his wide eyes searching mine, and then the two of them hurried off down the garden.

'Danny's hungry,' Edwin said, watching the retreating figures.

'Yes.'

'I hope Mummy comes back soon.' He helped himself to cornflakes, and I poured milk onto them for him.

Dominic ran back across the lawn within a few minutes, with Seraphine in his arms. He went straight to the phone in the hall.

'Ambulance, please. My wife's unwell. She's just given birth, she's very confused. I'm afraid she's going to hurt herself.'

I held my breath, watching Edwin's face. He stirred his cornflakes, frowning.

'On the cliffs,' Dominic said. 'No, she won't listen. I need someone here right now.'

He marched back into the kitchen and dragged me to my feet, the baby held firmly against his chest with his other hand. I had no choice but to stagger along behind him as he ploughed on into the day nursery. He lay Seraphine down at the opposite end of the moses basket to Danny, their feet alongside each other's. Both babies — the robust little girl and the fragile little boy — made moaning noises and turned their heads from side to side.

'What happened?' Dominic hissed at me. He glanced at Edwin, who hovered in the middle of the room, and managed to gain some control over his voice. 'Go back to the kitchen, Edwin, and finish your cereal. Now.'

I swayed on my feet, and Dominic caught me by the elbow, supporting me. He marched me back to the kitchen, out to the patio, propelling me onwards each time I stumbled. Edwin sat at the kitchen table and watched us pass, his eyes wide.

'Did you tell her about Danny?' Dominic said. 'She's not making any sense. You've got to come and get Vera away so I can talk to Ruth properly.'

He tried to hurry, but I couldn't keep up with him, and my legs buckled under me at the edge of the lawn. He crouched in front of me, gripping my hands.

'Please, Laura. We need to hurry. Vera's bound to be going on about the twins, and Ruth won't know . . . I need to talk to her alone.'

'I can't.'

'You have to. Something's wrong with her. With Ruth. I think she's hallucinating.'

Bright greenery whirled through my field of vision, and I closed my eyes against a surge of nausea.

'Please.' He half lifted me from the grass. 'You've got to come. She keeps saying — I don't know what's wrong with her — she keeps saying someone's coming to take her baby.'

I sank my nails into his arm, and he flinched. 'He's already taken her,' I croaked.

He let me drop back onto the lawn and stared at me, and then his gaze flitted to the day-nursery windows. 'You're . . . What's wrong with you? No one's *taken* her. You're not making sense.'

A siren sounded in the distance.

He gestured at the house. 'Both our babies are in there. Seraphine and Danny. I just need to tell her about Danny. Make her understand.' He gave me an agonised look. 'Please, Laura. Help me.'

I nodded, and struggled to my feet, but before we made it halfway across the lawn, I fell again. The spinning in my head was worse than ever. Dominic hesitated.

'Go,' I said. 'I can't. I'm sorry.'

A siren sounded louder in the lane, and then another.

'Where's Edwin?' Dominic said suddenly. I followed his gaze through the open back doors. Edwin's chair at the kitchen table stood empty. Something small and white on the patio caught my attention: a cereal bowl, just outside the kitchen doors, broken neatly into two halves which tilted away from each other, spreading milk and cornflakes onto the stone slabs.

'Edwin?' Dominic called. 'Edwin!' He turned a full circle, his eyes searching the windows, the hedge, the trees at the back of the garden. 'Edwin!'

I staggered to my feet. 'Is the back gate open?'

Dominic stared at me, wild-eyed.

Another burst of siren noise reached us, accompanied by pounding at the front door and raised voices. A man in green uniform appeared from the direction of the stable block as Dominic turned and ran towards the gate and the cliffs. The medic jogged over to me, and I pointed after Dominic.

'A little boy,' I said. 'Edwin. He's four.'

'We were called about a woman, miss.'

'Yes, but — I think he's gone to the cliffs as well.'

A police officer appeared behind him, and then another. 'Can you give us the keys to the front door, please, Miss . . . ?'

'Laura,' I said. 'Laura Silveira.' I took a couple of steps but was seized by a violent shaking. 'They're in the hall table. In the drawer.'

Someone caught me as I stumbled, and helped me as far as the patio, where I sank onto a chair. Harsh voices stuttered from a radio indoors. More sirens wailed in the lane, doors slammed, sharp questions shot back and forth. Men and women in uniform jogged out of the house and away across the lawn. None of them so much as glanced at me.

I didn't realise my eyes were closed until a woman in green shook my shoulder and made me jump.

'Is there any formula in the house, do you know? For the babies. They're mighty hungry.'

I shook my head. 'Is Edwin okay? Have you found him?'

She looked at me blankly.

Figures emerged from the trees at the back of the garden, and I sat up straighter. Two police officers hurried straight into the house, and the woman in green jogged over to meet her colleagues in the middle of the lawn where they held a murmured conversation. Louder voices rose inside the house. I closed my eyes again and concentrated on fragments of sentences.

' . . . fire engine along the cliffs from the boatyard . . . '

' . . . could be anywhere . . . '

'Is there any chance . . . ?'

' . . . too late.'

Above all of this floated a high-pitched, hungry wail that made me grunt as my insides contracted.

A young police officer came to sit with me, introducing himself as PC Martin Larch. He rested a large hand on my arm for a moment.

'Are you feeling all right, Miss Silveira? You look terrible,' he said.

'Have you found him?'

'Edwin? Not yet, but we will. We're checking the house and the garden — he's probably hiding somewhere.'

I struggled to sit forward. 'He went to the cliffs. I'm sure of it. He went to find his mum.'

'I need to ask you about Mrs Mayes, Miss Silveira. About Ruth. When did you last see her?'

I stared at him. I held on to the arm of my chair more tightly. 'Why? What's happened?'

He cleared his throat. 'I'm sorry,' he said. 'I'm very sorry to have to tell you that Mrs Mayes fell from the clifftop a short while ago.'

I shook my head. *Fell from the clifftop. Fell from the clifftop.* 'What did you say?'

He nodded, and he scrunched his face so tight for a second that his eyes closed almost completely.

Tears splashed onto my lap, and onto the cream Summerbourne patio cushions. Tears that I'd been holding back for hours. Tears that I'd been holding back since the night with Dominic, since the boat ride with Alex, since my first glimpse of the Summerbourne au pair advert which offered a new beginning I knew I didn't deserve. The young police officer, with the battle between his professional feelings and his personal feelings raging on his face, held my hand while the tears fell.

'Not Edwin?' I asked eventually.

'No, no,' he said. 'Vera — Mrs Blackwood

— saw it happen. Edwin wasn't with them. We'll find him. Did you see Mrs Mayes before she went to the cliffs? You were here with her this morning when she delivered the babies?'

I swallowed. 'Yes.'

'What frame of mind was she in? Did something happen to upset her?'

My field of vision swayed again, and his face seemed to part into two pale disks, and my eyes weren't sure which of them to focus on.

'I don't know,' I said.

He let out a puff of air.

'You really don't look well. Can I get you a glass of water?'

'Please,' I whispered. 'Find Edwin. They lost Theo. They can't lose . . . '

Martin Larch nodded. 'I know,' he said. 'Stay here.' He left me then, and I closed my eyes again, unable to separate individual words from the background murmur of voices and crackle of radios in the house behind me, unable to think coherently at all.

A while later, the woman in green tapped my shoulder. 'Are you okay there?'

I stared at her. 'Edwin?' I asked. 'Have they found him?'

'I don't know. Not yet.'

Uniformed strangers continued to bustle out of the house periodically and trot away down the lawn, while other people spilled out onto the patio — neighbours, acquaintances from the village, their bright eyes drinking in the scene. Several cast sideways looks at me, but none ventured near enough to speak to me.

Voices rose inside the house, and then a figure came jogging out of the trees. It was Martin Larch. He slowed as he approached the house, and his eyes sought mine.

'They've found him. Both boys, actually — little Joel Harris was up there too — ran off from his grandad and hid with Edwin.' He passed a broad hand over his forehead, and I realised suddenly that he knew them all: Ruth, Vera, Dominic, Michael. Martin Larch had probably known them all since he was a small child himself. 'The boys had locked themselves in the tower,' he said. 'Michael just got the door open, got them out.'

I brought my hands to my cheeks. 'And they're okay, the boys?'

He straightened his shoulders. 'They're fine. More than can be said for you, I think. Did someone get you a glass of water?'

'I just want to go home,' I said.

Michael appeared from the back of the garden then, leading Edwin and Joel by their hands. A brief surge of strength flooded into my limbs, and I struggled to my feet as they approached, holding my arms out towards Edwin. But Dominic ran from the trees behind them and caught up with them before they reached me. His face was white, but his eyes flashed as he scooped Edwin into his arms. The little boy buried his face into his father's shoulder. Dominic swept past me as if he didn't see me, disappearing into the house with his son. I sank down again.

Martin nodded. 'I saw your suitcase, and your

letter. We'll get you home as soon as we can. London, isn't it?' He placed one large hand on my shoulder as I tried to bring my breathing under control. 'It's the shock, miss. I think you'll feel better when you're home. I'm sorry about Mrs Mayes, I really am. They'll send someone to your home in London tomorrow to take a statement.'

And then Vera emerged from the trees, like an apparition from a nightmare. A police officer supported her on one side and a paramedic on the other. Her mascara ran in streaks down her face, and her mouth was skewed to one side. Her faltering steps brought her steadily closer. A tremor seized my neck muscles, and the more I tried to hold my head still, the more unsteady it became. I had to tell her. I had to claw into Vera's pain at this awful moment and tell her the truth about the new Summerbourne twins. I wasn't strong enough to carry the secret away with me unshared.

She stepped up onto the patio.

'Vera,' I said.

She stumbled sideways, the police officer dipping a shoulder to steady her. Her head swung in my direction, her gaze somewhere near my feet.

'The babies,' I said. 'I need to tell you something.'

Her expression didn't alter; I wasn't sure she could hear me.

'I'm sorry,' I said, a little louder. The words scraped in my throat. 'About everything. But the babies . . . '

Vera raised bloodshot eyes to mine, and for a second her brow lifted as if she was forming a question. *Whose? Whose babies are they?* I opened my mouth, searching for the right words. Then the paramedic cleared her throat, and suddenly, Vera's expression tightened.

'No,' she said. It was like ice sliding over my skin.

I swallowed. 'They're not — '

She lurched towards me, her face contorted, and I gripped the chair, pressing myself back into the cushion.

'I said no,' she hissed. Her face loomed over mine. 'You have nothing to say to me.'

I stared at her, my chest tight. Her gaze bored into mine; I was unable to look away.

'You don't belong here,' she said, and her voice dropped further as she leaned even closer. 'You have nothing to say that I want to hear. Get out of my house.'

The police officer supporting her frowned at me as she and the paramedic helped Vera straighten and shuffle away into the house. A gaggle of neighbours stood transfixed on the lawn, their lips parted, their eyes wide. Martin paused by my chair and lowered his voice so he wouldn't be overheard.

'Don't take it personally,' he said. 'She's lashing out. She'll talk to you in good time, I'm sure.'

I shook my head. I knew now that Vera would never talk to me about this, would never agree to listen. She must have suspected that something was amiss, but that expression on her face told me everything I needed to know. Vera wanted these babies — she needed these babies — and she would do everything in her power to keep them. The truth was unnecessary, irrelevant, when weighed against Vera and her Summerbourne twins.

A while later, Martin told me a taxi had arrived for me, and he carried my suitcase out to the lane where the driver was waiting. Two ambulances purred on the driveway with their back doors open, a baby being examined in each. Martin placed his broad hand on the top of my head as I ducked into the taxi's back seat. The driver was the same man who'd delivered me from King's Lynn station eleven months earlier, but neither he nor I acknowledged it.

I closed my eyes as we pulled away, but the image of Summerbourne's honey-coloured bricks bathed in swirling blue light haunted my dreams from that night onwards.

Ruth was dead. Kiara was taken. Dominic had no idea that Seraphine wasn't his. Vera had met both Danny and Seraphine, but I suspected a seed of doubt about their identities had been planted in her mind. And as for Alex — down the road in his cottage, falling in love with a baby that would never be reclaimed but who wasn't his — what had I done to Alex?

It's best for the children, I told myself, repeatedly, as the taxi bore me away. I was convinced that Kiara would be doted on by Alex. And I had to trust that Danny would be safe alongside Edwin and Seraphine — his half-brother and his non-sister — within the golden walls of Summerbourne. I had to believe that Vera, Dominic and Alex would always protect those children as if they were their own.

33

Seraphine

Laura's fingers curl around her locket while she talks, but they return to her lap when she stops. We sit in silence as her final words sink in, and I suspect we are all trying to process the same mental image: pulses of blue light on yellow bricks, the two babies that half belonged, the one baby that was taken.

Laura rests her gaze on the coffee table in front of her while she waits for us to gather our thoughts, and I blink with recognition. I have seen this same stillness in Danny when he's preparing for me to grill him for information.

'And did the police question you the next day?' Kiara asks eventually.

Laura nods. 'They came to see me at Mum's. I was in bed. I told them I didn't know why Ruth had run to the cliffs. I didn't know which private doctor she had seen in London. I didn't know what had upset her.'

Alex passes a hand over his eyes.

'And Dad never knew I wasn't . . . ?' I ask, my heart squeezing when I say his name as if I'm betraying his memory. *I am not the betrayer*, I remind myself.

Laura's forehead creases. 'I really don't think so. I don't think the possibility you might not be his would ever have crossed his mind.'

'And you never told anyone?' Danny asks. He doesn't look at her directly. 'You never tried to get us back?'

'I — ' Laura's hand creeps up to her locket. 'After Vera wouldn't listen to me, I thought — what would I achieve by telling anyone? I had nothing to offer you, either of you. Beaky would have kicked me out if I'd taken you back there. You were better off where you were, with people who could look after you. And after the first year or two . . . I mean, how could I?'

Danny grunts. 'So you — what? Moved on with a clear conscience?'

Laura gazes at him, but he won't meet her eye.

'Do you have other children?' Kiara asks.

'No, I . . . ' Laura presses herself further back into her chair. 'I stayed inside at my mum's house for months afterwards. I didn't tell them anything about you, of course. I literally stayed in bed for weeks. I didn't care about anything — I didn't have any *emotions* about anything.' She breathes deeply, in and out. 'My mum was so worried, at one point she asked my aunt to come and see me. But they're twins, my mum and my aunt, and they'd barely spoken in years, and it just made it worse — reminded me what I'd done. What I'd lost.'

'What about your A levels?' Edwin asks.

'Three As.' She sighs. 'But that was it. I couldn't face going out to the shops for a long time, let alone the thought of moving to another city, starting a degree course. I got a job with a local company eventually, when I started feeling stronger. In a small office, part time at first. It

371

took me another year to save up enough money to move out.'

'And after that?' Alex asks.

Laura shakes her head at him wordlessly. The silence lengthens, but just as it seems she's going to offer no further reply, she opens her mouth.

'I've been alone ever since,' she says.

Alex leans back and closes his eyes as if he's in pain.

Edwin is hunched on his chair at Laura's side, glancing frequently at the phone on the coffee table. He spoke to Martin briefly while I was persuading Danny to come back inside earlier, and Martin told him he might be allowed a short visit with Vera before the end of the day. I know Edwin's desperate to see her, but I'm not sure I'll want to go with him, and I doubt Danny will either.

Danny shifts restlessly on the sofa next to me as though he's considering leaving again. I reach out and touch his arm, but he shakes me off, turning on me.

'You know this is all your fault, don't you?' His eyes are red rimmed, furious. 'You heard what Martin said — Vera was here, arguing with Dad, and then she — ' He waves a hand.

Edwin's voice is sharp. 'Danny. Stop.'

Danny ignores him, and continues to glare at me. 'I bet Dad was dreading having to tell us I wasn't Ruth's son. But because of *you* he felt he had no choice. If he didn't say anything, he knew Vera would give Summerbourne to me, and then *you'd* make all our lives hell. If you weren't so fixated on this bloody house, there wouldn't have been an issue, and they wouldn't have argued, and Vera wouldn't have — '

'Danny!' Edwin roars.

My jaw hangs open. The injustice is like a slap to the face.

'Take that back,' Edwin says to Danny. 'We're not discussing what Gran's accused of until we know the facts. And none of this is Seraphine's fault.'

Joel slides his hand over mine, and I lean against him, keeping my eyes on Danny as he breathes rapidly, inches away from me, curling and uncurling his fingers. He won't look at me, and my chest feels too tight, and I fight back tears.

'Edwin's right,' Alex says suddenly, and even Danny looks at him, startled. I hold my breath. Is Alex about to defend me? Can I bear it if my stranger father has to protect me from the twin brother I have lost all claim to?

'None of this was Seraphine's fault,' Alex says. 'It was all Vera's fault.'

Danny rocks in his seat, and it's almost as if he's nodding. Joel's arm is warm against mine, and I close my eyes for a moment, thinking about the charges against Vera.

'Do you really think that?' I say, and I try to look directly at Alex, but it's easier to let my gaze skip to each of the others. 'I mean, really? Can you really believe Vera would have done those things?'

Edwin opens his hands in a pleading gesture. 'Come on. We need to be on Gran's side. Who'll defend her if we won't? What chance will she have? There are no witnesses — no one saw any of it.'

Next to me, Joel clears his throat. 'Actually, that's not quite true.'

Edwin stares at him. 'What?'

'That no one saw any of it,' Joel says. 'That day — we hid in the tower, do you remember? Your mum and your gran and my grandad — they were all shouting. Your gran told my grandad to go away, and he did, but we hid in the tower, you and me.'

Edwin frowns. 'The robin.'

Joel's voice is soft. 'We locked ourselves in. They were shouting, screaming at each other, Ruth and Vera. We were scared. You stayed at the bottom, Edwin, but I went up to the top and I saw them.'

'*The robin's dead,*' Edwin says slowly. 'That's what Gran was shouting. And, *Theo's dead. I can't lose another one.*' He leans back on the chair. 'Robin. Mum's brother who died.'

Joel sighs. 'I don't remember that.'

'What then?' Edwin says. 'What did you see from the top?'

'The thing is,' Joel says, 'I don't remember it. But last night, after Martin found out about Vera arguing with your dad, he dug out all the statements from when your mum died. And he came to see me, because he found something that Grandad had said . . . '

'Go on,' Edwin says.

'When Grandad was putting me to bed that night — just a few hours after your mum died — I told him I saw . . . ' Joel raises his palms.

'Apparently, I told him I saw your gran push your mum over the edge.'

Edwin stares at him.

'I'm sorry,' Joel says.

Edwin makes an effort to relax his muscles, forcing his shoulders down.

'That's what Martin meant by reviewing old evidence?' Edwin says eventually. 'Hardly something that would stand up in court. The word of a four-year-old child, reported by a man known for telling tall stories.'

Joel doesn't flinch. 'I know.' He continues to look Edwin in the eye. 'And maybe I was wrong. Maybe what I saw was your gran trying to catch your mum. The police evidently dismissed it at the time.'

Edwin tilts his head back, thinking. Next to me, Danny shakes his head.

Alex clears his throat. 'You know, Vera always was the pack leader. She must have been so happy when Dominic told her the family had twins again. If Ruth told her, on the cliffs, that she'd only had one baby, that she'd done something terrible . . . Vera must have seen her dream of having new twins at Summerbourne about to be snatched away from her.'

Kiara stares at him as if she hardly knows him. 'That doesn't mean she pushed her.'

Alex has the grace to look uncomfortable. I study him surreptitiously. This man is my father; he loved my mother, and he fought with her — over me. I drop my gaze when I realise Kiara is watching me. When Alex speaks again, he focuses only on Joel, as if finally remembering

375

who he is, or who he was all those years ago.

'Your grandfather,' Alex says. 'Michael. He still lives here? What did he say about his old statement when Martin dug it out?'

Joel tenses. I twist my hand under his so I can hold on to him.

'He wasn't lucid,' Joel says. 'He has dementia. He rambled on about twins and witches' cloaks and stolen babies.' He lifts his chin and looks at me rather than at Alex. 'It made me think — Grandad's obsession with the twin stories, and people falling over the cliff. I think that's where my nightmares about Theo came from. I mixed up my memories of seeing your mother fall with Grandad's stories, and started worrying that everything was my fault.'

I squeeze his hand, not knowing what to say. Perhaps if one good thing comes from all this, it will be that Joel can finally put the gruesome childhood tales about our family behind him.

'Poor Michael,' Laura says.

Edwin makes a noise in his throat. 'Just . . . let's remember,' he says. 'Like Joel said, Michael's statement might not reflect the truth. Gran might have been trying to *catch* Mum.'

'I don't think so,' Alex says.

The dining chair rocks backward as Edwin leaps to his feet. He looms over Alex, his fists curled.

'That's because *you* want to pass the blame,' Edwin snarls. 'It's your fault Mum was out there in the first place. Gran had no reason to push her. Much more likely she jumped — because of you.'

'Hey.' Joel springs up and catches hold of Edwin's arm. 'This isn't helping.'

Kiara shrinks further into her corner of the sofa, away from both Edwin and Alex, her eyes wide. Edwin takes a step back.

'I agree with Alex,' Danny says suddenly.

Edwin turns on him. 'You're talking about Gran here.'

Danny's voice is a roar. '*She's not my grandmother!*'

Edwin sways as if he's been punched. Laura holds a hand over her mouth. I feel all alone suddenly, with Joel up by Edwin and Danny radiating fury on the sofa next to me. Danny is so sure Vera's guilty, and Edwin is so desperate to believe she isn't. I feel trapped in the middle, uncertain and isolated.

Kiara looks across at me.

'Do you think she did it?' Kiara asks me. 'Do you think she killed them? Your mum and your — your dad?'

I want to hug her for calling him my dad. The others look at her, and then look at me. Danny's real twin sister will be much better for him than I ever was, I think. I draw a shuddery breath.

'I don't know,' I say. 'She said she knew something about us wasn't right. But she never knew exactly what. Why would she go to such extreme lengths when she didn't even know what the secret was?'

'Because she was frightened,' Laura says quietly, curling her fingers around her locket again. 'Vera was frightened that if the truth came out — whatever it was — it would tear your family apart.'

There is a pause, and then Danny says, in a voice that starts off low but swells to fill the room, 'Well, it looks like she was right.'

I stand up then, and I look from Danny to Edwin, and I am filled with more certainty than I've felt about anything since Dad died.

'We need to talk to Vera,' I say. 'Ring Martin again, Edwin. If she's innocent, she needs a chance to explain. If not, we deserve to know the truth.'

34

Seraphine

Martin is waiting for us at the imposing redbrick police station in King's Lynn, and he accompanies us into the interview room where Vera sits. Her back is straight and her chin is high. I try to read her expression, but my heart thuds painfully every time I come close to meeting her gaze, and I find myself scrutinising the rest of the room instead: the camera in the corner, the mug of pale tea by Vera's elbow, the row of three unpadded chairs that we hover behind. It's uncomfortably warm in here.

Vera draws her face up into a smile. 'Darlings.' She gestures at the mug. 'They've run out of Earl Grey, can you believe it?'

'Sit down, please,' Martin tells us. 'Mrs Blackwood, you have ten minutes.'

We waste the first sixty seconds in silence, and I stare at my hands in my lap. It takes all my will not to leap up and run out of the room, and I have to remind myself that I can do that at any point if I want to. Vera can't. Vera has no option but to stay here and endure this.

And then she speaks. 'I admit it.'

Martin shuffles his feet in the corner of the room, and Vera shoots him an annoyed look.

'Oh, for goodness' sake, Martin, not your ridiculous charges,' she snaps. 'The sooner we

379

get those dropped the better. No.' She composes herself. 'I admit I wanted to persuade Laura not to talk to you because I was afraid she knew something about you, something about your birth. I was just trying to protect you. As far as I'm aware, that isn't a crime.'

I glance at Edwin, wondering if he'll say something, but his expression is watchful, guarded.

Vera sighs. 'I always knew it was possible that one of you wasn't Ruth's. After what she said on the cliffs. But — it didn't matter, don't you see? I didn't want to know the details. And I certainly didn't want Laura telling *you* the details.' She pauses, twists her rings. 'But I admit I went about it in a . . . ' She pauses, and tilts her chin a fraction higher. 'In a poorly thought-out way. Which I'm sorry for. But I certainly didn't hurt anyone on purpose.'

'A poorly thought-out way?' Danny makes an incredulous noise in his throat. 'You dropped a stone on her head. You tried to set her on fire.'

When Vera looks at him, she ignores his words entirely, and if anything her expression is wistful.

'My Summerbourne summer-borns,' she says, and she smiles. 'You know, I was sure at first that Seraphine must be Ruth's baby — she was out there with Ruth on the cliffs when I got there. And I was frightened, when Ruth said she'd done something terrible, that maybe she'd stolen you, Danny. From a stranger, from the travellers, I didn't know. I listened to the news every night for months, waiting for a kidnap story, waiting for the police to swoop and seize you.'

Danny shudders. I glance at Edwin again, wondering if we should tell Vera the truth right now, but I want to hear what she has to say first. My new knowledge of our identities is painful, but my uncertainty over Vera's guilt or innocence feels like a heavier burden in this stuffy little room.

'You were so tiny and weak, at first,' Vera tells Danny. 'I worried, about who you were, where you'd come from. But then — as you grew, I changed my mind. You looked so much like Edwin and Theo, it was obvious you were their brother. I relaxed, began to forget. And you, Seraphine . . . '

When Vera turns her gaze to me, her smile broadens, and I'm shocked to feel tears rolling from my lashes.

'You reminded me so much of Ruth at times,' she says. 'So I made myself forget. I was desperate to forget all those doubts I had at the beginning. Of course you were both our children.'

Danny clears his throat next to me. 'Tell us what happened with Dad.'

Vera nods. 'We did argue that morning. It's true. I didn't want to say after the accident, because I realised . . . how it might look. It seemed unnecessary.' She sighs. 'Dominic told me there was something he wanted to tell us all — before I made a decision about Summerbourne.'

She glances at Martin, and I am gripped by a sudden cold suspicion that she's calculating exactly how much of the conversation Ralph might have overheard.

'Dominic mentioned Laura's name,' she says. 'I was . . . worried. I may have raised my voice a little — but only because I wanted him to tell me straightaway, and he insisted on waiting until we were all together. That's what Ralph must have heard — the silly boy parked up by Michael's cottage, so we didn't hear him coming.'

'And then?' Danny says.

'I felt bad immediately, of course. As soon as I'd sent Ralph away, I apologised to Dominic. And then, we discussed party plans for the weekend. The argument was forgotten.'

Edwin frowns. 'And what did you think Dad's announcement was going to be?'

Vera's gaze slides to me.

'You thought he was going to tell us I was Laura's daughter,' I say. 'Didn't you?'

In the seat next to me, Danny hangs his head.

Vera takes a deep breath and appears to reach a decision. 'I have to admit, I used to wonder — Ruth said someone was coming for her baby, and Danny looked so much like Edwin . . . And your colouring is similar to Laura's, Seraphine, and tall, long-bodied women like Laura can sometimes hide their pregnancies. I thought perhaps Ruth agreed to take you on, but Laura's boyfriend, whoever he was, was coming to claim you for himself.'

My heart knocks erratically. Which of us is going to tell her the truth?

Vera blinks at me. 'But it didn't matter. And Laura had the good sense to stay well away from Summerbourne — until now. Until *you* tracked her down.'

The events of the past couple of weeks jostle in my mind, and I think of the wadded shreds of paper I pulled from that smelly park bin.

'The letter,' I say.

Edwin and Danny both look at me. Vera inhales sharply through her nose.

'You wrote that to Laura, didn't you?' I stare at her, and even now I don't want to believe it. I want her to laugh, to explain, to say we'll get this all sorted out, don't worry. I dig my nails into my palms. 'You took her address out of my handbag, and wrote her that letter, threatening her daughter. You meant me, didn't you?'

Vera twists her rings, and then stops. 'I panicked,' she says eventually. 'I wanted to make sure she didn't talk to you. She tried to tell me something that day, about you two, after Ruth fell, and I — I wouldn't listen. But when you said you'd tracked her down, I tried to work out — what was she most likely to say? And I thought — your hair, your skin tone, Seraphine — perhaps you really were her daughter. I'm so sorry. I was trying to protect you.'

'Protect me?' I shove my chair back as I stand.

Vera begins to rise too, but at a gesture from Martin, she sinks back onto her seat.

'Yes,' she says.

'You wrote that message on the mirror.' Edwin and Danny both turn in their seats to stare at me, bemused. 'You burnt that word into the grass . . . '

'Your father . . . ' Vera says, then checks herself. She is no longer looking at any of us. 'Dominic was fine when I left him. We parted on good terms. I decided to take in the view along the cliffs before heading back to London. I rang Ralph from the boatyard, and he gave me a lift back to the station.'

There's a rhythm to her speech that makes her words sound rehearsed. I sway on my feet, waiting for either of my brothers to say something, but they remain silent. Martin is a large, calm presence in the corner, taking it all in.

'Dominic was fine when I left him,' Vera says again.

Danny gets to his feet then, taking his time, watching her. 'I don't believe you.'

Vera gives him a pleading look. 'When you rang me about the accident, I was back in London. I was so shocked. I always worried about Dominic using that ladder, but I never imagined . . . And then, by the time I got back to Summerbourne, the morning's events were the last thing on my mind.'

'I don't believe you.' Danny's voice is louder this time.

'He was fine when I left him,' Vera insists. 'You have to believe me.'

'And Mum?' Edwin asks, his voice cracking. 'Martin has old statements that say' — he swallows — 'someone witnessed you push her.'

Vera looks from him back to Danny. 'Your mother fell. Or jumped. It happened so quickly. I didn't — '

'She wasn't *my* mother,' Danny snarls.

Edwin leaps up then and grabs Danny's arm, turning him away from Vera. 'Danny, wait . . . '

I meet Martin's gaze, and his expression is alert, calculating. I have no idea whether we've had four minutes or forty in this overheated box of a room.

'What do you mean?' Vera pales. She reaches trembling fingers towards the mug of tea, but doesn't touch it. 'Who . . . ?'

Danny stutters, seemingly unable to name his biological mother. '*Seraphine's* your real grandchild,' he says in the end. 'She's Ruth and Alex Kaimal's daughter.'

Vera stares at him. Then looks at me. She shakes her head. And then her focus turns inward, as though she's scanning her memories, searching for something to prove or disprove this.

'Gran,' Edwin says. 'Dad and Laura. Danny's their son.'

Vera draws in a breath, her gaze flicking around the room, looking at anything but us while she thinks. Danny draws himself up, and steps closer to the table. He bends forward, bringing his face down to Vera's level, and finally, she looks at him.

'You killed them, didn't you?' Danny says. 'Mum and Dad. Ruth and Dad.'

Vera's voice is strained. 'No.'

'I don't believe you.' Danny draws a shaky breath. 'I hope they lock you up and throw away the key.'

Martin's colleague stands aside as Danny marches from the room.

The anguish in Edwin's eyes as he looks at Vera before setting off to follow Danny makes my heart ache. I glance over my shoulder as he tugs me through the door, but Vera isn't watching us leave. Her head is turned away, her expression distant; she has already retreated inside herself.

Only Martin watches us go, and there is a gleam of satisfaction behind his sympathetic expression. I don't know how helpful our visit has been to the investigation into Vera's alleged crimes, but I suspect the glimpse it's given Martin into the puzzle of the Summerbourne twins will make up for any official disappointment. Martin's colleague closes the door softly behind us, and we flee to the fresh air and freedom of the car park.

Edwin drives, and I sit in the passenger seat. Danny doesn't speak a word to either of us on the journey home.

35

Seraphine

I stand with Joel in the Summerbourne hall. He has offered to drive Laura back to her home in London tonight, to give us three — Edwin, Danny and me — a chance to sit down together and talk. Not that Danny is aware of this plan, since he stalked off towards the cliffs as soon as we got back from the police station, declaring he wanted nothing more to do with any of us. If he's not back by dusk, I will go and find him.

Laura is taking a stroll around the garden with Edwin before she leaves — for old times' sake, she said, although I suspect she wants to talk to Edwin alone. I'm surprised to find this doesn't bother me. The truth is exposed, and we each have to process it in our own way, and anyway, I'm inclined to see Laura less as a threat now, and more as an ally.

Alex and Kiara are out on the driveway, transferring items from Kiara's car to Alex's. They're going to drive back to Leeds together tonight, and arrange for Kiara's car to be collected during the week. If I turn my head now, I can see them through the hall window: Kiara closing the boot of her car and clutching a bag against her chest, Alex reaching an arm out as he walks towards her.

'You'll be okay,' Joel says, and I turn away

from the scene of my father hugging the daughter he wishes was his.

Joel stands at the bottom of the stairs, his thumbs tucked into his jeans pockets, watching me. The shape of him makes me think I would fit against him perfectly if I stepped closer — my cheek against his chest, his arms curved around my back. But a swell of memories makes me keep my distance: my shame at believing he might have been Laura's attacker; my horror that I caused the injury that gave him his scar; my lingering embarrassment about the night I kissed him and Ralph Luckhurst punched him.

A thought occurs to me. 'It's Ralph's fault,' I say slowly, and then I wince. Of all the people to bring up, of all the names to mention.

Joel tilts his head as if he hasn't heard me properly. 'What is?'

I cross my arms. 'It's Ralph's fault Laura was injured, isn't it? If he'd told the police, when he heard about Dad's accident — that Vera was here that morning . . . '

Joel nods warily. 'Yeah. It might have changed things, I suppose. But it's not like he lied. If the police didn't ask him . . . '

'I could have asked him!' I swipe at a tear on my cheek, annoyed by it. 'If I'd talked to him . . . It was too late for Dad, but I could have stopped Laura being hurt.'

'Seraphine.' Joel waits until I look at him directly. 'Ralph is responsible for his own actions. Don't blame yourself for any of this.'

'But we used to be friends. And I didn't know how to keep that, when we stopped — ' I wave a hand, appalled that I'm even attempting to describe my relationship with Ralph to Joel. I take a deep breath. 'What if he didn't say anything to the police because of me?'

Joel frowns. 'Why? To protect you? From finding out what your grandmother had done?'

'No, I mean — maybe he didn't say anything because it was my family, because he didn't want anything to do with me.'

Joel unhooks his thumbs and steps towards me, but I step back, and he stops.

'Ralph owes your gran a lot of loyalty,' Joel says. 'She's always helped his family out, hasn't she? Supporting Helen, Daisy's job. I'm sure he was just . . . he didn't want to cause her trouble. He was just putting his own family's needs first.'

A noise outside makes me glance again through the window. Alex and Kiara are peering into the boot of Alex's car now, heads close together.

'You're looking for ways to blame yourself, Seraphine, and you mustn't,' Joel says.

I turn back to face him.

'Doctor's orders,' he says. 'I mean it.' There's something in the warmth of his tone that eases the ache in my muscles. I frown at the scar on his jaw, the lift of his eyebrows, the hint of his smile.

'You saved her, didn't you?' I say.

'Who?'

'Laura. I put her in danger, but you saved her.'

'Well, I found her, yeah.'

I shake my head. 'You did more than that . . . You saved her life.'

Joel steps closer to me, and his voice is soft. 'I

guess I was in the right place at the right time.' He reaches out slowly and takes my hand in his. 'And do you know why?'

I watch his thumb stroke across my wrist.

'Because of Michael,' I say.

'Because of you,' he says. 'I could have waited for Grandad to come home, but I thought I'd go and look for him, because I wanted to clear my head. Not because I was particularly worried about Grandad. Because I was thinking about you.'

I look up at him, trying to resist the hypnotic nearness of him, trying to puzzle out his meaning.

'Are you trying to convince me that Laura was saved because of *me*?' I ask him. 'Nice try, but I'm not *that* gullible.'

His widening smile reminds me forcibly of carefree childhood days: heading out to pick blackberries, racing down the lane on our bikes, pedals pumping, the wind in our hair.

'What can I say?' He shrugs, and he's impossibly handsome with this glint in his dark eyes, this almost-laugh on his face. 'It's the truth. I was in the right place at the right time, because I was thinking about you.'

I shake my head at him, but I can feel my own smile responding to his.

'I'm always thinking about you,' he says.

And then I kiss him. I kiss Joel Harris, and he kisses me, and it turns out we do fit together perfectly.

Joel pulls away first. The front door creaks on its hinges behind me, and I press my forehead against his chest for a moment. Blackberries, hearts pumping, the wind in our hair. I don't want to see anyone but Joel.

'Seraphine.' It's Alex. My father. When I turn, his gaze drops to the floor tiles between us. I feel disconnected when I look at him, and I see a reflection of my bafflement in his own eyes.

Kiara stands just behind him on the doorstep, and she makes an attempt to smile at me. I squeeze Joel's hand tighter and wait for somebody to speak.

'Is Danny not back?' Kiara asks.

'No,' I say.

'Edwin and Laura are in the garden,' Joel says. 'Would you like me to go and get them?'

'No,' Alex says. His clipped tone echoes mine, and we make eye contact for a split second. I almost want to laugh; is this what we have in common? A genetic tendency to snappiness?

Kiara gives Alex a sideways look. I get the impression she's tempted to contradict him, to insist on saying goodbye to her newly found mother and half-brother, but it's clear that Alex is desperate to get away from us all and in the end she doesn't argue. She looks tired.

'Can we ring you?' she asks me. 'In a few days, maybe?'

I nod, not trusting my voice again.

Alex makes a brief gesture, flexing his fingers as if under different circumstances he might offer a hug. 'I'm sorry, Seraphine,' he says, and then they turn and trudge away over the gravel, and I shove the front door shut and lean against it.

'You'll be okay,' Joel tells me again, and I smile

at him, not because of what he says, but because he's here, with me.

When they re-enter the house, Edwin fusses around Laura, checking she's taken her painkillers, insisting she accept a sandwich and a flask of tea for her car journey.

'You do know Joel's taking her home by car, don't you?' I ask him. 'Not horse and wagon.'

Edwin gives me his stern big brother look, and the surge of relief it triggers in me takes my breath away.

'I'll walk down to Joel's car with them,' Edwin says. 'Check whether Michael needs anything. When I get back, we can go and find Danny.'

I happen to have spotted Danny through the window when I fetched Laura's handbag from the sitting room; he was lurking on the patio, no doubt waiting for Laura to leave before he comes back in. I nod at Edwin.

'Sure, okay.'

Joel curves his hand around my elbow and dips his face to mine. 'Remember what I said?'

I let my gaze run over his face, absorbing the details. 'I'll be okay?'

'Exactly.' He kisses my cheek.

When he steps back, Laura is watching me. Her lips suggest a trace of amusement, but underneath that is a sadness that makes my heart feel heavy. She has survived being attacked, and she has met her two grown-up children, and they have left her without even saying goodbye. We study each other.

'You remind me of her,' she says eventually. 'You're strong like your mother.'

I stand on the doorstep and watch them until they are out of sight.

Danny makes a cheese sandwich at the kitchen table, scattering crumbs and ignoring the butter-smeared knife when it clatters to the floor. He doesn't look at me. I open two beers and follow him through to the sitting room, and I sit on the same sofa as him and pass him a bottle.

'Thanks,' he murmurs, and the absence of the word 'sis' stretches like an abyss between us.

'I'm sorry,' I whisper.

He's still the same person. But he's not my brother. We share a half-brother. Different halves. That's as close as we can get.

'Kiara's my sister,' he says eventually.

'And Laura's — ' I say.

He waves his hand, cutting me off. 'And Alex is your dad.'

He finally looks at me. We stare at each other. Something shifts in his eyes then, and he drops his gaze.

'Well, you got what you wanted, I guess,' he says.

'What do you mean?'

'Summerbourne.'

My mouth falls open, but no words form.

'She'll give it to you now, won't she?' he continues. 'Once she finds out you're her grandchild and I'm not. You'll get the house you always wanted, from your murderer grand-mother. Congratulations.'

I shake my head. 'Danny, that's not fair. It's not like that.'

'It's why you started all this, isn't it?'

'No!' I sit forward, reach a hand towards him. 'That's not why! I wanted — I just wanted — ' I'm short of breath, and I can't gather the words together. 'If she gives Summerbourne to me, I'll give it to you, okay? I just — I knew something wasn't right. I just wanted to know where I came from. Who I was. Who I am.'

He tilts his head back against the sofa and closes his eyes, and we sit for a while in silence, waiting for Edwin to get back. My twin brother is not my brother. He has a new twin sister. And she's — a tear slides down my cheek — perfect for him.

The silence lengthens. The heat of the day is fading, and I rub my arms, too drained of energy to get up and find a cardigan.

Eventually, Danny sighs loudly. 'I guess I should have known.'

'What?'

'It's obvious, isn't it?' He rolls his head back down and shoots me a sideways look. 'I always wondered why I got all the good genes, and you didn't. Now it finally makes sense.'

I blow out a puff of air. 'Danny . . . '

'All those hours I wasted trying to teach you stuff. Trying to show you how to play cricket when you just wanted to read a boring old book on the cliffs. I should have realised then we weren't related.'

I shake my head, watching him through narrowed eyes.

He leans back again, and gives an even more exaggerated sigh. The corner of his mouth twitches. 'Thank God.'

He's still the same person. Even though my vision is blurred with tears, I manage to land a blow on his arm with my cushion. He lets out a huff of a laugh.

'Be very careful,' I say, my voice scratchy. 'I'm still older than you.'

He makes a dismissive noise in his throat, and settles his head back more comfortably, but his expression retains the trace of a smile. I retrieve my cushion and hug it to my chest.

Edwin returns, and the three of us drink beer and talk as the setting sun turns the Summerbourne sitting room orange and pink. I wonder what Alex and Kiara are saying to each other on their drive home. I wonder whether Laura will contact us again, or whether any of us will contact her. I wonder whether Vera will get any sleep tonight in her cell. I wonder whether Joel is thinking about me as much as I'm thinking about him.

'Did you notice the engraving on Laura's locket?' Edwin asks.

Danny and I shake our heads.

'It has three hearts with zigzag lines across. Like — broken hearts, I guess. But why three?'

'Who cares?' Danny says, and springs up from the sofa, waving away any further talk about Laura. He retrieves the old family photo album from the bookshelf, and as he passes it to Edwin, it falls open at the empty double page. Edwin quickly flips to the next page, and all three of us lean in to study it in silence.

Danny and I were always told this was the first picture taken of us after all those months lost to grief when we were born. It's a bright winter scene, the ground blanketed in snow, and five-year-old Edwin wears a navy blue duffel coat and bright blue mittens and no hat. The bare branches of the Summerbourne orchard are visible behind him, and he holds a carrot and stands next to a noseless snowman. Instead of looking at the camera, his eyes are fixed on two babies propped up in an old-fashioned pram.

I have a sudden memory of Dad telling me this was the brief stage when Danny and I were the same size; when he'd just caught up with me, before he surged ahead and left me forever the smaller one. We wear red bobble hats, almost certainly knitted by Vera, and we're zipped into quilted snowsuits, wedged in next to each other, and we stare out at the world — at the snow, the sky, our big brother — with matching startled expressions.

I run my thumb over a smudge in one corner that I never noticed before: something yellow poking up through the snow — an abandoned toy, perhaps, or early daffodils?

'I can almost remember it being taken,' Edwin says quietly.

Danny grunts. 'What is it you remember exactly — the chocolate cake they gave you afterwards to warm you up?'

Every time something makes me smile, fresh tears slide down my cheeks. It's exhausting. My thoughts are disjointed. I don't want to think about Vera and her crimes. The fact that she imagined she was in some way protecting us, protecting me, even as she wrote that warning on my bathroom mirror to frighten me. And I don't want to think about Alex tonight, and yet how can I not? He's my father. But I'm still mourning Dad.

We talk, and cry, and talk some more, until the room is in darkness. A thin crescent gleams in the sky outside the window like a glint from a silver locket.

'We're still family, us three — aren't we?' I say as we head upstairs.

'Absolutely,' Edwin says firmly.

Danny rolls his eyes. 'Whatever you say, sis.'

I pad away to my bedroom. The night is cooler than we've been used to, and I drag my sheets and duvet from the floor and make myself a nest on the bed, sighing as I curl up inside it to wait for the new day. We are still family, us three. I am still Seraphine.

Epilogue

Seraphine

EARLY DECEMBER 2017

Edwin helps Laura out of her coat as Joel bounds up the steps and joins them in the warm Winterbourne hallway. Steam from the kitchen wafts up the stairs, carrying the aroma of rosemary and garlic to the turn of the staircase where I hover in the shadows, watching them. Edwin kisses Laura on both cheeks. Joel declines to take his coat off.

'I'll get going to the station,' Joel says. 'It's a long enough journey down from Leeds. Much nicer if I can pick Kiara up, rather than her getting a taxi. Especially if she's by herself.'

He glances up the stairs then, although he doesn't give any indication he's seen me.

Laura says, 'Thank you, Joel,' and then, 'This smells so good,' as she follows Edwin into the kitchen. They're discussing goose fat and oven temperatures as they pull the door closed behind them.

I dash down the stairs to catch Joel before he leaves, and he's still standing by the grandfather clock, a half smile on his face, as if he was waiting for me all along. I haven't seen him often enough since I moved into Winterbourne three months ago — I have a long commute to work in the week, and he's been doing weekend locum jobs while he looks for a permanent position. He looks well today, his eyes shining, his freshly shaved skin glowing above his scarf. I stand close enough to feel the cold December air drift from his coat.

'Hi,' he says. 'How are you?'

'Good,' I whisper, and then the slow widening of his smile knocks whatever else I was intending to say out of my mind. We study each other as the clock ticks.

'It's great you managed to talk Danny into agreeing to this,' he says eventually.

'It was Brooke, really. She's good for Danny, I have to admit. She told him he has to give Laura a chance. He has to be here to support Kiara.'

Joel glances at the kitchen door. 'But Alex is still refusing to speak to Laura?'

I'm grateful that Joel still calls him Alex. I'm still prickly about Alex being referred to as my father, even though we have been talking, making tentative steps towards forming some kind of a relationship.

'He's struggling,' I say. 'He told himself all those years he'd done the right thing, and now — he feels guilty about my mother, guilty about me. He and Kiara are okay, I think, but the fact that Laura *knew* he was taking the wrong baby . . . It's just easier for him not to see her at the moment.'

Joel nods. 'And you're feeling okay about today? Having Kiara and Laura here?'

'Well. As Brooke says, we're all related one way or another. And we might actually like each other, if we give it a chance.'

'True.' He's so close to me I could reach up and stroke the scar on his jaw if I wanted to.

'Edwin said you've been looking at houses in the village?' I say, 'To be closer to Michael?'

'Yeah, I wanted to talk to you about that, actually.'

'Oh?'

He pulls a face. 'The old Collisons' place is up for sale. Alex's old cottage.'

I consider this. 'Where Alex set up a nursery for me, and ended up taking Kiara.'

'Yeah.' He shakes his head. 'It's too weird, isn't it? It doesn't matter. Something else will come up.'

'I'm going to move back into Summerbourne,' I say. 'Vera's solicitor wrote to me a couple of weeks ago. She wants me to have the house after all.'

Vera is still in custody, awaiting her trial for the attempted murder of Laura. Only Edwin visits her. She continues to maintain that she knocked the stone onto Laura's head by accident, and was then too shocked to rush down the staircase to help Joel carry Laura back to the house. She continues to insist that Dad was fit and well when she left him, that our mother committed suicide in front of her.

Joel watches me. 'You okay?'

I nod.

I'm coming to terms with the idea that we might never know the true extent of Vera's guilt or innocence. The Crown Prosecution Service has decided not to proceed with the other charges — Martin says there's not enough evidence in the case of Dad's fall, and really none at all in the case of our mother.

Joel's pupils are large in the dim hallway. 'Will Danny mind if she gives you the house?'

I smile. 'Can you imagine Brooke living out in the sticks? He's fine with it. And I'm going to put it in both our names anyway — if and when it ever does legally become mine.'

He dips his head closer to me. 'I'd better go. I don't want Kiara leaping in a taxi before I get to the station. Do you want to come with me?'

'No, I want to talk to Laura, actually, before anyone else gets here.'

'Okay.' He doesn't move. His gaze slips from my eyes to my lips and back again.

'Joel,' I say. The wool of his coat over his chest is faintly damp under my hands. He runs his thumb lightly across my cheek.

'Seraphine.'

We kiss then. I'm still getting used to this delicious feeling of being wanted by him. Like I said, I haven't seen him often enough in the last three months. He claims he's been in love with me for as long as he can remember, and whenever he says this, I tell him I don't believe him, and then he smiles his slow smile at me, and then I forget that it might not be true and decide to believe him after all.

The clock chimes, and we pull apart.

'I have a better idea for where you could live in the village,' I say.

He laughs softly. 'Oh yes?'

'At Summerbourne. With me.'

The laugh is still on his lips, and I kiss him again. We're interrupted by the kitchen door opening, and Laura exclaiming, 'Oh, excuse me,' before she ducks back inside.

Joel draws back, smiling. 'I really should go.'

'You'll think about it?'

'I'll think about it,' he says.

I stand for a couple of minutes after he's gone, waiting for my heart rate to settle, trying to synchronise it with the solid ticking of the clock. When I enter the kitchen, Edwin is shifting pans around on the hob and waves a spatula at me.

'Seph, for goodness' sake, can you let Laura get to the cloakroom if you've finished canoodling with Joel?' He grins as he turns back to the cooker.

There's something in particular I want to ask Laura about, and I examine her in brief glances once she returns to the kitchen. She makes small talk with Edwin about the meal he's preparing, but she checks her watch frequently, and I suspect she's more nervous of hearing the doorbell ring than I am. She offers to do some washing-up, but I step in front of the sink, blocking her access.

'Let me show you the Winterbourne garden,' I say, 'before the others arrive. There's something I think might interest you.'

We grab our coats, and she looks curiously into the other rooms as we pass them on our way to the back door, but she doesn't ask any questions. We shove our hands into our pockets as we stroll down the long central garden path, past the winter-flowering cherry trees with their frilly pink blossom. Autumn colours linger in the borders, and it's remarkably peaceful away from the traffic on the street.

'Thank you for this, Seraphine,' Laura says. 'For inviting me here.'

There's a tension around her eyes. She's about to sit down to a meal with both her children after twenty-five years of them not knowing she was their mother. Impulsive actions are rare for me, but I'm still floating from seeing Joel, and I tug one hand out of its pocket and hook my arm through hers. She did help my mother give birth to me, after all. She did tell me my mother's words, when nobody else could.

She's taller than me, and I smile up at her briefly, and we walk along together quite comfortably.

'Edwin thinks it's a nice way to mark his birthday,' I say. 'New beginnings and all that. Kiara wants to get to know you, doesn't she? And Danny — well . . . ' I'm not sure quite what to say about Danny. After weeks of emotional withdrawal, he has become fierce in his insistence that the revelation about our genetic identity won't damage our sibling bond, but I see him bristle every time Laura's name is mentioned. I blow out a puff of air. 'Danny will get there. You can't rush him.'

She nods, pressing her lips together. She glances at my necklace — a tiny gold angel on a delicate chain. 'This is pretty.'

'Brooke gave it to me. Because of my mother.' I sigh. 'She's a good influence on Danny. She's told him he has to at least say hello to you today.

Try talking to you.'

I flash her a quick grin, and she shakes her head, but there's a flicker of amusement in her eyes.

'Poor Danny,' she says. 'And you? Have you been talking to Alex?'

I still experience a dull jolt in my abdomen whenever his name is mentioned. I did consider cutting Alex off, telling him I wanted no contact between us, and at my lowest moments I wondered if he might actually be relieved if I did this. But I find myself drawn to Kiara, entranced by the myriad ways in which she reminds me of Danny. And I can see that Kiara loves Alex. He's been a good father to her.

I'm glad he left me behind. Of course I am. I'm glad I grew up with Dominic as my dad. Nothing that happens with Alex will ever change that. But we've met up several times now, and when we push all the complications of our family to one side, I think we do actually like each other. It surprises me how disappointed I am that he doesn't want to join us today. I realise Laura is watching me, and I grimace.

'Yeah, we've been talking. I went up there last week, actually. Saw both of them. It was okay.'

'Good,' Laura says. 'But he's not coming today, because of me.' It's a statement, not a question.

'He needs time,' I say, but I'm not sure she's listening.

'I wish — ' She shakes her head, as if acknowledging the pointlessness of such thoughts when it's all too late. 'I wish somehow

I'd managed to — '

My tone is firm. 'It's done. It made us who we are. We can't change it.'

A bright-eyed sparrow tilts its head at us as we approach the final section of the garden and the structure I want to show Laura. Four curved stone benches stand in a circle, looking in towards a large sundial on a raised stone platform.

'It was made to tie in with the folly at Summerbourne,' I say. 'On a smaller scale, obviously.'

Laura releases my arm and circles the sundial, examining the writhing stone sea serpents and the Latin inscription.

'*Fruere hora*,' she reads aloud.

'Enjoy the hour,' I say.

'No cannon.'

'We're a bit more restrained at Winterbourne.'

She rests a hand on the sundial and closes her eyes. I use the opportunity to lean closer and peer at the locket just visible between the lapels of her coat.

'Laura?'

She opens her eyes.

'Your locket's pretty too,' I say, stuttering slightly. 'Are they three broken hearts? What does it mean?'

Her hand reaches for it. 'I used all the money I saved at Summerbourne to buy this,' she says quietly.

I raise my eyebrows. 'But you could have used that money to move out sooner, into your own place.'

She looks back at the sundial and shakes her head.

I take a deep breath. 'Why a locket? What's inside it?'

She frowns faintly, and I half expect her to claim it's empty, but then something shifts in her expression, and I'm gripped by the conviction that I'm right: there *is* something inside it, and it has something to do with Summerbourne.

Her eyes search mine. I have a feeling she's trying to reach a decision. She lifts the locket and passes it backward over her head, tugging the chain loose from her hair.

'It was so long ago,' she says, and she stares down at the locket in her hand. 'It's silly, of course, to be so sentimental. I should let it go.' She presses the tiny button on the edge of the oval, and nothing happens. 'I never opened it, ever,' she says, 'after I put it in.'

She presses again, and suddenly, the front pops up, and she prises it open. I bend closer in the chill air to peer at the contents. Overlapping paper-thin shapes: pressed flower petals, the colour of pale tea with a tinge of purple.

'Sea lavender,' Laura says. 'From the beach at Summerbourne.'

'You kept it all this time?'

'Alex gave it to me.'

I gaze down at the fragile shapes until Laura suddenly flicks her wrist. The petal remnants flutter into the breeze, spinning and disintegrating into tiny shreds of papery dust. There's a low hedge of sweet box behind the sundial seating area, and Laura considers the empty locket for a moment and then tosses it into the dense greenery. It slithers between glossy dark leaves and disappears.

'I messed everything up,' she says. 'My whole life. I got pregnant in sixth form, and my boyfriend wanted nothing to do with it. He kicked me out. Beaky made me have an abortion.'

I stare at the hedge. 'The three hearts?'

She nods. 'I was never a mother to any of them.'

Tiny white flowers nestle in the hedge, and their sweet scent rises with the breeze and drifts around us.

'I was really ill afterwards,' she says. 'I missed my A levels. And then Beaky made me take the au pair job, to see how hard it was to look after a child. To teach me a lesson.'

I picture the form from the au pair agency: 'difficult circumstances at home'.

She looks at me then, almost smiles. 'But it wasn't hard. I loved it. Looking after Edwin. And then . . . '

I reach out hesitantly, touch her sleeve. 'Alex?' I say.

'I wasn't enough. I couldn't compete.' She swallows and gives me an apologetic look. 'And then Dominic . . . I'm so sorry, Seraphine. I messed it all up. Alex — he can't even bear to look at me now. I messed up your life, and Danny's and Kiara's. I'm so sorry.'

Her focus shifts, and I turn to the house to follow her gaze. Voices erupt from the back door as figures emerge, doing up coats and rubbing hands together and exclaiming.

Laura grasps my arm. 'I can't do this. I can't. I need to go.'

'Wait, no. We need to do this, Laura.'

She grips on to me, and I catch hold of her free arm, and I try to summon up a courage that I can somehow transmit to her.

'You're Danny and Kiara's mother,' I say. 'They've come here to see you.'

We both look across the lawn. Edwin and Joel stand on the back step. It's too far away to be certain, but I'm pretty sure Joel is looking directly at me. Danny and Brooke set off, hand in hand, down the path towards us. Following close behind them are two more people, and I'm surprised to find my cheeks rising in a smile. Behind Danny and Brooke are Kiara and the guest who said he wasn't coming: my father. Alex has decided to join us at Winterbourne after all.

Laura's arm twitches under my hand.

'If I let go of you,' I ask her, 'are you going to run away?'

She manages to tear her attention from the figures on the path to frown at me, but it's not enough to hide the shine in her eyes. She shakes off my grip and turns in a slow circle, her gaze skimming over the borders, the stone seats, the sundial, the approaching people who are part of our family now.

'Enjoy the hour,' she says. 'How are we supposed to do that, then?'

'Don't ask me.'

She takes a deep breath. 'Well. We've come this far. I suppose we could give it a go.'

Something like a smile passes between us then, and I link my arm with hers again, and the two of us set off down the path to meet the others halfway.

Acknowledgements

I feel incredibly lucky to have the wonderful Rebecca Ritchie as my agent; thank you, Becky, for being so enthusiastic about my book from the outset, and for your ongoing wise advice. I'm enormously grateful to Emma Beswetherick at Piatkus, and to Amanda Bergeron at Berkley, for the combination of your superb editorial skills and insights; thank you both for shaping this story into its best, final version.

Thank you to Suzanne Harrison, Val Watson and Jo 'the flying vet' Brand, for all the pep talks and cakes. Thank you to the staff and clients of the Cromwell Veterinary Group in Cambridgeshire, for being so gracious about my change of career and for cheering me on. Thank you to Danielle Feasby, for answering all my plant questions (although any horticultural mistakes remain my own). Thank you to Xanthe Randall, for your detailed feedback and positivity at every stage. And thank you to the kind people who gave me feedback on my very first writing attempts and encouraged me to persevere: Rachel Niven, Andrew Baron, Suzie Bishop, Charlotte Harrison, Ami Quenby and especially my brilliant mother-in-law, Susan Brown.

Thank you to my parents, Steve and Joan Smith, and to my sisters, Clare Redmond and Lucy Bell, for your unwavering support and delight during this whole process, and to my sons, William, Edward and Arthur, for celebrating all the highs with me. And finally, to my husband, who cheerfully rearranged our lives so I could chase my writing dream, and who still brings me that all-important cup of tea in bed every morning: I couldn't have done this without you, Brian (and I'm not just saying that because of the tea). Thank you.

We do hope that you have enjoyed reading
this large print book.

Did you know that all of our titles
are available for purchase?

We publish a wide range of high quality
large print books including:
Romances, Mysteries, Classics
General Fiction
Non Fiction and Westerns

Special interest titles available in
large print are:
The Little Oxford Dictionary
Music Book
Song Book
Hymn Book
Service Book

Also available from us courtesy of
Oxford University Press:
Young Readers' Dictionary
(large print edition)
Young Readers' Thesaurus
(large print edition)

For further information or a free
brochure, please contact us at:
Ulverscroft Large Print Books Ltd.,
The Green, Bradgate Road, Anstey,
Leicester, LE7 7FU, England.
Tel: (00 44) **0116 236 4325**
Fax: (00 44) **0116 234 0205**

THE SINGLE MUM'S WISH LIST

Charlene Allcott

Martha Ross dreams of being a singer, but she's been working in a call centre far too long. She's separating from her husband, the father of her son. And she's moving back in with her parents, toddler in tow. Life has thrown her a few lemons, but Martha intends to make a gin and tonic. It's time to become the woman she's always wanted to be. At least her mum's on hand to provide childcare — and ample motherly judgement. Soon Martha realises that in order to find lasting love and fulfilment, she needs to find herself first. But her attempts at reinvention — from writing a definitive wish list of everything she wants in a new man, to half-marathons, business plans and meditation retreats — tend to go awry in the most surprising of ways . . .

FOUR

Andy Jones

In the time they've known each other, Sally, Al and Mike have shared — well, almost everything. Sally and Al have been married for seven years, but now their relationship is hanging by a thread. Sally and Mike have been best friends since university. Mike and Al have been friends for many years. Yet with Al poised to become Mike's boss, their relationship is coming under threat. And now there's Mike and Faye. They haven't been together long, but Mike's pretty sure that this time it's the real deal. As the three old friends sit on a train heading towards Brighton to meet Faye, little do they know that after this weekend, the four of them will have shared . . . everything. They all know they have made a mistake. But they could never have imagined the consequences.